Matthew,
meet Matthew

GW00729087

Matthew, meet Matthew

SHARON MULROONEY

POOLBEG

This novel is entirely a work of fiction. The names, characters and incidents portrayed in it are the work of the author's imagination. Any resemblance to actual persons, living or dead, events or localities is entirely coincidental.

Published 2004
by Poolbeg Press Ltd
123 Grange Hill, Baldoyle
Dublin 13, Ireland
E-mail: poolbeg@poolbeg.com

© Sharon Mulrooney 2004

The moral right of the author has been asserted.

Typesetting, layout, design © Poolbeg Group Services Ltd.

1 3 5 7 9 10 8 6 4 2

A catalogue record for this book is available from the British Library.

ISBN 1-84223-151-0

Typeset by Magpie Designs in Goudy 10/14pt
Printed by Litografia Roses, Barcelona, Spain.

www.poolbeg.com

About the Author

Sharon Mulrooney was born in Galway
and moved to London when she graduated in
1987. After ten years of working in the field of human
resources in hotels, the music business and the drinks
industry, Sharon left corporate life to work freelance
and to fulfil her dream of writing. She is married
to Colin and has two children, Conor and Aoife.

ACKNOWLEDGEMENTS

Thank you to Linda Gibson, for your advice about the legal world, for taking all those loose pages on holiday, and for being a good mate.

Thanks to Clive Hayward for your insights into the world of acting, and your example of pursuing the dream through lots of adversity.

Thank you to the officers at Brixton Police Station for giving me a well-informed glimpse of another world.

Thanks to my sister Ina for your huge enthusiasm, and your invaluable advice on the ending!

Thanks, Mom and Dad, for being the best parents in the world – for giving me roots and giving me wings.

Ros Edwards, thank you for the energy you continue to give to a long shot!

To Claire Harcup and Louise Voss, for being there during the ups and downs and advising on the twists and turns.

Thanks very much to all the team at Poolbeg for your unstinting support and enthusiasm.

To Colin, my rock and my hero

PROLOGUE

Caroline

I've always liked the name Matthew. If you're going to have more than one man in your life, I recommend having two with the same name. You never have to think twice when you're talking about them. When you say, "You'll never guess what Matthew did ..." or "Matthew drives me mad when he ..." to someone like my mother, you never get it wrong. Mind you, my mother must think he's schizophrenic. Or maybe just the perfect man. Because if I took the good bits of each of them, that's what I'd have.

I've wanted to be a lawyer since I was small. I used to sit and watch courtroom dramas on the television and imagine myself pacing up and down, cross-examining the baddies in the dock. They always had jutting, unshaven jaws, and narrow ties, like clones of the Kray twins or Al Capone. I would have a tailored red suit on, with shiny black court shoes and a smooth blonde pageboy haircut. My chunky calves and curly dark hair never intruded into the dream.

"You're not clever enough to be a lawyer," my sister Maura used to say. "More like a teacher, or a nurse."

"Just you wait and see," I would answer back.

So I worked my socks off at college, and I didn't have much of a social life, but I did get a good degree. By that time I had discovered you have to be a certain kind of person, from a certain kind of background, to go to Blackhall Place in Dublin, to qualify as a solicitor, so I opted out of that bit and went off travelling after I graduated. To her credit, Maura didn't say, "I told you so," every time I rang her.

And I'm still determined to prove her wrong. Now, when people at parties ask me what I do, I want to say that I'm a Lawyer, with a capital 'L', but I'm still only doing my articles, which is a bit unusual for someone in their thirties. I just say I work for a law firm. It seems to work. People are usually impressed. After being away for so long and then temping in data-entry jobs, my mother is delighted that I'm back "in the system". She'd prefer if I was living around the corner from her in a nice new Celtic Tiger semi-detached box with a hankie-sized front lawn. But the cheap flights from London to Dublin mean that we're psychologically, if not physically, close.

"I was telling Joan that you're doing really well now that you've settled down a bit. Her son Mike is over in London now, you know."

Earning sixty grand a year as a trader with huge bonuses on top.

"Mmm," I say non-committally.

Honestly, once you're on the treadmill, you're expected to catch up with all the other hamsters so your mother can boast about you when she's working in the Vincent de Paul shop in town on Thursday mornings. My two sisters are married with kids, and Mam's focus has just shifted from the career prospects of their husbands to the number of teeth her grandchildren have sprung. I love my nieces, the three of them, but I have no urge to "settle down" just yet, and my life is a bit too complicated at the moment to think about such adult things. Dad thinks I'm just a lightweight who can't stick at anything. I gave up the piano lessons when I was eleven, and it's been all downhill since then, as far as he is concerned. I didn't tell him, or anyone else, that the piano teacher tried to get me to put my hand on his crotch while he was playing a piece for me. As innocent as I was, I knew there was something not quite right about that. I persuaded Mam to let me do Irish dancing instead, and she was happy enough with that.

3

I've lived with Matt for nearly two years. He's gorgeous-looking, brilliant in bed, and he can make me laugh like no-one else. I met him in India, at sunrise on the side of the lake by the Khajaraho temple. That's the one with all the Kama Sutra kind of carvings on the pillars. You wouldn't believe the human body could do such contortions. We were sitting by the edge of the water and we got talking, and one thing led to another. Kissing him was surreal. I felt like I was looking down on the two of us from some exalted place on the top of the temple. Two tiny, insignificant creatures surrounded by all the grandeur of nature and ancient architecture. I can't believe I did it, good lapsed Catholic girl that I am. He was a complete stranger, and anything could have happened. And lots did happen, but all of it was good.

"Do you want to have something to eat?" he asked me while we were lying there, looking at the still water disturbed only by the flies landing delicately on the surface.

"That would be nice, " I said to him, "as long as it doesn't have any coriander in it. I can't do coriander for breakfast."

He laughed. "Or cumin seeds?"

"Definitely no cumin seeds."

He stood up, and I followed him. "May I make a serving suggestion? How about some sunshiny cornflakes with cold milk, and three halved strawberries tossed carelessly on top, followed by white toast with the hot butter dripping on to your fingers as you sip your freshly ground black coffee?"

"No, you haven't?" My salivary glands were dancing a jig. For just a tiny second, I thought he was going to produce the ultimate breakfast from his rucksack. By now we were sitting outside a tiny shack with one rickety formica-topped table leaning against the wall.

"Sorry, Madam, the best we can offer today is some chapatti and the solidified remains of a 1960s jar of Nescafe." Matt's face brightened. "But we do have English marmalade." He pulled the jar out of his bag.

"Where did you get that from?"

"I won it," he said. "I was playing cards with this American guy on the train from Bombay and he lost big time, so he paid me off with marmalade."

"Bizarre," I said, but drooled at the thought of the chapatti disguised with a taste of real breakfast.

That day, we talked a lot, and laughed. We shared his lumpy hostel bed that night, and let's just say that, "not much sleep was had". We travelled around India for three more months, and we've been together ever since. From day one, Matt has made me feel really special. It's usually something simple, like making me a daisy chain, or giving me a little kiss on the nape of my neck when he's passing my chair. I never stopped to ask myself if he was Mister Right. It all just sneaked up on me and a little while ago I realised that I am at the stage where I should be thinking about these things. And then I discovered the other Matthew.

Matt

Caroline is changing and I'm not sure if I like it. It all started when she got that job. When I met her in India, she was so anti-establishment that a job in the City of London would have been an anathema to her. She said it was even worse than the old boy's network in Dublin. But that was three years ago, and people change.

I'll never forget seeing her for the first time by the lake at Kujarahah. The sun was rising, casting an orange glow everywhere. She was perched, silhouetted, like a little elf on a rock, staring at the water. It was her self-containment that appealed to me first. She didn't seem to need any human company to share her experience with. When I was travelling, I always made friends with people on the train, or waiting for the ferry. We would travel together for a while, and some of us promised to keep in touch when we went our separate ways. For me, the experience was richer for sharing it with other people, even strangers. The different perspectives that people bring to the same place make you look at it in another way. It's like in that poem, 'Tintern Abbey', when Wordsworth turns to share a breathtaking view with his wife, then remembers that she is gone and it somehow isn't so special any more. The most poignant memory of Kujarahah for me was when I lured Caroline into a conversation about the kind of people who must have built such an amazing temple. When I walked up to her first, she turned her shoulder slightly away from me, silently telling me to leave her alone. She didn't seem scared, even though we were the only people there, but I still wanted to reassure her that I was no threat.

"It's fantastic, isn't it?" I said. I meant it in the full sense of the word, as in fantastical, almost illusory.

"Mmm," she muttered back.

I didn't take the hint.

"Isn't it amazing the way the pillars look like they're floating on the water? They're glowing, as if they were on fire," I said.

Caroline didn't say anything. She just nodded. I was probably a bit like an eager puppy, looking for company and assuming that all humans would find me appealing. I sat down beside her and waited for her to thaw out. I sighed, but I didn't quite rest my head on my paws.

The first time I saw glossy photos of the temple, I was in my second year at university, and promised myself I would see and touch those pillars for real. I took my Arts and Drama degree at the University of London, because I thought that was where it was all happening. But it meant living at home, which was not such a good idea. My mother kept telling me that I was an adult now and no longer her responsibility – after all, if I had gone away to another university she wouldn't have known what I was up to. It didn't work because she hadn't managed to convince herself. She lay awake every night until she heard my key in the door. That's the problem with being an only child. I always told her when I was staying out, because otherwise I would be greeted at breakfast two days later by a ghostly shadow of her former self, zombie-like from lack of sleep. It didn't do great things for the spontaneity of my sex life. Can you imagine being engrossed in a good snog on a girl's sofa, desperate to get her upstairs, but wondering where the phone is, so you can tell your mother you won't be home? I felt like Ronnie Corbett in *Sorry*, that sitcom where he is forty and living at home with his draconian mother – though he's not exactly the right role model for a six-foot-four serious actor. No doubt there is some twisted Freudian interpretation, but I blame my mother for my obsession with sex in strange places.

On the edge of the lake, I got Caroline to talk back, eventually, and we sat for an hour or so, staring at the sculptures on the pillars and wondering about their origins. By then, I felt incredibly horny. I know that sounds a bit juvenile, and obvious, when I was surrounded by erotic carvings, but it wasn't just that. Caroline was sitting really close to me, and the sun was coming up and warming the rock we were sitting on. I could smell the freshness of her hair, and a light, lemony soapy smell from her skin. Once I got her talking and laughing, she relaxed, and I wanted to touch her, to kiss her. I didn't just want a self-gratifying shag. I really wanted to share something with her, there and then. She was very responsive, and we made love right there on the shore, exposed to the sky. It was a kind of primeval experience, and seemed to create some kind of bond between us. It's hard to explain. Afterwards, Caroline said she had never done anything like that before, in a kind of awed little voice, but she was giggling and grinning. We went for breakfast together and we talked and laughed a lot. I think it was the marmalade in my rucksack that clinched our relationship. Caroline asked me where I was going next and when I said Calcutta, she said that's where she was going too. We decided to travel together for a while. Afterwards, I found out she had already bought a train ticket for Agra, but she threw it away and bought another one.

If that was me, I would have given it away to someone, but Caroline was worried that I would see the ticket and realise that she had changed her plans to be with me. She's far too independent to admit to such a weakness. That's what I love about her. She's feisty and strong and self-possessed, but she can also let her guard down sometimes and that's when I think I see the real Caroline. She's a romantic at heart, and loves a soppy movie as much as the next girl. She saw *Sleepless in Seattle* three times, and bought the video of *Ghost* so she can watch it whenever she needs a dose of escapism. She voted for 'Unchained Melody' on the ITV top 100 singles for the last millennium. What she sees in Patrick Swayze I will never know.

When we got back to London first, I wasn't sure if we'd stay together. Caroline was very restless. She wouldn't move into my flat straight away. Having been away so long, travelling and living all over India and the Far East, she found it difficult to settle down to urban domesticity. All she could see was her twenty-something friends from Ireland making it good in professional careers. They were busy buying houses in suburbia, worrying about what company car they were going to get next, and spending huge amounts of money in Conran restaurants. It offended her socialist tendencies, especially after all the poverty she had seen, and at first she refused to join in the rat race. For six months, she insisted on being self-sufficient, temping in some really crappy jobs while she decided what to do next. Her mother was going mad, back at home, thinking she had gone completely off the rails, and I'm sure in her mind she thought I had led Caroline astray and persuaded her to come to London instead of going back home to Ireland. Finally, Caroline decided to use her qualifications and get a job in law. She figured maybe she could give away some of her money to help people instead of trying to just live on a pittance. In true Caroline style, she put everything into getting a job, and it only took a couple of months. For some bizarre reason, she went into the City to work in commercial law. I had expected her to go and work for Mencap, or Help the Aged. But it's all or nothing with Caroline, and she took to corporate city life like a duck to water. And that's when she started to change. She's very attractive, quite petite, and when I met her she had long curly dark hair and eyelashes that really set off her green eyes. She used to wear quite floaty, almost hippy kind of clothes, and her hair all wild and tangled. Until she cut all her hair off to fit some idea of corporate image, and started wearing charcoal-grey pin-striped suits and glossy tights. They say the clothes make the man. They certainly make the woman.

When she came into the living-room after being at the hairdresser, I looked up and just said "Fuck".

"Do you like it?" she said, tossing her head like a shampoo advert. Except there wasn't much left to shake – it was a very short bob, sort of falling forward on her face – I think they call it the gamine look in the magazines. And it was streaked with highlights. I could tell that she liked it, so I wasn't going to tell her that she looked ten years older and like a completely different person.

"Yes. Very corporate." I managed to make that sound like a compliment.

Even at weekends, she started wearing different clothes. More slimline, black trousers and clingy halternecks, and she chucked away all her hippy silver bangles and rings.

11

I feel like she is leaving me behind now. Before, I never thought of her as being five years older than me, because she didn't look it, and she certainly didn't act it. Now she has turned into a mother hen, nagging me about bills and housework and treating me like some kind of house-husband. It doesn't help that my nan's money has finally run out. I didn't tell Caroline, but my last Visa bill took the remaining few hundred pounds. So now I have to depend on her money, until I can get a decent acting role. The money was never important to me. I considered it as our money and, while I had it, I was happy to spend it on us. But now it's gone.

CHAPTER 1

Matthew

The day doesn't start well. Liz is frantic because she has had a bad night's sleep anyway, and then Jack wakes up at five am. Instead of guzzling a bottle of milk and going back to sleep until seven thirty, he decides that as the birds are singing and it looks bright outside, it's time to get up. Liz has optimistically slipped back under the duvet, hoping that a few minutes of grizzling will end in blissful silence. After ten minutes she gives up and flounces out of bed again, wafting cold air under the duvet in the process so that I will appreciate her great sacrifice. She goes downstairs with Jack, and I hear the television going on. At six, I hear the *Sesame Street* jingle and decide I might as well get up and use the early start rather than lying in bed, awake and frustrated. On the way to the bathroom I look into the boys' room, and see Ben blissfully spread-eagled on his bed, his Winnie the Pooh pyjama top riding up, exposing his little white belly, and his teddy clutched under one arm. I always find it amazing that Jack's antics don't wake him, but he must have some kind of inbuilt children's protective sensor, to safeguard his peaceful sleep. It would be nice to patent such a thing, and sell it to frazzled thirty-something career people who are trying to juggle too many plates, or balls, or whatever, and whose sleep always seems to suffer. I pull the bedroom door slightly closed so that my bathroom noises won't wake Ben, and run a hot powerful shower to banish the remnants of sleep from my body and my brain. As usual, while I stand under the water, I survey the grouting between the tiles, proud of the neatness of the job in most places, and irritated by the couple of irregularities, promising myself to dig them out and re-grout them soon. Liz keeps on saying we should just get people in to do these jobs. That's the whole point of us both going out to work; we earn enough to pay other people to do things we don't want to do. But I want to do them. Liz doesn't understand the therapeutic value of a bit of weekend DIY after spending a long week shuffling papers and doing meaningless corporate financing deals. I really enjoy the ritual of taking out my toolbox and measuring tape, planning the job, and going to Sainsbury's Homebase or rooting around in the shed to find leftover pieces of wood and screws from previous jobs. Liz would much rather make a few phone calls, get some quotes and have a guy in a van to come around. She says I should chill out at weekends, but she has no idea what a buzz I get out of building a fence, or painting a room. The end result is tangible and visible, and *mine*, unlike most of my weekday work. I kind of drifted into commercial law after I did my articles, rather than making a conscious decision about which direction to take. An element of it was probably prompted by the lure of filthy lucre, but mostly I think it just happened by osmosis. There was a slot in the commercial department at the practice where I had taken my articles, the partner had a good reputation, and I applied for the job and got it. I haven't told Liz about my increasing frustration, because she just wouldn't understand. I know that sounds like the "my wife doesn't understand me" cliché, but she really wouldn't. She's a Financial Controller for a big multinational, earning very good money, and with her eye on a seat on the UK board. For her, a career should always be moving onwards and upwards, and she has done exceptionally well, especially with taking two maternity leave periods in the last three years. My musings are interrupted by a screech from downstairs, and I pull on my dressing-gown and run down, anticipating the worst. Jack has now started a high-pitched wailing, and Liz is trying to calm him down, holding his head against her chest, stroking his hair.

"There, there, you silly thing, that's what happens. Mummy told you, that's what happens." She looks up at me, shaking her head. "He was doing his head-first kamakaze trick off the arm of the sofa, and I didn't grab him in time." She looks totally stressed out. It is only six fifteen a.m. and the GMTV presenters are just warming up.

I take Jack from her arms, and say: "You go and have a shower, I'll look after him for a few minutes." I flop onto the sofa, too lazy to change the channel to BBC for some decent meaty news, and Jack snuggles up to my chest and promptly falls asleep, his long eyelashes resting on scream-reddened cheeks, and his wispy blonde hair standing out on the back of his head. It's for these kinds of moments that I put up with a lot of other stuff – the grinding boredom of the daily commute and dull work, the snatched conversations with Liz over a Marks & Spencer's chiller-cabinet dinner before she goes into the study for another hour of work before bed, the broken nights. I stroke Jack's head, smoothing down his hair, and look at his little hand spread out on my chest; the perfect nails, the long fingers he inherited from Liz, the pudgy knuckles. I wonder what kind of person he will turn out to be. I am always fascinated by that idea – his personality and ability and potential are all locked away inside that head, waiting to grow and show themselves. I never thought about it so much with Ben, because the first child is such a miracle anyway that you don't really stop to think about it. But when Liz was pregnant with Jack, I kept wondering how can the same parents, with the same gene pool, produce another child totally different from the first? Even if it's the same sex, it will look different, have another personality, and grow up into another person. That's the true miracle. I think Liz would have liked a girl second time around, to satisfy her need for balance, and her neat idea of our little nuclear family, but she certainly won't want to try again – two interrupted years in her career is quite enough, and I think she finds the two boys quite a handful.

The telephone rings, and I calculate that Liz will still be in the shower, so she won't pick it up in the bedroom. I ease myself almost horizontally off the sofa to grab the receiver, and manage not to disturb Jack.

I murmur "Hello?" quietly, and hear Nicky, the nanny, coughing at the other end. "Sorry, is that Matthew?"

"Yes, hello, Nicky, how are you?" I say patiently, knowing what is coming. Liz will have a fit.

"Not very well, actually," she says, strategically inserting another splutter. "I've been up all night, coughing, and I think I'd better go to the doctor's today and get something for it."

"Sounds like it," I say.

"I wouldn't want to pass anything on to the boys," she says virtuously. She seems to spend most of her time catching or recovering from bugs she wouldn't like to pass on to the boys. Liz hasn't had time to do anything about it – she usually rushes in at exactly seven o' clock in the evening, when Nicky is due to finish, and Nicky is out the door in a flash, barely giving an update on what has happened during the day.

"So when do you think you'll be back to work, then?" I ask, knowing that Nicky is sighing with relief to get me on the phone instead of a hysterical early-morning Liz. "Probably a couple of days, I should think, depending on what the doctor says," she wheezes.

"I'll tell Liz. You've got her work number, haven't you, in case there's any change?" "Yes, thanks, Matthew, bye." She has hung up before I can wish her a speedy recovery. Liz appears in the doorway, immaculate in a new suit I don't think I've seen before. "That was Nicky. She's not well. A cough."

"So she's not coming in?"

"No – probably not for a few days, she said, but I told her to ring you at work and let you know."

"Shit!" Liz puts her hand to her mouth automatically, and then realises Jack is asleep.

We have made a vow to try not to use bad language, now that Ben is actively taking everything in and repeating it at inopportune moments. Liz takes the hands-free phone from me, and speed-dials the nanny agency. That's how often Nicky is ill – it was worth putting the number on speed dial.

"Yes, hello, it's Liz Turner. Again. Yes, I'm afraid so,

and I really need someone as soon as possible. I have an eleven o' clock meeting to get to, so do you think you could find someone to get here by ten thirty at the latest?" She manages to sound completely calm, even though I know her stomach will be churning, panicking about the presentation she is due to make. She stayed up until midnight with her laptop, finessing her Power-point slides.

"Great. Thanks, Anne-Marie, you're a saviour." She hangs up. "Can you hold on to Jack for a minute, and I'll go and change out of this suit?" She's already on her way up the stairs.

I stand up and follow her, thinking I can put Jack down in his cot and get dressed myself. My early start is fast diminishing and I really have to get on. Jack wakes up and screams as I lay him down, immediately waking Ben, who is not good in the mornings. He needs at least ten minutes of attention and cuddles before he is ready to face his day. He won't be a fire-fighter when he grows up, that's for sure. I can hear Liz's sigh of exasperation from the other room, as she races to pull on a track suit and trainers – the breakfast-feeding uniform. I sit down beside Ben, giving him a half-hearted hug, but that incenses Jack even more, and he stands at the bars of his cot screaming at me.

Liz comes in, swoops on Jack, plonks herself down with him on the other side of Ben, and says brusquely, "Go on, you'd better get ready for work."

"Don't you want a hand?" I say feebly, not really meaning it. I hate the children's morning routine, which inevitably involves the flicking of cereal around the kitchen and jammy toast being stuck to any item of furniture within reach. I enjoy the escape to the train station, buying my paper, cappuccino and Danish pastry and settling down for the forty-minute journey to Victoria. Sometimes Liz has morning meetings in London and she catches the same train as me and, to tell the truth, I hate it. I should be glad of the opportunity to spend some time with her chatting about domestic trivia like some of the other couples I see travelling together. But she sits across from me, getting stressed by the pastry crumbs falling on my suit, or the fact that I haven't polished my shoes for weeks. Anyway, this morning I get dressed quickly, kiss Liz and the boys good-bye and catch a train half an hour earlier than usual. At least I have salvaged some time from the unearthly start at six o' clock.

Caroline

Matthew was sent in at the last minute to negotiate a contract with one of my firm's clients, because a colleague of his was off sick. I was sitting across the table from him, just watching, because Baxter, our Senior Partner, was doing the talking and I was taking notes.

There was nothing appealing about Matthew's slightly shiny suit lapels, his messy hair and his crumpled trousers. He looked totally disorganised when he arrived, carrying a bulging briefcase full of dog-eared files. Baxter looked sideways at me as if to say, "Walkover!". He grinned snidely when Matthew flopped everything down on the table and knocked over a glass of water. It spilt all over the brown leather blotting-pad in front of him, and ran across the shiny surface of the glass table, dripping down into the crotch of his trousers. I caught his eye as he looked up, all flustered. He had beautiful brown, deep eyes, full of intelligence and I could see just a hint of him laughing at himself. I shiver at the thought of that moment. Then it was gone and we got down to business. I kept looking across at him, and then finding myself dreaming, so there were huge gaps in my notes. Baxter didn't notice. He was too busy going for the jugular. I alternated between fantasies of having Matthew's babies and hating him. He pointedly ignored me throughout, and I thought he might be one of those male chauvinists who treat women lawyers as glorified note-takers. Which I was on that occasion, but that's beside the point.

Matthew's voice is deep and powerful. If he was a singer he would be a baritone, and his accent would have qualified him as a BBC presenter before regional accents got trendy. He responded to Baxter's petty ripostes in a measured and masterful way. Apart from Brian, the bass player at university, I have never been turned on by the sound of someone's voice. Matthew listened like a blackbird, tilting his head slightly to one side, ready to pounce and stab the soil if a worm was unfortunate enough to poke its head out. He obliterated a few controversial clauses with a sweep of his pen, ignoring Baxter's attempts to confuse the issue. He captivated me. I sat in the meeting room by myself after he was gone, pretending to finish my notes. I stared out the window, my eyes in fuzzy focus on the grey clouds while I replayed his every gesture and turn of phrase.

Matthew rang me about an hour later to ask me to confirm a point from the notes. He said he couldn't get through to Baxter. He made his question sound much more complicated than it was, and then right at the end of the conversation, he said, "So how are you, anyway?"

I was thinking, 'You mean, how am I right now this minute, compared to how I was an hour ago?' But I said, "Grand, thank you," in a coquettish, little-girl kind of voice that I didn't know I had in my repertoire.

"I was wondering if you would like to go for a drink one evening, after work?"

I panicked. I put him on hold. I felt like a thirteen-year-old being asked to dance at the Loreto convent disco.

I took a deep breath and said, "Sorry, em, Matthew, I had a client on the other line. Yes, a drink some evening would be lovely." Just saying the familiar name out loud released the butterflies in my stomach. What was I thinking of? He wasn't even attractive. In fact, he was distinctly scruffy, as my mother would have said. But he wasn't wearing a ring. So he must be single. Like me. Not.

When I got home, Matt was sitting on the couch reading a men's fashion magazine. He looks like he should be on a front cover himself. He has very sleek black hair, arched eyebrows and green eyes with a dark rim around the iris. When he looked up and smiled at me, I wondered how I could even think about being attracted to anyone else. He is tall, with wide muscular shoulders and narrow hips, a tight bum and rock-hard thighs from cycling. I love hard thighs. He works out, and goes to Ceroc classes twice a week to keep fit, ready for the perfect acting role he always thinks is just around the corner.

"Did you have a good day?" He stretched sinuously like a cat that has been curled up by the cold fireplace all day, and is looking forward to the prospect of a warm body to purr against.

"Yes, it was grand," I said. I couldn't look him in the eye. I went into the bedroom and took off my suit, secretly examining myself in the full-length mirror. Like I had just lost my virginity. But this time, the invisible transformation was in my head. I could feel Matt watching me, and when I turned around he was standing in the bedroom doorway, grinning. He looked down, and I could see why. He took my hand. Afterwards we had a bath together, with a glass of wine and crackers and Cashel Blue cheese balanced on a plate. I told him about Matthew's accident with the water. He laughed. I laughed with him, but the spell of Matthew's eyes was not broken. I went to sleep drowning in those eyes.

Matthew

I have to admire Liz. I know she huffs and puffs about it, and sometimes she makes me feel most un-twenty-first-century man, by pointing out how little I do for the boys, but she is a fantastic mother. It wouldn't even have occurred to her to ask if I could wait until the agency nanny turned up. She sees it as her job, even though sometimes she is under more pressure at work than I am. In my less charitable moments I think she has a need to see herself as Superwoman, and all this juggling of home and work is part of the picture, but most of the time I really believe she is a devoted mother who also happens to want a good career outside the home. The only problem with that is that she hasn't got much time or energy left for me. I know, I know. But we haven't had a night out together for about six months, and I think the last time we had sex was about three months ago. Yes, it was, during the Christmas holidays when we stayed at her parents' house and they told us to have a lie-in and they would look after the boys. We did it in a hurry, with that slight feeling of rebellion you have in your parents' house, and I came too quickly, so Liz wasn't best pleased.

This is probably just a phase in our lives – small children, no sleep, careers important, high stress levels, no time for each other. But when you're in it, it seems all-encompassing and looks as if it stretches ahead to infinity.

When I got into the office there was a flap because Anthony Trevelyan had had a bad car accident the night before, and was in hospital. Judith, his fifty-five-year-old veteran assistant, was madly rescheduling his diary, organising flowers and trying not to cry. I stood by her desk waiting for her to finish a telephone call. There was a stack of files she had obviously prepared for the day's meetings, and on top sat the folder for the e-commerce deal he had been talking about for weeks – negotiations were due to start that day.

"Are you all right?" I asked Judith, as she hung up and reached for a tissue. Her mascara had stained one cheek, and her normally immaculate hair looked dishevelled.

"Yes, thank you, Matthew. It's just so upsetting . . ." She looked as if she was going to dissolve into tears again.

"Do you need some help? Diana won't be too busy today, so she could give you a hand." I actually had quite a lot of work lined up for poor Diana, but none of it was urgent. "I should probably review these files and make sure nothing falls through the gaps," I added, lifting the pile.

Judith's face brightened a little. "Thanks, Matthew – I didn't like to ask, but I wasn't sure what to do with some of them."

I was confident that if left to her own devices, Judith would have competently prioritised the files, highlighted any issues, and come to me or Roger for guidance. "Do we have any kind of prognosis on how Anthony is doing?" I asked.

"Not yet. His wife promised to call later when they know more," Judith sniffed.

Anthony is a really nice guy, but a very reckless driver. He has a Ferrari, which he drives too fast, and throws around corners as if he was at Silverstone. Luckily, he tends to drive into the office at about six in the morning, so the roads aren't too busy, but he really does take chances. I wasn't surprised that he had come a cropper, but it was unsettling, because he had almost seemed invincible when he was recounting some of his closer shaves.

"Which hospital is he in?" I asked. "West Middlesex – we don't know which ward," Judith said. "The shop wouldn't take an order for flowers until I could tell them the ward." She was speaking like a child, in a trance.

"I'll send Diana over to you. Stop for a minute and have a cup of coffee." I touched her shoulder. "There's nothing that can't wait while you catch your breath." I took the pile of folders to my office and asked Diana to decamp to Judith's desk. It took half an hour to review the files and decide on how to delegate them. I summoned a couple of the Assistants, and persuaded Roger, the other partner, to take one file. I kept the e-commerce deal myself and called Hare, Wood and Baxter to tell them I was coming instead of Anthony and would be a few minutes late. Judith looked calmer as I went past her desk to brief Diana on the way out. She managed a wan smile, and I told her to take it easy. She was usually so ruthlessly efficient and self-composed that I was surprised to see her so rattled.

The meeting went fine, after an initial fluster when I spilt water all down the front of my trousers. My client, whom I had only just met in the lobby and so had the lift journey to instil with confidence in my ability to take up where Anthony had left off, must have been cringing. I could see Baxter smirking, but I could feel sympathy emanating from the very attractive female colleague sitting beside him, who had been introduced as Caroline. She offered me a napkin from the coffee tray on the credenza behind her, and caught my eye as I started to use it and then realised it was leaving white fluff all over my crotch, which was only marginally less embarrassing than a dark water stain. I opened the file and focussed on the task at hand, the essentials of which I had tried to absorb in the taxi on the way over. Baxter was irritating. He was condescending to his client, making an issue of explaining in lay terms some of the technical legal issues as we addressed them. With me he took the slightly hectoring tone of a public-school headmaster about to give one of his charges a good thrashing. But it served the purpose of getting my adrenaline flowing again, which had been defeated by a sudden wave of tiredness that hit me as I sat down. After three hours of slogging through the detail, I had redeemed myself, and we had made significant progress towards a deal. The client said on the way out that he was pleased with the result, and could I pass on his regards to Anthony if I spoke to him in hospital.

All through the meeting, every time I looked across at her, Caroline's head was down, and she was busily taking notes. Her shiny hair hung slightly forward, and her body language said in the most subtle way that she was only playing the part of being Baxter's diligent acolyte, but she wasn't in tune with him. In the taxi on the way back to the office, I tried to analyse how I felt. Stirred up. Discombobulated, as my old dad would have said. How could I feel such a magnetic attraction to a woman whose voice I had only briefly heard, the top of whose head I had seen more than her face, and about whom I knew nothing at all?

I went through my own notes when I got to my desk, and jotted down a few more points. Baxter had promised the draft contract by afternoon, and I wanted to be able to respond quickly and get the file off my desk so I could get back to my own deals. I couldn't stop thinking about Caroline. It was as if she was imprinted on my brain. I picked up the phone, having found a query in the notes I could ask her about. I wanted to hear more of her voice. When she came on the line, sounding all business-like, I was momentarily thrown. But within seconds, her warm Irish accent came through, and I melted. I managed to frame some kind of question, and waffled on for a few minutes, feebly trying to keep her on the line. Before I knew it, I had asked her out for a drink. It seemed the only way to keep the tenuous link between us going. She put me on hold, and my heart was pounding. What had I done? I was like a gauche teenager, asking for my first date. I was married with two kids, for God's sake – what was I thinking? Maybe she would say no and save me from myself. She came back and said another call had come in, but yes, she would go for a drink sometime. She told me to call her next week when work would be a bit lighter. Shit, I thought. I've done it now. I've started something and I don't want it to stop. I hung up, my leg muscles all watery from the rush of unused adrenaline.

When I get home, Liz is already there, comforting Ben who has just dropped a tin of Ambrosia creamed rice on his big toe, and is alternating between crying and staring fixedly at the black bruise developing under the nail. Liz gives me a wan smile. She looks tired.

"How was your presentation?" I ask, stroking her head as I pass to the fridge to get a Coke.

"Not bad. I was only twenty minutes late so they gave me a later slot in the meeting. It wasn't ideal, because some of the issues they were discussing beforehand would have been clearer if I had already taken them through my bit. I think it went down well though."

"Good."

Jack comes bustling into the kitchen then, pushing his new truck, making the engine noises he has learned from Ben. He smiles at me, and then demands to get onto Liz's knee with Ben. I'm not good enough, and he cries when I try to take him and give him a hug. Liz smiles.

"Sometimes, only Mummy is good enough," she says, sighing. Her tone of voice has that particular cross between martyred mother and Superwoman that she has perfected, and which really annoys me. If I'm supposed to be a better father, as she keeps telling me, she will have to let go a little bit, and let me into the cosy exclusive club she has created with the boys.

"Shall I start cooking?" I ask, opening cupboard doors and the fridge to look for inspiration.

"Yes, and if I could leave Ben down here with you, I can get Jack into his pyjamas." Liz sits Ben down on his special chair and tells him to draw a picture for Daddy. "Something nice and bright," she says, and hauls Jack upstairs, wailing because he thinks he's missing some action.

Ben and I have a nice chat about his day, including the vicissitudes of being friends with Oscar, who seems to be the soul of generosity with items from his lunchbox one minute, and a complete bully the next.

"He hit me on my head today, Daddy," Ben says.

"Did you tell the teacher?" I ask, unable to remember her name.

"No, because Oscar told me not to." Impeccable logic, I think.

"Why did he hit you?"

"I don't know." Ben is radiating innocence, but with a twinkle in his eye that makes me wonder. It's amazing how children so young can have a range of facial expressions to rival adults'. Even Jack, who is only eighteen months old, has his 'I am just about to tip my cereal bowl upside down and I know it's naughty' face, and his 'oh yeah?' face for when you tell him not to do something. I start to sauté onions and garlic, gulping down my Coke and moving on to a glass of red wine from the fridge. I nibble on some olives and root around for sun-dried tomatoes in the cupboard. Ben has his head down, concentrating furiously on colouring between the lines in his colouring book. His hair, parted roughly where Liz has been stroking his head, reminds me suddenly of Caroline's. My stomach lurches. I am going to see her again. I feel a nervous thrill. My life is too dull. Yes, these moments with my children are special, but hardly exciting. Conversation with Liz revolves totally around her work or dull domestic details like the need to get the outside of the house painted now while the weather is good. I am looking forward to being someone else, to having good conversation over dinner and a bottle of wine, to joking about silly things, and finding out about someone new. I won't have to be Matthew, solid husband, doting father, reasonable boss, reliable friend. I can re-invent myself and be scintillating and interesting and challenging, and even unpredictable, if I want to.

Ben holds up the picture for my approval.

"Fantastic – you're getting really good at colouring, aren't you?"

Liz comes back in with a clean-faced Jack, his wet hair sticking out in all directions. "Can we swap?" She takes a bottle of milk from the fridge and hands it to Jack. I know the routine. I sit with him quietly while he drinks it, and then put him to bed while Liz has 'quality' time with Ben. I suppress a sigh and turn off the gas, my pasta sauce only half made. When will I ever get a chance again to play my music really loudly while I chop and cook, slurping back the wine and olives and slowly unwinding? Never. This evening routine will go on forever – with slight variations maybe. Homework, school projects and hobbies will have to be supervised. Crises with schoolmates and not getting on to sports teams will have to be discussed before bedtime, which will get later and later. I sit on the sofa with Jack, trying to watch the seven o'clock news headlines on the television. He reaches his hand up and strokes my hair, which is a habit he has had since birth, and involves me cricking my neck downwards so he can reach. So I listen to the commentary, staring at Big Bird's face on Jack's pyjama front, thinking about how I should really not meet Caroline for a drink. I am looking forward to it too much.

CHAPTER 2

Caroline

In the morning, while I was snatching a quick breakfast, Matt told me that he had been rejected for a part in a fringe production. He said he hadn't told me the night before, because he didn't want to ruin the evening. I hugged him, and tried to think of nice things to say to him. Work was going so well for me, he said, and if he could just get a lucky break, maybe we could think about buying a place together, or even going on another trip. I nodded, munching a piece of wholemeal toast that was rapidly turning into carbon-tasting crumbs in my mouth.

"Maybe your agent should look at some different types of parts for you? I know you don't really want to do Rep, but maybe that's where you need to focus just for now.

That seems to be where most people start out. Then the critics would see you and rave about you and you could get bigger parts, and the TV stuff." I have made this speech before. Often. Poor optimistic, idealistic Matt. He thinks he can just walk into TV parts based on his good looks and charm. I personally would love to watch him on telly, and of course I tell him that, but what do I know about it?

On this occasion he just muttered something under his breath. I'm not very good at conversation in the morning at the best of times, and this discussion definitely did not qualify as small talk. I kissed him good-bye and ran down the road to the tube station, forgetting my umbrella and regretting it as soon as the rain started spitting at me. The usual crowd of misfits was hanging around outside the station. I grabbed *The Independent* off the newspaper stand, threw the exact money into the guy's hand, and started down the steps. I always have the right change for him, and I always arrive at the station before the digital clock said 7:38. I'm a bit superstitious about things like ladders and cracks in the pavement too. Matt always laughs at me. Mammy used to worry that I was autistic when I was small, because I had strange fixations, and she couldn't break them no matter how hard she tried. I had to visit the stag beetle in the drain beside the house before I went to school, and I would only ever drink the first glass of milk that was poured out of a bottle. It was in the days before homogenised milk, and I loved the cream off the top. These little habits went on for years. Luckily no-one ever stood on the stag beetle, and he didn't move to another drain down the road. Havoc would have ensued. I hoped that if I ever turned up a minute late to the tube, or lost my change for the newspaper, that I would behave in a rational, adult way and calmly proceed to work. But I had never tested it.

That morning, I got on to my usual carriage and sat in my usual seat, on the end of a row, near the door, so that I only had to touch shoulders with one person, on my left. I got engrossed in the front-page article about a police experiment in Brixton to ease off on cannabis smokers and focus on tackling the class 'A' drugs trade. Good move, I thought – we might have Amsterdam-style coffee shops soon. Starbucks could put that in their pipe and smoke it. I looked up from the newspaper and realised we were at Oxford Circus, and the doors were just about to close. I jumped up.

"Excuse me, excuse me," I said to the unyielding pinstriped backs. They shuffled, and harrumphed, and moved, but not quickly enough, and the *"beep, beep, beep"* of the closing doors mocked me. There is nothing more humiliating than desperately trying to get out of a carriage and then being stuck on the train until the next stop. No-one makes eye contact, so you couldn't accuse them of laughing at you, but they are. If any human sound was to be heard on the tube, which of course it isn't, it would be sniggering. But there is only the rasping sound of a personal stereo playing the Brand New Heavies, the odd foot shuffle and the loud rattle of the carriages as they whisk you through the darkness. It's not like on a bus, where people talk about the weather or the best stop to get off for Selfridges. The tube has this power to silence people. Even Italian tourists who get on the train happily yakking away are subdued into silence, or maybe the odd self-conscious remark about how many more stops they have to go. I finally shuffled off at St Paul's station, which I hate, because it's so busy in the morning, and worked my way against the flow of eau de Cologned bodies to get out. The communal morning smell is nice. Soap, shampoo and the latest designer fragrances are only occasionally overlaid by a singular underarm whiff of someone who doesn't believe in deodorant. The lunch-time smell is more varied, with take-aways, and lots of non-working people who don't have to smell pleasant to avoid the condemnation of their fellow wage slaves. Slight alcohol fumes and the subtle undertone of trainers worn all day add an extra nuance to the evening smell.

The cold outside air on Ludgate Hill dispelled the lingering odours from my nostrils, and replaced them with a lungful of carbon monoxide.

I got into the lift at work and pressed the button for my floor. My stomach sank as the lift went up. I looked at my watch and remembered that I was supposed to be in an eight o'clock review of a big banking deal. Twenty past eight wasn't even close. I tugged down my jacket, and brushed the non-existent fluff off my sleeves, because the lift doors open right outside the glass-sided meeting-room where they would all be sitting. Should I look flustered, like I had run eagerly from the tube, or saunter out casually and act surprised to see them all sitting there? I had to go to my office anyway to get the papers, which would take another five minutes. I'd bluff it and say I thought the meeting was at eight thirty. I composed my face and tucked my hair behind my ears. I must practise my feigning skills, because my look of surprise and puzzlement didn't work. I got a filthy look from Baxter, who pointedly stared at his watch when I slid into the room. Someone else was talking, so I couldn't casually say, 'Ooops, I thought we were meeting at eight thirty?' with any credibility at all. The meeting droned on for two hours and I was gasping for a coffee by the time we finally came out. There was a message on my desk to call Matthew, and my heart jumped. Then I read the rest of the note, which said to ring him at home. The other one, I thought. Matt was already relegated to the status of *the other one*. I must get a grip on this, I thought, forgetting my desperate need for caffeine and ringing home, full of contrition. Maybe he had been called for an audition, or even offered another job. "Hello," he said. "I was just wondering what shopping we need. I thought I'd be a New Man and go down to Waitrose for you."

Apart from my urge to say, '*For me?*' in a sarcastic squeaky Miss Piggy voice, it was a nice surprise. But I couldn't help wondering why Matt didn't just get on with it. Why did I have to rack my brain to remember if we needed tea bags or washing-up liquid, when he was sitting at home and could just open the cupboards and check? I gave him a makeshift list, feeling stupid as I noticed Alison, my assistant, sniggering at her PC.

"Matthew doing the shopping for you?" she asked when I hung up.

"Yes, is that all right with you?" I snapped at her, totally unnecessarily.

She offered me a coffee. Alison knows me so well. As I sipped it, my irritation subsided. Those butterflies were busy flitting around and waiting for Matthew to call. Why should he call again today? Butterflies are not renowned for their logic. I made a list of things to do for the day, to focus my mind.

As usual, I had come away from the earlier meeting with most of the action points. It seems that the more junior you are, and the less experience you have, the more work you get. You spend most of your time unproductively wading through files and references checking the finer points of law, which if you had more experience would take you two minutes. But as soon as you have the experience, you step up the ladder and start passing things back to the person on the rung below you, while you keep your beady eyes on the next one up. By the time you're a Senior Partner, you just swan into meetings, adding credibility and weight and status to the proceedings, and walk out with nothing to do until the next meeting. Or lunch. My newly-found career ambition was based on this theory. It must be worth serving your time in the lowly depths of juniordom to later reap the rewards of seniordom. Or is it juniority and seniority? I suppose that is the principle that makes the corporate world go around. I had a great conversation with a lawyer in another firm a while ago. He was Irish too, and we were sort of flirting across the telephone, like you do. He had a lovely deep voice, a Mayo accent, and a really sexy laugh. I can't even remember his name. We were talking about a licence application for some software. He said, "Do you ever wonder, if we all stopped negotiating how to give each other permission to do things, so you didn't have to get my advice, and your client didn't have to get your advice, and his customer didn't have to get his advice, then the whole infrastructure of work and society would break down?" I must confess that I said no, I had never thought about that, but it was quite depressing, really. Especially when I have only just cottoned on to the whole working-for-a-living thing. The philosophising lawyer asked me out for a drink, but I turned him down. Maybe I was giving off 'available' signals, or something. Maybe I wasn't as happy with Matt as I thought I was.

Sitting there, staring blindly at my list of things to do, I thought: Matt has changed in the last six months. He used to be really laid back, generous and always up for a good time. But since I got the job, he seems to be different. Maybe he feels like a house-husband or something, now that I work long hours and kind of expect him to do things like laundry and washing-up. I don't think that's too much to expect, now that I am earning the money. I keep telling him that he needs to find some work, to help to pay the bills. He always agrees, but there is a distinct lack of evidence to support his claim that he is really looking hard. He buys *The Stage* magazine on a Thursday, and trawls through *Production and Casting Review* and he even gets the occasional audition. His agent never seems to call him. I thought agents were supposed to try and get you work. I guess it didn't help Matt's ego that I was told by the senior partners that I am a 'hi-po', meaning someone with high potential and a bright future. It also means that I'm expected to work long hours with a big smile to show how motivated and committed I am. Clever psychology. So clever that it works, even when you know what's being done to you.

With a guilty start, I focussed again on work. I gulped down the coffee, adjusted the rictus grin on my face, and went to Baxter's office to apologise for being late. He was full of the caffeine of human kindness, having escaped, as usual, from taking any work away from the meeting.

"Don't worry, Caroline, you are doing really well. We are very optimistic about your future with the firm. Perhaps you just need to –" here it comes, I thought, "concentrate a little bit more on your timekeeping."

"Yes, of course," I said demurely, looking down at the blue floor tiles in a good imitation of a public-school boy being 'carpeted'. The nuns gave me plenty of practice at this skill and I have found it is also the best way to deal with middle-aged men of a certain background. As long as it never goes to spanking, I can play the game as well as the next guy. I went to the library to do some research and managed to forget about both Matthews until lunch-time.

The library is my favourite part of the office. It's a circular, open space, taking up the whole top floor. It has a wooden mezzanine, lined with shelves of dusty old tomes. There's a glass dome on the top, like a miniature imitation of the reading room in the British Library. Muted, greeny light penetrates through and softens the harsh fluorescence of the artificial lighting. In the lower section, the computers and microfiche machines take up nearly all of the space, and that's where I usually end up working. But it's nice sometimes to look up at the old mahogany shelves and imagine leafing through those books, looking for the precedent that will clinch a legal argument. Using the computer to find information is a bit like travelling on the tube across London. Your schematic map bears no relationship to the actual location of the stations, and if you were to rely on it above ground, you would get well and truly lost. In the same way, magical keywords will take you through the databases and on-line legal updates to your end-point, provided you use the right ones. But it's not as much fun as flicking through books and scribbling notes, and finally pouncing on the thing you were looking for. Maybe I should have been born in a different era. I could amble through the back alleys of the City of London, like Salt Lane and Costermonger Street, savouring the journey rather than hustling to the destination. Then I would lock myself away in the library, licking my index finger to turn the thin fragile pages of my law books, making notes with my goose-quill pen.

I suddenly realised I was starving. I went downstairs to grab my handbag before going out to get some lunch.

Alison looked up from her desk, and with her mouth full, which really irritates me, she mumbled through her French-bread crumbs, "Can you call Matthew, please?"

I had just stopped myself from saying, 'Which one?' when she handed me a message slip with the number. It was him! Him! I did a mental jig, smiled at Alison, and went into my office to call. She obviously swallowed her lump of Camembert and grape baguette, because she said loudly after me, in an interrogative sort of way, "He sounded a bit funny, I thought? Is he all right?" She has a huge soft spot for Matt, and I know she would give me such a hard time if she thought I was two-timing him.

But I wasn't.

So I was a bit abrupt with her. "He's fine, thank you." I was hoping the possessive, defensive tone would put her off, but she appeared at the door.

"Has he got a cold, or something? His voice sounded quite husky today."

"No, really, he's grand, honestly." I smiled tightly at her and refused to dial the number until she left. She knows my home number as well as I do, so she must have been curious about where Matt had called from.

"MalloryandTurnerscanIhelpyou?" the bored voice of the receptionist intoned in my ear.

"Hello, can I speak to Matthew Turner please?" Believe it or not, I hadn't clicked before that he must be one of the partners. I know. I have a lot to learn. Baxter's snide comments came back to me, and now I understood them. 'It doesn't take much to get to partner in a small firm . . . It's not like the old days where you had to serve your time . . .' He couldn't handle the fact that a thirty-something lawyer could have become a partner when he himself was at least forty-eight before the firm bestowed the honour on him.

"Can I ask who's calling please?" I knew by her tone that the receptionist must have asked once already, and I mustn't have heard her.

"Sorry, Caroline Connolly. From Hare, Wood and Baxter," I said. Better make it sound like a business call. Maybe it was. Maybe he was checking another point on the contract. Maybe he didn't even like me, and he was calling to explain that the drink invitation was a mistake. I chewed my nail while I was waiting to be put through.

"He's at lunch at the moment, can I take a message?" His assistant sounded like she had just swallowed her Camembert and grape baguette in one piece. Or maybe it was just a large plum. Why can't people just talk in normal voices? Do they really talk like that at home?

"Can you just let him know that Caroline Connolly from Hare, Wood and Baxter, returned his call?" I am always tempted to say *Hare, Wood and Fox*, or *Hare, Wood and Beagle*, just to see if anyone would react. But she didn't sound like she had a sense of humour. She was probably in the Countryside Alliance and went hunting at the weekends and looked forward all year to the Hunt Ball so she could get pissed on Stirrup Cup, or whatever they drink.

"Certainly, can I take your number?"

"He's got it." Obviously he's got it. He just called me, you silly cow, I thought.

"Thank you. Good-bye." She wasn't going to volunteer when he might be back, or if he would call that afternoon, or if he was going to be in meetings until midnight.

I grumpily stuck some lipstick on my chapped lips, and went to get a sandwich. Alison didn't even look up when I went past. She was in 'dealing with Caroline with PMT' mode, even though she could have quite easily worked out that it wasn't the right time of the month for that. Her tactic is to avoid eye contact, make lots of coffee, take efficient messages and never have any typos. I am sure she has refined this as a survival technique, having had women bosses for most of her career. She says she prefers women to men, because they're more predictable. Meaning that she only gets on the wrong end of irrational, inexplicable behaviour for a few days a month, instead of all the time. She's great. But one more phone call from Matthew and she would have sussed me out. I needed to get some fresh air and plan my strategy.

"I'm just going to get a sandwich. Do you want anything?" I asked.

Alison waved a chocolate muffin at me and shook her head to reassure me that she was stocked up with enough calories to get her through the tedium of the afternoon. At least she didn't talk with her mouth full again.

I love walking down Gray's Inn Road. Even though the traffic is manically busy, and you inhale foul fumes as you fight your way across the street to Prêt à Manger, there's a real sense of history there. My favourite building is the old Tudor-fronted shop with the bowed front walls that look as if the black timbers will collapse like a heap of burnt gingerbread. And the big old black gates with the small wooden door you have to stoop to go through, like

Alice stepping into the hallowed courtyards of Temple Inn. I sometimes walk through there, just to inhale the oldness of it, and to play out in my mind some of the scenes from the *Barchester Chronicles*, or *Nicholas Nickleby*. I imagine Mr Toogood coming bustling down the stairs to advise poor Josiah Crawley on the matter of the Stolen Twenty Pounds. Sometimes, I get funny looks from people passing by with manila files or bags of sandwiches. Then I realise that I have been standing in one of the cobbled courtyards, looking up at the windows with a very gormless expression on my face, for longer than a sane person would be expected to do. I get embarrassed and shuffle off before they summon the constabulary.

Today, as I bent my head and climbed through the little black door, I was smiling, thinking what a silly English word "gormless" is. When I heard Matt using it for the first time, I teased him, asking him could you be gormful, or with gorm? I remembered Matthew's eyes again, and his hands, one resting on the glass table, and the other waving his Waterman black and gold pen as he made a point. The butterflies fluttered. They hadn't had a good outing in a quite a while. I love Matt, in a comfortable, take-him-for-granted sort of way, overlaid with occasional frustration and occasional real passion. It was ages since I'd had that distracting, almost uncomfortable feeling of anticipation mixed with uncertainty that you get when you first really fancy someone. (It was a bit like being a seven-year-old, wiggling a loose tooth that really hurts, but it's a nice sort of pain and you know if it falls out, the tooth fairy will come.) I really tried hard to make the feeling go away. I told myself I was in love with Matt, and living with him. I could not be attracted to another man. It had never happened before. Why was it happening now? I tried to read my book, but I only got through three pages. My eyes kept drifting out of focus. That happened a lot at university. I spent endless hours in the library staring at legal texts, but really dreaming about Brian, the bass player in the college band. He was tall and skinny and had a very cool Dublin accent that I found irresistible. I was eating an apple one lunch-time, and had just taken a bite, when Brian walked into the refectory. I swallowed it in one lump, and started choking. He came up and said, "Are you OK, Caroline? Did something go down the wrong way?" I just nodded furiously, hoping he would go away, but a mighty reflexive cough dislodged the offending lump and it landed with a slimy bump on the table. I just smiled, blushing to my toenails. "Apple, was it?" he said, insisting on scrutinising it. "Yes, sorry," I said. I picked it up and threw it into my polystyrene coffee cup which wasn't quite empty and sloshed its contents onto the table top. He asked me to dance a couple of nights later, in a student club in Rathmines. He called me Snow White, which I thought was very sweet. I'm sure she didn't throw up in front of the handsome prince. I always thought of myself more as the Ugly Duckling. I think my dancing convinced him of that, and I saw him skulking out the door with some Goldilocks a few hours later. I had already realised when I got up close to him that I couldn't bring myself to kiss his cool, but very stubbly and spotty face. The bass line of that song, 'Stand By Me' can still turn me on.

Matt

I rang my agent, but he said there was nothing on the horizon. So I cooked this Chinese meal, and chilled a bottle of wine to mellow Caroline out before I broke the news to her. I heard her key in the door as I dabbed on some of her favourite aftershave. She was standing in the kitchen with her coat on, looking a bit flustered, when I came out of the bathroom and it was only the next morning that I found the discarded Chinese takeaway in the bin. Anyway, I persuaded her to relax in the living-room with a glass of wine while I stir-fried the chicken, and tossed the odd witticism in her direction to set the tone. It didn't work. She was still really uptight and distracted when we sat down at the table. Suddenly I had this overwhelming feeling that it would not be a good idea to tell her the bad news tonight. It seemed like some tight wire inside her was about to snap, and I didn't want to be the pliers.

"Did you hear the one about three blondes?" I said, doing my best non-PC wicked grin.

"No. But you're going to tell me?" She was trying hard to join in the spirit of things, but was failing miserably.

"There were these three blondes, and they were walking through the woods, talking about blonde things. . ."

"Blonde things?"

"You know, hair, nails, all-over-body moisturiser, that sort of thing."

"This sounds like a boy's joke to me," she said.

"It is, but that's never stopped me before. Anyway, they get to this river in the middle of the forest, and they're pacing up and down, trying to work out how to cross it. They don't realise that they're standing under a magic tree, and when the first one says, 'I wish I was ten times more intelligent, so I could figure out how to get across this river' – *pow!* She turns into a brunette and swings across on a vine that's hanging from the tree . . ." I could see that Caroline was trying not to smile. My strategy was working. "So the second one stands under the tree and says, 'I wish I was a hundred times more intelligent so I could figure out how to get across this river. ' *Kebang!* She turns into a redhead and runs across, balancing on this tree-trunk that's fallen across the water . . ."

"Why do I think I know the end of this?" Caroline said in this world-weary tone, taking the fun out of the punch line, but I gave it to her anyway.

"The third one asks to be a thousand times more intelligent, and *Wham!* She changes into a man and walks across the bridge!" I laughed, but Caroline just gave me this wan smile. "Did you have a bad day at the office?" I said, even though I swore I would never ask that. House husbandry, here I come, complete with wok and apron.

"No, not really," she said.

"Have you got something on your mind?" I might as well get to the bottom of this, rather than suffer the faintly disapproving and dissatisfied look on her face.

"Not really. No. Any luck today with jobs?" Caroline always knows how to sharply turn the conversational tables.

Suddenly I had this inspiration. "Actually, yes. That's why I cooked this nice meal. To celebrate. I spoke to my agent today, and I've been offered a really good part in an ITV drama that's starting filming in the autumn."

"Wow!" Her face lit up, and I felt mean for thinking she was mentally putting me down. She wants me to succeed as much as I do. "Why didn't you say? What kind of thing is it?"

"A detective thing, as if we need another one, but I'm not complaining. I'm getting the sergeant sidekick role."

"That's fantastic!" Caroline jumped out of her chair and came around the table to kiss me. She hugged me around the neck. "Why didn't you tell me straight away?"

"I was building up to it," I said, feebly, but she didn't notice the feeble bit. "I suppose this could be the beginning of something."

She toasted me: "To new beginnings!"

As we curled up on the sofa with the bottle of wine, I wondered what kind of trouble I had got myself into. Getting work isn't as easy as it looks. Caroline says she would love to watch me on TV, and so would all her friends. As if they were an accurate sample of casting directors. She just can't understand why I'm not getting the parts. I suppose I should have been a bit less choosy when I left RADA. But all through college, the tutors told me that I had the perfect face and physique for television. The talent scouts who came to see the end-of-year shows were very positive about me. So I turned my nose up at a spear-carrying job in the Royal Shakespeare Company for the season after graduation. I wanted to go travelling, and in my innocence, or arrogance, I thought that once my TV career was launched, I wouldn't have time to travel because I would be in such demand. Ironically, the guy from my class who took the spear-carrying job ended up covering Romeo, who promptly developed glandular fever and disappeared, leaving my friend in the limelight. I don't envy him, because I never wanted to do RSC, but it does show you how fate takes a hand in these things. When I got back from India, I rang around all the decent agents and got one quite quickly. That was encouraging, especially when he got me a part, three weeks later, in an episode of *Sherlock Holmes*, on BBC 2. I was on for about ten minutes, and everyone said I made a great baddie. Then I worried about being typecast, and turned down a bad guy role in *The Bill*. My agent would have bullied me into it, if he was any good. But he's a wimp, and here I am four years later, and the only TV part I'm likely to get is the fantasy one I've created to get Caroline off my back. Still, I've got four months before the filming is supposed to start. I'll get something before then, and worry about telling Caroline nearer the time. I suddenly realised that Caroline was stroking my stomach, tracing her nail from my chest down and down, and down . . . Maybe it was the second bottle of wine, or the adrenaline rush of bonking a TV actor, but she was like a tiger.

Caroline

I went back to the office and the afternoon passed quite quickly. I was working to a deadline on the banking deal. The computer network crashed for an hour, but I managed to get a sixteen-page fax to our associate offices to go through the machine first time, which is a miracle, and was packing up at five forty-five feeling satisfied with a good day's work. I could squeeze in a quick visit to the gym on the way home and get a Chinese takeaway for dinner. I waved at Alison, who was down at the other end of the office corridor, on her knees, doing some long-awaited filing, and grabbed my gym bag from under my desk.

"See you tomorrow," she yelled, and went back to her task.

I put a note on her desk, saying: *Sorry for snapping at you earlier on. Thanks for doing the filing, C.*

Baxter was preening himself in the lift mirror when the doors opened on my floor. He looked a bit embarrassed and then covered it by saying, "You're off early, aren't you?" as if to say, don't we overwork you enough?

I smiled my happy, dedicated Legal Exec smile and said, "Yes, I got through all the banking stuff and faxed it off. I'll be in early tomorrow to review any amendments." "Off to the gym?" he said, in an attempt to appear human. He was on his way down to the basement carpark where his chauffeur would be waiting with his polished Bentley to whisk him home to St John's Wood. The most exercise he gets is strolling around a golf course doing the old-boy thing while someone else carries his clubs. Maybe he occasionally swings one for effect.

"Yes. Healthy mind and a healthy body," I said brightly. Clichés are such useful things in a lift-type conversation. That took me to the ground floor and I wished him a nice evening with my best smile.

As I passed the reception desk, the security guard called to me, "Caroline Connolly?"

I said "Yes?" and from under the desk he produced a cellophane tube with a single red rose, wound around with a red silky ribbon.

"It only arrived five minutes ago, I was just about to give you a call," he said apologetically, but with that universally recognisable smug male grin.

I acted dead casual, and took it, saying very coolly, "Thank you," and turned away so he wouldn't see my burning face.

The note was really simple. It just read: *"I will call you – soon. Matthew."*

And his mobile-phone number. What class! I could see his deep-brown eyes with the eyebrows raised as he asked the question, a little smile playing on his lips. Now I was on dangerous ground. No more pretending that I didn't fancy him, or maybe he didn't fancy me, that it was a professional relationship, that I wasn't cheating on Matt. A surge of adrenaline rushed to my arms and legs, and I could feel my heart pounding. I needed time to think. I definitely needed a trip to the gym on the way home.

The gym was packed and I was mad that I had forgotten how busy Tuesdays are. Everyone with new week's resolutions would really like to exercise on Mondays, but they are too knackered after the excesses of the weekend, and they think that the gym will be busy anyway. So they all pile in on Tuesdays, to get the virtuous feeling early in the week that will carry them through to the weekend again. If you ask how often someone goes to the gym and they answer in an agonised tone, "Well, I *try* to go twice a week," you know they're a Tuesday person.

I wangled myself into the corner of the changing room, turning my back to the bench where a woman was posing with her all-over-body moisturiser, and crammed my stuff into the last available locker. Honestly, you need the first five minutes of exercise just to work off the stress of the changing room. I went into the ladies-only section of the gym, not because I am modest, and need to hide my body from the men, but because it is palpably less competitive in there. I inhale enough testosterone all day at work. I like to potter around the machines and do twenty-seven push-ups or ninety-nine strokes on the rowing-machine. That's just to prove to myself that my other obsessive little habits are purely voluntary and I could give them up any time I like.

On the running-machine I declined Matthew's offer politely, and told him that I was in a long-term relationship. On the rowing-machine I dumped Matt, so I would be free to see Matthew with a clear conscience. On the bike, my heart was pounding as I clocked up a speed of eighty revolutions a minute and I decided to wait and see what happened. I felt totally de-toxed after forty-five minutes, and I jumped into the shower just before the six-thirty aerobics class came piling out. I hate queuing while the Tuesday exercisers, who have spent most of their time in the aerobics class standing and gasping for breath, then spend twenty minutes cooling down in the shower. I know. I'm old and miserable before my time.

I had completely forgotten that Matt was doing the shopping. He had cooked a fantastic Chinese meal. I discreetly dumped the takeaway straight in the bin, in an excess of remorse and wastefulness. He had set the table with a red cloth and slim white candles, and had *Turandot* playing in the background. He does the best chicken in black bean sauce in the world. I challenge any Chinese chef to beat it. To my shame, I was thinking how nice the red rose would have looked in my bud vase in the middle of the table, and I was sad that it was lying, all lonely, in the bottom of the bin at the gym. I still had the card, though, tucked away in my purse.

Matt was in great form, because his agent had called him about a part in some new ITV drama that was being filmed in the autumn. He poured some Chardonnay, saying, "Maybe this is the beginning of something really good."

I smiled, and held up my glass, "To new beginnings," I said, and I felt only a little bit guilty. After all, I still hadn't *done* anything.

CHAPTER 3

Matt

It occurred to me in the morning, as Caroline was getting dressed, smiling indulgently at me, that I still hadn't broken the news about the money. Maybe I should do it now, while she was still basking in the glow of living with an actor on the brink of great success.

No, I couldn't face shattering the dream just yet. Maybe tonight, I thought, as she kissed me on the way out, looking very business-like in her new navy suit.

I rang the bank and made an appointment with the manager, to try and get a loan. Just to tide me over until the autumn, when the money would start coming in. Or so I would tell him . . .

"I'm afraid we won't be able to give you a loan, Mr Hughes," the bank manager said, trying to sound sympathetic, but half standing up, like the conversation was over before it had started.

"Why not?" I said. "The lobby is full of leaflets offering people money to buy cars and go to college and pay off credit-card bills. Why can't I have some?"

"Because you are not doing any of those things. You want to use it for daily living expenses, and you have no source of income with which to pay it back."

So much for being honest on the application form. I should have pretended I wanted to buy a car I couldn't afford. "But I'm a good prospect. Think of it like a student loan, investing in my future."

"But you're not a student, Mr Hughes. You're twenty-five, and you haven't earned any money to speak of since you graduated. You don't even have a track record to go on." I sighed. I couldn't even threaten to take my business elsewhere. Nan's money was well and truly gone. It was so depressing. The UK is becoming Americanised, with credit ratings dictating your every move.

I stood up to go. There was no point in trying to persuade him. Bank managers these days are just lackeys of bank policy. They have no power. He was only about thirty. It was just too humiliating to be turned down by someone who could have been at school with me, rather than some grizzly, wise old man who knows what's best for me, sir. I left the bank and wandered down the High Street, looking at all the things I couldn't buy in the shop windows. Caroline's birthday wasn't far away, and I had no idea what I would buy for her. I thought about ringing Mum and asking her for a loan, but she would wonder where Nan's money was gone. She said at the time that I should invest it, and I probably should have, but it's too late to think about that now. Anyway, I've never been quite sure if Mum was pissed off that Nan left all the money to me, rather than to her. Mum would never admit it, of course, and it's not the sort of thing you can ask. But she certainly wouldn't appreciate being tapped for a loan now. There was no way around it, I would just have to tell Caroline, and go with the flow.

I got back to the flat and picked up all the post off the hall floor and sorted it into piles. For some bizarre reason, every day I expect the post to bring me some good news, but of what kind I have never stopped to think. Most of the envelopes contained tacky prize-winner's notifications from the *Reader's Digest* for Nigel upstairs and there were a couple of clothes catalogues for Mel in the basement flat. Mike in number three had two envelopes and, as I put them on the hall shelf, I realised that one of them was a cheque book. He hadn't picked up his mail for a few days, so he must be away, I thought. And the other, one of those carefully anonymous white envelopes with no logo and a post-box number for a return address, very obviously contained his cheque card. Before I even stopped to think, I had shoved the cheque book and card into my jacket pocket and gone upstairs. I had never done anything like that before, but it seemed like Lady Fate was offering me a way out of trouble. My heart was pounding when I got into the flat, and I pulled the curtains across the living-room window in an excess of paranoia that one of the neighbours across the road could see me. Once I had ripped open the envelope, there was no going back. I told myself that Mike was a jerk, and that the bank would be liable for the loss anyway, and would refund him, so I would only be temporarily stealing from him. Barclay's could well afford a few quid to get me through until I landed a decent part. There would be no electronic alarm out on a cheque card, so I could write cheques without worrying about getting caught. I wouldn't go mad. Just use it for essential expenses. Like Caroline's birthday present. And I could do the food shopping every week, as my contribution to the bills. That would stop her nagging me. I practised a signature – *Michael S Grant* – until I was happy that it was convincing, and then signed the back of the card. The best hiding-place for the card was in my wallet, where Caroline would never see it, but I couldn't decide where to hide the cheque book. Finally I used the pocket of the revolting striped dressing-gown that her mother had sent me the previous Christmas. Caroline knows I hate it, but it hangs in the wardrobe in the silent, smug knowledge that it can't be thrown away or put in a charity bag. Instead of remorse or shame, I felt a huge elation, like I had committed the perfect crime. I still didn't have any money, but psychologically I had access to it. That made all the difference.

I now had a plan: use the credit card where I could, to pay my share, and worry about clearing the balance later, when I had some money. The cheques could be carefully doled out to get me through the next few months. They would be stopped, but if I was careful they wouldn't be traced back to me.

The other key part of the plan was getting a job. I knew it was pointless, but I rang my agent again. His assistant said he was out, but I knew by her tone that he was sitting there drinking coffee or doing something else too important to interrupt for me. I made a cup of tea and turned on the television, a very bad afternoon habit I have recently developed. I am hooked on *Ricki Lake*, *Montel* and the *Oprah Winfrey Show*. I started off thinking they were a good way to gain an insight into the sadder aspects of human nature, which could be useful in some future role I might play. The pure, unadulterated exhibitionism of the guests exposing their personal problems and dilemmas to an audience of millions has always fascinated me. Teenage street gang-members abandon their colours for love, cheating partners confess to each other, traumatised transsexuals are deserted by their friends, adopted children meet their birth parents. The whole gamut of trivia to tragedy is encapsulated in a half an hour of stage-managed empathy. I love it. But this time, Ricki was reuniting High School sweethearts now in their thirties, laughing at their year-book photographs and reminiscing about the sexual exploits of the cheerleading team. Too boring for me, even in my current state of complete frustration. I flicked through the channels and ended up watching an Open University sociology documentary, talking about the effect of unemployment on people's morale and motivation. I have never thought of myself as unemployed, probably because until now I had enough money to insulate myself from the idea. I have never signed on, and I am always waiting for the next acting job to come along. I say next, as if I have a stash of credits to my name, an agent made rich by my toil, and a scrapbook bulging with programmes featuring my face and my witty biography and list of awards. All I have is that one TV role in *Sherlock Holmes*, and the two gigs I did for no money to help out a friend from college who was doing fringe at the Brockley Jack pub theatre. I played a roaming gypsy, ducking and diving in petty crime, trying to hook the virtuous heroine, a local lass in some Midlands town who is attracted to this good-looking ne'er-do-well but afraid to trust him. Great role – I really enjoyed it. The intimacy of the theatre, with only about twenty-five people sitting in a square, practically touching me as I worked the tiny centre stage, really made me feel like an actor. Caroline keeps telling me I should try and do Rep, to build up a profile, before trying to break into TV, but she has no idea what that actually means. There is the thrill of playing small theatres, bringing 'the Arts' to provincial towns and seeing your face on the posters, but you have to stay in grotty B&B's, and eat crappy meals in greasy-spoon caffs, unless you want to spend every penny you earn just existing. The camaraderie of being on the road soon wears off when you are stuck with the same people for weeks on end, and rinsing out your underwear and hanging it over the shower-rail to dry overnight. TV work is much more my style – decent money, probably based in London, and instant profile without all the slogging. I just need someone – the right person – to see my work, and I know that other jobs will follow. I just need one break. I switched off the television in a fit of self-righteousness and decided to go out and look for Caroline's birthday present. I should make it something special, to help with softening her up for the news that I had no money left.

I went to Bond Street on the tube, as much to pass the time as to find any particular shop. I had to smile because there was a caramelly sort of smell in the carriage that I knew Caroline would have loved, and I looked around until I found the source. She was a skinny girl eating a bag of those caramel-covered nuts they sell on the corner of Oxford Circus, stirred around in a big hot copper pot with a wooden spatula, and scooped into a bag when someone stops to buy one. A lot tastier than the burnt chestnuts you get at Leicester Square, but not quite as 'London' – if pretzels are New York and chestnuts are London, then those 'chou-chou nuts' should be Paris or Milan, and not invade the savoury taste-buds of our city.

The girl looked homeless. She had that translucent look to her skin of someone who is permanently cold, not eating very well, and probably smoking. She got off at Bond Street as well and for some reason I walked behind her, slowing down my pace, curious about what she would do next. She looked in all the boutique windows with the same air of nonchalance, or maybe detachment, that rich people cultivate to hide their interest in anything. Maybe she came from a well-off family, or she was consciously copying the other window-shoppers, or she was just in some kind of daze. From behind she looked even skinnier, her thin legs in navy leggings truncated by chunky scuffed Nike trainers, and her straggly hair tossed over her narrow shoulders. For some strange reason, I was interested in her. I wanted to know her. She turned into a side street and walked down to Davis Street, and I followed. It was too early in the day for her to be looking for a doorway to settle down in, and I had a feeling she was on a mission rather than just wandering aimlessly. There were no shops here for me to pause and look into, like they do in the movies when they're following someone, so I slowed right down, dawdling along behind her, feeling a bit stupid, but drawn to follow. Then she disappeared into a doorway, and only when I came level did I see that it was a hairdressing salon – Toni and Guy's. She must be looking for a job I thought, as a junior, washing people's hair or sweeping up, and I admired her gumption. She wasn't going to just sit around begging. She was going to get herself a job and somewhere to stay and escape from the trap of homelessness. I saw her standing at the reception desk, being subjected to a down-the-nose look by the receptionist, who seemed to be checking in a diary or book of some kind. The girl looked out through the plate-glass front window just as I passed, and caught me staring. I gave her a sheepish smile and kept on walking. I felt like a voyeur, probing into her life without any logical reason at all.

I worked for a few months as a volunteer in a homeless shelter a couple of years ago, to alleviate my guilty conscience about not earning a living. I could cope with seeing the older men shambling into the shelter at night, usually stinking of drink and that unique street smell of dried urine, raided bins and stale sweat. For some reason, I could rationalise that they had made a choice about living on the street, and that some of them wouldn't take a permanent roof over their heads if it was offered to them. That generation, in their fifties and sixties, seemed more like the tramps of my childhood, idealised in storybooks as free spirits who wandered the countryside relying on people's good will for food and sleeping in sweet-smelling haystacks. They washed their socks in bubbling brooks, made tea in battered billy-cans and dispensed wise advice about life to little children, who weren't scared of them. The stark reality that faced me in the shelter bore no relationship to these childhood images, but I could talk to these old men, give them soup and clear up after them without the gut-wrenching feelings of pity that assailed me when I came across the pale, thin sixteen-year-olds. They always had a story to tell – of parental abuse, problems at school, or escape from children's homes. For some, the story was their currency of exchange, their way of proving their right to be part of this disjointed, sad little temporary community under one roof for a night. They never seemed to make the obvious connection when they sat beside the older ones, that they hadn't really escaped from their old life. They had just exchanged one set of desperate circumstances for another. I think that's why I was less shocked by the poverty and begging in India than Caroline was. It took her months to adjust, especially to the apparent resignation of the people to their lot in life. We often talked about the old chestnut of religion being a form of social control – why else would they passively accept such depths of poverty, unless they thought it was destined for them?

Memories of the hostel came flooding back as I walked up Bond Street, looking out for something to buy for Caroline. There was one girl of about seventeen who tried to bring her two dogs into the hostel, and was told she would have to leave them outside. She said she would rather sleep rough than lose the dogs. It was freezing, and it snowed later that night. I wondered as I crawled into my warm bed where she had ended up. There were some real characters too – Old Willy was a classic cockney comedian. He always had a one-liner for every situation and never seemed to be depressed or down.

Looking in the windows of jeweller's and designer clothes shops lost its appeal after about ten minutes – I went home. I shouldn't lie to Caroline. I should just be straight, tell her I had no money, and pull my finger out and get some work. That was my resolution as I walked from the station. I shouldn't let it drift any longer. I owed it to her to tell her. And what about the ITV role – should I admit I had made it up? Maybe not yet, there was still time.

I called my agent again, and I could hear by the way his assistant was chewing her bubble-gum that she couldn't care less and had no intention of putting me through. "Can I have a meeting with him, please?" I asked. "I want to get some advice about a change of direction." I figured if I could get in front of the guy I might convince him to put some energy into finding me work. 'Out of sight, out of mind' is a saying that probably came from the world of performance. I had absolutely no profile – how was the guy supposed to sell me to a casting director? The assistant flicked through some papers, trying to make them sound like the pages of a diary, and told me I could see him next month, on the fifteenth, at ten o'clock. She was probably hoping I would just give up, and say forget it, but I swallowed and said, "Fine, thanks, I'll see you then". I decided to set that as my target. I had a month to get sorted out, and if nothing good had happened by then I would tell Caroline everything.

Matthew

I sat in my office, staring out at the stark branches of the London plane-tree that stood guarding the entrance to our building. The buds were just visible as a lime-green haze at the tip of each twig. A pigeon sat on one of the branches for a moment, and then swooped downwards, having spotted a crumb dropped by a sandwich-munching passer-by. The sky was grey and heavy and it was difficult to be inspired by the pile of papers on my desk. I couldn't summon the energy to go out and get something for lunch but, on the other hand, I never had time to eat after work on Wednesdays. It was a rush to get to the Law Centre by six o' clock, and there was always a queue of clients (the "druggies and drop-outs of Brixton" as Liz called them) waiting.

I stood up and stretched. Maybe some fresh air would revive me and I could tackle the problem of the legal jurisdiction applying to my client's situation with more enthusiasm when I got back. Jack's antics during the night had well and truly broken my sleep, and as usual it took ages to get back to sleep, once I started thinking about work and feeling guilty about Caroline, and even some of my case work at the centre. In my usual feeble attempt to incorporate exercise into my day rather than devoting any special time to it, I walked down the three flights of stairs to the lobby. I started thinking about Jermaine as I went down Ludgate Hill to get a sandwich from Antonio's on the corner of Carter Lane. He would undoubtedly be at the centre tonight, wondering if I had magically found a way of solving his housing-benefit problems and preventing his eviction at the end of the month. I couldn't think of any other way of helping him. I had contacted his local councillor, who had promised to raise the case at a meeting with the benefits payment agency. She said the agency's backlog of paperwork was so big that there was a very low chance of resolving his case within two weeks, but she would continue to advocate for him in the meantime. Unfortunately, Jermaine doesn't help himself by ignoring letters, summons and statements he receives, until they reach such a threatening tone that even he is moved to take action. He is dyslexic, and only in desperate circumstances will he admit to it, and ask someone to read his correspondence for him. Then he ends up coming to see us at the Law Centre and expects us to wave our magic wands and get everything sorted out. He was due to appear in court twice in the following week, on Tuesday for the appeal on his housing-benefit claim, and on Friday at the magistrates' court for theft. I paid for my tuna and grated cheese sandwich and ready-salted crisps, and made my way to Finsbury Circus to find a free bench beside the bowling green. I wondered what Caroline was doing for lunch, and then guiltily thought of Liz. She would be working manically, maybe taking thirty seconds out to ask her PA to go and buy her a sandwich, but worrying that she was leaving work at five o'clock today to get home and relieve the nanny. Nicky was still off sick, and Liz was tempted to fire her and take on Sylvie, this French temporary girl who seemed to have settled in really well. So Liz was trying to get home on time, to keep Sylvie interested. I had offered to leave early, and then remembered it was Wednesday, so I had to ring Liz and withdraw the offer. She wasn't impressed, and our conversation was very brief. She can't understand why I do the Law Centre work. She keeps telling me I don't need to prove anything to anybody by representing "druggies and drop-outs".

When I first met Liz at university she was full of youthful idealism and socialist principles. We used to bemoan the fate of the miners and deliver leaflets for the local Labour Party. But then her career really took off, so she never had time to do anything else. Fifteen years and two kids on, we both seem to have changed beyond recognition. I know I used to be a lot more fun, and I was always the life and soul of the party when we got together with old university friends. I could tell a really good story and have everyone laughing, especially Liz. She's beautiful when she laughs, and she has a really contagious giggle. I realised as I sat on the bench that I haven't seen Liz laugh for quite a long time. She's always tired, and stressed out by work, or by the children. I haven't told a funny story or made anyone laugh for a while, either. Though, I had surprised myself the day before when on the spur of the moment I called a florist's and ordered a single red rose for Caroline, with a message saying I would call her. It had felt good. I wondered how long I should wait before calling her.

At ten to six, as I changed onto the Victoria line to go to Brixton, my phone gave a brief pip to say I had a message, but I didn't have time to check it, and forgot about it as I rushed down Electric Avenue to the Law Centre. It's right on the corner of Brixton market, and I love the noisy throngs of people, the smell of fruit and vegetables and even the slightly off-sweet odour of the piles of meat on the butchers' counters. Loud reggae music blared from a ghetto-blaster on the CD stall.

There were six people waiting on the orange plastic chairs in the waiting-room and I recognised a couple of the faces. No sign of Jermaine yet. Maybe I had misjudged him. I settled in behind the desk and had a quick look at the three files which had been put out by

Gloria, one of the assistants. I smiled at her.

"How are you today, my dear?" she asked, flicking the switch on the kettle beside her desk. "Tea?"

"Lovely, thanks, Gloria. I haven't had time for any tea this afternoon."

Gloria is a glamorous Nigerian lady whose enormous girth is always clad in swathes of vibrant fabric, and her lips painted a glossy burnt orange. "Adrian just left, he said he was sorry to miss you, but he had to get off home. He saw about four or five this afternoon."

It is always busier in the evenings, even though most of our clients don't have jobs and could come in any time during the day. "Thanks, Gloria," I said as she put a mug of tea and a digestive biscuit on the desk. She is the only paid member of staff in the centre, which is meagrely funded by the local council and the single regeneration budget. The legal professionals are all volunteers, and although we try to have a regular commitment to the project, sometimes work pressures take over, so the cover is scanty.

Just after eight o'clock I said good-bye to the last client, and sighed with relief. Sometimes I can be there until ten, and it takes an hour to get home. Gloria had left already, so I quickly rinsed out my mug and locked the files in the cabinet. I pulled the outside shutter halfway down, to make sure no-one else came in, and went out the back to the toilet. We operate from a railway arch, so the facilities are primitive, and it was freezing out there. As usual there were no paper towels, so I shook my hands dry, locked the back door and went to get my coat. I thought I saw feet walking slowly past the bottom of the shutter, but didn't pay any attention. Atlantic Road is quite a busy thoroughfare at all times of the day and night.

I bent down to stoop under the shutter and was just straightening up outside when a heavy blow landed on the back of my neck, and a shock of electricity seemed to turn on a blinding light in my head. I collapsed on the pavement, and I can just remember the surreal vision of my own face looming closer in a dark puddle as I fell. They took my wallet, my mobile phone and my brief-case, which luckily didn't have any confidential files in it. My watch was gone too, but luckily I don't wear a wedding ring, so they hadn't had to chop my finger off to get it.

When I woke up, I was temporarily disconcerted when I couldn't place the flowery curtains that surrounded me, but when I saw the white uniform of the nurse leaning over me it all fell into place. I was on a stretcher trolley in the Accident and Emergency depart-ment of Kings College hospital. The nice Irish nurse told me I had been there for about half an hour. I tried to read her name badge and couldn't figure out what it said. She reassured me that it wasn't concussion and loss of ability to read. No-one knew how to pronounce 'Niamh'. She said that Liz was on the way.

"Now, I'll just go and call the doctor to have a look at you." She rustled out of the cubicle.

I stared at the polystyrene tiles above my head, counting them to reassure myself that my brain was still functioning. I lifted my head half an inch, but the shooting pain down my neck stopped me trying anything more adventurous. I recognised Liz's footsteps as she walked down the corridor, and I heard her anxious voice asking the desk nurse where I was. She swished aside the curtain, her face tight and white, and gave me a little nervous smile when she saw that I was awake.

"They told me you were unconscious," she gasped, and she kissed me, looking into my eyes, and cupping my face in her hands like she does with the boys when they're upset.

"I just woke up." I didn't feel up to a conversation, so I just lay there, and she sat beside me, obviously torn between wanting to know what happened, and not wanting to tire me out. "We'll just wait for the doctor," she said, holding my hand. "I got Mum to come around to look after the boys. Lucky she was in, it's her bridge night tonight, but her partner was sick."

"You got here very quickly," I said.

"It doesn't feel like it, believe me. I feel like I've been trying to get here for hours. First Mum didn't answer the phone because she was in the bath, so I thought she'd already gone out. I was frantically ringing Sylvie's mobile to see if she could come back, when the other line beeped and it was Mum. She'd heard the phone and done 1471 and rung me back. Then Jack threw up just as Mum arrived so I couldn't leave her to cope with that, but Ben played up when I tried to go out the front door, so I had to do 'huggies' and 'big huggies' before he would let me go. Even then I could hear him wailing as I got into the car." She was talking in long, breathless sentences, and her voice was croaky with stress.

"Don't worry, I'll be fine," I said, through gritted teeth. The pain in my head was worse than anything I've ever experienced before, and I wanted to be sick. "Can you see if they have one of those bowler-hat things to get sick into?" I gasped, but it was too late. As Liz bent down to look under the bedside locker, I threw up all over the sheet.

She called the nurse, and started ineffectually mopping at the sheet with a tissue from her sleeve. "You poor thing," she said, giving up with the tissue and stroking the side of my face instead. "I brought you some clean clothes, in case you need them." "Thanks," I said, smiling wanly at her.

She couldn't sit still. "Will you have a glass of water, to get rid of the taste?" she said, holding the glass to my lips, almost like a dental nurse ministering to a very young or very senile patient.

"I can hold it," I said, taking it off her, but when I lifted my head and tilted it to drink, a shock of pain made me drop the glass.

The nurse bustled back in just then, saying, "Oh dearie me, you're making a right old mess there, aren't you?" She bent to the bottom drawer of a cabinet in the corner and took out a clean sheet, unfolding it as she came back to the bed. "Now, Mrs, eh – ?" "Turner," said Liz distractedly.

"Mrs Turner, if you could just support his shoulders while I whip this out." She pulled away the pillows, and the top half of the sheet, and had slipped the fresh one underneath in seconds. Then she did the bottom half, saying, "There we are, that's much better, isn't it? The doctor is on the way back to see you, make sure you're all right to go home. Can I get you some more water?" She took the jug and was gone before I could reply.

Liz sat tentatively on the edge of the bed. "I'm parked miles away. When he releases you, I'll take you down in the lift and leave you in reception while I go and get it. It's still raining out there."

I just stopped myself from nodding, and said, "Thanks."

"Can you talk about it yet?"

"There's nothing much to say. I was just locking up when I was clunked on the back of my head by a person or persons unknown," I said, in a parody of the style we use in the magistrates' court.

"You didn't see anything?"

"No, except for a pair of average-looking Nike-type feet attached to a pair of track suit bottoms. And they might not even belong to the guy who hit me."

"Why would they do that, Matthew, when they know that you're helping them?"

Her naivety astounded me. "What do you mean, helping *them*? Do you think there's some kind of protective halo that you get when you do a bit of work in the community that makes you immune to being attacked just like anyone else?"

"No, of course not, but you were in the Law Centre, and very obviously coming out from working in there –"

"And the guy who took my stuff to sell for his next fix is really going to care about that?" I snorted. Sometime, he would probably come in looking for advice, or maybe he had already sat in front of my desk, looking at my Rolex and guessing how fat my wallet would be.

"Sorry." She looked downcast and I felt bad. "But I still think you should stop doing the Law Centre work – there must be something safer you can do," she appealed to me and held my hand.

A female doctor pulled aside the curtain and said hello. She stooped down and lifted my eyelids one at a time, asking me to look up, down and sideways. A very slight hint of perfume was almost masked by the clinical hospital smell and I thought it was familiar. *Contradiction.* Caroline. I looked into the little light as instructed, and answered the doctor's questions about the pain in my neck, while she looked into my ears and took my pulse. If I had been on one of those heart-monitors I wonder if it would have jumped when I thought of Caroline, and then settled back into a steady rhythm of medium-sized blips. Liz drove me home, and I dozed through most of the journey. I found it easier to escape that way than to find reasons to justify why I would continue to work the Law Centre. The doctor had provided a useful interruption and I had no intention of bringing the subject up again.

The house was dark when we got home. Liz's mother had left a porch light on so we could see where to put the key in the front door, but was obviously saving energy by switching off the hall light when she went to bed. It was 1.37 on the digital clock radio as I put my head gingerly on the pillow, and Liz kissed me gently and rolled over.

I hadn't even said 'Thank you for coming to collect me'. Maybe that's what the problem is between us – taking each other for granted.

CHAPTER 4

Matthew

"But it's morning time, Daddy, get up!" shouts Ben on the morning following the attack. I can hear Ellie, Liz's mother outside in the hall, reluctant to intrude into the bedroom.

"Sorry, Matthew, I couldn't keep him distracted downstairs," she says tentatively at the door.

"Daddeee!" shouts Jack, toddling in, thinking he's missing out on the action.

Ben has pulled himself onto Liz's side of the bed, and is prodding me. "Daddy, tickle me, Daddy! Grangran stayed in our house last night. She said I could have a treat later if I'm a good boy. Am I a good boy, Daddy?"

Jack is pulling at the duvet, trying to scale the height

of the bed, and failing. *"Daddeee!"* he wails.

"You can come in," I call out desperately to Ellie, unable to lift Jack onto the bed, or push Ben off it.

She peers around the shared burgundy dressing-gown that hangs on the edge of the door, ready for middle-of-the-night excursions to see to one of the boys. "Sorry, Matthew. Come on now, boys, time to get ready for the park!" She tries to sound enthusiastic, but just sounds hesitant. Little boys have a built-in sense of smell for lack of authority. They ignore her. Ben has now climbed onto my chest.

"Come on, horsey! I want you to be a green horse today, so I can fall off."

I look, cross-eyed, down my nose at him. "Daddy's not very well today, Ben, so he can't play horsey. I have to stay in bed until my neck is better."

"Did the baddie hit you with something hard?" he says, and I jolt painfully.

"Who told him that?" I ask Ellie.

"He overheard Liz on the phone to your office. She was telling your assistant that you'd been mugged and had a nasty bump on your head." Ellie reaches across me and lifts Ben off the bed. "Come on, Benny boy, time to have a wee-wee and get your coat on."

"Noo-oh!" he wriggles and kicks.

Ellie stands up. "Right, Jack, we're just going to have to leave Ben behind – come along, we'll just take those doughnuts I brought yesterday and feed the ducks." She takes Jack by the hand, and he trots along beside her, trying to say "*duck, duck, quack, quack!*".

Ben shimmies across the bed and slides his feet onto the floor. "I'm a bit busy now, Daddy – I'll come and play with you later, when I'm finished," he says importantly, and scampers out of the room. I sink back on the pillows, and close my eyes. My eyelids are throbbing.

The slightest movement of my head sends a shooting pain down through my vertebrae. I've been given some anti-inflammatory capsules. They help the pain, but give me dizzy spells and a queasy stomach.

I'm conscious that I need to be better by tomorrow. I desperately want to meet Caroline after work. But Liz won't want me to go back to work so soon.

It will be difficult for the boys today, knowing that I am in the house but they aren't supposed to disturb me, and for the first time I understand Liz's claim that it is easier to go to work when she feels ill than to stay at home in bed. For Ben and Jack, our bed is the castle where the dirty rascal is vanquished by the king, or a ship surrounded by crocodiles and sharks that will bite off their toes. Sometimes it's a dinosaur nest, and Daddy Dinosaur helps them to fight off the monsters. But it's certainly not a place for sleeping, especially when it's bright outside.

Liz said she would try to be home for six, but her mother has promised to stay for the day, since the French nanny got herself a permanent job and Nicky is still off sick. Liz got all anxious about yet another strange person looking after the boys, and I have to say, I agreed with her. Ben thrives on a routine, and if he's not going to have one, he might as well be with his grandmother, being spoilt rotten. Poor Liz, she takes it all to heart so much. There is no way that any woman can do the whole job-and-mother thing without losing out somewhere. In Liz's case, I think it's our relationship that loses. She is a really great mother, and I know that while she is in her high-powered meetings, and navigating the Sargasso Seas of corporate politics, she thinks about Ben and Jack all the time. When she first went back to work after Jack, she was in a taxi with one of her male colleagues on the way to a meeting at Warburg's in the City, and they passed some roadworks. She said instinctively, "Oh, look, a digger!" pointing at the JCB which was scooping out a drain channel. She laughed and tried to cover it up, but the guy looked at her like she was mad. She says she quite often smiles in meetings and people wonder why, when they're discussing some dull financial reporting issue. She's remembering Jack's first step, or Ben's story about the worm he met on the garden path. Despite all this, she says she's not cut out for full-time motherhood, and I can see why. She is very bright, very interested in people – adult people – and found her time off work more dull and tiring than going into the office. But now that she's gone back, it seems like she has absolutely no headspace left for me. Or even heart space. I get a peck on the cheek when we leave for work in the morning, and a peck in the evening, offered from the sofa, where she is entwined with the boys as they drink their bedtime milk and watch a *Thomas the Tank Engine* video in their pyjamas. Ben doesn't like when we try to have an intelligent conversation, and starts wriggling around, or throwing things to get our attention. If he's feeling virtuous, he'll say, "Mummy, 'scuse me, 'scuse me, *'scuse me*, Mummy!" until Liz looks at him, and she says to me, "Can we talk about it over dinner, when they've gone to bed?"

I nod, and we talk to the children, or through the children, and by the time we've had dinner, and cleared up, and watched the news, we are both so tired that we fall into bed, kiss – another tight dry peck – and roll over. Sex just doesn't happen. Sometimes she laughs, a sort of sad, wistful, 'if only' laugh, when I make a tentative advance on her as we flop on the sofa. She stays for the news headlines at ten, and then goes bustling into the kitchen to prepare milk, put on the dishwasher, write out the cheque for the milkman or make sure that the kitchen bin has been emptied. It's difficult to recreate the mood after that. It must happen to everyone who has children, I suppose. Maybe it doesn't bother them so much, or maybe it just passes. At the moment I feel like I have a pleasant but platonic relationship with Liz. I am horrified at the thought that this is it. Maybe the quiet companionship my parents share could have started when they were in their thirties, and is not the result of forty-five years together but the result of having children! No-one warns you about that bit. They say that lack of sleep is a killer, and that you stop having a social life, but they don't warn you that you lose your sex life completely, and feel like you're drifting further and further apart.

I am very rarely ill, so I am not very good at lying in bed doing nothing. I try to sleep. I remind myself how difficult it is to get up for work at 6.30 a.m. How I have not had a full night's sleep for over three years. How my body needs rest to recover.

I slide out of bed, trying not to move any muscles in my neck, and switch on the portable television in the corner of the room. We haven't progressed to a remote control, because we're afraid we'll turn into 'Terry and June' even quicker than we are already, and go to bed every night at nine o' clock to watch television. Without a remote, you have to really want to watch the programme, and hop out of bed to switch off the TV before you fall asleep, thereby retaining a modicum of discernment and youthful vigour.

I hope that Liz reported my stolen wallet last night, rather than waiting until this morning. The guys who steal them don't hang around, and no doubt my credit card will be on to its third user by now.

The news programme finishes and some guy called Montel starts interviewing transsexuals about how their former partners reacted when they made the change. What is this voyeuristic obsession we have with other people's sad lives? I thought about Caroline, and wondered if she had got the flower. Now is the time to stop it all before it gets out of hand. Liz has been so loving and worried about me, I can't betray her. We just need to talk about stuff and work out what is going wrong. It's not like we have massive rows or anything. We don't talk enough for that. I lie back and remember Caroline's smile across that conference-room table. When the water was dripping down onto my crotch, I looked up and caught her eye. I got a hard-on.

She knew. I laid the paper napkin on my lap to disguise it, shifted my chair further under the table. Someone to my left finished mopping the table and poured me a fresh glass of water. I sipped it, and looked over the rim of the glass. She was watching me. She looked down and made a note of the date on the top of her pad of paper. Her left hand was spread on the pad, holding it firm on the glass surface. Pink, small round nails on tiny hands. No rings.

The telephone rings on the bedside table and I forget about my ribs and stretch across to answer it. So the person on the other end just hears a loud grunt of pain. "Hello? Are you there?" a concerned but official-sounding female voice asks.

"Yes, sorry, I'm fine," I say.

"Could I speak to a Mr Matthew Turner, please?"

"Speaking."

"Good morning, sir, it's WPC Somers here, from the robbery squad at Brixton police station. I'm calling to let you know that we have recovered some property which we have reason to believe may be yours."

"Oh, that was quick," I say. "I wasn't even sure if my wife had reported it yet."

"Yes, sir, the report was filed in the early hours of this morning."

Good old Liz. She always stays calm and does the right thing in a crisis.

"Are you able to come into the station, sir, to identify your property?"

I swing my legs out of the bed and inhale sharply with the pain in my neck. "I don't think so, not for a couple of days. My neck is really painful and I can't drive at the moment. My wife is out at work."

"That's fine, sir, I understand. Perhaps I could give you the station number and you could call when you feel up to it, and arrange to come in?"

"Yes, I'll do that." I scribble down the number on the pad beside the bed, and promise to call in a few days. "Just as a matter of interest, what have you recovered?"

"We can discuss that when you come in to the station, sir. Have you cancelled all your credit and debit cards?"

"Yes, I think my wife did it this morning."

"Well, we'll see you when you come in, and I wish you

a speedy recovery."

"Thanks for the call." I wonder if she is working her way down a long list of calls, tidying up the paperwork in the aftermath of another night of street crime in Brixton. They have probably caught a "runner", one of the kids who act as couriers between the drug-dealers and handlers. A mugger will go to a drug-dealer with mobile phones, credit cards and store cards, and hand them over in straight exchange for drugs. A mobile phone will only buy one rock of crack, which doesn't go far if you have a serious habit. The dealer will disappear with the goods, and send a runner back to the punter with the drugs. The runner takes the valuables to a handler for cash, which he then brings back to the dealer. These kids are sometimes as young as twelve, and they ride bikes or mopeds like they're playing a video game, swerving around people and obstacles, and frequently crashing. The police look out for these accidents and rush to help the kid, knowing that in the process they will find a stash of drugs, cash or valuables in panniers or backpacks. Often, that is the only way that street-crime victims are reunited with their property. As I lie on the bed, I wonder which kid has been caught this time, and if he is sitting in the youth detention cell in Brixton station, waiting for his "appropriate adult" to turn up. More likely to be a social worker than a parent or relative. I had a twelve-year-old boy in to see me in the Law Centre a few months ago, a runner for one of the drug-dealers on Electric Avenue. He'd already had a caution for carrying stolen goods when he crashed his bike into the side of a car coming down Atlantic Road, and was "rescued" by a friendly town-centre police officer. They had confiscated the bike and he wanted my advice about how to get it back. Some front – he'll go far, and probably in the wrong direction. In only nine years, Ben will be the same age as him. Even in the 'safe' suburb of Bromley, our boys will be exposed to things I would never have known at the same age.

Caroline

He still hadn't called. How soon is soon for him, I wondered. Strange man – he sent me a red rose, and then ignored my thank-you message on the phone. I couldn't ring him at work – the deal we were working on had been taken over by his colleague and I had no reason to ring him there.

Anyway, I wasn't going to chase him – he might have had a change of heart, or met someone else, or anything. I just felt stupid. My message was a bit gushy. Maybe he thought I was too keen.

On Thursday night Matt suggested we go to a movie at the Ritzy, and there was only one film we could agree we wanted to see, so I booked it on my credit card, and we walked down to the Z bar for a drink beforehand.

As we wandered down Acre Lane, Matt reached over and took my hand, saying, "You're a bit preoccupied – are you OK?"

I hadn't even noticed we weren't holding hands. I was just wondering what it would feel like to walk down the street with Matthew. He's taller and bigger all over than Matt, and I would imagine that his hand would dwarf mine, making me feel all vulnerable and girly, and protected by my big strong man. Matt is slight, and has narrow hips, and a neat little boy's bum. Funnily enough, he has quite short fingers, even though he is tall. We drew around our hands once, on a piece of paper like kids do, and my fingers were longer than his.

"Hmm? No, I'm fine, really. Just thinking about a deal at work," I said, smiling at him, wondering how long I would be able to hide it from him.

"You're very busy at work these days. Is it going to get any better, or will I have to find another girl to take to the cinema soon?" Matt squeezed my hand, and smiled at me.

I stumbled.

"It's OK, I was only joking," he said. "I'm sometimes jealous that you have work, and I'm sitting around festering."

"It's only a couple of months until that other job starts though," I said, grinning with relief.

I had been staying late at work, waiting for a call from Matthew, standing beside the phone until the very last moment. I knew it was the only place he could call me. I had also started topping up my lipstick when I went out, in case he turned up outside the office.

We stopped outside the Traidcraft shop for a quick look in the window. A shadow loomed over us and I looked up to see a grey sweater hood and skinny black face with a goatee beard.

"Got a light, mate?" he asked, holding out a cigarette to Matt, his stale, unwashed breath wafting past my face. I recoiled. "Wha's your fucking problem?" he snarled at me, his beard twisting like a snake on his chin. I couldn't speak, so I just stood there, afraid to take my eyes off him to see what Matt was doing behind me.

"No. Sorry, mate, I don't smoke," said Matt, and I could feel him pulling my arm.

We stepped away from the window, Matt with his arm around my shoulders now, and turned to walk away.

"Fuck you!" he shouted from behind, and charged us, driving his head like a battering ram between our bodies, his shoulders impacting at the level of our waists, and I felt his rigid arm thumping into my left kidney. We all fell down, and I instinctively rolled away from him as we hit the pavement. I lifted my head and he looked directly at me, a mixture of desperation and frustration in his eyes. He scrambled to his feet, slipping on the greasy pavement in a parody of a breakdance, and scuttled off around the corner.

Matt jumped up and put his arm around me. "Are you

all right?" His forearm brushed off my coat sleeve and he winced. He held it up and we could see a long graze along the underside, with a dark black punctuation mark at the wrist.

"That looks deep." I winced, and steered him towards a streetlamp so we could get a better look.

"I think it's OK," he said. "Come on, I need a drink." He let his sleeve fall back down and limped beside me.

"Did you hurt your leg as well?" I asked as we reached the corner, and I had an urge to look around it and make sure the guy wasn't lurking there waiting for us.

"I might have sprained my ankle on the edge of the kerb. Bastard! Did he hurt you?"

I felt my kidney, pressing it with the heel of my hand. "I might get a bruise, but I'm fine. He didn't get my bag, either. I landed on top of it. We were so lucky."

"Lucky?" Matt said. "Brixton is getting worse. I used to think we were safe because we weren't out drug-dealing on the street at two o' clock in the morning, but you see those yellow witness-appeal boards sprouting up on every street corner these days."

"We could have been stabbed, and he didn't get away with anything," I said, pressing the pedestrian-crossing button, too shaken to think about crossing the road without the reassuring presence of a green man beckoning us.

We pushed open the doors of the cinema, and I got Matt to sit down in the bar, while I bought two beers.

As I turned to go back to the table, I looked over at Matt. His face was pale and drawn with pain, and he was peering at the puncture-hole in his arm, prodding the edge of it with his forefinger. I put the cold beers down on the zinc-topped table, adding ours to the rings of liquid from previous filmgoers.

"Do you want to go to casualty?" I asked. "Just to get it checked out?"

"No, we'll be there for hours, and they'll probably just tell me to take paracetamol and keep it clean."

I looked more closely. The hole was tiny, but very black and looked deep. "You were lucky it missed a vein. Do you think there's any chance of glass being stuck in it?"

He turned on me. "Why do you keep saying we're lucky, and I'm lucky? We've just been attacked, and knocked down in the street. I've got a bloody hole in my arm and a twisted ankle, and you got whacked in the kidneys. That is not my idea of a pleasant Thursday evening out."

"Sorry," I said, unable to summon the energy to justify anything. "I've got a headache now. Will we just go home and forget about the film?"

"Yeah," Matt said, draining his beer. "Do you want this?" He held up the other bottle, which I had barely touched.

I was already standing up, ready to go. "No, you have it."

He drained that one too, and grabbed his coat off the back of the chair.

We fought our way through the bar, which was suddenly full of people coming out of the earlier showing of the film, eager for another beer before they went home. It was really hot in there, and the cold air hit my cheeks as we came out. Matt's knees suddenly buckled under him, and he leaned heavily on my shoulder.

"You shouldn't have drunk that beer so quickly," I said, looking around to see if a black taxi might miraculously appear. I edged my shoulder under his armpit, and we shuffled to the edge of the footpath.

Matt was as white as chalk and I was just wondering if we could stagger down Coldharbour Lane to the minicab office, when a Ford Granada pulled up and a Jamaican voice said, "Minicab, dahlin'? Where you goin'?"

I broke all the rules for sensible girls in the city and nodded. A fifty-something black guy hopped out and came around to open the back door of the car. He helped Matt into the back seat, and waited until I shunted in beside him before closing the door and going back around to the driver's side.

"He had too many beers?" he asked, as he pulled away from the kerb.

"No, yes, sort of . . ." I stuttered. "Can we go to Evelyn Gardens, please? Number 47."

"Sure, dahlin', anywhere you wanna go," he said, turning down the radio.

"We got mugged," I found myself blurting out, trusting him just because he had a Kurt Franklin gospel song playing on his car radio. Matt was slumped against the side of the car.

"I fink you wan' the hospital, man. Get him check' out, jus' in case, you know what I'm sayin?" He put his arm across the back of the passenger seat and leveraged his neck around to look at me, his eyebrow raised, waiting for the word. The traffic light changed to green, and a horn blared behind us.

"No, it's OK, I'll just take him home," I said, thinking a warm bed and a good night's sleep would be a better cure than sitting on a plastic chair in casualty for hours.

"Whatever you say, dahlin'." He drove down Brixton High Street and I realised I was looking at everyone's face. How would I react if I actually recognised the mugger?

"Them take your bag?"

"No, we were lucky," I found myself saying again.

"The Lord, he lookin' afta you. You not hurt too bad and nothin' taken," he said, turning the radio back up, as Benny King announced the next song. "I do like dis one," he said, humming along as he indicated to turn onto our road.

Matt groaned when he was getting out of the car, and I was terrified that I had done the wrong thing. Maybe I should have taken him to the hospital after all.

"No charge, dahlin', you got enough on you' plate,"

the driver said as I held out a fiver. Matt managed to climb the front steps and just leaned against the wall as I opened the door. He was still very pale, but his eyes looked alert now. "I think those beers just went to my head a bit too quickly," he said, as we went inside. I got him to sit on the edge of the bed, pulling off his boots and jeans as if he was a child or an old man. I made an ice-pack for his ankle, which had gone blue and swollen, and found the iodine in the bathroom cupboard to clean the graze and the puncture-hole in his arm. He smiled at me, with that special wounded but brave expression that men reserve for these occasions. I turned on the television and climbed into bed beside him. We drank hot chocolate and ate ginger-nut biscuits, watching a dreadful Channel 5 movie about a teenager who murdered a classmate with a samurai sword. We didn't talk about what had happened. I think that Matt's pride was hurt, and I didn't want to push it. We went to sleep with me cradling his head in my arms.

CHAPTER 5

Matt

I woke up the morning after the mugging and felt much better. The puncture mark in my arm didn't look too bad in daylight, and I pushed away the nagging doubt that it could have been a contaminated needle or something that would give me tetanus. Caroline was humming in the shower, and had *News Direct* blaring out over the sound of the water. I went into the kitchen and put on the kettle for tea and looked out the window. A squirrel was running down the trunk of a tree in the back garden. The next-door neighbour's black cat was huddled under a bush, pretending indifference, but the flick at the end of his tail gave the game away.

Caroline came into the kitchen wrapped in a fluffy

peach towel, her feet shoved into the flat blue silk mules I had given her for Christmas. "How are you feeling?" she asked, lifting up my arm to have a look.

"Better. Thanks for looking after me last night," I said, turning her around and lifting the towel. "How's your kidney?" She had a purple bruise just above her hip, and it made her seem so vulnerable. I touched her soft, moisturised, scented skin, and she flinched.

"Fine. Matt, have you got any change? I only have notes, and you know I hate queuing up in the tube station in the morning – it's a nightmare." She grabbed her tea and was already on her way out to get dressed.

I started to say, "Yes, my wallet should be on the . . ." and then remembered the credit card. "No, hang on," I called and followed her into the bedroom.

She was picking up my jeans, feeling in the pockets. "It's not here, Matt, did you . . .?"

We both realised at the same time.

"You didn't notice it was gone, last night?"

I could hardly believe it myself. I had been a bit dazed, and just worried about Caroline's bag, and my ankle and my arm . . . and those beers had really messed me up.

"You'll have to report it, and cancel all your cards." Caroline was pulling on a pair of tights. She slipped a Jaeger dress over her head, and immediately transformed herself from tiny, gorgeous, caring Caroline into corporate Supergirl, short hair already dry, diamante earrings glittering on her soft earlobes. She pulled on her trainers, which I always think looks ridiculous, and gave me a peck on the cheek.

"You should be quick, Matt, because they'll ask why you didn't report it last night," she said, picking up her briefcase.

I sighed. Shit, I didn't want my wallet to be found. Not by the police, anyway. And now, the delay in reporting the theft would look even more suspicious. But I called the credit-card company and the bank, and cancelled my cards. The credit-card company told me I had to get a crime number from the police, unless I wanted to be liable for the spending on the card. I got dressed, my heart pounding, trying to think of a way around this. Caroline would ask me if I had reported it, the credit-card company would insist on a crime number. I was trapped.

I got the bus to Brixton and went into the police station before I had any more time to think.

The double glass doors were surprisingly heavy, and as I went in a tiny Indian woman came out, distraught and weary, even the red dot on her wrinkled forehead looking dusty. There was a queue of people waiting to be seen.

A blind man with a dog was rattling the handle of the door to an inner office, saying "'Scuse me, can you get the door, please?" in the general direction of the reception desk.

A Scottish woman turned around from the front of the queue and said loudly, as if he was deaf, "There's no-one at the desk, love." Then she said to the woman behind her, "Honest to God, the phone is ringin' off the hook, a load of us been waiting for ages, and not one person there, behind the desk."

A desk sergeant appeared, and said briskly, "Right, who's next?"

As I joined what I thought was the back of the queue, a young guy and a middle-aged woman materialised from nowhere and pushed their way in front of me. There was a big argument going on now at the front, about who was next in the queue.

The Scottish woman was slagging off a tall, gangly dreadlocked woman with a scraggy mongrel on a lead. "There is a queue here, you know, you can't just walk up and ask what you want."

"It's just a very quick thing – my keys, I've lost my keys," said the dreadlock queen, in a surprisingly posh drawling voice. She tossed her burgundy-coloured hair over her shoulder and it reached to her backside.

"It doesn't matter, does it, we're all in the same boat." The Scottish woman looked back at the rest of us, hoping for allies.

"Oh, get a life, why don't you," her adversary drawled, looking down her nose.

The smaller woman managed to look her up and down, even from her considerable height disadvantage, and said, "I've got a life. But I'd suggest you make a visit to the laundrette, eh?" It was the kind of 'eh?' that precedes a head-butt in a Glasgow kiss joke.

A female police officer came to the desk and said, "Did you skip the queue?"

"She did," spat the blonde Scotswoman.

"You shouldn't really skip the queue, but I can confirm that no keys have been handed in," the well-ironed WPC said.

"Thank you, you've been nice – unlike some others I could mention." The tall one swished her ankle-length mud-caked coat around and pulled the dog past me, leaving a smell of unwashed hair and coconut musk behind her.

"I'm here to see if my brother is lying."

There was camaraderie now, between the women at the front.

"I've lost my income support money."

"Well, my brother's gone to the Post Office this morning, got a load of money out, supposed to be for me, and he reckons he got mugged. Going to Scotland now, for God knows how long, with my money, most likely. If I find out he wasn't mugged, I'm going straight home to sort him out."

"Next, please," shouted a new face from behind the counter. Suddenly there were four officers on duty and the queue started moving again. I looked at the posters on the wall. The Crime Stoppers telephone number was emblazoned everywhere. *Carrying A Knife In The Street Could Slash Two Years Off Your Life*, said one orange-coloured poster with a jagged black mark down the middle.

Stop The Killing, said another one.

Maybe Caroline was right and we had been lucky after all. I crossed the *Wait Here* line and stepped up to the desk.

"Can I help you, sir?" asked a skinny guy with a number-one shave all over. He looked about nineteen. I must be getting old when police officers look too young.

"Yes, I want to report a mugging," I said, quietly. It seemed cowardly, somehow, to admit to being a victim in this place.

"I'll just need to take some details, sir," the police officer said, and he stepped over to a computer behind a desk and sat down.

"Your name, sir?" he asked, raising his voice to project it across the desk and over the counter. I couldn't believe he was going to take all the details there, with people listening.

I muttered my name, and had to repeat it. I could feel the young guy behind me listening. I could feel his interest burning a hole in my back as I leaned as far as possible over the counter.

I gave the officer the main details and when the two-fingered typing was finally finished, he stepped back up to the counter. "Did you get a good look at the perpe-trator's face, sir?"

"Well, yes, I suppose but …"

"Would you or your girlfriend be able to identify him from photo-ID?"

My stomach turned. I just wanted a crime number. "I really don't think I saw him well enough, to be honest," I said, feeling like a middle-class wimp in front of my audience in the queue.

"Perhaps you could ask your girlfriend?" he asked, standing in front of me now, and being a bit conspirato-rial. "We have a special Robbery Squad. That's all they do, concentrate on robberies. Could you have a word, and see if she could come in, maybe do an identification on our WADS system?"

"What's that?"

"It's like a computerised photo-ID system, sir."

"All right, I'll ask her, and should she just come in, or make an appointment?"

"Ask her to give us a ring, and use this number." He finally handed over a slip with a crime number on it.

"Thanks very much." I turned away, and the guy behind me was already pushing up to take my place at the front. He looked more like a criminal than someone who would be reporting a crime, and I was almost tempted to sit down and watch. But the smell of ciga-rette smoke, BO and Jeyes Fluid was getting to me. My arm was throbbing in the heat of the confined space. I escaped onto Brixton Road, desperate for a coffee, and strangely, a cigarette, even though I stopped smoking years ago.

Caroline

Still no message from Matthew. I sat at my computer, one minute resigned to the fact that he had lost interest, and the next minute wondering if he hadn't got my message thanking him for the rose. Would it be really pushy if I left another one?

Then Alison called across, "Matthew on line one, Caroline – do you want to take it, or call him back?"

I had told her I needed an hour to wade through my seventy-two e-mails and asked her to take my calls. My heart jumped.

"Hi, gorgeous."

Matt.

"Hi, how did it go?" I had switched from flirting to factual mode, before I even opened my mouth. I felt myself blushing. The redundant adrenaline seeped into my ankles and seemed to weigh down my feet.

"OK. They want to know if you can go in and do an ID thing – from photos – because I said you got a better look at the guy than I did. I know you didn't really, but I can't remember his face at all . . . so if you feel you could . . ."

Matt sounded like he was opting out of this.

"Will you come with me?" I asked, feeling a bit scared at the prospect.

"If you like . . . but I honestly don't think I'd recognise the guy . . ."

"Sounds really heavy going, doesn't it?" I said, deciding that I really did feel scared. "Did they have any news on the wallet?"

"No, but they said if it wasn't recovered in the next twenty-four hours there wasn't much hope."

"How are you doing?" I asked, feeling guilty that I hadn't asked before.

"Fine. The little hole looks like it's healing up, and I don't think there's anything stuck in it."

"So what do I have to do – ring the station?" I asked.

Matt read out the number, and I wrote it down.

"Are you home for dinner tonight?" he asked.

I often go out for a drink after work on a Friday night and one always leads to another. Dinner is usually a kebab on the way home. I felt trapped. Matt needed me. He was still feeling a bit sorry for himself. I should go home, but one of the partners was having a drink to celebrate getting married. A freebie in the boardroom, and everyone was expected to show their face and eat lukewarm mini-quiches and greasy peanuts with their champagne. Usually that would lead to a session in the local wine bar, topping up the expensive bubbles with cheaper ones. I hesitated.

He knew. Obviously not," he said, "Well, don't worry

about it. Have a nice drink. I might be in bed when you get in."

I was shocked that I didn't even feel inclined to explain, or make any excuses. What was happening to me?

We hung up and the only thought that crossed my mind was that I would win him over in the morning, and we could still have a nice weekend. I rang the police station and arranged to go in on Saturday morning to do the identification. Then I got down to answering those e-mails. I hate it when my whole screen is covered in highlighted, unread messages. It disconcerts me, even though most of them are circular information-only ones, or sent by someone who is busy covering their arse, copying in everyone who might be remotely interested what they're doing.

Matthew

I wasn't popular Friday evening when I called Liz to say I would be home late.

I was already unpopular for insisting on going back to work so soon. Liz was quite angry with me. Of course, she was right – it was stupid.

Friday nights are supposed to be sacrosanct for us. They're not even for going out together. They are preserved for the ritual flop, eat, drink and talk session which clears away the week and lets us be a family at the weekend, rather than two stressed-out, high-powered parents who rediscover their kids after five days of hard work and office politics.

"I'm really sorry, darling, but this has got to be finalised today, because the deadline is the end of the month, and that's Sunday," I said, knowing that Liz would never suggest my working over the weekend, even without her concern about the ill effects of the mugging. We do have some rules we both try to keep.

She sighed. "OK. I'll see you when I see you, then," she said, and I could hear in her voice that she was too tired to even protest. She would do the whole bath and bedtime routine, tell them stories, reassure them that Mummy and Daddy didn't have to work tomorrow, and agree with them that it would be OK to come into our bed in the morning, because it was Saturday.

While I was having a shower at the office after work, changing my clothes and smoothing aftershave balm on, Liz would be up to her arms in soapy water, refereeing the splashing matches in the bath, and half-heartedly listening to her mother's debrief on the day while partaking in a farewell glass of wine. We had a new nanny starting on Monday, so my mother-in-law would be gone when I got home.

I had rung Caroline and found her at some kind of work freebie. She had agreed to meet me afterwards in the Cork and Bottle in Leicester Square.

I was late, because I had forgotten how long it takes to get anywhere on a Friday night in the West End, with the throngs of tourists and partying Londoners. I had decided to walk from Holborn and completely misjudged the distance too, so I was a rude twenty minutes late. She was surprised that I wasn't in a suit, and that pleased me. I was trying hard to be someone else – the carefree, late thirty-something Matthew with endless possibilities before him. A little bit late was good, because the other, responsible, serious Matthew would never be so inconsiderately late for a lady.

I tried to drink the white wine that Caroline had ordered, but failed after one glass, and ordered a bottle of red Burgundy – aware that I really shouldn't be drinking while I was taking the anti-inflammatory capsules. We sat there, each with a bottle of wine, talking and laughing, until she suggested that some food would be a good idea.

"I had lots of champagne before I got here, I really need to eat," she giggled and smiled at me and I desperately wanted to kiss her.

I had a hard-on under the table and her eyes taunted me that she knew, and was I going to do anything about it? We ate something, I can't remember what, and towards the end of the meal I decided that I had to sleep with her. I know it sounds really calculated, and predatory, like she didn't have a choice in the matter, but she was giving me all the signs. I may have been married for seven years, but I am still "programmed to receive" the signals she was definitely sending me. I almost kissed her as we left the table, but I had a feeling I wouldn't be able to stop there, and I'm not the type to book into the Strand Hotel for a quickie. I decided I would do it when the time was right, and I had covered all the bases, as they say in the movies.

Liz was asleep when I got in, so I didn't have to explain why I had changed my clothes to work on a contract until midnight. I hadn't thought of that one in advance, and had a panic on the way home. I even thought about changing back into my suit in the toilet on the train, and then stopped myself. I hadn't done anything wrong. Changing my clothes back would be admitting to myself that I had something to hide.

Caroline

The boardroom drink was the usual boring do. It was slightly redeemed by the in-house butler, a really camp guy from Liverpool called Liam, who wears white gloves and calls everyone sir and madam, even if they are ten years younger than him. He loves me because I'm the only Irish one in the firm, and he kept topping up my glass. I must have had a fair few when my mobile phone vibrated against my hip. I fished it out of my bag and said "Hello?" really quickly, thinking the assembled partners would not be impressed that I hadn't switched it off for this august occasion.

"Caroline?"

That voice. I gulped. "Hi, yes, it's me," I stammered, moving to the door so I could get into the hall before Alison or someone else started listening over my shoulder. I thought I could open the door with one hand, while still holding a champagne flute. I twisted the handle, spilling champagne all down the wooden panelling, and making a puddle on the shiny parquet floor. "Oops," I said, hoping that no-one had noticed and, if they had, thought I was just a bit clumsy instead of completely pissed. Baxter, of all people, came to the rescue, and opened the door for me. He made a face and pulled out his hankie as he let go of the sticky handle. He raised an eyebrow at me, obviously trying to work out how many drinks I'd had.

"The speeches are about to start, Caroline," he said in a voice brooking no disobedience.

I nodded, and waved the empty champagne flute at him, pointing with one finger to my phone. "Won't be a moment," I said. Outside the room, I put the glass down on a French-polished mahogany table beside a huge display of waxy-looking exotic flowers. I took a deep breath, and said, really concentrating on it, "Hi, sorry about that, just had to extricate myself from a drinks thing at work – so, how are you?"

Matthew must have wondered what on earth I was

doing. "Fine. Well, not really fine, I was mugged in Brixton a few days ago."

"Matt?" My champagne-addled brain went into overdrive.

"Can you hear me? Are you losing reception?" That was Matthew's voice. Definitely. "Sorry. You were mugged?"

"Yes, in Brixton. I've only just got back to work today, and I didn't have your number at home. Sorry I didn't call you sooner."

"Are you all right now? What happened?" This was too weird.

"Maybe we could meet up and I can tell you all about it?" he suggested.

"Yes, fine, that would be nice," I said, ineffectually. I could hear clapping from inside the function room. "I have to go now, I'm afraid. The speeches have started."

"What about later on this evening?"

I knew I shouldn't. I'd had too much to drink already. I would make a show of myself, and anyway Matt needed me at home. But he wasn't expecting me. The demon drink spoke for me before I had a chance to think. "Sure, where do you want to meet?" We settled on the Cork and Bottle in Leicester Square. Easy to get home from there, and no-one from work would see me. My brain was still working to that extent. I sneaked in the door of the boardroom and discreetly leaned against it.

Alison caught my eye, and mouthed, "Are you OK?"

across the room at me.

I nodded and smiled. Oh, yes, I was most definitely fine. Baxter was watching me from another corner of the room. I ignored him and clapped enthusiastically at the end of the predictable 'Boy's Own' speech.

I did the obligatory well-wishing and escaped before Alison could knobble me. In the ladies', I looked at myself in the mirror and, apart from my cheeks being a bit too red, which always happens when I drink champagne, I thought I looked passable. I put on some lipstick and mascara, and brushed my hair. I was wishing I had my new suit on, and higher heels. On the tube to Leicester Square, I tried to read my book and not think about what I was doing. It was just a drink, after all, and I was in control. I wasn't being unfaithful to Matt. He has drinks with people all the time.

I was surprised when I was the first to arrive at the wine bar. I am so used to Matt always being early. He knows I hate waiting by myself. I ordered a bottle of the recommended new Australian Reisling, and got a table with a good view of the feet coming down the spiral staircase into the basement. I am interested in shoes, because I think they say a lot about people. I had a few false alarms with shiny black brogues, before a pair of black, well-worn Doctor Marten boots came down the stairs, twenty minutes late. They were topped with dark blue Gap canvas trousers and an almost trendy sweater. He had a leather jacket on as well. I was so surprised by the missing pinstripe suit that I nearly let him go past the table before I touched his arm and he looked down.

He smiled at me. "Hi, sorry I'm so late, my train was stuck in a tunnel just outside Holborn." He pulled out a chair and squeezed into the tiny space between us and the next table. He picked up the wine bottle, and checked the label.

"I thought I'd try their recommendation. It's nothing like a German Reisling," I said apologetically, sensing his disapproval.

"Not a black nun or a blue tower in sight, then?" he said, and it took me a second to get it.

"No, only Our Lady's milk," I said, and found myself blushing as I poured him a glass.

"Cheers, to the grape-growers of Australia," he said, and we clinked glasses.

"Should you even be drinking? After being knocked out, you know?"

He smiled wryly. "Let's hope a little won't do any harm." And then proceeded to drink a lot.

We sat at that tiny table for three hours, talking and laughing, and just barely avoiding brushing our knees. I didn't tell him about our mugging. In between, I prodded my slowly congealing Spaghetti Carbonara. Why hadn't I ordered something else to eat on our first date? This little oasis of candlelight, chat, wine and food had somehow turned into a date. On the way home in the taxi, I justified it to myself as professional networking.

Essential for the go-ahead career girl.

Back home, I brushed my teeth and cleansed my face and my head was buzzing with more than just alcohol. I felt like someone had opened a huge dusty filing cabinet in my brain. Loads of ideas and words I hadn't used for ages were jumping up, trying to get my attention, to be first out of the drawer. Snippets of conversation kept coming back to me.

"Do you think that people consciously seek out the media which support their views on life, or is it the other way around?" I had asked Matthew when he said he always judged people by the newspaper they read. I didn't mention that I judge them by their shoes.

"I think we subconsciously look for all kinds of justifications for our own views," he said. "Did you know that those full-page newspaper adverts for cars are designed as much to reassure people who've already bought that model of car, as to persuade anyone to buy a Mercedes, or a Renault Clio, or whatever?"

"I never thought about it like that, but you're right – it's like when you buy a new pair of shoes, or change your hairstyle, you spend your time looking at everyone else's, to reassure yourself that you made the right decision."

"Reducing the cognitive dissonance of the consumer," he said, and I was at a loss for a follow-up to that one.

I never thought that just talking to someone could be such a turn-on. I kicked myself. Why couldn't I think of better examples than shoes and hair?

When I got into bed, I couldn't believe it when Matt rolled over and started stroking my thigh. I nearly went along with it, but the guilt took over, and I said I had a headache from too much champagne. I couldn't get to sleep. I replayed all the evening's conversations, and made up witty and intriguing remarks I could have dazzled him with. He probably thinks I'm a complete dizz, was my last waking thought at about four o'clock in the morning. Matthew told me that he plays the piano, and I was imagining those long tapered fingers stroking the keys, forcing them to yield their music to his power . . .

CHAPTER 6

Caroline

Matt woke me up by nibbling on my nipple, and I had about five seconds of post-sleep, pre-waking bliss, thinking it was Matthew. I gasped when I opened my eyes, and Matt pursued his course of action, having made the very reasonable assumption that I was an eager participant in subsequent events. We had our usual Saturday morning soak in the bath, freshly ground coffee and croissants, and then Matt went out to get the Saturday papers. I sat with my mug of coffee, curled up in the window seat overlooking the back garden, and mulled over the evening. Especially the last ten minutes. I had this really strong feeling that Matthew wanted to lean across the table and kiss me. I could imagine the taste of the rich red Burgundy on his lips, and smell the hint of coriander and lemon sorbet on his breath. I could even feel the slight evening rasp of his cheek as I put my hand up to touch his face. But he was the soul of propriety and, when finally he eased his way out from the table, he stepped behind me and took my chair when I stood up. I turned, with my gracious 'I am used to this kind of treatment' smile, and he smiled back. He has the warmest, sexiest, most kissable smile. But he has to go first.

Sitting there, listening to the chirping of some unidentifiable bird in the shrubs outside the window, I wondered if Matthew was thinking about me at all. Probably not. Maybe he did fancy me a little bit, but I probably put him off by talking too much. Nothing worse than a yabbering female, especially one who gets even more talkative as the demon drink takes control of her tongue. I had all that champagne, then most of the bottle of Reisling because it turned out Matthew didn't like white wine, and then shared his bottle of red. I must have been incomprehensible by the end of the night. And he hadn't kissed me.

It was time to look for a silver lining. Maybe the only reason Matthew was put in my path was to make me stop and think if I was with the right man. I stood up from the window seat with great intentions. I needed to review my life. Well, review living with Matt. Soon. Not

117

now, but soon. I immediately felt better. There's nothing like a plan to do something later that you really should do now. I went to the sink to rinse out the cafetière and suddenly remembered that I was supposed to go to the police station.

I left a note for Matt and walked really quickly to Brixton, determined not to think about Matthew again. He was a catalyst in a chemical process. He had done his job, making me think about things, and now he was redundant. He could go back to lurk in his brown reagent bottle on the top shelf and I would go back to my busy, fizzing overflowing life.

Matthew

I wake up on Saturday morning with Jack's heels rammed into my kidneys, and after the initial flood of relief that I'm not facing the other way and being kicked in the ribs, or even lower down, my first conscious thought is of Caroline. I can hear the shower going, and the giggles from the bathroom mean that Ben is in there with Liz, probably wreaking havoc with the shower hose. This also means that if I don't move a muscle and don't wake up Jack, I may get anything up to three minutes more of peaceful slumber. I put my head back down on the pillow and sigh. I detect a slight red-wine hangover, but it is no worse than the usual for a Saturday morning.

Liz and I often polish off more than a bottle between us on a Friday night, usually accompanied by an Indian takeaway because we're both too tired to cook.

And so I am lying with the soles of my son's feet resting against my back, listening to my other son talking to his mother, explaining how a caterpillar changes into a butterfly, and plotting how I can see Caroline again, at a time and place that could spontaneously lead to other things, without seeming too contrived. Needless to say, I am not very practised in these matters, and I haven't made much progress when a wet towel lands on my face, accompanied by wild shrieks of glee.

"Wake up, lazy bones!" Ben is climbing on top of me, standing on my arm as he pulls himself onto the bed, and collapses on top of the sleeping Jack. Through the wails of protest, and more delirious laughter, I can hear that Liz trying to tell me something from the bathroom.

"Sorry?" I try to lift my head out from under Ben's entire body weight. I know I've brought it on myself by playing 'beat me up' tickling games on the bed, but sometimes I want to shout at the boys and tell them to go away until at least ten o'clock so that I can have a leisurely shower and shave, and come downstairs for a civilised Saturday morning breakfast with the papers. Liz is better than me at extracting the enjoyment from the children that is supposed to compensate you for the loss of the child-free pleasures like reading newspapers, doing DIY jobs or eating a meal while making intelligent conversation. Liz can see the boys mucking about in the paddling pool or the sandpit, or crayoning vigorously with the tips of their tongues showing, or saying a new word, and her face softens, and she smiles in a way that only mothers can. She says those moments make up for everything else – the stress of rushing around every-where, the lack of sleep, the lack of sex. She didn't say the last one, but it must be true. I still can't hear what she's saying from the bathroom, and I give up and just grunt my assent. It will be something mundane about the house or the children, and she will nag me about it again if I'm expected to do anything. Otherwise she'll do it, and I might find out afterwards that she was annoyed, but it's certainly not worth worrying about now. I decide to join the boys rather than try and resist, and we have a great tickle-and-roll game. There are two kings of the castle and one dirty rascal, who is always me, and the role involves me writhing around on the floor having been evicted from the bed, trying to grab the kings' toes as they bounce around on the bed. Then we have the usual episode of tears, followed by an apology extracted with difficulty from Ben, who always bounces too high so that Jack will fall over. Liz sighs as she dresses herself. I've stopped asking why every time she does it now – her sighing has just become part of the background noise of our family. She takes the boys downstairs so I can have a shower in peace, and I listen to Radio 4 for ten minutes, the volume on very high so I can hear it over the water and then the electric shaver. They are talking about the role of fathers in modern family life. "Ironically," one speaker says, "as women have entered the workforce outside the home, the men have withdrawn even further from their family duties, and lo and behold, women are trying to do both." I think about it. I rarely take the boys somewhere by myself at the weekend, because we are so busy trying to be a family that we do everything together. So I suppose Liz doesn't really get any time to herself. But then, I only get Monday nights for squash with Andrew, and he'll be out of commission for a while after his accident, and the occasional night out for a beer after work. Maybe we should try giving each other a morning off over the weekend, every so often. I know what I would do – have a lie-in until about ten, then go to Starbuck's Coffee with a big fat Saturday paper, then Border's bookshop, and . . . I suddenly realise that I don't know what Liz would do if someone gave her four hours to herself. Probably go and see her mum. Sad, but true. She doesn't really enjoy reading, she's never been a big shopper, and the idea of going to a gym would completely leave her cold. Although she could do with it. She has never quite lost the post-baby flabby bit on her tummy, which is not the most attractive part of her, I have to say.

I make a resolution and go downstairs full of good

intentions. "I just had a great idea," I say, flicking on the kettle.

Liz is sitting with one boy on each knee and they are all sharing the same cereal bowl. Muesli and cornflakes litter the floor. She loves having both of them close, clamouring for her attention. "Yes? What's that then?" she asks. "Going to the city farm?"

"No, but it could be part of the plan,'" I say, irritated despite my good intentions. Why can she not let me have a family-related idea all of my own for a change?

"Farm?" says Jack.

"I don't want to go to the smelly old farm," says Ben.

"Who lives on the farm?" asks Liz, brightly.

"Lion!" says Jack.

"No! Silly bumhead," says Ben. "Rabbits and hens."

"Don't call him names," Liz and I say simultaneously. We are sometimes still on the same wavelength.

"So, do you want to hear my idea?" I ask, my grumpy Saturday feeling returning. I need some caffeine. The kettle boils and I fill the large cafetière. We've got into the habit of making a huge amount of coffee on Saturdays and reheating it in the microwave as the morning goes on. Unfinished mugs of lukewarm drinks are among the other pleasures of having children.

"Yes, of course," says Liz, in what I call her affirming voice.

We went to an evening parenting class at the GP's surgery, and we both found it so nauseating we gave up after three weeks. Affirmation and reassurance featured a lot more than discipline, which is what we had gone to find out about – not having mastered it and thinking we were missing some critical piece of parenting information that wasn't in our genes or covered in the numerous books we had bought. Liz uses this special affirming tone when she is humouring the boys, and has increasingly started to use it with me.

"I was thinking we could give each other a few hours off, every other weekend, and take the boys out somewhere," I say.

"That's a great idea," Liz replies. "I've got loads of work to catch up on this weekend." "Do you want to start this weekend, then, and I'll take them to the Natural History Museum, or somewhere?" I ask solicitously, thinking how sad – I knew she wouldn't do anything enjoyable or relaxing. Her mother only left last night, so she wouldn't rush over there now, and work was the only alternative.

"Do you want to go and see the dinosaurs, boys?" Liz asks.

"Yeah, dinosaurs, they eat you all up and then they bite you and then you're dead!" Ben says with glee. He jumps off Liz's knee and runs to get his shoes on.

"I wish you hadn't got them going quite so quickly," I say, grabbing the toast that has just popped up and smearing it with butter. "I have to go to the police station in Brixton this morning. I thought I'd do that first, and get some stuff in Brixton market for lunch, and then I could take them out this afternoon."

Liz says that is fine, but not before emitting a sigh, and manages to calm Ben right down again by producing chocolate-chip muffins to distract him.

Matt

I gulped when the WPC introduced herself on the phone. When she kept talking I told myself that if they had found anything incriminating, they would surely have turned up on the doorstep.

"We believe we may have recovered some of your property, sir, and wondered if you could come down to the station to identify it?" she said, and I agreed to come straight away.

I could hopefully catch up with Caroline who had already gone there, and we could have lunch. I walked to Brixton out of habit, and then thought I would probably miss Caroline and should have caught the bus. But just as I climbed the steps of the police station, she pushed the doors open and came bouncing out, smiling at me. I was delighted when she said she was going to do some shopping – they might have found Mike's card with my stuff, and ask me about it. I had some chance of bluffing it without Caroline around, but she would smell a rat. I joined the queue, which almost seemed familiar.

There was a similar cast of weirdos to my first time, and the perennial argument going on about who was next. This time it seemed to be between a Rastafarian with an enormous stripey woollen hat, and a Nigerian woman with a coloured turban which nodded emphatically when she spoke, almost with a life of its own. If it came to physical contact, the headgear would be in an even match. I smiled at the thought, and caught the eye of the guy ahead of me in the line. He fitted in even less than I did, with his brown loafers, chinos, and white Ralph Lauren polo shirt. His clothes were a bit crumpled, and I wondered if he was a solicitor in mufti, maybe just finishing night duty.

"Hi," he said, nodding and rolling his eyes at the two combatants at the front.

I smiled. "Nice way to spend a Saturday morning," I said, hoping he'd confirm my theory about his job.

"Yes, I have to identify some stolen things," he said in a drawling, confident voice that could have been a lawyer's, or a doctor's.

"Me too," I said, probably not sounding much like an out-of-work actor.

"Mugging?" he asked, sympathetically, and I nodded. "Me too. When was yours?"

"Thursday, about nine o'clock in the evening."

"Mine was Wednesday."

I felt like we were schoolboys exchanging details on a sporting fixture.

I lowered my voice. "Around here somewhere?"

"Just around the corner. I do some work for a legal advice centre in Atlantic Road – you know, just under the Arches?"

"I knew it!" I said, and regretted it as soon as the words escaped. I'm always doing things like that.

"Knew what?" he asked, raising his eyebrows in an almost theatrical gesture of bemusement.

"Sorry, I always try and guess what people do for a living, and I thought you were a lawyer." I was embarrassed. "I should explain – I'm an actor, and it's one of the things we're taught to do, to identify the characteristics that are recognisable, so that we can copy them when we need to."

"I never would have guessed you're an actor, so you have one up on me," he said, laughing. "I'm Matthew Turner." He stuck out his hand to shake mine, with all the confidence of public-school and old-boys' networks, but I couldn't find it in me to dislike him for that.

"Matthew . . . Hughes," I said, after a pause.

"This is starting to get a little spooky, don't you think?" he said.

I nodded, and we began to compare details of our respective muggings. Then I realised the queue had moved on really quickly. "You're next, I think," I said, anticipating the people behind lynching us for chatting rather than moving up the line.

He grabbed the door to the inner sanctum as

instructed by the desk sergeant with the buzzer, and disappeared after a brief wave in my direction. I was ushered through a few minutes later, and went into a room that looked like a normal open-plan office, except for the large table in the corner with plastic bags laid out in neat rows, obviously containing people's recovered property. Small white labels stuck to the front identified the most likely owner. Another WPC, this one a very attractive blonde, with unusually slim ankles for a copper, took me over to the table and explained what happened. "We often recover a batch of stolen goods, which may include mobile phones, wallets, credit cards, store cards and jewellery. Some of it is easy to identify because it has the owner's name on it, like a card for instance, but some is completely anonymous. What we would ask you to do, is look at the contents of the bag with your name on it, and confirm if the property is yours. Then you should look at this other stuff, and if you think any of it is yours, we will cross refer to your crime report, and then ask you for some means of confirming ownership, before returning it to you."

I saw the little bag with my name, and shook out the contents. My two credit cards, debit card, wallet with my name engraved on it and my actor's Equity card were all there. No sign of Mike's. Thank God. I smiled hugely.

"You know of course that as your cards are cancelled, they have no worth," the WPC said, probably confused by my unalloyed delight.

"It's the Equity card I'm delighted to see," I said, and should have won an improvisation prize. I glanced at the rest of the items on the table, even though I hadn't lost anything else except the cash in my wallet. There it was. Mike's card. All alone in a plastic bag, covered with my fingerprints. I looked at the WPC. "Thanks very much, I wasn't missing anything else," I said, waving my little bag at her. "Is that it then?" My legs were wobbly suddenly, and I wanted to escape. I'm not cut out to be a criminal, I haven't got the nerve.

"Yes, if you could just sign here, please, to say you have recovered all your property?" She pushed a little white file-card in my direction, with my name and crime number on it. I signed it with a slightly shaky hand, and exited stage left. My nan's voice rang in my ears, as I skipped down the front steps of the police station. 'Count yourself lucky, young man, and learn a lesson from that,' she said, in her soft Derbyshire voice, and I was transported to her back garden, where she had found me on the ground under a tree, completely winded after a fall from a high branch where I had been stealing her apples.

Caroline and I spent the afternoon in IKEA, which is not my idea of fun, but we managed to find a coffee table we both liked, and escape without having a row or spending money on anything else, which is unusual for us.

I cooked again on Saturday evening, this time a little Jamie Oliver number, with lots of haphazard handfuls of fresh herbs, crumbly feta cheese, grilled tuna steaks and some very fine egg noodles. Sounds bizarre, but it was delicious. Caroline loved it, and came out of her reverie long enough to say so.

"I've got something to ask you," I said, and she looked up from her plate, with a startled expression.

"Yes?" she said, and I wondered why she flushed, and looked guilty.

I was supposed to be the guilty one around here. "Would you still love me if I told you I had done something terrible?"

Caroline looked at me with her head cocked on one side, like she was trying to figure out if I was serious. "What kind of terrible thing?"

"No, that's not answering the question," I said, wishing I hadn't started this. I'd never be one of those Americans who took the fifth amendment. I have too much to say for myself.

"It depends," said Caroline.

Which of the terrible things do I tell her? That I have no money left? That I lied about the TV part? That I stole Mike's card? "I shrank your new silk top in the wash," I said. "Oh Matthew!" she said, exasperated. She only calls me Matthew when I'm in trouble. "Sorry, but do you still love me?" I did my best sheepish grin, and it won her around, as it always does. It only occurred to me later, as I drifted off to sleep, that Caroline didn't say that she still loves me.

Caroline

I had never been into Brixton Police Station before, and it was a bit of a shock to the system. There was a group of people who could only have been refugees from the Centre around the corner, with about ten children sitting quietly on the benches, or on the floor at the adults' feet. The thing I noticed most about them was their silence. I felt like I recognised them from the news, even though I couldn't tell you which country they came from. I wondered what would happen to them next. The queue of people at the desk was noisy, with a row going on about who was next. Matt said the same thing happened when he was there. I only had to wait about twenty minutes, and when I explained I was here to see DC McInerney from the Robbery Squad, I was buzzed through a huge heavy door into a corridor that smelt even more strongly of the disinfectant my nostrils had just got used to in the waiting area. The detective was a woman, and I wondered if they did that on purpose: allocate women police officers to talk to women victims. She showed me into a little interview room like you see on television, and brought me a cup of scalding hot tea in a polystyrene cup.

"There you are – I'll just go and get the laptop," she

said in a Glasgow accent, and disappeared for a few minutes.

I looked around the bare yellowy-white walls and wondered what it must feel like to be interviewed in here, under suspicion, or even guilty of something. Do they give suspects cups of tea, or do they save it for victims and witnesses?

The DC came back in, and took a minute to plug in the computer and set it up. "This is called WADs and it's just a computerised version of the photo ID albums we used to use. It can cross-reference files though, and fingerprints, and criminal records, so it is a lot more useful than just a mug-shot album."

I nodded, and felt strangely nervous. What if I identified the wrong guy, or just thought I remembered what he looked like?

"What I'd like you to do is use the mouse to go through all the pictures in the gallery, taking your time, and making a note of the number of the file if you think the person might be the one we are after. Then you can go back and have another look. Don't worry if you don't see someone resembling your man – he could be new to the area, or a new offender. You might not find him in here."

I nodded, and clicked the mouse to look at the first mug-shot. After twenty minutes, the faces all started to look the same. They all looked like criminals, which I suppose they had to be, to get in there in the first place.

But maybe they put some placebos in there, like in clinical trials, to trick you into thinking you've found your man. There might be some perfectly respectable civil servants or even policemen, wearing woolly hats or hoods, to show us how we stereotype the baddies. I had already noted three file numbers and I went back for a second look before going on. I still wasn't convinced by any of them. The DC was sitting beside me, not speaking, and I was surprised to pick up a really fresh shampoo smell from her hair, and a musky, quite strong perfume when she reached across to show me how to save a file. She had short, dark hair and tiny gold and diamante earrings that seemed too feminine, somehow. I was wondering what she did with her friends, and if she had a boyfriend who worried about her when she was at work – or she might even have kids. That must be difficult, I was thinking, working shifts and – the face jumped off the screen. The snake beard was there, and the eyes.

"That's definitely him!" I said, my heart pounding as if I had just yelled and pointed at him in the street.

The DC made a note of the file number. "You're sure?" she asked, but she knew by looking at me that I was sure.

I shoved the laptop away from me and the legs of my chair screeched on the floor as I pushed away from the table. The little tilting blocks under the computer folded and it banged flat on the table. I could feel a flush creeping up past my neckline. All I could think about was the way the guy looked at me when we were both lying on the footpath.

"Good," she said. "We know him. We should be able to pick him up. If we do, we'll ask you and your partner to come in and finger him."

I nodded. "That's grand with me. I'll tell Matt."

"OK, I'll just show you out. I'm on this case, so please contact me if you remember anything else relating to the crime." She pressed the round, white release button for the door to the outside world, and held the door open for me to go through.

Matthew was standing right in front of me. "Hello!" he said, and sort of leaned towards me. If we hadn't been in a police station, I'm sure he would have given me one of those old-friends-meeting kisses on the cheek.

"Hi," I managed to mumble.

The policewoman said, "I'll leave you here, then, Caroline – I'll be in touch."

I didn't even answer her. I heard the door clicking shut, but otherwise the waiting area seemed very quiet. "Thanks for dinner last night," I said, and he reached out and very lightly stroked my cheek with those beautiful fingertips.

"I really enjoyed it," he said, and my enzymes started fizzing again, not to be relegated to some anonymous back shelf in the laboratory while the rest of my body dealt with the situation. Then, "What on earth are you doing here?" he asked.

I kept myself together and managed not to tell him I was in to identify a mugger. That's not the kind of thing you talk about when you are surrounded by dodgy-looking people who could all be muggers themselves, by the look of them. "Helping police with their enquiries," I said, trying to sound mysterious and witty, but I ruined the effect with a hysterical little laugh.

He smiled. "They've recovered some of my stuff," he said. "I'm just waiting to go through and identify it. Have you got time to go for a coffee afterwards?"

I hesitated. I shouldn't. I looked at my watch. It was almost half past twelve, and Matt would be waiting for me to get back so we could go to IKEA and buy the new coffee table.

"I'd love to, thanks, Matthew, but I'm in a bit of a hurry. I've got loads of things to do today." I couldn't believe I actually sounded like that casual, busy girl who could take it or leave it, rather than the desperately infatuated bundle of confusion that I was.

"May I call you?" he asked.

I nodded. I couldn't trust myself not to gush.

"See you soon then?" he called as I pushed open the double doors onto the street.

And had my second heart failure of the day.

Matt was coming up the steps.

"Hiya! Great, I was hoping you wouldn't be finished yet," he said, and kissed me. I turned around and saw that the doors had just closed. "They called to say they've got my wallet back. They wanted me to come and check the stuff." He kept on walking up the steps and was sort of holding my arm and I was walking up with him, without even realising it.

"Tell you what," I said, just as he put his hand out to push the doors open, "I'll just run across to Marks & Spencer and get some bits for lunch, and meet you at the bus stop."

"Oh, come in with me, I'm sure it won't take long," he said. "I was going to treat you for lunch, anyway."

"I need some underwear too," I said, desperately latching on to the only other thing I ever buy in Marks.

"OK, but come back here afterwards, because I want to take you to lunch in that new Mediterranean place next to Barnardos."

I could hear the irritation in his voice. I was taking control, as usual. I didn't kiss him, terrified that Matthew would loom behind him in the doorway any second. I dashed across the road, nearly making a boy with a hooded sweatshirt fall off his bike. His peripheral vision must have been lousy because he nearly crashed into the opening door of a parked car after he swerved around me.

I browsed in the tiny underwear department in M&S for twenty minutes. I must have looked like a shoplifter, because I noticed that one of the assistants had found a compelling need to rearrange everything on the hangers beside me. I moved on and she followed, finding a really interesting shelf of boxed bras to occupy her. I started feeling guilty, and I had to fight a brief mischievous urge to stuff a pair of knickers in my jacket pocket just to see what she would do about it. Eventually I found a bra and two little grey vests that were surprisingly trendy, and bought them, thinking I had to buy at least three things to justify abandoning Matt.

The lunch was nice, but I kept looking out the window all the time, wondering if Matthew would walk past.

"You're very distracted again. Are you OK?" Matt asked, with his mouth full of Thai chicken (very Mediterranean). His table manners are one of the things about him I wouldn't miss. He always seems to have some really important thing that can't wait thirty seconds for him to empty his mouth before saying it.

"Yes, fine," I said. "I'm just thinking about those people in the police station."

"Which ones?"

"All of them, really. Did you see those refugees, though? The poor kids were just sitting there, waiting for the next shitty thing to happen to them, not knowing if they'll even eat today."

"The desk sergeant came out and took them to the canteen for some food."

"Did he? That's incredible. How can they do that?"

"I asked exactly the same thing. He said they're not

supposed to, but when the refugee place is closed, and there are kids involved, they can't turn them away from a hot meal."

"Wow, the human face of the police force," I said. "I bet that would never be on the news. Especially about the Brixton police station. There's far more mileage in talking about street crime and drug-enforcement policies."

"That's exactly what the guy in front of me in the queue said. He's a lawyer in the City, but he does pro-bono work with the Law Centre on Atlantic Road."

"Really? What was he in there today for? One of his clients?" It was hard to pretend I wasn't really interested.

"Same reason as me. Getting his stuff back. He got mugged on Wednesday, but a lot worse than us. He was off work. Couldn't move with bruised ribs, and they cracked him on the back of the neck, so he had to stay in bed for a couple of days. You were right when you said we were lucky." Matt held up his hand and showed me the little hole, which was almost sealed up.

"Did you check if all your cards were in the wallet? Not that it makes any difference when they're cancelled."

"Yes, everything was fine," he said, and then stood up suddenly. "Shall we make a move? Get this coffee table?" He waved for the waiter to give us the bill, and we were out on the street in about two minutes flat. No dessert, no coffee. Not like Matt, but I didn't think anything of it at the time. I was too worried that I hadn't had a chance to make sure the coast was clear before we wandered down Brixton Road.

IKEA was packed. It always is on Saturdays, but we successfully negotiated the single-item queue and escaped while still being civil to each other. This is often a challenge for us, after wandering around with no idea where to find anything, picking up loads of things not on the original list, and then fighting about the money, and where everything is supposed to fit in a tiny one-bedroom flat. As you can imagine, I'm the spender and Matt is the champion of minimalism. But we still don't have enough chairs if more than two people come around. When we have a dinner party for six, one ends up sitting on the laundry basket (also from IKEA) and the other one is perched on the very edge of the wicker chair from the bedroom, which is very deep and comfortable for reading a book, but does not work as a dining-chair. Matt refuses to entertain the idea that two spare director's chairs could be folded up and stuck under the bed until they were needed.

"We have too many things stashed under the bed. We need to move to a bigger place and get a proper dining-table," he says, to kick-start things.

"If you were earning any money, we could get a bigger flat, or even a mortgage on a house, with a dining-room," I inevitably interject at some point.

After a few more exchanges Matt sulks, and then tells

me what he's done about looking for a job that week, and I apologise for being a bitch, and we then get stressed together about the length of the queue, and how long it takes to get out of the carpark. By the end, we are exhausted, at least a hundred pounds poorer, and Saturday is nearly over, but we are still a couple, proud owners of some new item of furniture or trendy gadget, and we have achieved all this *together*.

Today, we avoid all that, because I am preoccupied with my thoughts about you know who and, looking back, Matt is also quiet and reflective, and we manage to find our way to the coffee tables, pick one, and get through the checkout without picking up one other item. Not a recycled aluminium magazine-stand, a toothbrush-holder or a kite. Not even a roll of Christmas paper, or a mega-size pack of Swedish Dime bars at rock-bottom prices. I spent the whole time wondering what Matthew was doing – what do single thirty-something guys do on Saturday afternoons when there is no football on? He doesn't seem like the DIY type, working on the house he has bought for silly money because it needs complete re-wiring, re-plastering, walls knocked through and a completely new kitchen and bathroom. He could be the Tate Gallery type. He might be having a look around the latest special exhibition and then having lunch with married friends in Fulham, godfather to their kid, and popular because he always brings a cool present. Or maybe he was watching the cricket at Lord's, in a corporate enter-tainment box, drinking champagne and doing old-boy back-scratching stuff. He certainly wasn't sitting in the queue to get out of the carpark at IKEA, trying to stop thinking about me like I was about him.

Matthew

After lunch, and twenty minutes of finding shoes, spare nappies for Jack, and stuffing a rucksack with all kinds of superfluous emergency supplies that Liz keeps handing me, we are ready to go. I manage to drink a whole mug of rewarmed coffee while this is all going on, and still have a piece of onion bread in my hand as I open the front door and start lifting the push-chair over the threshold.

Jack suddenly realises when I say, "Shall we wave to Mummy?" that Liz isn't coming, and starts wailing.

Ben, never to be outdone, says, "I need a wee-wee, Mummy."

Liz has to take him upstairs and then give him big hugs before he agrees to come out with me, like I was some ogre that was trying to steal him away from home and family. Jack cries for about thirty seconds after the front door closes, and then gets all excited about the prospect of going on the train. "*Choo-choo!*" he yells at the top of his voice, competing with Ben, who has decided we are a fire engine on the way to put out a fire, and makes very realistic "*dee-dah*" noises in case the neighbours are in any doubt. The old lady from three doors up gives me an indulgent smile as we pass her, and I'm sure she's thinking I am a model father, taking my share of the child-care burden, bonding with my children and giving Liz a well-earned pampering session in the beauty salon. The train is a novelty for the boys, who usually either walk, or are driven by the nanny to nursery, playgroups and friends' houses. It's great pointing to different kinds of houses, churches, shops, lorries and cars. Jack repeats everything back, in his lispy, baby voice and I smile, enjoying the feel of his soft little cheek against mine as we look out the window together. Ben insists on sitting by himself across the carriage, looking out the other side of the train, and his legs stretch all the way across the seat, the soles of his trainers facing the stern-looking woman in the opposite seat. She probably thinks I should have kept him with me, but boys need a bit of space and freedom, according to that parenting teacher, and it was one of the few points on which I could agree with her. They are really well behaved until we get onto the Underground at Victoria, when Ben tries running down the carriage, just as the train starts moving, and falls over, splitting his lip against the pole in the middle. I grab Jack around the waist and stumble over everyone's feet to reach Ben, abandoning the push-chair, which falls over because of the rucksack hanging on the handles. I get to Ben and, for some reason, instead of being sympathetic, I shake him by the arm, telling him he should have stayed beside me. He sobs, leaning against me and I hug him to me. A totally inadequate parent, I am hunched on the floor of the carriage, holding on to the pole with one hand, and trying to embrace both boys with the other arm. The train stops at the next station and a flood of people get on, looking at me askance as they follow the driver's instruction to "move right down inside the carriages, using every available space, and mind the doors, the train is ready to depart".

"Come on, we have to get back to the push-chair," I say to the boys, and I carry Jack and hold Ben's hand. I manage to keep my balance in the rocking train as we find our way through. I get lots of sympathetic smiles from women, and one really nice woman even picks up the push-chair and puts the rucksack on the seat beside her. "Here," she says, "sit one of the boys down here."

She lifts the bag and I plonk Jack down, grateful to be relieved of his weight. He wails and demands to be picked up, so I sit down and put him on my knee.

"Hold on to the pole, good boy," I say to a very subdued Ben, whose upper lip has now swollen to twice its normal size. He is feeling it with his tongue, and sticking out his lower lip in the very familiar way he has when crossed, so that his lips almost match.

"Never mind. We'll buy an ice cream when we get out

of the train. That will cool it down." I'm doing exactly what I give Liz a hard time about, bribing him with a treat. Jack is wriggling around on my knee and, as I desperately try to stop him from accidentally kicking the nice lady next to us, I catch her expression of pity.

I don't need any pity. I'm having a lovely day out with my boys, and a little accident isn't going to spoil everything. I'm coping, we're nearly there, and there is absolutely no problem at all. She looks like the marrying kind, but doesn't have a ring on her finger, so maybe she's divorced and thinks I am too, doing my weekend-access duties rather than just being a daddy. She has it all worked out. I hate her for it. Because I should be better at this. I should have anticipated Ben running down the carriage and stopped him, I shouldn't have shaken him, and most of all, I should know by now that a push-chair with a bag on the back will fall over. That was the biggest giveaway of my novice status. I pointedly don't make eye contact with the nice lady. We manage to get off at the right station, and not fall down the gap between the train and the platform, or trip on the escalator.

"Can I have my ice cream now, Daddy?" Ben asks about six times on the way up the escalator, and I feel like shouting at him again by the time we get to the top. I have an ominous wet patch on my jeans, which could only have come from Jack, and I'm trying to remember how long the walk to the museum is, and where the toilets are. Ben runs ahead down the Victorian pedestrian tunnel that very cleverly links all the museums and avoids the huge traffic congestion in South Kensington. I have a feeling it won't not have resident ice-cream sellers, and we will emerge at the museum ice-cream-less. Not anticipating quite how much of a problem this will be, I follow Ben, trying to keep up so that he stays in sight. I've forgotten to reiterate the "going out for the day in London" rule about staying in sight, preferably holding on to the side of the push-chair, which Liz faithfully recites whenever we go out. I have a momentary panic when I realise there is an exit before ours, and I can't see Ben, but then he reappears from behind a large woman with numerous shopping bags who looks like she would have been happier in a black cab rather than slumming it with us in a subterranean tunnel.

When we arrive at the Natural History Museum, the end of the queue for the dinosaur exhibition is actually coming out the door, having doubled back on itself several times inside the lobby. I ignore it and steer the push-chair towards the toilets to get Jack changed. Ben is now, thankfully, holding on to the push-chair, having apparently forgotten the i-c-e-c-r-e-a-m. There is no baby-changing station in the men's toilet, and I kneel down and change him on the floor of one of the cubicles, while desperately trying to stop Ben from holding his fingers under the flush for the urinal. He is fascinated with them. It's extremely difficult to explain to a three-year-old that something is dirty when it clearly involves running water, which he is constantly told to use to wash his hands. We escape unscathed from the great changing adventure, and the dinosaur queue is moving relatively quickly, so we never have to actually stand still. I manage to convey my limited knowledge of dinosaurs to Ben, who is staring at the huge skeleton in the lobby, asking me if I think it is a Tyrannosaurus Rex or a Brontosaurus. How does he know these things? I ask myself as he tells me that one is a meat-eater and the other is a plant-eater. That's the sort of thing his daddy should be telling him. I should be his fount of dinosaur-type knowledge. We should have our own little jokes, that other people don't understand, and make us giggle together, enjoying the exclusivity of our dinosaur club membership. He is so innocent, staring up with his neck stretched to its limit, his mouth open and his eyes wide. I want to pick him up and hug him, but I don't want to spoil the moment. Jack has obligingly fallen asleep, and I am grateful. I don't think he could have coped with waiting much longer in the queue, and he will probably wake up as we come out and miss the whole thing – but that's life. We'll come back lots of times, I decide.

Ben gets bored watching the immobile skeleton, and starts fidgeting.

"Can I have my ice cream now, Daddy?" he asks, and I have to explain that we're in a queue now, and we can get one when we come out.

"But you said we could have one when we got off the train. We got off the train now." The tone is changing with every word, from polite enquiry to irritable whinge. Liz warned me that an afternoon outing would probably be too tiring for him, but I didn't listen.

"Tell you what," I say, down on my hunkers, in my best 'reasonable daddy performing parenting duties in front of a large crowd' voice, "we'll go and see the big dinosaur eating the other dinosaur first, and then we'll have an ice cream."

"I want it now!" Louder.

Another section of our audience tunes in to the entertainment. Every parent there manages to convey with eyebrows or twitching feet that they are delighted it's not their kid who is about to showcase in the lobby of the Natural History Museum. Every grandparent manages to convey their disbelief that children these days have no discipline, and no understanding of boundaries.

"Ben, darling, you're going to have to wait until we come out the other side," I say, knowing that my tone is too hopeful, and not authoritative enough.

Ben loses it, and throws himself on the floor, kicking the push-chair and waking Jack, who looks around startled and then starts crying himself.

"Ben, stand up right now!" I yell, while trying to calm Jack down.

"No!" he shouts back, his chin jutting out. And then

146

he spits at me.

Liz has told me about it, but I haven't witnessed it yet. A habit he picked up at nursery apparently. I am appalled. I grab him by his upper arm, and wheel the push-chair out single-handedly, bumping it down the two steps at the front of the museum.

"We're going home," I say, calmly, holding Ben by the wrist now, desperately trying not to give him an inadvertent Chinese burn, as he is wriggling around so much. We'll never get back to the tube station like this. He refuses to apologise for spitting. I yank him down the road for another few yards. I'll get hauled away for child abuse at this rate. I take a deep breath and find myself promising that if Ben is a good boy all the way to the station, he can have an ice cream. He says sweetly, "OK Daddy," and he holds on to the handle of the push-chair, and trots along beside me, pointing out a JCB digger in the middle of some roadworks.

"Did you hear that siren, Daddy?" he asks when a police car shoots past.

I'm hyperventilating, and he's passing the time of day like we have just spent a pleasant afternoon browsing through dinosaur fossils. Jack is asleep again by the time we get to the shop, so I don't buy him an ice cream. Ben sucks his multicoloured overpriced stick of ice happily on the tube until we get to Victoria and then solicitously puts the lolly-stick in the first bin he finds. I lift the push-chair up all the flights of stairs, bruising my shins in

147

the process, and we get to the mainline rail station in time for a four o'clock train. Liz won't be expecting us until at least six thirty. I hate to admit failure, so I take them to the local park. I feel ridiculous and angry. Ben has completely forgotten about the dinosaurs, and Jack is happily poking sticks into drains, and chasing squirrels and pigeons. The boys completely ignore me, except when they want to be pushed on the swings, or they get stuck climbing up the chains on the pirate's ship.

I sit on a bench in the playground and fantasise about sleeping with Caroline. I haven't even kissed her yet. When she came out of that door in the police station, I couldn't believe it. I got a hard-on when I was talking to her. She had a tiny little black vest top on that clung to every curve. Her hair was gelled and mussed up, and she had no make-up on as far as I could see. She blushed a little bit when she saw me and it just made her look better. I desperately want to call her, and take out my phone several times, and search for her number. I don't call. The boys have an unerring instinct for interrupting phone conversations by making dramatic leaps from high places, whacking each other on the head, or just yelling so loudly that you have to hang up. I take them to McDonalds at five thirty, to show Liz that I know when they have their tea, and they get themselves covered in tomato ketchup and have spaceship fights with the plastic freebies in their kid's meals. It crosses my mind that this would be a typical Saturday for them, if Liz and I split up, and I saw them only at weekends.

The thought makes me so sad that Ben looks at me with his head on one side, takes a sip of his drink through the straw, and asks, "Daddy, are you happy?"

"Very happy, Ben, because I'm with you," I say, forgetting I am supposed to be angry with him about spitting. And not saying 'sorry'. And not wanting to see the dinosaurs with me.

"And you're happy to be with Jack?" he asks.

"And Jack, of course," I say. "Come on, let's get home to Mummy now."

They slide off their seats and let me clean their faces and hands with a napkin. I hold both their hands as we walk to the bus stop, Ben skipping, and Jack tripping over his feet trying to copy him. There is nothing better than the feel of your own child's hand in yours – the size of it, the innocence of it, the trust it conveys.

The boys race into the conservatory and find Liz, and Ben is in the middle of describing the huge dinosaur skeleton when I catch up with them. I kiss her, and she says, "So, it sounds like you had a great time."

"Mixed, but yes, it was good," I say, and realise she must have been sitting there staring into space, because there wasn't a book, newspaper, laptop or telephone anywhere within reach.

"What did you do?" I ask, and it comes out more as a

challenge than I intended.

"Some work, and a bit of pottering," she says, and she sounds sad too. Maybe the same thought has crossed her mind about future Saturdays.

CHAPTER 7

Matthew

We take the boys to Godstone Farm on Sunday, to see the newborn lambs, and they love it. Ben is very well behaved, and even helps Jack to climb a gate so they can stroke one of the sheep. Liz takes some photographs of the boys leaning over a pig-sty, trying to count the wriggling piglets. Then she balances the camera on the rusty bonnet of an old tractor, and sets the timer, so that we can all pose as a happy family on a bale of straw. Will we look at those photos together in the future, as a reminder of happy days, or will they become a symbol of what we have lost? We hold hands as I help Liz over a stile into the fields, but she lets go as soon as she is over, and fiddles with the zip on Ben's coat, which looks perfectly fine to me. I can't seem to think of anything to say to Liz any more. The mountain of things we haven't said over the last few years is too big to climb. We stick to the trivialities. When we're on outings like now, Liz is totally focussed on nappy-changing and feeding opportunities. Her only criterion for selecting a café used to be the brand of coffee they served. Now she checks for high chairs, baby-changing facilities, and whether they hand out crayons and colouring paper to children.

She takes Ben behind a bush for a wee, and I put Jack on my shoulders so he can see over the high hedge.

"See the cows, Jack? Brown and white ones. Eating grass." My pidgin English is coming along nicely, I think, as I stroll with him along the edge of the field, inhaling the sweet smell of open grass and hawthorn hedge. When I look back and see Liz and Ben following us, hand in hand, I have a huge revelation. This is it. This is the whole point. The children, not us. We have been put on the planet to procreate, subsume ourselves in our children, and pass the world on to them. In terms of nature fulfilling its objective, it doesn't matter if we don't communicate with each other, or experience complete happiness, or even achieve our petty career goals. So Liz and I have done our bit, by producing two healthy males, and now we just have to give them warmth and shelter and a bit of nourishment, and they will grow and we will die. Great. One should feel uplifted by profound insights into the nature of the world, but I am immensely depressed. Not helped by the sudden dampness percolating around the collar of my polo shirt. Liz was right, we should have changed Jack's nappy before setting off on the walk. I lift him off my shoulders and grimace as the offending whiff passes my nose on the way down.

"You were right," I say to Liz, trying not to laugh as I shrug off the enormous rucksack full of a week's provisions and six changes of clothes, to try and find a dry nappy. She finds one immediately in a side pocket, and extracts wipes and nappy bags from two other secret zipped compartments. She smiles at me, and changes Jack while he stands there, fixated by Ben's antics with a dandelion.

"Piss in the bed, piss in the bed!" sings Ben, and Liz and I look at each other in horror.

"Ben, where did you learn that?" I ask, trying to sound stern.

"Nursery. That's what you say when you pick a lello danmelion," he says, holding the flower under Jack's nose. "Smell, smell, Jack!"

Liz snorts with laughter, and hides her face in the top of the rucksack, while I try to stop smiling and have a serious father-to-son conversation.

"That's not a nice thing to say, Ben, so I don't want to hear you saying it again, OK?"

"OK, smelly pooh-pooh head!" says Ben, and runs off down the path. So much for that.

"This is nice, isn't it?" says Liz, and she slides her hand into the crook of my arm. Jack reaches down from his reinstated position on my shoulders and ruffles her hair. "S'nice, Mummy," he says.

I squeeze Liz's hand with my elbow, but don't say anything. I have just been wondering if Caroline prefers the city or the countryside, having come from a rural Irish village. She certainly seems a natural in London, but there might be another side to her.

A tractor and trailer go trundling down the lane on the other side of the hedge, and Ben fights his way into the undergrowth to peer through. He yelps in pain and starts dancing a jig. "*Owwww, Mummeeee!*" he wails, and I see the end of our countryside idyll fast approaching. Ben's poor legs are covered in nettle stings, which are already swelling on his skinny little shins. I put Jack down and pull at some dock-leaves, spitting on them and scrunching them up in the palm of my hand. Ben is curious enough to stop wailing for a second, and I explain that I am making a special magic potion to make the pain go away. I swab the stings, leaving green streaks down his legs, while Liz digs in the rucksack for a distracting packet of chocolate buttons. Both methods seem to work.

Predictably, Liz suggests we should go back to the car, and we turn around, fifty yards from our starting point, and go back to the gravel carpark.

I use the cover of listening to the cricket on the car

radio to avoid conversation on the way back, and plot where I will take Caroline for a nice meal, still perplexed by the problem of taking her somewhere afterwards that won't look like a tacky ploy to get her into bed. Which is exactly what I want to do. I want to kiss her beautiful soft white neck, make her arch it backwards, lifting her pert chin and gasping for breath as I work my way down her body, down, down, down.

"*Down, Daddy, down!*" Ben shouts from the back seat.

"What?" I turn the volume on the radio up.

"Window down, please?" he says, fiddling with the window control on the rear door, which I have locked for that very reason.

"No, Ben, it's dangerous," Liz and I say in harmony, and he subsides, knowing when he is beaten. He pokes Jack instead, and pulls his blanket off him. Shouting and screaming ensue. I just drive the car and let Liz handle it. There have to be some advantages to being the driver. They finally fall asleep just as we turn into our road, and Liz sighs with that martyred air I now find really irritating.

"This is going to be the half an hour from hell," she says, as she gets out of the car and unbuckles the sleeping Ben. He's almost too heavy for her to carry now, but she always tries to do everything, so she picks him up and staggers to the front door, without even waiting until I have the key in the door.

"Liz, don't try and do everything, hang on a minute,"

I say, and push the door open in front of her.

She just flicks her hair at me in a dismissive way. "If you could do Jack, that would be great."

"No, actually I was planning to just leave him there in the car with the door open, in the rain, so you could come back down and get him in ten minutes or so," I say, really annoyed now. I haven't been as "hands on" as some fathers, but she should give me credit for a very basic understanding of what is required. I carry Jack, his little sweaty face serene in sleep, up to his cot, and strip him, change his nappy and put his pyjamas on without waking him up. I turn on the yellow elephant night-light beside the cot, and put the blackout blind up on the window. Then I just stand and look at him. He's not even talking properly yet, and I love every inch of his tiny person, the twinkle in his eye, the gung-ho way he waddles down the garden, his pudgy little hands with the fattest knuckles you've ever seen.

CHAPTER 8

Matt

I went up to the West End again on Monday, looking for inspiration for Caroline's birthday present, and to my shame I was annoyed that I had lost Mike's card, just when it might have come in useful. Someone up there is trying to save me from myself, I reckoned. On Oxford Street, a familiar face came towards me, and I was just racking my brain to put a name to a face as she got close enough for me to notice her clothes. It was the homeless girl I followed to the hairdresser's. She obviously hadn't got the job, and she was doing the same slow, deliberate window-shopping that had fascinated me before. I named her Chloe in my head, because it conjured up for me her delicate bony face, and the skinny legs that would be shapely if she had a bit more flesh on her. I wanted to talk to her, but couldn't think of a pretext, and I let her walk past, leaving a slight aroma of white musk oil on the air behind her.

I went into the gadget shop hoping to find something for Caroline that would be funky and different, and not instantly identifiable as cheap. But my budget wouldn't stretch to the only thing in there she would have liked – a very retro rocket-shaped lava lamp with red amoeba-like bubbles undulating up and down.

Chloe was actually sitting on the steps of the tube station, begging, as I started down. I stopped.

"Have you got a few pence for a cup of tea?" she asked, looking up at me with big liquid green eyes, a tendril of her mahogany-dyed hair hanging down over her face.

"I'll take you for a cup of tea, if you want," I said.

"Why, do you think I'll only spend it on drugs?" she asked, her eyes narrowing a little, but still big enough to bewitch me. She was standing up as she said it, which I took as an acceptance of my invitation, so I turned and led her back up the stairs, to the frustration of the flood of rush-hour commuters which had suddenly started flowing down the steps.

"It's like a switch, at five o'clock," she said. "They come out of nowhere."

We battled through them, past the man on the *Evening Standard* stall with its bizarre collection of rubber animals having an orgy on the top of the pile of papers, preventing them from blowing away.

"Café Nero OK?" I asked, pointing at the nearest coffee shop.

"Fine. I'd love a coffee, actually." By the time she had ordered her latte with an Italian emphasis and her pain au chocolat in an immaculate French accent, my intrigue had turned to downright curiosity, and I was determined to satisfy it. I ordered a large espresso, and we sat at one of the shiny mock-aluminium tables outside, watching the wage-slaves striding past with their briefcases and tiny handbags.

"Thanks for this," Chloe said, with meaning. "It hasn't been a great day for takings, so I didn't have any lunch." She was younger than I had first thought. Maybe seventeen.

"Where are you staying?" I asked, remembering my time at the shelter. You don't ask homeless people where they live.

"Oh, at home," she said, and now I was completely confused.

"Why are you begging then?" I asked. "Is it drugs?"

"No, no!" she said, and laughed.

"What then?" I didn't have any right to ask, and she could have just told me to bugger off, but I sensed she was enjoying this.

"I'm doing a project for my Sociology 'A' level. It's about homelessness and I want to experience it first hand."

"But you're living at home?"

"Well, my mum doesn't know that I'm begging. She'd kill me. I told her I needed to look poor, and not wash my hair and stuff, so I could walk around and do the research, but I have to be home by seven o' clock, before it gets dark, so she knows I'm OK."

Her naivety was so touching that I wanted to cry. But I also wanted to shake her, and show her the homeless fourteen-year-olds who didn't have a mother, or whose mothers didn't care. It wasn't a game to them, not to wash their hair for a week or two, or miss their lunch. I swallowed all the indignation that rose into my throat, and took a deep breath. Who was I to judge, sitting on my arse all day and dreaming about success and fame?

A mobile phone rang with a telltale Nokia tone, and she started, guiltily. She slid it out of the tapestry bag on her lap, and answered it, "Hello?"

If she started giggling and talking to her mates, I was going to walk away, I told myself. What a gullible idiot.

"Yes, Mum, I'm fine, I'm just having a coffee with someone."

Great, I thought. Her mother will think I'm a child molester, or a pimp trying to pick her up. Here it all comes.

"No, he's not, he's …" She blushed, and looked away when she caught my eye. "I'll call you back, Mum. Promise." She punched the off button and shoved the phone into her bag. The blush was just fading.

"I don't chat up under-age girls," I said, more gruffly than I intended.

"I'm not under-age, anyway," she said, and then blushed again, realising how that sounded. "My mother rings me every hour, and it doesn't look good when you're trying to beg, does it? No wonder I hardly get any money."

"Look, finish your coffee, and then I really think you should go home, and do your research in the library, or on the internet, or whatever turns you on. But it is very dangerous to do what you are doing, and I'm not surprised your mother is ringing to check up on you."

"I'll be leaving home next year anyway, to go to university," she said indignantly, and I sensed this was a well-rehearsed argument. "I'm going to be a social worker, I think."

"What does your dad think of all this?" I gestured towards her sticky hair and tatty Nikes. If she were my daughter, I wouldn't let her do it.

"He's my stepdad and he doesn't count. I hate him. He's really creepy. My mum only married him for his money. She couldn't possibly love him. He's awful."

"But he disapproves?"

"I haven't told him. I avoid him if at all possible and it's none of his business anyway. I can't wait to leave home and get away from him." She gulped down the last of the coffee, and wiped her fingers on the paper napkin. "Are you going back to the tube station?"

"Yes, I was on my way home," I said. "But shouldn't

161

you ring your mother back? She'll be worried."

"In a minute," she said sullenly, and I could see that for all her surface charm and confidence, she was still a teenager, who didn't want to be told what to do.

"What's your name, by the way?" I asked. "Mine's Matthew."

"I'm not supposed to give my name to strangers," she said, archly. "Thanks for the coffee, though." She couldn't escape her nice upbringing, even when she tried.

She stood up and put the strap of her shoulder bag across her body, and tossed her hair back over her shoulders. I watched her disappearing down into the tube station, and then settling on a corner of the steps. She bowed her head and held up a piece of cardboard with some black crayoned writing on it.

I took the bus after all that. The tube was too claustrophobic at this time of day, and I needed to clear my head. While I waited at the number 3 bus stop, next to Dickens and Jones, I watched glamorous women walking past with their Jaeger shopping bags draped on their arms and tourists heaving bulky Hamley's bags into taxis. A pale teenage boy lurked across the street, and I knew by his body language he was waiting to "*pick a pocket or two*". In the face of all that ostentatious wealth, who could blame him?

When I got home, I called CityScope, the charity for homeless young people, and got the answering machine. I wanted to do something useful. When I finally spoke to the manager, he said they were desperate for volunteers, and I could come in any time for a chat, to see where I could be most useful. I went there directly.

They decided I could do speech and drama classes, which really scared me. I hadn't managed to make a living out of being an actor, so how could I possibly teach other people how to do it? It wasn't about that, said Peter Wycross, the co-ordinator for volunteers. These kids needed to build their self-confidence, and learn how to relate to other people so that they could get themselves a job and a place to live, and try and leave behind their sad histories.

"So what kind of stuff do you want me to do with them?" I asked, still hoping for clues. I never paid much attention to the actual classes at college. It was so long ago . . .

"Maybe role plays, or little dramas they could act out?" he said, sounding as clueless as I felt.

"And telephone manner, that kind of thing, so when they ring up about jobs, they sound OK?" I suggested.

"Yes, great, and how to talk about themselves positively in interviews," said Peter.

"OK, I'll have a think about that," I said, and I felt quite fired up by the idea. I'm not a great tea and sympathy type of person. I would rather be doing something. Maybe if I got some practice, I could apply for real jobs teaching drama, to fill in between acting parts.

As usual, I got carried away on my own PR, and had

to tell myself to come back down to earth. I said I would have a think and get some ideas, and then come and discuss them with Peter. He was delighted. He said it would be great to have a real actor in, to inspire the kids. I groaned – they would probably ask me had I been on telly, and was I very rich, and what kind of car did I drive. A little bit, no, and none would be the short answers there.

I decided not to tell Caroline about what I was doing, because I wanted to get some results first. She would probably think it was a really flaky idea, and I should be out looking for real work instead of preening in front of a bunch of awestruck teenagers. As it happened, she was a bit tearful when she got in from work, so it was not the time to tell her. I wondered again what was up. It takes ages to get anything out of Caroline – she says she has to "process things" before she can talk about them. So I would just have to wait until she was ready to tell me.

Caroline

Matthew rang my mobile phone just when I was arriving in the office on Monday morning. I was so flustered I waved at Alison with the other hand, forgetting I was holding a Cappuccino Grande, which slurped out through the hole in the lid and splashed on the sleeve of my suit.

"Oh great," I grunted. I swung my laptop case off my shoulder and on to my desk, still holding the phone to my ear.

"Sorry?" He was probably wondering if he had got the right number.

"No, I'm sorry, Matthew," I said. "I've just spilt coffee all over my suit. Never mind! How are you, anyway?"

Alison was hovering in the doorway, holding up a napkin and a bottle of fizzy water from her desk. She definitely looked curious. Was I talking like this to Matt? I could see her wondering.

"Thanks, Alison, you're a honey," I said, nodding towards the desk. She put them down and went out with her ears flapping.

"I'm fine. Sounds like you're not having a great start to your day," he said and, I had to admit, his voice just turned me on so much.

"No problem, I'm grand. How was your weekend?"

"Great, thanks. I went to a museum on Saturday after I bumped into you, and had a walk in the country on Sunday, so it was the best of urban and country living. What about you?"

Did he go on his own? With friends? Were they single ones or married ones?

"Not much really, just pottered around and went to buy a table, and had some nice meals at home, so it was very relaxing."

"Good. So, what's your diary like this week? Shall we

try and get together for a drink?"

We settled on Thursday. It felt weird, nearly like a work arrangement – he's quite formal, and I don't know why, but I think he's a bit nervous. He must have had loads of girlfriends, surely – he's at least thirty-seven and he's not bad-looking, even though he's a bit scruffy.

CHAPTER 9

Caroline

I went shopping on Tuesday after work instead of going to the gym. I wanted something new to wear for my birthday. Matt usually organises a special meal or something, but he'd been a bit quiet on the subject this year. Maybe it would be a weekend away, and I wanted to be ready, in case he sprang something on me. I started trying on things I don't usually wear, like skinny sleeveless tops that don't do me any favours, and flimsy skirts cut on the bias. I looked at myself in the mirror in the changing room at Karen Millen's. Why on earth was I trying on a pale blue little dress that I would usually walk past without even thinking about it? I sometimes miss the me who went travelling. I would wear the same pair of baggy trousers for a week, with different coloured T-shirts and my canvas sandals. I would just put my hair up in a scrunchie, and half the time I didn't even brush it from one day to the next. Here I was, staring at a slightly plumper version of me, in a goodie-two-shoes dress and strappy, high-heeled sandals, with a spiky grown-out crop by Paul Michel and the lipstick of the month from *Red* magazine. That's what Matthew would expect to see. I finally admitted to myself that I wasn't buying a birthday outfit, but something for my date with him. I hit the credit card with a hundred and eighty pounds and only felt a tiny bit guilty. My days of student poverty and low-budget travelling are still fresh enough in the memory. I am still amazed to be in credit at the end of the month, and I'm delighted every time the cash machine gives me money. I went back to work to drop off the Karen Millen bag. As I was hanging the dress on the back of my office door, I realised I had crossed the line. From that moment on, I was betraying Matt. I should tell him that I wasn't sure where our relationship was going. Sow the seeds. Maybe it was time to finish with him. He was starting to really frustrate me now. Even though he had that TV job lined up for the autumn, I thought, who knows what will happen after that one? Were we going to spend our lives together with me being the Steady Eddie breadwinner, and him always waiting for the next big break? When do aspiring actors resign themselves to doing an ordinary job like other people?

If you love someone, are you supposed to just accept everything about them, or is there a point where you have to be hard, and say it's not working? Having been on a high, smiling at myself in the mirror and imagining my intimate dinner with Matthew on Thursday, I now felt like I had a lump of lead in my stomach, and I couldn't imagine ever eating another thing. I got the tube home.

Matt was sitting in his usual place, on the couch reading a magazine, and he looked up and smiled when I came in, like he always does. I flopped on his knee, and he stroked the back of my neck. I felt cosy, curled up on his knee with my eyes closed and his big strong arms around me. He kissed the top of my head, and I could feel tears squeezing out between my eyelashes. Why did it have to be so difficult? When I sat up he asked me what was wrong. He stroked my cheek really gently with the back of his finger. The concern in his eyes made me want to cry even more. It doesn't feel good to realise you are not a nice person.

"Just a tough day at work, and hormones, I think." I smiled at him and escaped to fill a hot bath.

"So, how was your day?" I asked him later when we were sitting watching a police documentary, eating pasta.

"Fine, really," he said, and didn't volunteer any more information.

This is one of the things that drives me mad. I couldn't imagine, if I was ever unemployed, me sitting in the flat all day, doing nothing, just waiting for Matt to come home. He seemed to have lost all his hunger to do anything. It had definitely got worse since he heard about the ITV part, as if he was sitting back, just waiting for that to happen. But it was four months away – enough time to go temping, or try and get some voice-recording work, or anything, I fumed to myself. I was tired of lecturing him. I was tired of trying to sound supportive when I was really frustrated, so I didn't ask questions any more. We never had arguments before and I didn't want to start having them now. Especially when …

Well, who knows what will happen with Matthew? I thought. I'll have to make a decision soon. Very soon.

CHAPTER 10

Caroline

I was surprised on Wednesday when Matt told me he was going out the following evening, before I even had a chance to make an excuse about working late. He never goes out by himself. I was afraid to ask where he was going in case he wanted me to go with him, so I changed the subject.

We're supposed to be deciding where to go on holiday, and we're having the usual unrealistic fantasies about going somewhere exotic, to remind us of when we were travelling. On the way home from work I had picked up loads of brochures about canoeing down the Amazon, and boat trips to the Galapagos islands. I still prefer to turn the pages of safaris and sunsets in a brochure instead of going on the internet. Matt wasn't very enthusiastic. Last year, we went on a walking safari with the Masai Mara, which was brilliant. I had only two weeks off work, and I was a bit unsettled when we came back to muggy, miserable old London, but it didn't last long. Matt was teasing me about it, saying I was really an urban girl at heart. I'd love to do something in South America this year, and the Amazon trip is one of Matt's dreams, but he wasn't really interested in even looking at the pictures.

"Do you not want to do anything, any more?" I asked, nearly bouncing on the sofa with frustration.

"It looks really expensive," he said, and in all the time I've known him, that's the first time he's ever mentioned the cost of something.

"Well, if you're a bit tight for money at the moment ..." I said, tentatively, waiting to see if I would get a reaction before going any further.

"And I should probably just be around, in case some work comes along, too," he said.

"Wouldn't it be awful if I missed out on something, just because I was away on a two-week holiday?"

"Yes, of course it would, Matt, but you can't put your whole life on hold. The phone isn't hopping off the table every day with your agent begging you to take parts, is it?" I said, flinging the brochures on the floor beside the sofa, trying to look like I was aiming for the magazine rack. I really wanted to roll one up and wallop him around the head with it.

"Are you annoyed with me?" he asked, managing to convey a mixture of incredulity and woundedness in equal measure.

"No, I'm grand," I muttered, and went into the kitchen to make a cup of jasmine tea. "Do you want a cup?" I asked, leaning out the door and trying to be friendly.

"No, thanks," he said, and I could hear in his voice that he was trying not to be sulky.

We huddled up together on the sofa and I sipped my tea and Matt stroked my leg while we watched Chris Tarrant hosting a "TV blunders" programme. Matt loves them. I know he's fantasising about featuring in one some day – the urbane, darkly handsome actor who is a household name, embarrassed by some silly faux pas, but able to laugh at himself. Dream on, my friend, I thought to myself. Then I swallowed a mouthful of jasmine tea leaves, and I had to stand up spluttering and rush into the kitchen to spit them into the sink. Punishment for my uncharitable thoughts.

Later, it was Matthew's beautiful hands with their long fingers caressing me that I imagined as Matt and I made love. I was ashamed and turned on at the same time.

Matt

I had told Peter I would come back in a week, but as I sat at the computer in the library, trying to come up with ideas about how I would structure a drama session, I realised that I had no feeling for what these kids were like. I should spend some time with them before arbitrarily deciding what kind of teaching they needed. I was so fired up by the whole thing that I left the library at once and got the bus to the CityScope hostel in Streatham.

I introduced myself to Steve the supervisor, a striking-looking man with ebony skin, dreadlocks and a baritone voice. I told him I just wanted to have a look around, chat to the kids a bit, and get a feel for what might work. He gave me a quick tour, talking non-stop about what the shelter did, and how they try to reintegrate the kids into society rather than just giving them a roof over their heads. He kept saying, 'Great,' and 'Wonderful,' and 'Cool' every time I answered one of his questions. I told him I had some experience of working in a shelter.

"Fantastic, come in here – this is the common room, with the TV and games and reading corner. Some of the kids hang out here during the day, especially when it's raining. We don't allow them access to the dormitories before about eight o'clock at night. Some of them would sleep all day and then be up, needing supervising when the rest of us are trying to sleep!"

He didn't seem to be conscious of the fact that all of the occupants of the room could hear him, and I felt a bit uncomfortable, like we were talking about animals in the zoo. But he was the professional, and he obviously had a good relationship with some of the kids, because they looked up when he came in and smiled, or gave him a high five as he passed.

"Put the kettle on, Jason, will you?" asked Steve, and a tall skinny kid stood up, his eyes still glued to the TV screen as he edged out of the room into a galley kitchen and flicked a kettle-switch.

"They all love the X Files," Steve smiled and pushed a bunch of newspapers away from one end of the table.

"Have a seat." He pulled out an orange plastic chair and I sat down and looked around the room.

Steve had to answer his pager, and excused himself. A slight figure hunched in the corner, hair hanging over her face, her hands clasped around her bony knees as she sat on the bean bag, staring at the stained green carpet-tiles. Jason made a very decent cup of tea and handed it to me, managing not to spill it while still fixated on the television screen.

"Cuppa?" I asked the girl, holding out the styrofoam cup, the steam curling off it in front of her face as she looked up.

"Chloe?" I said, searching her face. Her face was paler, and her eyes were rimmed with black circles from lack of sleep, but it was definitely her.

"No. You must be thinking of someone else," she said, and took the tea. "Thanks."

"It is you. Don't you remember me from Oxford Circus? We went for coffee and a bun. Your mother rang you on the mobile phone."

She snorted. "Oh, yes, when I was pretending to be homeless." Her voice had deepened, and sounded hoarse. Her big green eyes had narrowed and dulled.

"What happened?"

"He raped me. Mum doesn't believe me. Or doesn't want to, maybe. So I came here. The staff were really friendly before, when I was doing my project."

I sat down beside her, leaning against the wall.

She looked into the cup, and then nibbled around the edges, making semi-circular marks with her teeth, and holding it up to study the effect. "I've always had uneven teeth," she said, pointing out the odd dents with a grubby fingernail that still boasted the remains of a childish pale-pink polish. "Mum wanted me to have braces when I was fifteen, but I thought no-one would want to kiss me so I said no. They're not that bad, anyway, are they?"

"No," I said. "They're fine." Unlike the rest of her, which looked distinctly unwell.

"He used to come into my room and just look at me, when he thought I was asleep," she said, looking down again, and fixing on a spot on the floor.

"Are you sure you want to talk about it?" I wasn't sure if I was ready for this.

"No, but it won't go away, will it?"

"No, but there are women volunteers here too, if you felt …"

"It doesn't make any difference, really," she said, and I sensed that she had found a way to distance herself from the whole situation. I hoped it wasn't with drugs.

"I used to hear his breathing. He's really fat, and he'll probably die of a heart attack soon. He used to creep into my room and stand there, breathing heavily, and watch me. I was afraid to open my eyes and see what he was doing, but I could guess."

She blushed, and I could feel the anger burning in my chest and my stomach, like an acid invading my body. A girl her age should blush when she's caught smoking by the head teacher, or talking to a boy she really fancies, or presenting her school project to her whole class. These should be the "most embarrassing moment" stories that enable her to grow, and gain her confidence.

"Did you tell your mother?" I asked, swallowing the bile.

"She didn't believe me. She said he was just checking on me, that I should be glad he wanted to, like a real dad." The tears came then, and found their way down her dusty face and ran along her chin. I didn't dare put my arm around her, but I settled against the wall so that my shoulder rested lightly against hers. She leaned over a tiny fraction, accepting my support but not surrendering totally.

"I went home after I spoke to you that day. Mum was out visiting a friend, and I was in my room. I had my stereo on really loud, and I was reading a magazine, so I didn't even notice him coming in."

I sensed someone looking at us from across the room, and I looked up. Steve gave me a nod, and I acknowledged it without moving. I didn't want to disturb the flow, and Chloe was staring at the carpet, obviously replaying the nightmare in her head.

"Next thing I knew, he was sitting on the end of the bed, and I pulled my legs up, to get away from him. He's never touched me before. I never get close enough to him. He looked a bit weird. His face was all hot and sweaty and his eyes were all dark. He reached out and stroked my leg, and I had short pyjamas on so I could feel his hand on my skin. It was horrible. All rough."

She shuddered. I stayed still, even though my leg was starting to ache and I was desperate to change positions.

"I tried to get away, but he's really big. He just got on top of me and I couldn't move." Her voice quavered and she angrily wiped away more tears as they ran down her face. "He raped me and really hurt me, and do you know what the worst thing was? He kept saying that I wanted it. 'This is what you want, isn't it?' He kept on saying it and saying it, in that horrible raspy voice. I tried to fight him, but I was flat against the bed, he was so heavy.

Then he just rolled off me like a fat pig and pulled up his trousers and went out. He didn't even look back at me. Whitney Houston was still singing." Her voice had turned sing-song now, almost as if she were in a trance. "It didn't take long. It was the same track. I looked on the CD cover – 'And I Will Always Love You.' Five minutes and twenty-nine seconds long."

I pulled up my knees and held on to them, like her, and we sat there together for a long time, saying nothing.

"By the way, my name is Zoe, so you were nearly right," she said. "Thanks for listening." She stood up and went towards the girls' dormitory. I just nodded at her, unable to speak.

CHAPTER 11

Caroline

All day Thursday, the Karen Millen dress accused me from the back of the office door, when I was trying to concentrate on my computer screen. Its pale blueness stood out against the dark mahogany-coloured door, and hovered constantly in my peripheral vision. I kept running my fingers through my hair, and even nibbled the corner of two of my nails. I am really proud of my six-month-old nails, a major achievement after not having any for about ten years. Alison kept popping in and offering to make me a coffee, or get a Coke from the machine, and she was bursting to ask me what was wrong. I went to the ladies' at about three o'clock, and I couldn't decide whether to sit down or throw up. I looked in the mirror and my hair was sticking up every-where.

Alison followed me in. "Are you OK, Caroline?" she eventually asked, and gave my arm a brisk but caring stroke, catching my eye in the mirror, and desperately hoping I was going to confide in her.

"Grand, thanks, I think I must have a tummy bug or something," I said. "I feel a bit light-headed."

"Probably all that coffee I've been giving you," she said. "You didn't have any lunch, did you?"

"No, I want to finish on time tonight, I'm . . ."

"Going somewhere nice with Matthew, are you?" she asked, and I nodded, sticking to my childhood habit of not telling lies out loud, so they don't count.

"For dinner, so I didn't want to eat too much today," I said. "Some new trendy restaurant in the Aldwych."

"Early birthday treat, is it?" she asked, knowingly. "These new places are difficult to get into at the weekend."

Had she guessed what was going on or was I just being completely paranoid? "Mmmn," I muttered, putting on lipstick and nodding and rolling my eyes at her in the mirror. I am so good at not lying out loud. It all goes back to me asking Mam when I was about six what the worst sin was, and she said it was lying. I haven't been able to do it out loud very well, ever since. The reason I was so anxious about this date with Matthew was the realisation of how easy it had become for me to lie. I usually can't do it to save my life. It's one of the things that I just know about myself. It's part of being me. Am I changing into some sly little slut overnight?

Alison stood quietly beside me, not even washing her hands or pretending to fix her make-up. Just being there in case I needed her. She smiled at me in the mirror.

I opened the door. "Thanks, Alison," I said, and smiled back at her.

She probably thinks I'm either pregnant or I've got another job. She was watching me for the rest of the afternoon. She knows I'm hiding something.

I was nearly late, because I wanted to wait until my section of the floor was empty before I came out of the ladies' in my new outfit. I suddenly felt really self-conscious, and I couldn't face the thought of Alison or anyone else seeing me teetering along in those ridiculous little heels, with the new tiny matching handbag that holds nothing but a lipstick, a credit card and a really small mobile phone. I stashed all my other stuff in my laptop case, thinking I could leave it behind. Then the blinding realisation hit me that I couldn't go home at the end of the night dressed like this. It was supposed to be my new birthday outfit. I'd never have time to come back to the office and change, and anyway, Matthew would think it was really weird. He'd probably want to send me home in a black cab. He's that kind of guy. Change in the cab? Give the cab-driver a thrill? I stood staring at myself in the mirror. What on earth was I thinking of? I ended up tipping everything out of my gym bag, stuffing in my work clothes and my normal-size handbag, and leaving my smelly trainers and crumpled shorts under my desk. No self-respecting cleaner would touch them with the end of a hoover, never mind steal them. Now I just had to contend with looking ridiculous, carrying a huge black gym bag down the corridor. Baxter was in the lift. I have the precision timing of an accomplished criminal.

"Off somewhere nice?" he sneered, looking down at my previously never-seen-in-the-office thighs, exposed even more by the strange position I had taken up, trying to look as if I carried heavy gym bags around with me all the time. I nodded and smiled at him, and then concentrated on fighting the rising tide of scarlet coming up from the cleavage of my dress. I'd just have to get to the restaurant first, dump the bag in the cloakroom, and worry about getting it back and changing later, when I'd had a few glasses of wine and could think straight. A cab came screeching around the corner on cue as I stepped out of the office door, and I hailed it.

"The Aldwych, please," I said, sinking back on the seat, with the first flutter of excitement rather than nerves. I kept thinking about Matthew's hands. And his voice.

I looked out the window, and indulged the butterflies. People were scurrying towards the tube station to avoid the rain, and the orange streetlights glowed in the wet twilight. I love London in the spring and the autumn, when the days are stretching or shrinking, and change is in the air. As the cab pulled up and I rooted with my fingers in my glittery useless handbag for a folded-up tenner, I glanced out the window and for one second I thought I saw Matt. But it couldn't have been him. This guy was walking along with a young girl, and they were talking very intently. He was totally engrossed in the conversation. The guy was just dressed like Matt and had the same hair. I found the money, got my change and tried to slide elegantly out of the cab before hauling out my bag. Matthew was standing there when I turned around, and he took the gym bag so naturally, I wasn't even embarrassed. He put his hand in the small of my back, and ushered me into the restaurant, and as we were shown to our table, it felt like we had always been together.

"So, has your week improved, since we spoke on the phone?" he asked, flicking open his crisp white napkin and putting it on his knee.

His hands, I thought, I just love everything they do. I followed his long brown fingers as they reached across the white tablecloth and picked up the leather-bound wine list, and was mesmerised. I flicked my eyes into focus and looked up at his face.

"It was grand, really. I always seem to be spilling things when I'm on the phone to you," I said. My coquettish smile was a bit rusty, but I think he got it. He asked if I liked Sancerre, and I found myself saying no, I would prefer a nice oakey Chardonnay, not caring if he thought I had no taste. I knew he would drink red anyway, so why should I try to impress him by drinking a white wine I hated? He is one of those people who can't summon a waiter with an almost invisible nod of the head, so it felt like forever while he craned his neck around, grinning at me, trying to catch the eye of the very fast-moving waiter. He finally ordered the wine, and then there was a little hiatus. We both knew this was really the beginning. Neither of us knew what to say. Where do you start when you want the other person to know everything about you already, so you can just talk?

We started talking about Islam, like you do. There was a Nigerian woman on the news who had been sentenced to death by stoning, because she had borne a child out of wedlock. I saw her on the television, with her beautiful tiny baby, coming out of the court of appeal, which had upheld the sentence. She only has a few months to live – until her baby is weaned. I was surprised by Matthew's reaction.

"Well, she's got to live by the laws of the country," he said, "otherwise chaos would reign. If we could pick and choose which rules to follow, there wouldn't be any rules."

"But it's barbaric!" I said. "Sharia law has only been reintroduced to Nigeria in the last few years, as a backlash to all the corruption that Nigeria has got itself famous for. So who has the right to suddenly impose a set of laws that weren't there before?"

"That's the difference, I guess, between law and religion – our laws are fundamentally influenced by Christian values, and we accept them on that basis. But who's to say they're any more right than Sharia law?"

"But we don't chop off people's hands, or stone them to death!" I said. "And we don't just impose a whole set of new laws, willy-nilly!"

"The Muslim majority voted that government in," said Matthew, "so it is democracy in action."

"Not really, when the effect on the minority will be so drastic," I said.

"Only the Muslims will be punished according to Sharia law," said Matthew.

I hadn't known that, but I wasn't about to back down on this subject. "But the adultery law targets women –"

Luckily, the waiter turned up with the wine at this point and we went through the ridiculously serious tasting ritual. Only once have I seen a wine sent back, and that was by Baxter trying to impress us all at a Christmas lunch. This time I was grateful for the interruption and neither of us pursued the argument when the waiter dissolved into the background again.

Matthew told me all about the Law Centre where he does pro-bono work. He managed to make the most outrageous recidivists seem harmless and funny, the way he told their stories. I haven't laughed so much for ages. Matthew does a surprisingly good "Sarff East Landan" accent. There was the six-foot-six drug-dealing schizophrenic who had just spent three hundred pounds on a chunky gold bracelet, and came into the Law Centre to tell Matthew he thought he had been 'skanked, man'. The guy wanted to know if he had any legal rights, because his friend had told him the bracelet wasn't even gold. Matthew, tongue-in-cheek, asked him if he had a receipt from the shop where he bought it, and he said, 'No, man, it wasn't in a shop, right, it was on the street, but what I'm sayin' is, it's not gold, man. I been right skanked.'

Matthew just had to agree with him, and suggest that he probably shouldn't wear jewellery like that in the street anyway, or people might wonder where he got the money from, with him being on benefit, and all that. I wondered if Matthew put on the London accent when he was talking to these guys, or if it was just to make me laugh.

I ordered the most delicious vegetable tarte with onion marmalade, and guinea fowl with redcurrant gravy. The meal passed in a blur, and I drank the whole bottle of Chardonnay without noticing. Matthew had done equal justice to his bottle of red, and when I stood up to go to the bathroom, I wobbled on the stupid little heels of my sandals. I hate that. I concentrated really hard and made it to the ladies' without incident, and leaned against the multicoloured marble vanity-stand, staring at my reflection. My cheeks were very pink, my lips were full and red, and I looked as if I had just had an orgasm, my hair slightly mussed, and my eyes all glazed. I was shocked at how horny I suddenly felt at that thought, and went to the loo wondering for the first time if I would go home tonight. I didn't need any lipstick or blusher when I came out, so I just brushed my hair and put some eyeliner on, staring into my eyes, and vaguely condemning myself for my wicked thoughts. When I got back to the table, a tiny, steaming espresso was waiting for me, and Matthew was delicately sipping at his. He looked at me over the rim of his cup, and just raised one eyebrow. I haven't done the tasteful 'date moving on to sex' thing for a long time. Matt and I bonked practically on first sight, so we never engaged in the niceties – I can't remember if this has ever happened to me before. I always seem to have been in the right place when sex entered the equation, and it just happened. No elaborate arrangements required. I decided to raise my eyebrow back at him, and stick to my old-fashioned girl principle. It was up to him to make the first move.

"My friend has a flat in Pimlico that he lets me use, from time to time," said Matthew.

I recoiled. Was I just one of a line of tarts he bonked in his friend's pied-à-terre? My heart started pounding. I could feel my neck burning.

"Oh, yes, handy for a bit of bonking, is it?" I said.

Matthew had the grace to look shocked. "What? I didn't mean it like that!" he said, "I just meant –"

"You're not telling me you were suggesting that we go all the way to Pimlico for a cup of coffee, are you?" I asked, wondering how we could have got from both wanting desperately to sleep with each other, to him denying it and me acting like a nun whose honour has been compromised.

"Well, I . . . sorry, Caroline, I've probably had too much to drink and it didn't come out right. I really like you, and I just didn't want the evening to end, that's all," he said, and he was so humble and embarrassed that I knew I had completely overreacted.

"I'm sorry, too," I said, but I managed to keep enough control to stop there.

Matthew immediately caught the attention of the waiter, who was hovering. We were the last table in his section, and he had already asked about three times if we wanted anything else. I looked at my watch. Twenty past twelve. My taxi would cost a fortune. "Could you ask the waiter to call a cab for me, please?" I asked in my best-behaved voice, and then I had a quick look in my minis-cule bag to make sure I had enough cash.

"I'm going to get a taxi and charge it to the firm," he said. "Shall I drop you off?"

I refrained from commenting on how expensive a cab to the outer reaches of Bromley would be, and I nodded at him. "That would be nice, thanks."

We were both a bit subdued while we were waiting. The rampant hormones had gone back into their boxes, and we were at the anti-climatic stage of the evening, with just the prospect of a snog in the taxi before it was all over.

"Thanks for a lovely evening," I said, and he said he enjoyed it, too.

Guilt had set in now. What if I had stayed out all night? Even the easy-going Matt would be unlikely to believe I was suddenly involved in some all-night contract deadline. That would be that, with him. Life turned upside down, and for what? Maybe things wouldn't even work out with Matthew, and I would have thrown away a lovely guy, a great relationship, for a passing flirtation. I slumped further down in my seat, and Matthew asked if I was OK.

"Just a bit too much to drink, I think," I said, and sat up again. He was quiet too, and I wondered for the first time if he had someone to have a guilty conscience about, as well.

The waiter brought our coats, and the *bag*. It looked as if it could have a body hidden in it. The pink cloak-room ticket stuck on with Sellotape was dwarfed by the huge expanse of black canvas. I ripped it off. How was I going to get changed, if I was sharing the taxi? Drunken flitters of ideas swept in and out of my head. Change in the bushes outside the house? Matthew would probably be the gentlemanly type who would wait until I was in my front door before letting the taxi drive off. Change in the lobby, when I got inside? What if one of my neighbours saw me? Or Matt heard the front door and then came down to meet me, or just waited in bed, wondering why I was taking ten minutes to climb the stairs? Could I pretend I had a ferocious mother at home, who didn't approve of me going out, and change here at the restaurant? Ask for my own taxi?

Matthew looked at his watch. "Look, it's very late, I think I'll stay in Pimlico anyway, and just ask the taxi to take you home after dropping me. Would that be OK with you?"

"Yes, yes, fine, grand!" I said, with a huge sigh of relief. A quick wriggle in the back seat and the humiliation of the driver knowing my secret was a significant improvement on the other options.

We finally got into the taxi, and I didn't know whether to sit beside Matthew or not. My big black bag was sitting on one of the jump seats, like my conscience, mocking me. Matthew slid across the seat and took my hand, and just held it in his, like a novice sixteen-year-old not sure what to do in the cinema. We went to Pimlico like that, not talking much, but I could feel every centimetre of contact between our hands. His fingers were soft but firm, and when I looked down, my hand looked tiny in his. I felt safe. Protected.

When we pulled up outside a mansion block of flats with Corinthian pillars flanking the black shiny door,

Matthew just kissed me really gently on the lips, and said, "Thanks, I really enjoyed this evening, take care," and got out, managing to close the door without slamming it – a difficult thing to do in a black cab. He waved at me in a sort of salute, through the window, and went up the steps. He didn't look back.

As the cab drove away, I did. The black door was already shut, and "Take care" was echoing around inside my head. That's what you say to neighbours, isn't it, or old people who are a bit frail? What happened to "See you soon," or "I'll give you a ring," or "How are you fixed next week?". Maybe he didn't want to see me again. Maybe that was good. Did I need this complication in my life? I did the Superwoman change in the back seat to distract myself and get it over with, and even remembered to take off some make-up to simulate exhausted career woman rather than thwarted tart. Matt was asleep when I got in, so my efforts were completely wasted. I wondered how people could seriously conduct affairs, if this was what it took. I slid into bed, exhausted with the turmoil in my head, and the queasiness in my stomach that always strikes me when I'm stressed.

Matthew

She is gorgeous. I can't stop thinking about her. She's funny, and charming, and so unaware of how attractive she is, that I am completely disarmed. We had a heated discussion about Islam at dinner, and sometimes I thought she was just playing Devil's Advocate to provoke me. It worked. Liz and I never have those kinds of conversations any more. Work and domestic trivia, and how we really must make more of an effort to see our friends seem to be the best we can manage these days. I could tell you all about Liz's Board Directors, their partners' names, and what their views on shareholder value are. I don't know what Liz thinks of the troubles in Iraq, or the situation in Kashmir. It's a terrible thing to say, but I'm not even very interested to find out. Liz has become a two-dimensional being, super-executive and super-mother, and has no energy left to be anything else. Sometimes when we're watching the ten o'clock news, I comment on a headline, and I can see that she hasn't been listening, because she looks at me blankly – she's either planning her strategy for a meeting the following day, or deciding what to put in Ben's sandwiches for nursery. I do know that she can't put in peanut butter or Nutella because someone in his class has a severe peanut allergy and even being touched by a child who has eaten peanuts can set off the reaction. I do know that Ben has been invited to a birthday party next Saturday morning, and Liz is taking Jack swimming for some quality time on his own. I know that Jack said 'Shoes on,' today, which counts as his first sentence, and I know that Liz has to go to Copenhagen next week for a two-day conference and her mum can't look after the kids. She got a letter today confirming her share option grant for this year, and it is worth ten thousand pounds if the share price continues to perform. And she has been asked if she will consider taking on the management of another department, which is struggling and needs a good sorting out.

Caroline must think I am so crass. I'm extremely out of practice – I probably wouldn't even be able to seduce Liz these days, it has been so long since I bothered – she's always too tired. I know that Caroline wanted it as much as I did – I could see it in her eyes. But I wasn't exactly subtle. How can you be, when you're in a restaurant in the middle of the West End and have to get to Pimlico? I wonder if she'll see me again.

Matt

I told Caroline I was going out on Thursday evening, and she didn't even ask where I was going, so I didn't have to lie. I wasn't about to tell her about the homeless shelter yet – if I changed my mind and decided it was not for me after all, I didn't need her looking down her nose at me for 'yet another' unfinished project, or off-the-wall idea. Her career path is so much more straight-forward – work hard, use your brain, follow the rules and you're pretty much guaranteed not only to have a job, but to be promoted. As an actor, so much is down to Lady Luck, and not having a bloody cold on the day of your audition, that it's amazing anyone gets anywhere. If I was going to do something a bit more predictable, like teaching, maybe, I figured I'd had nothing to lose by working at the hostel. I'd done some research, and gone back to my old college notes, and I had some ideas now, to try out with the group. I had told Steve I would do the first class on Thursday evening.

I got there before six and looked for Zoe. I was relieved at first when Steve said she hadn't been seen since the day before. She must have decided to tell her mother, and gone home, I thought. Tommy, one of the seventeen-year-old boys whom Steve thought I could help, was lying on the floor of the television room, biting his nails, his long skinny body hardly seeming to make contact with the carpet-tiles.

"Hi," I said, flopping onto a beanbag. He was watching *Changing Rooms*, but with the vacant expression of one who is somewhere else. What interest could a homeless teenager possibly have in middle-aged neighbours swapping keys so they can be filmed painting each other's houses in horrible colours? Tommy grunted and took another nibble at the edge of his thumbnail as if it was particularly appetising.

The television presenter was delighted with the blood-red shade of the new paint under the dado rail in the hall of a tiny terraced house in Leeds.

"Disgusting, isn't it?" Tommy muttered, not taking his eyes off the screen.

"Yep," I said. "You seen Zoe around?"

"No, mate. She said she was going up North to see her nan."

That was news to me, and obviously to Steve, who had just walked in.

"Did she say where, up North?" I asked, wondering which grandmother it could be.

"Gateshead, or Sunderland, somewhere like that I think." He pointed at the television. "Can you believe they spent five hundred quid to make it look that bad?" he said, as the neighbours hugged each other, tears in their eyes at the miraculous change that had been wrought on their dingy hall.

"Did she say how she was planning to get there?" Steve asked.

Tommy shook his head. "Train, prob'ly."

"She didn't have any money, when I spoke to her before," I said, and looked at Steve.

"She's good at begging. She was going to get the money outside some theatre she reckoned had a play on that would make people give her money. She's not stupid, that girl," said Tommy, going back to his thumbnail now, which had had a five-minute respite from the onslaught.

Steve went to his office and he came back with a London entertainment guide. We went through the

West End Theatre listings. Nothing looked likely. Then I happened to notice an advert for Shelter, the homeless people's charity. The takings of one night's performance at the Garrick Theatre were being donated to the charity. I checked the date. Last night. She probably got her train fare in one night, appealing to the guilt-ridden theatre-goers on the way out from the show.

"Shit!" I said, and was surprised how much I cared. Steve looked at me askance. "She's probably there already, if she got a train this morning," he said. I could see he was wondering why Zoe was so special – I just hadn't become inured yet to the pain, as I guess you have to be when you do his job, or you'd go mad. "She'll be sitting in her nan's front room, drinking tea and eating sticky buns, and wondering whether to ring her mum."

I was surprised at Steve's cavalier attitude. Zoe obviously hadn't told him what had happened. It wasn't up to me to tell him. Why hadn't I told her to report it to the police? I knew perfectly well why I hadn't. By nicking that card I had crossed the line of 'them' and 'us', and being on the other side, even briefly, had changed me. Now I had to find her, and redeem myself. I grabbed my jacket off the back of a plastic orange chair, and pulled it on. Steve lowered his voice so that Tommy wouldn't hear over the noise of the advertisements for Miracle Grow and paint that does what it says on the tin.

"Sometimes, kids like her just leave home for a little while to make a statement, assert their independence, and show their mums who's boss. They rarely stick it out for more than a few nights. Zoe had quite a romantic notion of homelessness when she started doing her project, and I have a feeling she'll be back home before the week is out."

I just knew he was wrong. I zipped up my jacket, told Steve I would be back in time for the class at eight and caught a bus and then the tube to Leicester Square. She was huddled at the side of the steps, already with the glazed look of someone who has no hope.

"It was last night," I said to her, putting my hand under her elbow, and gently pulling her upright.

"I know," she said, and sobbed, and when she turned her face to me, one side was completely swollen around a purple and red gash on her cheek.

I took her arm. "Come on, let's go for a coffee down on the Strand, and you can tell me all about it."

She leaned on me, like an old woman, trying not to put any weight on her left foot. We hobbled down to a twenty-four-hour coffee house on the corner, and I had to help her to climb onto one of the high stainless-steel stools.

"Will you be OK there? Cappuccino and a pain au chocolat?" I asked, and was pleased to see that she could manage a grin. When I came back, she was staring out the plate-glass window at the stream of preoccupied commuters grimly stomping to Charing Cross station, and the meandering tourists avoiding the puddles which would stain their bright white holiday trainers.

"So, what happened?" I asked, as she took a sip of the hot coffee, and her whole body shivered so violently she nearly dropped the cup.

"I was going to see my nan. She'd never stand for what's been going on. She's my dad's mum, but we haven't seen her for years, not since my mum and dad split up."

I just nodded, and tasted my coffee.

"So I thought if I just got the train fare, and went up there she would tell me what to do." She nodded her head in a direction I took to be North and said, "She lives in Durham."

"Did you ring her, or anything, to find out if she was still living in the same place?" I asked.

"I didn't have any number or address, but I remember how to get to her house from the station. We used to go there all the time when I was little."

I nodded again.

"So I needed a lot of money, like more than fifty quid, to get there, so I thought I'd beg outside the theatre when that special Shelter thing was on, and I got there really early, like six o'clock, to make sure I had a good place to stand."

I pointed to her pain au chocolat. "Have something to eat. The story can wait."

She devoured it in four bites, and then licked her fingers, the flakes of pastry clinging delicately to the tip of her pink tongue before she swallowed them. "Thanks, that was lovely." I almost expected her to come out with a childish "May I leave the table, please?"

"Would you like anything else?" I asked, and she shook her head. I knew it was just politeness, and I should have just gone and bought another pastry, but we were playing an elaborate game of pretending this was normal, and I didn't want to break the spell.

"There was a guy there already, on the steps and he must have had the same idea as me, and he looked really annoyed when I turned up. I was trying not to look too homeless, so the theatre people wouldn't send me away, so maybe he wasn't sure about me either. I brushed my hair, and I had clean jeans on."

"But surely you did want to look homeless, so people would give you money?" I said, confused.

"Yes, but it was still early, and I didn't want to get sent away, if they had a bouncer or something."

She had obviously never been taken to the theatre, and thought it operated like a Soho nightclub.

"So what happened then?" I took a bite of my chocolate brownie.

"The guy kept shuffling his feet, and walking up and down and glaring at me, hoping I would just go away, I suppose," she said. "After a while, he asked me what I wanted, and I just said, 'Nothing,' so he said, 'Well, fuck off then, this is my gig.' I said I had a right to be there too, and he just sneered at me, so I turned my back on him. He came right up to me and leaned over my shoulder and sort of hissed in my ear, 'You've got five minutes to piss off, right. Don't hang around or you'll get what's coming to you.' I just thought he was bluffing, trying to scare me, so I ignored him.

"Then I felt him lifting me up, and he pushed me around the corner, into that alley beside the theatre, and he whacked me in the face." Zoe's eyes filled up with tears and she just put her fingertip up to her cheekbone. "It really hurts."

"I can see that," I said. "Did you go and get it seen to at the hospital?"

She shook her head. "I didn't know where the nearest one is, and anyway, what can they do?"

"Why were you sitting outside there again tonight?" I asked, "It's just an ordinary theatre night."

"I know, I just couldn't think of anywhere else to go, and I didn't want to go back to the hostel. Tommy and all them will think I was making it up about my nan. People do that when they're homeless, you know." She looked at me earnestly, and I thought she was going to start giving me a psychology lesson in the middle of all this.

"I know. Everyone needs to feel like they belong. Is there no way you would talk to your mum? I'm sure she'd be horrified if you told her what had happened."

Zoe shook her head emphatically, and then winced.

"She won't believe me. She knows I hate him, and she'll think I'm making it up."

I wanted to go to the cash machine and give her the train fare, but I knew I was over my cash limit, and there was no point. I couldn't bring her home.

"Come back to the hostel with me, and get a night's rest, at least," I said. "Maybe you will think of something tomorrow."

She just nodded, no resistance left, and slid down off the high stool like a rag-doll who is not convinced her legs will hold her up. Then she turned back and licked the cappuccino froth off the lid of the cardboard cup. She grinned at me like a child. "That's the best bit," she said. "I always save it for last."

I put my arm around her shoulders, and we walked through the drizzling rain with our heads down, to the tube station.

The workshop went really well. I was surprised at how nervous I was when I saw six of the kids sitting on the floor in the common room, with the television off and an air of expectation about them. I wished Zoe were there, but Steve had given her some painkillers for her face injury and sent her off to bed.

I did an icebreaker where they all had to stand in different parts of the room, representing a ship, and tell the group which part of the ship they were on, and why. Sean, a skinny black boy who looked about fourteen, wanted to be the captain, but Jamie, a glum Scot who was towering over him, and about twice his weight, said that I had to be the captain, otherwise we were going nowhere. On one level it was quite reassuring, because it meant they were entering into the spirit of things, but on another, it was frightening. They really expected me to lead them, and give them something new.

Justine said she had been good at drama at school, and one of the others snorted: "Yeah, we know you're a drama queen, you don't need to tell us that!"

She didn't rise to the bait, but I saw her face as she turned around, and she looked really sad for a couple of seconds, before she tossed her hair in a Miss Piggy gesture, and said, "That's the trouble with frogs, they have no imagination, humph!"

Everyone laughed, and then I got them to settle down and listen to a piece of music, and asked them to draw a picture representing what they heard. Peace descended, and all I could hear was the sound of Ravel's 'Bolero', and the scratching of pencils on paper. They silently took coloured pens from the pot in the centre of the circle, and then returned them, and I was just marveling at their total involvement when the door opened and they all looked up.

Tommy was standing there, his hair all wild, his jacket hanging open.

"What's this, mate, nursery school?" he asked, obviously high.

Jamie and Sean chucked down their pens, ashamed of being caught.

I took a deep breath. "Do you want to join in, mate, or not?" I asked, desperately hoping he would just go to his room.

"I want to watch telly, actually," he said, in a mocking imitation of my voice.

I have become aware of my accent since I started coming to the hostel, and to them, it must smack of privilege and snobbery.

"Steve said we could use the room for a couple of hours," I said, and realised how pathetic it sounded.

"Steve says jump, Steve says touch your toes," Tommy mocked, lifting one Doctor Marten boot up, and tapping it with his finger.

All the pencils were down now, and I knew this was one of those moments where you have to win. But I had to allow him to keep face too.

"I've got a video for later, but we could put it on now, if you want," I said, standing up to get it out of my rucksack.

"Nah, cheers, s'all right, mate, I'm gonna crash," he said, and backed out the door.

'Bolero' was still building momentum, and after a collective sigh of relief, it soon lulled everyone back into their artistic efforts. Afterwards, we discussed their pictures, and I was surprised by the kids' openness. I thought it would be weeks before I could build enough trust for them to really engage in this stuff. Justine had drawn an easily recognisable Albert Hall, with spirals of colour encircling the dome. She said that each one represented an instrument, and when they all came together at the top, they exploded into a huge firework display, against a black crayon sky. I wondered where her life had gone wrong. She was like another Zoe, articulate, confident, and so obviously not meant to be in a hostel for homeless kids. She said she wanted to be an actress, and had been hoping to study drama at 'A' level. But she stopped there, and I didn't push her. Sean's mum left him with his crack-dealing dad when he was seven, and he said he'd had enough by the time he was twelve, and ran away. His dad used him as a runner for the drugs, and he figured he was better off on his own. Now he was seventeen, showing all the signs of lack of nutrition and care, but wiry, and surprisingly mature. Jamie wasn't ready to talk about himself, and it crossed my mind that he was only joining in because he didn't have enough confidence to stand up and be different, like Tommy. The others, two guys and a girl, didn't have much to say, either, but they did participate, and I hoped we'd make some progress the next week. I wanted to come back the next day, and keep going, but there was no point in rushing things.

I realised when I got home that I'd left the CD in the player at the hostel, and kicked myself. It was unlikely to be stolen, but could easily get lost, when it got tossed out and replaced by someone's Eminem CD. It would probably be left on the side, and have coffee spilt on it when I went back the next time.

CHAPTER 12

Caroline

Matt seemed very preoccupied when I was getting ready for work. I wondered if he had noticed anything different about me? He got dressed before me. He had such an air of purpose about him that I asked him if he had an audition, even though I knew he would have told me.

"No, just a few bits and pieces to do, today," he said, sort of half smiling at me. "Have you got a busy day?"

"One or two meetings, and one bit of work to finish by the end of the day. Not too bad, I hope," I said. I was wondering if he was going to ask me to come straight home instead of going out for a drink after work. Then I figured that Matthew was unlikely to ask to see me so soon, and I could get a few brownie points under my belt with Matt. "Would you like to go for a curry, tonight?" I asked him, quickly putting on my make-up. My eyes were bloodshot and I had that swimmy head feeling of an imminent hangover.

He hesitated, and I looked over at him. "Yeah, sure, that's a good idea." He went into the kitchen to put on the kettle. He didn't ask me what time I got in, or if I was tired after working late, or if I managed to get everything finished last night. Maybe he suspected something.

I followed him into the kitchen and poured a bowl of cornflakes. Maybe he was just planning something for my birthday, and trying not to give the secret away. He drank his tea with his hands wrapped around the mug, and I couldn't help comparing them with Matthew's. Fingers not as long. Nails not as nice. A little bit too hairy. That's the only downside of his dark colouring – too much hair in a few places.

I actually shook my head when I thought that, and Matt looked at me. He came over and started nuzzling my neck and kissing the top of my ear, and I nearly flinched. What was happening to me? I put down my spoon and turned around to hug him properly. I felt a huge wave of sadness washing over me. What was I going to do?

Matt ruffled my hair, which irritated me, because I had just spent five minutes gelling it and trying to get it to sit the right way.

"Got to go, nearly late." I rinsed my soggy cornflakes into the sink and gave him a quick kiss. "See you about seven. Have a good day."

"You too," he said, as I slammed the door and ran down the stairs. I was a little bit behind schedule, but I knew I had the right change for the newspaper in my coat pocket.

A text message beeped onto my phone just as I was getting into the lift at work, and I read it with my heart in my mouth: *Sorry re last night, CU 4 a drink soon? M.*

I quickly sent a '*yes*' reply, and the sending message logo whizzed across the screen as I was turning the corner in the corridor. Matthew was standing there, talking to Baxter on the way into his office. His suit pocket beeped at him as I was walking past, trying to pretend I hadn't seen him.

"Are you all right?" Claire asked when I marched into her office and sat down on the edge of her desk.

I couldn't decide whether to hate her for noticing, or tell her everything. She's the same age as me, but she's married and has one kid, and one on the way. We would probably be even closer friends if our lives weren't so different. She races off after work to let the nanny go home. Sometimes we go for a drink after work, and she really makes me laugh. But she's sensible with it. And she doesn't fancy Matt, like Alison does, so her judgement wouldn't be clouded. Just what I needed.

"Yes, no, not really." I was running my fingers through my hair, making it stand on end again. "Do you want a coffee?" I asked to buy myself some time. I shouldn't tell her. Then I would have to make a decision. As long as it all stayed in my head, I could live with being a two-timing bitch, but if I said it out loud, I couldn't live with myself.

Claire nodded. "Shall I come with you?" She stood up and followed me to the machine at the other end of the corridor. I punched the buttons distractedly and got a tea with milk instead of a very strong coffee with sugar.

"You're not OK, are you?" Claire asked. "Is it work?"

"No," I sighed. I'd have to tell her something.

"Matt?"

"Sort of. I think I fancy someone else, and . . ."

"Ohhh, the guy from Mallory Turners," Claire said, the light of understanding dawning in her eyes. She looked back down the corridor. "Shit."

"Exactly," I said, and knew I couldn't tell her any more.

"Is he single?"

"Of course he's single, I wouldn't . . ."

She just put her head on one side and looked at me. "You haven't?"

"No, but it I nearly did, last night."

"Last night!" she almost yelled, and I grabbed her arm.

"Shut up! Alison will hear you." I pulled her out

through the fire door into the lobby.

"What's his name?"

"Matthew."

"No way."

"Yes."

"What are you going to do?"

"I don't know. I don't want to lose Matt. I think I could be in love with two people."

My stomach was in a knot. The tea tasted of tepid dried-milk powder. I wanted to throw up.

"Is he really that great?" Even though she doesn't have a crush on Matt, she probably couldn't believe I would do this to him.

"I think he might be," I said, "but I haven't *done* anything yet."

Claire was torn between enjoying the huge juicy scandal and feeling sorry for me, or maybe even for Matt. I could nearly see the emotions running across her face.

The swing-door opened suddenly behind her back, and Alison was leaning through.

"Matthew Turner wondered if he could have a quick word, before he goes," she said, knowing fine well that something was up. Claire and I don't make a habit of behaving like schoolgirls gossiping in the corridor.

"Just a sec," I said, and started licking my fingers to flatten my hair.

"Caroline, leave it," Claire said in a cross voice, and pushed the door open, walking quickly after Alison and leaving me to take a deep breath and follow her. That blue carpet-tiled corridor has never seemed so long. I felt like Alice in Wonderland, walking in slow motion from tile to tile, trying not to step on the lines while Matthew loomed at the other end, looking through a folder, pretending to be completely absorbed in it.

Alison made herself busy at her computer screen. I took Matthew into my office.

He closed the door behind him and I wished he hadn't. We never close our doors. Even performance appraisals are done with the door half open. I couldn't get up and open it now, or it would look even worse, but I blushed, wondering what Alison must be thinking.

"Hi," he said. "I just wanted to say sorry in person. I came in to see Baxter anyway."

"Nothing to say sorry about. I really enjoyed myself last night."

"Me, too."

I had a bizarre urge to say, 'Me, three,' like I used to do with my sisters when we were small.

"So, would you like to do it again, sometime?"

"I'd love to." I must get him out of the office. "Tell you what –"

My mobile rang. I automatically picked it up. "Sorry, I should have turned it off," I said, glancing at the screen: *Mattmob*. Shit.

"Answer it, I don't mind," Matthew said, walking over to look out the window, to give me the notional privacy of not standing in front of me.

I froze. It kept on ringing. I switched it off. "It's OK, really, I know who it is. I can call back."

Matthew turned around. "Would you like to do something tomorrow?"

"What, on a Saturday?" I must have sounded like I was being strangled.

"Yes, I thought we could go to the Tate Modern in the morning, and then have some lunch?"

"I'm busy, I'm afraid," I gabbled, "hectic social diary – you need to give a girl a bit of notice for these things." I nearly mentioned that it was my birthday, but I managed not to.

"Never mind. Maybe another time," he said, pulling out a small shiny black electronic organiser. "Shall we try another evening, then?"

The phone on my desk rang. I was fumbling with my filofax and waited for it to transfer through to Alison on the third ring. I got to the right page for next week, and Alison knocked on the door and poked her head in.

"Sorry to interrupt. It's Matt, he's locked out." She looked at the two of us, standing poised with our diaries. "Shall I put him through?" Only Alison could make that question sound accusatory. She glanced at my big black desk diary, sitting closed and mute on my desk.

"I'll call him back in a second – is he on his mobile?" I asked.

"Yes, I'll tell him." She disappeared.

My flatmate? My brother? My cousin? I decided to bluff it out and not say anything.

"Wednesday is good for me," I said, clearing my throat. Matt was out at his Ceroc classes on Mondays and Wednesdays and I could just make sure I got back home before ten.

"Can't do Wednesday, I'm on duty at the Law Centre."

"Monday?"

"Fine, what do you want to do?"

"Let's talk on Monday. I'll have a look in *Time Out* over the weekend."

I wanted him to go now. Poor Matt was locked out. I'd have to courier him my keys or else he'd have to come all the way in on the tube and collect them. What a pain!

Matthew was struggling with the palm-sized chrome-plated organiser, prodding at the screen with the little metallic pencil, and getting more and more annoyed with himself.

"I must admit, you didn't strike me as the electronic-organiser type," I said, laughing at him.

He looked up, with his hair all tousled, and said, "I'm not. Someone gave it to me, and I'm determined to master it." He snapped it shut, and shoved it in his pocket. "I give up. I don't know why I need to put it in, anyway. I won't forget I'm seeing you." He opened the door. "You'd better ring your friend back," he said. "It sounds urgent." He smiled at me and went out, leaving a slightly lemony soap and aftershave smell lingering on the air.

"Fine, see you then, thanks very much," I said for Alison's benefit.

"Bye, thanks," Matthew said and smiled at Alison as he took his briefcase off her desk.

"He's nice," she said, as he walked away, and she looked at me out of the corner of her eye. I went back into the office and dialled Matt's mobile.

"Hi, gorgeous, sorry to interrupt your meeting. Mary next door isn't in so I can't get the spares."

"Do you want me to bike them to you, or do you want to come in to the office?"

"I forgot to bring my wallet out too. It was only when I got to the tube station and tried to buy a ticket, that I realised."

"At least you had your phone," I said. "Don't worry, I'll get Alison to bike the keys over. It will probably be about half an hour."

"Great, thanks, and I'll get the curry tonight," he said.

That makes a nice change, I thought, knowing I was being ungracious. Matt hasn't treated me for ages, and I hadn't really thought about it before. He must be getting short of money. He's probably too proud to admit it, because he knows I'll just nag him about getting a job. I know I shouldn't, but I can't help it. Maybe secretly I'm jealous that he's still a free agent, and I'm a wage slave. I gave Alison my keys and sat down to do some work. Somehow it had got to ten o'clock and I still hadn't done anything useful.

Matthew

When I got in this morning, Diana was standing behind my desk, just finishing a call and writing in my diary.

"One moment, please, Mr Turner has just walked in, and I will be able to confirm." She put the call on hold. "I wasn't sure whether to go ahead, but you are free this morning. Would you be able to go along to see Mr Baxter at nine?" She looked up at the clock over my office door. "It might be a rush, but it seems there is something urgent to resolve."

I glanced at my watch. 8:22.

"Yes, that's fine, I'll just grab the file and go straight away," I said, and while Diana finished the call, I unsnapped my briefcase, and took out the files I shouldn't have taken home and put them on my desk. Diana does a great sideways look that takes everything in, but she doesn't follow through and raise her head make eye contact with me. She wouldn't see it as her place. She is aware of my breach of the rules, and is undoubtedly offended by it, but wouldn't dream of saying anything. This morning she will just quietly file them away in the right place, removing the slips of paper which confirm that I have temporarily taken the files from their green hanging spaces.

"I'll just get that file for you," she said briskly, and swept up the other three bundles in her arms as she went out. "Have you got time for a coffee?" she asked solicitously as I quickly checked my e-mails. Should I send one to Caroline, apologising for last night? No, her secretary might read her e-mails.

"No, thanks, Diana, I'd better go now." I picked up the dreaded electronic organizer that Liz gave me for Christmas, and slipped it into my inside jacket pocket. I must try harder with it.

"See you later then. I'll be back in plenty of time for my eleven thirty," I said as I went out, secretly hoping I could get the meeting over quickly and persuade Caroline to come for a coffee somewhere. Maybe I should send her a text message, to get the apology over with, and then if I bumped into her, could casually suggest a coffee? It took me most of the taxi journey to type it in, fighting the predetermined text setting which I don't know how to switch off, and which produces the most bizarre words – it must be teenage lingo I have yet to master. I finally sent it just as the taxi pulled up outside the office block, and sighed with relief. I forgot to get a receipt from the taxi driver, and swore as he drove off. I'm always doing that. I must have spent thousands on unclaimed expenses. I'm not a receipt-collecting sort of person. I went up to Baxter's office, and as we walked in I could sense Caroline behind me. A little electric shock hit me in the base of my spine, and reminded me of the Tens machine Liz used when the boys were being born, to zap the pains of the early contractions. She got me to test it, sticking the sensor pads on and turning the power up to the maximum. The vibrations exploded in my lower back and raced to my brain, leaping across every synapse on the way like black-cloaked highwaymen hurdling fences to escape from pounding pursuers. The pain of contractions must be bad to choose that as an alternative. Now, the high-waymen were back, and I resisted the urge to turn and face Caroline as she passed me by. I completely missed what Baxter was saying, but murmured some bland reply, and then she was gone. I really had to work hard to concentrate for the next forty minutes, but I held it together, and Baxter took a call as I left his office, so I was able to take a diversion via Caroline's secretary on the way out. She was very helpful, and disappeared down the corridor, saying she thought Caroline was just getting a coffee. When I looked up from the file, Caroline was walking slowly down the hall, and I couldn't tell if she was glad to see me. Her one-word text reply hadn't given me any clues. I followed her into the office, and closed the door. She intoxicates me. I inhaled the smell of her space, a mixture of freesias on her desk, her perfume, and a trace of the cleaner's polish. She looked uncomfortable, and was blushing – she must hate when that happens, I thought, as I moved towards her. She looked towards the door. Surely she didn't think I was going to do anything stupid? I said sorry again, and she said she'd had a lovely time, so I smiled at her, and asked if we could do it again soon. Her phone rang and she got really flustered, holding open her filofax, and switching off her phone, and then her desk telephone went. We had just settled on Monday for a drink when the secretary poked her head in, and said that someone was locked out. I took out my electronic diary while she was dealing with that, and tried to get the stupid thing to go to the right date. I was still fumbling with it, looking like an idiot, when I looked up and realised Caroline was watching me. She laughed and said I didn't strike her as an electronic-organiser type. I wondered why it hadn't occurred to Liz, after fifteen years of knowing me, that her gift would end up torturing me, either by trying to master it, or with guilt for not using it. I put it back in my pocket without ever getting into the calendar, because I knew I would spend the next three days just counting the hours until I could see Caroline again. It was hardly an appointment I would forget. I was disappointed that I had to wait that long. For some stupid reason, because I was liberated for a Saturday morning, I had expected that Caroline would be free too. Who makes social engagements on Saturday mornings? When I was single, I just spent Saturday mornings recovering from Friday nights, reading the newspapers in the launderette while the tumble-drier tumbled, and eating a cooked breakfast at the local greasy spoon. It struck me then that I don't really know much about Caroline. Maybe she plays tennis in a club on Saturdays, or goes to an aerobics class, or even visits an old aunt in Mornington Crescent.

I made a hasty exit before I was tempted to do anything stupid, and said good-bye to the secretary, who had the look of an interested party, checking me out. Maybe I had already been discussed, which would be a really good sign. Women do that kind of thing more than men.

"None of my business, old boy, but don't you think you ought to be a bit careful?" would be as much as male protocol would allow. I got through the day, with back-to-back meetings carrying me through the hours until six, when I packed up my briefcase again, feeling like I should do some work at home if I was going to have the house to myself in the morning, and said good-bye to Diana, who was finishing off her weekly filing ceremony. I should be home in time to see the boys before bedtime, and I was really looking forward to seeing them.

I love it when I open the front door, and after a ten-second pause, I hear a jubilant shout of "Daddy!" and the sound of bare feet coming bounding down the stairs. Now there are two sets of feet, as Jack tries valiantly to keep up with his brother, and his sibilant shout is nearly as loud as Ben's. I get a huge hug around my legs, and it's all I can do to persuade them to let go so I can walk up the stairs and take off my suit.

I'm never sure if it will be the nanny or Liz who is standing at the top of the stairs, hair damp from the steaming bathroom, arms full of discarded clothes ready to throw in the laundry basket, and face smiling in anticipation of the imminent bedtime routine that signals the end of the working day. So I never shout anything affectionate, or race up the stairs and grab her in my arms. It's all very measured. If it's Liz, we give each other a peck on the cheek, and smile at the antics of the boys, who have pushed past me on the stairs to get onto Mummy and Daddy's bed for a game of "beating up".

I barely have time to get my suit off before I am pummeled into submission, and we spend fifteen minutes rolling around throwing pillows at each other, and sliding into the "gnu poo" that surrounds the bed.

Whether it is Liz or the nanny, they take the opportunity to empty the bath, draw the curtains in the boys' room and turn back their bedcovers, before setting up the video and preparing the milk. Then, when the boys and I are exhausted, we all decant downstairs and snuggle up on the sofa for the wind-down before bed. I am unfailingly filled with huge feelings of love for the boys for that magical hour every day, and that's when the guilt about Caroline hits me the worst. What could I be doing, to jeopardise all this? I could lose it tomorrow. Liz would be completely unforgiving, because she would just not be able to comprehend the betrayal. She would take the boys away, give me my reasonable access, but fill the new void in their lives with her endless love and security, and ultimately replace me, emotionally if not physically. That would be my punishment.

Tonight, it is Liz who hovers at the top of the stairs, and I am so pleased. When she arrives home late from work sometimes, to the kitchen left soullessly clean and tidy by the nanny, and the sofa occupied by a three-headed sleepy creature emanating dozy contentment in front of a Noddy video, I know how she feels. The adrenalin rush of work has diminished and, especially on a Friday, has been replaced by the anticipation of a cosy family weekend. The focussed, effective, respected working person she has been all day is no longer required. Her fuzzy edges can be displayed, as she peels off the work-clothes and throws them on the bedroom chair.

The children's magic is almost palpable, like the sprinkles of glittering dust that Big Ears uses to cast his spells for Noddy. She wants to be the one who is snuggled up with them, one arm around each as they guzzle their milk, and not the one who comes in later, drawing in the cold outside air, and disturbing the warm mass of bodies to wriggle onto the sofa.

I kiss her on the lips, and she looks surprised, but smiles at me as I am jostled against her by the two cannonballs who are careering around the newel-post and racing onto the home straight down the hall to our bedroom. Liz dumps the mud and chocolate-encrusted clothes into the laundry basket, and goes back into the bathroom. I join in the fray on the bed and, half an hour later, the four-headed sofa creature is absorbed in the trials of Peter Rabbit trying to escape from Mr McGregor's garden.

When the boys have gone to bed, Liz and I polish off our Friday-night bottles of wine, and she fills me in on the latest crisis in the boardroom, revolving around two directors who are suspected of fraudulent accounting practices. The auditors had been called in, and a full-scale investigation was going on, while the press were being fobbed off with bland assurances that all was well.

Liz sits on the other sofa, with her feet up, and I look at her, full of animation as she recounts the dramas of the day, and when she jumps up to emphasise a point, I realise she has lost weight, and looks younger and more fragile than my internal image of her allows. She's so resilient and strong, and so good in a family crisis, that I think of her as a rock, steady and fairly predictable, occasionally fraught, but mostly just tired, and now I see her in her baggy silk combat trousers and loose-necked top, full of energy and laughter, and I remember the Liz I fell in love with. I pat the sofa.

"Come over here," I say, and she sits down and leans

against me. She keeps fidgeting around, because she wants to look at me, and get my reaction to her punchline. She stands up again.

"Guess what? They've asked me to be acting Finance Director, while they sort all this out!" Her dream is on the brink of coming true. No wonder she can't sit still.

"Wow, that is incredible!" I say, standing up and hugging her, but a huge part of me is thinking, 'How can she do this? Is it humanly possible for her to take on any more?'

"Well done, Liz, I knew you'd get there. What does it mean, though? Will they give you the job long-term?"

"I don't know yet," she says, her eyes shining, "but even if they don't, and they might not think I'm ready yet, it's on the cards for the future – it must be, and they must rate me – especially as things will be really difficult while we get through this crisis."

"And you're a safe pair of hands," I say, realising the massive understatement as I utter it. "I mean, they trust you to hold it all together, to lead the team, to restore things to normal . . ."

"I'm really thrilled, Matthew, but I'm a bit anxious too – in a way I would have preferred if this had happened in a few years' time, when the boys are a bit older, and at school. But I can't turn down an opportunity like this. It's once in a lifetime stuff."

"I know," I say, "and I'll do whatever it takes to support you. Maybe we should get an au pair, to live in, so the boys have some continuity, and you don't have the stress of not knowing if the nanny will turn up. You can't make excuses when you're a board director – especially when you're trying to prove yourself."

"I know. I just worry about finding the right person for the boys. Maybe Mum could move in for a while, just as back up . . .?"

My stomach sinks to my knees. "Perhaps she could stay, for a little while, but I don't think we should be too dependent on your mother." I'm trying not to spoil the mood. She is one of the inevitable routes to an argument between Liz and me. Even talking about her makes us argue. What would we be like if we were all under the same roof all the time? We both decide to leave that one hanging.

"Let's just enjoy the moment, and we'll work out the logistics later." I stand up, holding up the dregs in my wineglass. "To success!"

We clink glasses and I place mine on the coffee table, take hers out of her hand and put it down, and we kiss, and stand swaying like dancers to some silent music, and the familiar shape of her, and the feel of her soft hair against my cheek, and the way her body moulds to mine fills me with love for her. I hold her so tight she pushes me away, gasping for breath.

"Sorry," I say, and kiss her again.

We go upstairs, after a short delay to gather milk supplies, teddies and other necessities to survive the night and early morning, and even after all that passion-killing tedium, we make love for the first time in a long time.

Matt

I kept thinking about Zoe, that I should encourage her to report the rape to the police, that the stepfather shouldn't get away with it.

I headed for the hostel on the tube, totally preoccupied with how I could persuade her, and nearly missed the change at Stockwell. I jumped out as the doors slammed shut behind me, and had to pull out the tail of my coat, which was trapped between the black rubber seals. The doors *beep-beeped* again, and opened and shut quickly and aggressively before the train pulled off, and I made my way to the Northern Line platform.

I must spend some time with Steve today, going through more of my workshop ideas, instead of traipsing all over London after Zoe, I thought as I sat down on the train.

"Can you make dead men come alive?" a poster asked me from the opposite wall, just as I was pulling my book out of my coat pocket.

Teaching. I'd always thought of it as such a pedestrian profession, and the current shortage of teachers didn't really inspire me to think it was the happening place to be. I didn't think I could do it. I watched a great fly-on-the-wall series about teachers on the telly once, but they never seemed to be teaching – they were all in the staff room bitching about the paperwork and each other. I'd hate that. Might as well be in an office job.

I got off at Balham station and meandered to the hostel, preoccupied with how I would put my ideas across to Steve.

"Hello, it's great to see you again," he said, shaking my hand. "Lots of people get fired up when they do something for the first time, but most of them get involved in their busy lives again and forget about us."

"My life isn't very busy at the moment," I said, and felt a bit pathetic. "I've got some more ideas for the workshops."

"Great," said Steve and he led me through to his office, and gave me a chipped mug of coffee, with a yellow smiling face logo. "Sorry, the milk is off, so I hope you take it black."

"Fine," I said, and took out my notepad.

We spent half an hour going through various role-plays and confidence-building exercises I could run, and I said I could do another session on Wednesday evening.

"How's Zoe?" I asked as he showed me out.

"She stayed last night, but was up bright and early this morning, and gone before I got a chance to talk to her."

"I need to see her," was all I said.

Steve looked at me. "Be careful, mate. I know what

227

it's like. One of them gets under your skin and you want to solve all their problems for them. Keep your distance, for her sake as well as your own."

"If she comes back tonight, could you give her my number?" I asked, handing him a torn-off piece of my notebook page with my mobile number scribbled on it.

"Are you sure?" Steve asked doubtfully, and when I nodded, he stuck it in his back pocket. "They don't even get my mobile number, Matthew."

I knew that he was right. I was probably crossing some invisible line.

Just as I was thinking that, he said, "And by the way, when you come again, you'll need to fill in a child-protection police-check form — it's standard procedure for anyone who is working with children."

I nodded.

"We'll need your birth certificate, so if you remember to bring it on Wednesday, that will save some time," he said, trying to be brisk now, because he could see that I was completely deflated. "It's not personal, Matthew." He patted my shoulder.

All I could think of was that Zoe's stepfather didn't have to fill in any forms to invade her life. The system couldn't reach into her "safe" family environment to protect her.

"I know," I said, and wishing that I could tell him.

I suddenly remembered that it was Caroline's birthday the next day, and I still didn't have a present. If I paid for the curry, I would be lucky if my Visa card would take it.

I was walking towards the tube station when I heard a vaguely familiar voice.

"Hey, mate, how's it going?" Tommy was coming towards me, and I was surprised at his enthusiasm. He had struck me as the type who wouldn't voluntarily engage in social banter with an adult.

"Fine, Tommy, how are you?"

I was just about to ask him if he knew anything about Zoe, when he said, looking around with the shifty expression of a market trader without a licence, "You've got a girlfriend, ain't you, mate?"

I said I did.

"Do you wanna buy som'fing nice for 'er?"

"Yes, I do," I said, temporarily impressed with his telepathy, and then realising that we were talking specifics, as he held out a silver bracelet, dangling on the end of his grubby index finger.

"Where did you get that from?" I asked, knowing that I sounded like one of Billy Bunter's schoolmasters.

"You don't wanna worry about that, mate. Like it? I'll do it for a tenner."

I pulled out a ten-pound note and handed it over, pocketing the bracelet in the same movement.

"Cheers, mate, see you around then," said Tommy, who had barely broken his stride to talk to me and now resumed it, loping off towards the hostel.

I tried to convince myself that the transaction had

been purely done to build Tommy's trust, so that I could work better with him next week, but failed. I took out the bracelet as soon as I was sitting down on the tube and then put it away quickly, just in case.

I must have criminal tendencies, I decided, when I got home, and dug around in my sock-drawer to find the black dickie-bow that I have had since the end-of-year ball at college. I dissected it carefully, and it gave me enough velvet to line a small box. I used cellotape to lift off the years of dust from the velvet, and was quite pleased with the end result. Then I had a good look at the bracelet. I wouldn't try to pass it off as new, but could tell Caroline I had found it on a stall in Portobello market. It was quite chunky and modern, and had a silver hallmark, so I polished it a bit and curled it up in its new home.

Maybe I'm schizophrenic or just a bloody hypocrite, I mused as I sat in front of *Countdown*, wondering how Carol Vorderman could bear to be still presenting the maths bit of a word-game after umpteen years, when she had so much other stuff going on. 'How could someone who was so pissed off about being mugged, and just had a close shave with the police, then go and buy very obviously stolen goods a few days later, and not even blink an eye?' I lectured myself, hearing Caroline's voice in my head. She would leave me for my stupidity, not my badness, if she ever found out.

'One lie leads to another,' I heard my mother's voice now, and I tried to banish it by concentrating on making a word out of the letters on the television screen:

F–W–R–C–Z–O–I–P–E–U.

Zoe leapt out at me, and that was it. I got up, put on my coat and went into the West End. I had to see her. Despite Steve's advice. I knew she had got under my skin. I felt like it was my job to save her.

CHAPTER 13

Matthew

I wake up on Saturday morning, and it's just Liz and me in our bed. I look at the clock. It says 6:17 and I realise we have slept through the entire night for the first time in living memory. Then I wonder if it's just me, or whether Liz has been up with the boys. She opens her eyes and looks at me sleepily, and we edge across the bed for a hug. This is what it used to be like every morning, I think, as I feel her body sliding against mine.

"Did I imagine it, or have we all slept through the night?" I ask, and she giggles.

"It must have been the bonk. They've probably been crying all night and we missed it," she says, rolling over and stroking my stomach. Surprised, but ever hopeful, my body responds accordingly. "In your dreams, mate," Liz murmurs, as we hear the sound of Ben's bare feet padding across the hall carpet.

"Morning, Ben," she says, and sits up so that he can climb in behind her to his spot in the middle of the bed. He never says a word for the first few minutes. He just snuggles up to Liz's back and drinks the first shot of milk for the day, and we lie there on Saturday and Sunday mornings, wondering who will break, and offer to get up first.

"Maybe we should extend the Saturday morning thing, to –"

"Include getting up first?" says Liz, laughing. "I'm getting up anyway, so you're lucky. Come on, Ben, let's go and watch cartoons downstairs."

She pulls on the dressing-gown that is hanging on the edge of the door, and closes the door so I won't hear the morning mayhem that will start as soon as Jack wakes up. I stretch, thinking I am almost ready to get up myself, I feel so refreshed, and the next thing I know I'm staring at the clock, which now says 9:21. I wonder if my brain is inverting the first digit so I squint at the black face until I am convinced. The house is very quiet. Usually the boys would have got impatient by now, and come to find me. I wonder if Liz has taken them out. I jump out and put on Radio 4 in the bathroom, thinking I have already wasted some of my free morning, lying around in bed.

Home Truths has its usual mix of family horror stories, laconically recounted by John Peel. I get engrossed in a tale of children being farmed out to relatives in Trinidad, and then discovering unknown parents and cousins, and mysterious letters being uncovered to vindicate a banished older brother. The shower drowns out the end of the story, and I feel a bit cheated, but not enough to turn the shower off and endure the cold stream of air from the window, which is slightly open. I stay under the hot water for ages, enjoying not having to peer around the shower-curtain every two seconds to see if the toothpaste is being squeezed into the potty, or an electric toothbrush being used to prise open the toilet seat. Finally, I get out and dry myself, looking forward to the prospect of a whole mug of hot coffee and a slice of toast all to myself. The kitchen is eerily quiet, without the sound of the endlessly reversing tape-player singing about the colours of the rainbow, and with no bickering, or battery-operated toys skittering across the floor. I look out at the garden while the kettle boils, and smile at the empty turtle sandpit. It is surrounded by piles of discarded sand, abandoned trucks and various mud-coated seaside accessories.

Although a newspaper to read would be the icing on the cake, I decide against walking down the hill to get one, because I can't believe the boys will be out for much longer, and I really want to enjoy that mug of coffee. Twenty minutes later, when I am refilling it from the cafetiere, I realise that this is it, my Saturday morning, and I should get on with doing Saturday-morning things. I have a list of DIY jobs that have loomed over me for months. Every time I decide on one, I think it would be a nice one for Ben to help me with. He would enjoy holding the screws for the new handle on the bathroom door, and helping me to screw them in. He would love to paint the inside of the walk-in cupboard under the stairs, and I could let him loose in there, knowing he would have a ball and do no damage. And most of all, he would love to help me sort out the shed, stacking the wood into neat piles of pieces the same size, and sorting the nails and screws into the glass jars I have been saving for the purpose. I'll keep the jobs for later, I decide, when he'll be around to help me.

So that leaves reading, and I have just finished my book. I have some paperwork, which has to be done at some point over the weekend. Liz would not appreciate me disappearing upstairs on Sunday to do it, so I decide to get on with it.

Three hours later, I snap shut my briefcase. I am getting peckish, and wonder if they will be home for lunch. The cat is lurking around, obviously as disconcerted by the peace and quiet as I am. I shove the briefcase under the stairs and enjoy a moment of satisfaction that a tedious task hasn't been too bad.

I potter around, and at one thirty decide to heat some soup. Liz is such a stickler for feeding the boys at the right times that I know she must have taken them somewhere. It would have been nice to know, I think, a bit ungraciously, as I stick a bowl of carrot and butterbean soup into the microwave. The groceries are obviously due to be delivered, as there is no cheese, ham, olives or any other niceties to be found in the fridge. A curled-up half of a red pepper and a blackened mushroom are the only occupants of the salad drawers. The stale bread is only redeemed by dipping it in the soup.

I have just cleared up and am getting the paint ready when I hear the car pulling up outside.

The silence of the house is shattered by a loud wailing as Jack pursues Ben along the hall, trying to retrieve his blanket.

"My pangint, my pangint!" he yells, as Ben drags it along the floor, just out of Jack's reach.

I feel a surprising wave of relief washing over me. Now it feels like a Saturday. Liz comes breezing in, her cheeks pink and her hair windblown.

"Daddy, Daddy, we went to the woods!" shouts Ben, picking up the stirring-stick from the pot of paint and waving it around.

"Ben!" Liz and I yell simultaneously, while I lunge at him to grab the stick before he can drip white paint on the blue carpet. Too late. Three blobs had already landed. Ben sulks, while I apply paint-remover to a cloth, and Liz holds Jack back from putting his whole hands into the paint-pot.

"Why are you only starting this now?" Liz asks, and I am annoyed by her tone of mild irritation, finely balanced with wifely tolerance. Why does she have to spoil things when they were going so well?

"I was saving the job so Ben could help me. I thought you'd be back sooner."

"Well, I thought you'd appreciate a nice long morning off," she snaps back, taking the good out of the gesture as far as I'm concerned.

"Sorry."

"Me, too."

But it was too quick, and we both know we were only going through the motions, trying to reset the tone for a nice weekend.

"Ben, come and put your painting clothes on, and you can help Daddy," Liz shouts up the stairs, where Ben has disappeared to sulk.

Now she's even taking away the fun of getting him involved. Ben refuses, and watches a video while I grovel around under the stairs for an hour, swiping the paint-brush in all directions, knowing I should have rubbed the walls down, and put masking tape around the edge of the door. I bang my head several times, and just manage not to swear. I emerge, grimy but quite triumphant, and Liz has a cup of tea ready for me, and a fairy cake from the batch the boys made at seven o'clock this morning. Not a trace of flour, smashed eggshell, or sticky baking tin had left a clue for me when I got up. The buns had already been cooled and stashed in the cake tin, by the time I got downstairs.

"So, where did you go, this morning?" I ask Jack, and he grins at me through a mouthful of crumbs.

"The woods," he says, pleased that Ben isn't answering for him, for a change.

"Was it good fun?" I ask.

He nods emphatically, with even his enormous capacity for talking with his mouth full frustrated by the last biteful of bun. Liz tries to make me laugh by telling me about lifting Ben out of his wellies when they got stuck in the mud, but I'm still a bit annoyed with her for spoiling my plans to paint with Ben. I also have the horrible thought that those three could survive better without me than I could without them.

CHAPTER 14

Caroline

I spent the whole weekend just looking forward to Monday, and when my mother rang me on Sunday night, and asked her usual question, "So, did you have a nice weekend?" I said yes automatically, and then couldn't think of a single thing we'd done.

"But what about your birthday?" Mam asked. "Where did the lovely Matthew take you on Saturday?"

"No, we're going out on Monday instead, I –"

"Oh, a special show, or something, is it?" she asked.

I suddenly felt seasick. How could I do that?

"Sorry, Mam, I must be hung over or something. Matt took me out for a meal last night."

"That sounds nice."

239

"Yeah, it was OK – we didn't stay out late. Listen, I need to go and blow my nose, Mam. I must be coming down with something. Tell you what, can I ring you one night during the week, and have a proper chat?"

Even my obtuse mother would soon cotton on, at this rate, I thought, when I hung up, feeling guilty.

It was true that the meal on Saturday night was very unmemorable in most ways. It was even worse than that – I couldn't believe it when the waiter came back with Matt's card, saying the payment wasn't authorised. I had to pay, which I didn't mind, but Matt was very ratty after it, and he just wanted to go straight home, instead of having one for the road in the new wine bar around the corner.

"It's no problem, Matt, it happens to everyone, at some stage," I said to him, trying to physically drag him into the wine bar. "It happened to me in Sainsbury's once, and I had to leave a full trolley at the checkout."

"No, you don't understand. I wanted to treat you. It's your birthday. I am a completely useless failure, with no career, no money, and no prospects."

I know it's mean to say this, but it really annoyed me that I had to spend the evening of my birthday placating him, reassuring him that he's not a failure, and that the TV part will be the making of him.

Then, on the way up the hill, with me gasping for another glass of wine, and trying to remember if there was a bottle in the fridge, he told me the TV thing wasn't happening, and that he'd made it up, because he wanted me to back off from nagging him. But that's Matt all over. Selfish, self-centred, worried only about himself. It's not the money. He could be penniless as far as I'm concerned, he would still be the Matt I love. Or loved?

"Why couldn't you just tell me your granny's money was running out?" I demanded when we got home.

He put the key in the front door. It opened before he had a chance to turn it, and Mike from the flat upstairs went out past us, checking his pockets for keys and money and not really paying any attention to us.

"Because I feel stupid," Matt hissed under his breath as we went up the stairs. "It's gone, and I have nothing to show for it – not even a tiny deposit for a flat, a few quid stashed away in some building society."

"But we're supposed to be in all this together." I was still trying to make him feel better even though I was incredibly mad with him.

"All what, together?" he said, and I didn't answer him.

"Where's the trust, if you can't tell me stuff like that?" I asked him as we went in, and I went straight to the fridge. No wine. I got a bottle down off the chrome wine-rack, and opened it, flung two ice-cubes into a glass, and filled it up.

"I don't want to keep living off your money," he said.

I couldn't resist saying he was living off it anyway, so telling lies was just going to make it worse, not better.

241

That was the end of our evening. He went off to have a bath, and even though I desperately wanted a pee after two glasses of cold, watery wine, I held on, and went to bed without brushing my teeth. I hate that.

He got up early on Sunday and said he was going to the library, which was very bizarre. I didn't even know they were open on Sundays. He was just trying to avoid me, I know.

"The back issues of *PCR* and *Stage* are there. I can't afford to buy them any more," he said.

What was the point of looking for work in back issues of magazines? I couldn't summon the energy or interest to ask him. I felt like sulking around the flat for the morning with the Sunday papers, and it suited me fine that he was going out. I could browse through *Time Out* and come up with some ideas for Monday night. I read all the *Review* and *Lifestyle* magazines, painted my nails and had a quick look at the *News of the World*. I can't resist buying it on Sundays to counteract the arty reviews and exotic travel articles. A bit of gossip is what you need while you're waiting for your finger and toenails to dry. I couldn't find any inspiration for a cool place to go on Monday evening, but I reckoned a Thai meal in a nice little cosy restaurant on Maiden Lane would go down well. Matt and I had been there before, with one of my sisters when she was over, and the food was fantastic. That was unless Matthew came up with a better suggestion.

When Matt came back, we both apologised and made an effort to be civil. It wasn't the time to talk about money, so I suggested that we went for a walk. Brockwell Park is always good for a bit of escapism, because there are several places on the path where all you can see is rolling hills, horse-chestnut trees and uncut grass, and you can pretend you're in the middle of the country. Even the traffic noise doesn't really penetrate there, and when the weather is a bit chilly, not too many kids go whizzing past on their roller blades. Even though my birthday had been ruined, I felt strangely liberated by our argument on Saturday night. We don't really argue, and the fact that we had a big one might just be a sign that Matt is not the one for me. The huge lie he had told was another brick in the wall. His admission that he was more worried about my nagging than he was about actually getting a job was the biggest indicator of all.

It all fell into place. I would see how things went with Matthew for the next few weeks, and then possibly take the plunge and leave Matt. No change in strategy there, really, except that I wouldn't have to feel so guilty about seeing Matthew, because now I had a plan. The only problem about the plan would be leaving Matt with no money. I would feel terrible about that. The unfortunate thing I was starting to realise about Matt was that he needed a big kick up the arse to make him do anything, and I might be doing him a favour by leaving him. I thought all these thoughts while we were walking around the park. Matt didn't really have much to say for himself, apart from telling me that he hadn't found any jobs to apply for. Why couldn't he go and fill supermarket shelves or work in a restaurant, or a bookshop? That's what actors were supposed to do when they were 'resting,' wasn't it? Four fifty an hour wasn't much, but it would get him out of the flat, and really he was vegetating without anyone to talk to during the day. He was a born extrovert, but he got all depressed and moody if he didn't go out and see other people. That's why I was going off him, I thought. He had nothing to say for himself any more, apart from the gossip from magazines, or the plots of daytime television programmes. I was usually buzzing when I got in from work, and I wanted to have a real conversation about stuff that mattered. It was as if his personality was draining down the back of the sofa. This money thing had obviously been playing on his mind as well, because I'd noticed him being a bit preoccupied for a couple of weeks now. He must have been really dreading telling me. Was I such an unsympathetic dragon?

I was wearing my new bracelet as a peace offering, and because I really liked it, and Matt looked down at my wrist as we were walking around the duck pond.

"It's nice on you, it suits you," he said, and I lifted up my hand and shook it so the bracelet swung around on my wrist.

"I think it's great – I'm surprised anyone was selling

it," I said, and he just nodded and looked away at the ducks. Maybe he was embarrassed that isn't new.

"You were clever to find it, before someone else snapped it up," I said. "You have to get to Portobello Road really early to get the good stuff, on a Saturday."

He nodded again. I wondered when he found it. I couldn't remember the last time he had a Saturday morning to himself. Maybe they had a market day during the week as well.

Matthew

Caroline sent me a text message on Sunday night at ten thirty and the beeping noise filled the hall, where my jacket was hanging with my phone in the pocket. Liz was just on her way through from the kitchen, with a cup of tea, and she fished the phone out and handed it to me.

"Strange hour of the night to be sending text messages," she said, and I could see she was curious. If I didn't read it, she would think that even more strange, so I quickly opened the message, and started deleting it almost before I had finished reading it. Caroline was suggesting a Thai meal in Covent Garden. I hate Thai food, but the thought of constructing a reply with an alternative, while Liz watched me, was too daunting. I could live with a bit too much garlic and lemongrass for one meal.

I just texted *"fine,"* back, and flipped the phone shut.

"What was it?" Liz asked, only half interested. She was reading one of the Sunday papers, which was spread out on her lap to collect the biscuit crumbs as she nibbled a digestive.

"Just a work thing. I'll be late back tomorrow night, I'm afraid."

She looked up, with a look of incredulity on her face.

"Tomorrow night?" she yelped.

"Yes, oh, sorry, have you got something on? Am I supposed to be baby-sitting?" I asked, panicking. I had never got into the damn electronic diary, so it could have anything lurking in there. Liz sometimes updated it for me, especially with baby-sitting requests, when she was travelling or having late meetings.

Her face closed. "Just our anniversary," she said, in the cold voice that had got her where she was today.

I bluffed. "No, that's Tuesday night," I said, smiling at her as if she was trying to wind me up. "I was going to ask you what you wanted to do."

"It's in your diary. It's a surprise. Is there any chance you could rearrange the work thing? I have tickets." Her voice was trembling now, and she sounded like a little girl whose party has been spoiled. She sipped her tea, with her hands clamped around the mug to hide her face. "I've got Mum coming to baby-sit, so I was hoping we could meet in town."

"I'll change the work thing. I'll ask Roger to sit in for

me, if it can't be changed. Don't worry!"

"Did you really think it was Tuesday?" she couldn't resist asking, because she knew me so well.

"To be honest, Liz, I struggle with that diary thing, and when I tried to get into it to look at Monday, I gave up."

She grinned at me, and said, "I suppose I should just accept that you are a complete technophobe, instead of trying to change you."

"Yes. So, are you going to give me any clues about this surprise?" I was trying desperately to think what I would say to get out of seeing Caroline.

Liz smiled enigmatically. "It's in the West End, but that's all I'm going to tell you. And it's the perfect thing for an anniversary night."

"Can you believe we've been married for eight years?" I asked, and she put her mug down and snuggled up against me.

"Sorry if I've been a bit preoccupied with work, recently," she said. "It's all absorbing when I'm there, embroiled in everything, but as soon as I walk in the door of the house, I feel like I'm living in a parallel universe, because it's so different. Sometimes I find it hard to adjust."

"I know how you feel. I get it when I'm at the Law Centre, talking to Jermaine or one of the other boys after a day of meaningless corporate bullshit."

"I wonder what the boys will remember when they grow up," she mused.

"What do you mean?"

"Well, our mums were always around when we were little. We never did very much, apart from playing in the house and the garden, but it was very stable. Look at our two. They have had four different people looking after them in the last six months, and they are constantly going for coffee mornings with other nannies, or play dates with other kids. It seems like they're hardly at home, sometimes."

"It's probably good for them. It will make them more confident – I was incredibly shy when I went to secondary school – it took ages for me to settle in, because I wasn't very good at making new friends."

"I suppose so," she said. "I'll tell you something. I never would have thought raising kids would be harder than working, but it is."

"I think that's because it changes every few months, as they get older, and need different things, whereas in a job, most variables stay the same, and if there are changes, they're predictable and quantifiable."

"That's two words that will never apply to the boys," Liz said, wriggling off the sofa and picking up her mug to take it to the kitchen. "Let's go to bed. We're always knackered, but we never go to bed early."

"Two nights' sleep in a row has an amazing effect, though, doesn't it?" I said, wondering if Liz might be persuaded to stay awake for a bit longer. When her softer side comes out, she is the most attractive woman in the world, and I wanted to make love to that Liz again, before she slipped off to allow Superwoman back on the stage.

CHAPTER 15

Caroline

"Bastard!" I looked up from my mobile phone just as I was saying it, and Baxter was standing there. "Sorry, I just got some bad news," I said sheepishly, grinding my heels into the carpet under my desk in complete mortification. I could feel the heat spreading out over my collar like a volcano erupting. The flag was up. Caroline was embarrassed.

"Just wondered if you could come along to my office in about ten minutes," he said, flicking up his blue stripey cuff to look at his watch.

I nodded. I didn't trust myself not to babble.

He turned around to go out, and said over his shoulder, "You are aware, of course, that such language is inappropriate in a professional work environment?" but he didn't stop to hear my answer.

I stared at the phone: *Sorry cant make tonite will call ltr. M.*

I had just spent three days looking forward to seeing Matthew tonight, and all my fantasies were wiped out at the press of a 'send' button. I rang the Thai restaurant and left a message to cancel the table, and went to the water cooler to fill the bottle that I keep on my desk. I gulped down mouthfuls of cold water, and told myself to get a grip. Alison popped her head in the door of the office.

"Did Mr Baxter find you?" she asked, and she managed to convey in her tone, as she always does, that she hasn't actually said the word 'Mister', although technically it has passed her lips, according to protocol.

"Yes, thanks. I have to go and see him in a minute," I said, and then started mentally running through all the work I had on, wondering if I had screwed up somewhere along the way.

"Good luck!" said Alison brightly, plonking a coffee a little too firmly on my desk, so that it slurped over the edge of the cup onto the front page of a client brief, thus confirming my inclination to think that today might go down as a bad day at the office.

After a quick sip, I stood up, braced myself, and decided against putting fresh lipstick on. Baxter had only just seen me, and might take it as a sign of vulnerability.

I walked down the corridor, and I could see two other people sitting at the meeting-table in Baxter's huge office. I just stopped myself from raising the shield of my black leather note-case, embossed in gold with the firm's logo, and clutching it across my chest. I held it firmly at my side, and smiled when Baxter looked up. He smiled back, and waved me to a seat. His personal assistant asked in hushed tones if I would like a coffee. Something about the day was changing for the better. Lavinia Edwards does not offer to get coffee for just anybody.

Baxter introduced me to two thirty-something guys, Steve Hartigan and Andy Miller, who looked about as comfortable sitting at the mahogany table with their gold-rimmed Harrod's teacups as Eskimos fishing in the jungle. I discreetly unbuttoned my suit jacket while Baxter was talking, to try and look a bit less formal, but they still sat like schoolboys in trouble, with their hands clenched together, leaning slightly forward and listening to every word. Andy's nails were bitten to the quick, and he had acne scars all over his face. His hair was very short, and I noticed that his black shirt and grey tie had seen better days. Steve was wearing dark navy branded sports wear, and had a tiny gold stud earring in his left ear. He had the beautiful ebony skin and enviably high cheekbones of East Africa, and a girl would have killed for the precise arch of his eyebrows. He spoke with a resonant baritone voice that matched his build.

Even sitting down, he looked about six foot six. His

fidgeting reinforced the schoolboy image, and I sensed a huge amount of energy, desperate to be released. I was intrigued. I looked at Baxter with what must have been a very transparent question-mark on my face.

"This is Caroline. She is on our corporate team, and has been involved in a number of deals which give her the ideal experience to work with you," he said, after clearing his throat. He wasn't giving me any clues. Baxter sat back in his seat, very obviously handing over to me.

"So …" I said, not knowing what else to say.

The two guys leaned forward even more, if that was physically possible, with expectant looks on their faces. I opened my note-case, starting to sweat a bit. Baxter was testing me. Second bastard of the day, I was thinking, just before the adrenalin rush kicked in.

"Would you like to start by telling me a little bit about yourselves, and what you are trying to achieve?" I asked, with my pen poised a bit theatrically.

I was looking at Steve, because his eyes drew me, and he had a presence that dwarfed his much smaller companion. But it was Andy who answered, in a voice that surprised me. He spoke really clearly, without a trace of the cockney accent I was expecting. His speech was soft and sibilant, and almost musical. West Country, I decided, after a few seconds.

"We've been referred to your firm through Business Links, on the understanding that you do some pro bono work for charities," he said.

I nodded, but I was still a bit mystified about what I could do for them.

"We run a charity called CityScope which helps homeless young people to reintegrate," said Andy, "by providing them with hostel accommodation and work for a limited time, until they build the confidence to do these things for themselves."

I scribbled some notes. He had obviously made this little speech a few times before.

"Yes …" I said in the tone that says 'I get it, and you can move on'.

Steve chipped in here. "Our problem is capacity."

"Or rather, lack of it," said Andy. "We are looking at expanding in London and opening up to three more hostel properties in the next year."

Did they need help with leases? I didn't stay very long in the conveyancing seat during my training, because it bored me to tears. An opportunity had come up to transfer early to the corporate team and I had jumped at it.

"So how are you going to expand?" I asked, trying to buy some thinking time. It would have been so much easier if I wasn't conscious of Baxter hovering behind my left shoulder, watching my every move.

"We're looking at a couple of partnerships with other charities – ways we can grow without a lot of extra capital," said Andy, and I was starting to get it now.

I know even less about charity law than I do about conveyancing, but it was beginning to sound interesting.

"And you need our help to structure those partnerships?" I asked hopefully.

"Exactly," said Steve.

I breathed a sigh of relief. Baxter sat forward again, and cleared his throat in the way he does to assert his authority over a meeting. We all looked at him.

"I think Caroline will be more than capable of taking this forward, gentlemen," he stood up, and his patronising tone was aimed at the three of us.

Now that I knew what I was supposed to be doing, I should have felt grand. But I didn't. I wanted to get us out of Baxter's office as quick as I could to get away from his air of condescension.

"Why don't you guys come back to my office, and we can start scoping some of this out," I said.

Baxter just nodded at me as I showed them out.

"Please let me never become like him," I was saying inside my head the way I used to say my prayers.

I spent about another hour with Steve and Andy, really getting into the detail of what they were trying to achieve, and I came out buzzing. This was my first solo run, and even though Baxter would notionally oversee it, I knew that he wanted to have as little to do with the whole unsavoury business as possible. This was my chance to make my mark, and in the process, I could help some people who really needed it.

Matthew

Unusually, I wake up before Liz, and hear Jack humming to himself. I should fish him out of bed before he wakes Ben, I think, as I check the clock radio. 6.32. Not bad. We don't bother setting the alarm any more, because we can rely on the boys to wake us within a ten-minute window of time. I shrug on my dressing-gown and tip-toe into the boys' room. Jack is sitting up in his cot, his chubby fingers turning the pages of a cardboard book with fluffy inserts. He can't see me, and I stand there for a second, inhaling the sweet smell of their night-time breath in the room, and watching him. He strokes the puppy's tummy on page two, and then turns to the rabbit's tail on page three. The *Thomas the Tank Engine* night-light glows orange, and for some reason it draws Jack's eye at that moment.

"Hello, Tang Chung Chung," he says amiably, waving at the plug socket. He turns his head, "Hello, Daddy," he says, reaching up his arms to be lifted out.

"Hello, Jack," I cuddle him close. He has recently developed the art of proper hugging, rather than just passively accepting ours, and now he stretches and puts his arms around my neck, leaning his cheek against mine. For how long will my boys do this, I wonder as I stand there, just holding him and savouring the moment. Then Ben wakes up. When he sees his brother being given undue attention, he immediately leaps out of bed, and grabs my knees.

"I want a hug, Daddy."

I bend down to try and hug both of them together. Jack shoots a well-aimed foot at Ben's head on the way down and chaos ensues. The precious moments are often measured in nano-seconds, I think, as I separate them. I distract them with the offer of Cheerios, and we stagger downstairs, with me carrying both of them, my convalescent ribs protesting every step of the way.

Liz appears as we sit at the table, with Jack trying to climb out of his high chair, bored with throwing soggy Cheerios around.

"Didn't you strap him in?" she asks, striding across the room and grabbing him as he finally gets the leverage to stand up on the seat and lunge towards her. She pushes him back down, managing to ruffle his hair, kiss him, and strap him in, all in one fluid movement. The soft and lovely Liz of last night is well and truly banished, and Superwoman is back.

"Sorry," I mutter through a mouthful of cereal.

She flicks on the kettle, noisily grinds some coffee beans, and shoves two slices of bread in the toaster.

"Busy day ahead?" I ask, knowing from the abruptness of her movements that she's mentally already at work. Ben jumps down from the table and grabs her legs in the rugby tackle he has figured out is the best way to bring busy parents to a complete standstill and get some attention.

Liz picks him up, grunting with the effort, "You are getting to be such a heavy boy." She kisses him, and he grimaces, wiping his cheek. She doesn't bother to answer my question, knowing it was meant to be rhetorical, and silently pours me a cup of coffee.

"Do you want to shower first?" I ask.

"You can go first, I don't have to leave until eight today. Happy Anniversary, by the way."

"And to you," I say, and stand up to give her a peck on the cheek.

"I'm really looking forward to tonight." She is smiling at me, intending to tease, and I just smile back, having still not worked out an excuse for Caroline.

We agree to meet at Charing Cross station at seven o'clock, Liz still determined not to reveal our ultimate destination.

On the train, I tried to call Caroline's mobile, but got her voicemail and decided a text message was better. I would have to try to speak to her later. Two of the regulars who always catch the same train as me, and often sit in my carriage, plonked down opposite me and launched into a conversation about their weekend activities. Usually it doesn't bother me, and I can block out their voices and focus on the *Financial Times*, but today, odd words and phrases kept penetrating my consciousness.

"I still love him, that's the problem," the older one said. She's probably only in her early forties, but she looked quite haggard this morning, and if I had never seen her before, I would have confidently said she was fifty. Her younger companion nodded, and unusually for her, didn't say anything.

"He says it was a one-off, he's never done it before, and he'll never do it again."

"But what if you hadn't found him out?" the friend asked.

"I know, that's what I keep wondering. I didn't sleep a wink all weekend."

"I'm not surprised. Where was he?"

"Oh, he was there too. It was horrible. We can't go on like this. But I just can't talk to him about it yet. I keep bursting into tears, and not being able to say what I need to say." She took out a tissue and wiped her nose.

"I know what you mean, that's what happened to me and Alan. But you have to talk eventually, if you want to save the relationship."

"I know." The older one blew her nose and took a deep breath. "Anyway, how was your weekend?"

The conversation reverted to the usual bland exchanges and I was able to block it out again.

Diana was frantic when I got into the office at eight thirty. "Your taxi has been waiting for ten minutes," she said breathlessly, handing me a folder and looking at me expectantly.

I had completely forgotten about a nine o'clock

meeting in Park Royal. That stupid electronic diary again.

"Diana, when I get back at lunch-time, I want us to sit together and extract all the information from this bloody thing, and put it in a proper diary. Can you get me one while I'm out?" I threw the electronic organiser onto her desk, and it skidded across the surface and landed in her paper-recycling bin.

"Sorry, but that is the right place for it," I said, smiling at her as I reached down to pick it up. I placed it with exaggerated care on top of her desk diary. The aggrieved but tolerant look she gave me was the one she saves especially for those who have not yet seen the Lord. It is always especially pronounced on a Monday morning, when she has just had her Sunday injection of holiness and goodwill to all mankind.

"Sorry." I stuffed the folder into my briefcase.

"Anthony said he would meet you there, so that at least one of you is there on time," Diana said, as I turned to retrace my steps to the lift.

"Fine, see you later," I said, already working out my tactics for the meeting.

I shouldn't have been so short with Diana, and I made a mental note to apologise properly when I got back. I spent the taxi journey refreshing my memory from the client file, and the meeting was dull but quite productive. I had three messages on my voicemail when I came out, and spent most of the journey back replying to them. Anthony was quiet, and when I asked him if he was all right, he just nodded.

"Do you want to grab a quick lunch before we go back to the office?" I asked, and he agreed. We sat in an Italian sandwich bar, momentarily daunted by the size of the Ciabatta wedges full of miscellaneous red, green and pink ham-coloured filling.

"I didn't expect it to be this difficult to get back into things," he said, washing down his first mouthful with a gulp of bottled mineral water.

"It was the first meeting on your first day back, Anthony," I said, shocked at his defeatist tone. This was a man who had been on his death-bed only six weeks ago, and now he was back at work, seemingly expecting to pick up just where he had left off.

"The meeting was fine. I'm not talking about that. I'm talking about the whole thing. Its relevance. The point of it all."

"Ah," I said, knowing exactly how he felt.

"I had a lot of time to think, when I was lying on that bed, in traction," he said, and I nodded. "This is going to sound like such a cliché, but I realised that I have been rushing around pursuing some notional idea of wealth and happiness, without actually knowing what I was looking for."

"I often wonder what I'm doing it for." I knew I sounded feeble.

"This is more fundamental, I think," said Anthony. "I

am totally disinterested in the outcome of the negotiations we have just sat through. I used to really care. It really mattered to me to get the best deal for the client, and to represent their interests in a way they couldn't do themselves. It seemed important. Now it doesn't."

"Do you think that if you give it some time, you could get back into the groove, so to speak?" I asked.

"That's what I'm afraid of," he said, looking at me intently. He had let his hair grow a bit longer while he was off, and the loss of weight on his face suited him. He looked younger, and even the wrinkles around his eyes seemed to have diminished slightly.

"I think I would get back into the groove, as you describe it, and not question what I'm doing. Earn the money, spend it on nice holidays, cars, a cottage in France, whatever. I need to do something now, while I feel like this, or I might never get another chance."

"Chance to do what, though?" I asked, unsettled by his conviction. I have always admired Anthony's love of life, his risk-taking, and his boundless energy. He is also a very able guy, with an astute mind, and a way of distilling a problem down to the essence, which has made him a brilliant lawyer.

"Don't know yet, but it's not sitting in endless pointless meetings debating the finer points of intellectual property rights," he said.

I had a flashback to my Cambridge days, sitting on single beds, or on the floor of someone's room in the halls of residence, discussing the meaning of life in the way that only nineteen-year-olds can do. It had been twenty years, I realised, since I had stopped to ask myself the questions that Anthony was posing.

"What does Marianne think?" I asked, and Anthony shrugged.

"I haven't really vocalised it before," he said. "I think she'd be supportive, but I need to have a clearer idea of what the alternatives might be."

I agreed with him. It might be a tad unsettling for her, having thought only a few weeks ago that he might not survive, to now find him questioning the whole meaning of life.

Diana had already extracted all the electronic meeting dates she had painstakingly entered for me only two weeks before, cross-referenced them with her desk diary, and entered them into a slim-line pocket diary from WH Smith. She handed it to me silently, and I took the reproach on the chin. I picked up the electronic organiser as well. It must have cost Liz a fortune and I couldn't just throw it away.

"Diana, I'm really sorry about this morning. I just get so frustrated with these things," I said humbly, and she generously forgave me and brought me a coffee as a peace offering.

Roger and I had a partnership strategy session all afternoon, and we decided it was time to recruit at least two new associates. We needed some fresh blood, and there was a lot of work in the offing. Considering the general downturn, we seemed to be picking up quite a few new clients.

Roger suggested we make Anthony a partner. "We should have done it last year, really," he said, "but the time wasn't right. Things are picking up now, and if we want to keep him, we'll have to make it an attractive offer."

I didn't have the heart to share my conversation with Anthony, which could be just a temporary aberration anyway. Time would tell. At five, I suddenly realised I still hadn't spoken to Caroline, and closed my office door, telling Diana I needed ten minutes without interruption. Caroline answered immediately.

"Caroline, hi, it's Matthew," I said, and waited for her response.

"Hi, Matthew," she said, non-committally. If that had been Liz, I would have known even from those two words what her mood was, and how to handle it. Not so with Caroline.

"Sorry about tonight – something important came up at work, and I can't avoid it," I said.

Silence.

"Can we rearrange?" I asked.

"Sure." Neutral tone.

"When would suit you?"

She suggested Wednesday.

"I've got the Law Centre, but I could meet you after that, at about eight?" I said, thinking that would be ideal. I could just tell Liz I was going out for a bite to eat with one of the other volunteers.

"Grand. Do you want me to come and meet you there? I've been meaning to go and see it for ages." Her voice was warming up now, and I was surprised how much it mattered to me.

"Great. It's on Atlantic Road, do you know it?"

"Yes, it's in under the railway arches, beside the carpet shop, isn't it?"

'Yes, see you Wednesday, then?" I said and we hung up.

I had to leave the office then, to go and find a present for Liz. There is a Jigsaw on the corner of the Strand opposite Charing Cross station, and I was hoping there would be something there. I should be able to get a card and a bag with a fancy handle in the stationery shop next door, and have time to spare.

Diana smiled at me as I left, obviously approving of my husbandly activities, and she said, "Have a lovely time, and give my best wishes to Liz."

I looked at myself in the lift mirror. Everyone around me seemed to be asking themselves what life was all about, and whether they were spending it with the right person. I felt a huge sense of contentment that I seemed to be able to have it all. Work was boring, sure, and as Anthony had said earlier, often begged the question of how relevant it all was. But I had the Law Centre work to keep me grounded, and give me a sense that I was "putting something back", to use that corny phrase. Liz is fantastic in lots of ways. She's bright, and energetic, although less so recently, and attractive. She's a great mother, although she beats herself up about it all the time. But she's so good at everything that I feel sometimes I am just one of the elements of her busy life. And just as I was starting to resent that, along comes Caroline to fill the gap. She makes me laugh, and reminds me of the healthy cynicism of youth, which seems to disappear when you get married and have children. Although I am only eight years older than Caroline, I feel like I occupy a whole different generation. It sounds ridiculous for a thirty-nine-year-old man to say that a woman in her thirties makes him feel young again, but she does . . .

These were the thoughts that were churning around in my head as I browsed through the racks in Jigsaw. I found the perfect present; a long slinky skirt in a dark red fabric, with a matching shawl to drape over the shoulders. The shop assistant approved of my taste, and when I said it was a gift she took extra care wrapping it in layers of tissue paper, and sticking it with a tiny branded sticker to hold it all together. She put it in the kind of bag I had been prepared to spend a fiver on in the stationery shop, so I was very pleased with myself as I stepped next door and bought a card. With plenty of time to spare, I went into Starbucks to write the card, and have a shot of espresso to keep me awake.

Liz would no doubt have booked tickets for a show, and I always fall asleep during the first act, the darkness and the close theatre warmth too compelling to resist. It really makes her cross. I was counting on the espresso to save me from the struggle with my eyelids that blur my view of the play to the point of not knowing what is happening to the characters.

A teenage girl was balanced on one of the tall chrome stools, sipping a cappuccino and staring out at the people passing on the street. I wondered if she was waiting for a date, and then when I looked closer I realised that she was probably homeless. Her clothes looked like they had been shrunk by repeated drenchings in the rain, and her trainers had seen better days. A scuffed green rucksack sat crumpled at her feet, and it looked as though it had originally been quite expensive. She had her hair tied up in a matted pony-tail, and when she turned her head slightly, something about the tilt of her chin, and the back of her neck, white and exposed where her hair was pulled up, made her look very young and vulnerable.

I caught a glimpse of her face as she turned, and she was pretty, with a pert little nose and nicely shaped eyebrows. Her upper lip had a trace of frothy cream on it, and a hint of chocolate stained the side of her mouth. I smiled at her, and she gave me the tight smile of a well-brought-up girl who doesn't want to be rude, but also doesn't want to invite further attention. She intrigued me. She hadn't been homeless for very long, I guessed, partly because she was still coming into a coffee shop, and didn't seem to feel self-conscious about it – she hadn't moved completely onto the fringes yet. Suddenly she sat upright, like a dog who has picked up a scent, and she tried to tuck a few strands of loose hair behind her ear in the nervous gesture of a schoolgirl who has seen the boy she likes coming down the corridor. A tall, dark-haired guy passed the window and his face broke into a huge smile when he caught her eye. I could see why she would want to fix her hair for him – he looked familiar in the vague way that people on television do. Maybe he was in a TV soap, or something. This was getting more interesting by the minute. I checked my watch, and realised I would have to go, if I didn't want to keep Liz waiting. I took a final sip of the espresso, tipping the tiny paper cup right back to get the last drop. I stood up, picked up my briefcase and put my mobile in my coat pocket. I was so busy watching the couple in front of me, that I forgot the bag with Liz's present. The guy had embraced her in almost a brotherly way, and up close I could see that he was probably twice her age. He was holding her hand now, perched on the stool beside her, and looking intently into her face. As I passed, I noticed an ugly raised red scar at her temple, which looked as if it could be infected. The guy reached up to touch it and she flinched away. He went to the counter and ordered two coffees, and finally I had to leave. I was crossing the road, dodging between two black cabs, when I heard a shout behind me. I reached the concrete central reservation on the road, and turned around. The man was standing on the opposite kerb, holding up the Jigsaw bag.

He pointed at it, and yelled, "Is this yours, mate?" and when I nodded, he nipped between the cars and handed it to me, smiling.

"Zoe spotted it," he said, nodding back at the mystery girl.

"Thanks, it's a present for my wife." I nodded towards Charing Cross station, as if he would know that I was meeting Liz there.

"No problem, mate," he said, already turning to cross back to the girl. He looked really familiar now, and I felt a pang of jealousy for his obvious assurance, and his athletic build, in black designer jeans and a black polo shirt. I could see Liz hovering in the entrance to the station, and caught her checking her watch before she spotted me. Her face lit up. She gets anxious if she's running late, but she is so used to my poor timekeeping that she is almost reconciled to it.

"Hi, darling. I nearly lost your present," I said, waving back towards the coffee shop. "A guy had to follow me across the road."

She reached up to kiss me, and I said, "Happy Anniversary," in that moment totally happy to be with her.

The play was *An Ideal Husband*, and she was delighted when I registered the appropriate surprise and pleasure as we walked up Haymarket and I spotted the theatre bill-boards.

"I've spoken to Mum, and the boys are fine. They're in their pyjamas already, and watching a Noddy video."

"Great." I stifled a yawn. I should have had another espresso, I thought, as we settled into our seats and I could feel the familiar lassitude creeping into my bones. Maybe just forty winks would do the trick, so I should just surrender for a few moments early on in the play, instead of trying to fight it.

"I thought we could go for dinner at Zoroastra, afterwards," Liz said, "or do you think it will be too late?"

"If the show finishes by ten thirty, it could be eleven by the time we're eating – that is a bit late, isn't it?" I said, feeling lame. I know it was our anniversary, but it was also Monday, with a long week ahead and the boys not known for their ability to adjust their biological morning clocks to accommodate late nights.

"Are we getting boring, or what?" Liz said, but she laughed. "Have I got time to look at my present before the lights go down, do you think?" she asked, patting the bag.

I checked my watch. "Should do, if you're quick," I said, as eager as her to see it open. I thought she would love it.

Her face fell when the tissue paper came away. "Red?"

she said, looking at me quizzically. She never wears red, as I perfectly well know. It totally draws the colour away from her face, and doesn't suit her at all.

"What?" I said, looking into the bag. "They must have put the wrong one in the bag!" I was making it up as I went along. "They didn't seem to have your size in blue on the rack, so I asked the assistant to get me one out of the storeroom so I could just see the size, and she took out a red one. But she must have thought I wanted the red. I must admit, I took a call from work as I was standing at the counter and didn't see her wrapping it up."

"Oh, well, maybe we can change it," she said, disappointment radiating from every pore. "It looks like a lovely skirt, though." Liz has an amazing capacity for making the best of things.

I kissed her. "I'll try and get it changed tomorrow. Sorry about that." I seemed to have spent my whole day apologising to women. The most disconcerting thing about the whole episode was that I realised I had been thinking about Caroline when I bought the clothes. Red really suits her complexion and her hair colouring. She looks stunning in red.

Matt

After spending most of Monday traipsing around the West End, and even sitting for a while on the steps of

Oxford Street station, where we had first met, I finally found Zoe in a coffee shop. I had decided to keep going until seven o' clock, and then call it a day and go home. I was heading for the number three bus stop on Whitehall when I glanced into Starbucks on the Strand, and there she was, sitting on a stool looking as if she didn't have a trouble in the world. She smiled when she saw me, and I did a funny Marx brothers double-take outside the window, just to make her laugh. I was shocked by the gash on her head though, which looked as if it had gone septic. It was weeping very unpleasant-looking pus, and Zoe wouldn't even let me touch the area around it. I bought her another coffee, and we were just catching up on her adventures of the last few days, when I noticed the guy who had been sitting further along the counter had left, forgetting a carrier bag on the floor. He had just reached the middle of the road when I caught up with him. I handed over the bag, and when he spoke to me, I recognised him as the lawyer who was in the queue in front of me at Brixton police station. He was off to meet his wife – no doubt going to a West End show. He was a typical city type, in a pin-striped suit and pink shirt, but I noticed his shoes were shabby, and his raincoat was crumpled. Somehow he didn't quite live up to the shiny-shoed snotty picture of commercial lawyers that Caroline paints when she talks about the older guys in the office.

Zoe had been sleeping in a doorway just around the

corner, having already figured out that some places were better than others, depending on the direction of the wind. She looked pale, and her face was developing a recognisable grey sheen of unwashed skin and permanent tiredness.

"I've been thinking, Zoe," I started, and she shrugged and raised her eyes to heaven.

"Listen, will you?" I said, trying not to show my frustration.

"I'm not going to the police. They won't believe me, and I never want to see that creep or my mum ever again, so it doesn't matter. Leave it. I'm going to get on with my life."

"What life?" I asked. "Before long, you won't be allowed to set foot in here, because you'll smell, and put the other customers off. You'll be completely on your own, with no money, no address to sign on, or get a job, and your clothes will eventually fall off you."

Her eyes filled up with tears, but her tone was defiant. "It's better than going back to where I was before – I'm better off on my own."

"Zoe, this is not the time to try and prove you can go it alone – at least come back to the hostel and get a decent night's sleep and a shower." There was no point in pursuing the police route, but I should at least get her under a roof where there was some chance of protecting her.

"I know what they're like. That Steve will be on and

on at me to talk to my mum, and tell her what happened."

"If I promise that Steve won't do that, will you come back?" I could hear the wheedling tone in my voice.

"Did he say he wouldn't?"

"Yes." I would just have to get to Steve first, and tell him to leave her alone.

Zoe drained her coffee and ran her index finger around the inside of the cup to collect the foam clinging to the sides. She stuck the grimy finger in her mouth, right up to the knuckle and sucked it with great relish. "Please, thank you, Matthew," she said, and I almost expected her to say, "May I leave the table, please?" We went back to the hostel, and she signed in while I went to find Steve and tell him she was all right.

"Great, cheers," he said, off-handedly when I told him I had found her and brought her back. "Are you in again later this week? The kids are really into these workshops. Not that they would admit that to me," he said, looking around to make sure no-one would overhear. "Tommy asked, dead casual, if you were coming back."

"Definitely still on for Wednesday. Did you find a Ravel CD by the way? I forgot to take it home last week."

Steve snorted in derision. "Are you joking, mate?"

"I know, but it's not exactly their kind of music, is it?"

"Doesn't matter, mate, it's the principle. Something there to take, they'll take it. Put it under their bed and never look at it again, but it's theirs."

I shrugged. I would have to invest in another one, and I wasn't exactly flush with funds. Zoe was lying on the floor in the television room watching *Pop Idols* when I went to say good-bye, and she barely lifted her head in acknowledgement when I told her I was going, and would see her on Wednesday. Tommy was occupying a chair by lying at a forty-five-degree angle to the floor, with the fewest possible contact points between his body and the seat. He nodded imperceptibly at me when I glanced in his direction. There was no sign of the CD, and I refused to humiliate myself by asking if anyone had seen it. I waved at the room in general and left, with mixed feelings. I told myself that Zoe didn't have to be grateful. I had spent a day looking for her out of a selfish need to know that she was all right, as much as out of a desire to help her. She was not my responsibility, but I still felt responsible. Steve told me on the way out that he is a qualified first aider, and he would try and persuade her to let him clean the wound, and advise her to go to hospital.

"But it's her choice, mate. They might not be considered adults in legal terms, but they're more than capable of deciding things for themselves. Don't treat her like some rebellious teenager. She's been through more already than lots of people go through in their whole lives. She's got inner strength, that girl." That was the longest speech I had heard Steve make, and he went up in my estimation. His previous casual acceptance that Zoe might have disappeared, and his indifferent response to her safe return had really wound me up. He was refraining from pointing out the obvious. He had seen all this before, and I was a newly transmuted do-gooder with not the first idea about anything.

CHAPTER 16

Caroline

Matt was acting very strangely. He was spending loads of time at the library, he said, researching things, but he was very vague when I tried to pin him down. Maybe he'd found another woman? One minute I said to myself that would be fantastic, because it would relieve my guilt about Matthew. The next minute, I was devastated at the thought of losing him. He was usually so straight and transparent that I found it difficult to deal with him being secretive. I felt like I was interrogating him, which I probably was, and for the first time in my life, I felt completely out of control. I was certainly not in emotional control. Matthew filled every waking moment, and lots of the sleeping ones too. I felt so bad when I woke up and the internal image of his face was overlaid with the sleeping face of Matt, snoring beside me, oblivious to everything. I kept grabbing him and hugging him at strange moments, because I was so scared of losing him, and then I betrayed him the next second by wondering what it would be like to be lying in bed beside Matthew. How could I be like this? I kept thinking back to all the conversations I'd had with girls who'd had the same dilemma. I was so judgemental.

"If you love him, you can't betray him. It's as simple as that. The very thought that you want to be with someone else means that you don't love him. Move on. Be fair to everybody, including yourself."

I felt like I had two alter egos. One was the fun-loving, idealistic, don't-give-a-damn girl who slept with Matt by the lake, and lived out of a rucksack for three years. The other was the intelligent career woman who wanted to make a mark in a male-dominated, intellectually challenging environment where money is king. I couldn't be both, but I didn't even know which person I wanted to be myself, never mind which Matthew was the right one. These were very scary thoughts when I was lying awake at night beside one Matthew, fantasising about sleeping with the other one, and getting wet at the prospect.

On Wednesday morning I woke up with gritty eyes and that tell-tale lethargy in my whole body that told me I wouldn't be leaping into bed with Matthew, and would probably not be awake past ten o'clock in the evening. Great. I've always been cursed with really heavy periods, and the pill helps, but the absolute weariness is still the same. Scintillating I am not. I dragged myself into the bathroom and tried to put in my contact lenses. The pain was excruciating. Conjunctivitis, I decided, and resignedly stuck my glasses on the end of my nose, seriously thinking about cancelling the date with Matthew. I keep meaning to get new glasses, but I only use them for reading in bed at night, and for emergencies. Not being in the recent habit of dating, it hasn't been top of my list of priorities to go and get more trendy ones. Now I was kicking myself. I have a personality change when I put on my glasses. I get all clumsy, and regress to being fifteen again, when I was a bit spotty and nobody fancied me. Matt, bless him, knows the signs, and he just came up behind me and gave me a hug, pressing his whole body against mine, and wrapping his arms around me. I could feel his erection pressing through his boxer shorts.

"Got any meetings on this morning?" he asked, nuzzling my neck.

I pushed him away. "Matt, please, I'm going to be late," I said grumpily, and started brushing my teeth.

"I'm out tonight," he said casually, and my first reaction was delight, because it would be one less lie to tell about why I was going to be late home. Then my suspicious mind started wondering what he was up to.

"That's nice, are you meeting up with anyone?" I

asked, trying to match his casual tone.

"A few people. I shouldn't be too late. I'm looking forward to it, I haven't been out with them for ages."

"That sounds nice," I said, wondering whether I could get away with seeing Matthew and getting home before Matt. It was worth a try. I could always come up with an excuse if I needed one later.

I pulled on my shirt and suit, and checked my change. I left in time, but I found myself walking down the street more slowly than usual. The lenses of my glasses have a distorting effect if I haven't worn them for a while, and everything looks as if it has curved edges. That's all fine, except when you try to step onto a kerb or walk around someone coming in the opposite direction. It feels like driving on the wrong side of the road; familiar but disturbingly different.

I spent most of the day dealing with the charity partnership contracts, and I was pleased with the progress I'd made by six o'clock. I e-mailed the latest amendments through to Steve Hartigan, and promised to turn it around quickly as soon as he had approved them. If it all went through, CityScope, my client, would be able to open three new hostels in London within a year. My client. That's a nice phrase. I guess that's what we were all supposed to get excited about. But I was getting even more of a buzz out of the idea of helping the charity to expand. I pushed my chair back and bent down to pick up my bag, and suddenly I felt a bit dizzy. I folded my arms on the desk and put my head down, just to rest my sore eyes for a minute and let the low-blood-sugar moment pass. My head shot up again when I heard the tell-tale discreet cough that Baxter uses to such effect.

"Caroline?" he asked, in what was supposed to be a solicitous tone. "Are you ill?"

I sat up, and adjusted my glasses. "No, Mr Baxter, I'm having some trouble with my eyes so I was just resting them," I said, grateful for the first time all day that I had my glasses on as evidence.

"Do you need to consult a medic?" he asked.

Why can he not just say "go to the doctor", like everybody else? "No, I think I have a touch of conjunctivitis. I'll call into a chemist on the way home and pick up some drops. I'll be grand," I said, smiling bravely.

"Everything going all right with our homeless friends?" he asked.

"Yes, thank you. We've got a first draft, and the other two parties are considering it. They should get back to us in the next few days."

"Excellent." He didn't offer to review the contract, or any other such practical support, but he must have felt he had done his bit. As he was leaving, he just said, "Perhaps an early night tonight?"

"Yes, sir," I said. I saluted and tried to do 'mocking funny', but I think it came out as 'mocking insubordinate'. I decided to call it a day. I caught a glimpse of myself in the lift mirror, and I wished that I had gone at lunch-time to an optician with a one-hour service where I could have ordered new glasses. I would still be clumsy and the world would still have curved edges, but I might feel a tiny bit more confident.

I had loads of time to spare, and got to Brixton at six forty-five. It wasn't a place I wanted to hang around with one arm longer than the other, as my mother would say, so I decided to go straight to the Law Centre, to wait until Matthew was finished. Then it occurred to me in a panic that I hadn't asked Matt where he was going out tonight, and it was as likely to be Brixton as anywhere else. I sneaked around the corner from the tube station and then glanced quickly up Atlantic Road, and across to the bar where we sometimes meet up before we go to a movie. This whole date thing was not auguring well, and I was literally dragging my feet like the fifteen-year-old I had turned into, when I arrived at the Law Centre. Through the plate-glass window, I could see Matthew sitting in a "booth" created by two maroon-coloured office screens, talking intently to a skinny black teenager with a Nike logo shaved on the back of his head. The kid was nodding, but not looking at Matthew, who was leaning further and further forward to try and make eye contact. There was a line of chairs in a waiting area, and it looked as if there were about eight people waiting to be seen. I looked at my watch. He would never get through them in an hour, surely? A glamorous black lady behind a makeshift reception desk smiled at me when I pushed the door open, and I whispered that I was going to wait for Matthew until he was finished.

"You going to be joining the team, then?" she asked, nodding at my briefcase, and obviously deciding that I looked like a lawyer.

I just gave her my special non-committal smile, and asked if it was OK for me to sit at the end of the row of chairs.

Matthew glanced up and smiled at me when he caught my eye, and I could see the receptionist's eyebrows lifting when she saw the look between us. She nodded sagely and looked down at her papers. A minute later she asked if I would like a drink, and made me a coffee in a chipped black mug emblazoned with a yellow *Action for Employment* logo. The coffee was scalding hot and tasted awful. I avoided looking into the mug so that I wouldn't see the hard-water scum floating on the top.

The young guy with Matthew finally stood up and shuffled out the door, muttering, "Cheers, mate," as he went, and Matthew nodded to his next client, a huge African lady wearing the full green and gold head gear and regalia and carrying a tiny baby. Her voice was so loud I couldn't help overhearing, and it seemed her husband had left her and she wanted advice about how to claim money from him for child support.

Matthew gave her some contact numbers and made some suggestions, telling her to come back if she had no luck. I started reading my book, but I couldn't resist listening in to some of the conversations, and I had to stop myself from staring. There was a young teenager, about thirteen, I would say, called Jose who told Matthew he was in a children's home on the Angell Town estate, and wanted to know how he could get out. Jose had been attacked the night before by an older boy, and although the police were after the other kid, Jose wasn't confident they would catch him.

"If he comes back, man, I'm dead. But my social worker won't do nuffink. She says it's down to the police, but they're fucking useless. I need to get out, man."

He was looking around as if he was the fugitive, and when I heard the next bit, I could understand why. Jose had thrown a knife across a room at the older kid, and it had stuck in his calf.

"Why were you throwing the knife in the first place?" Matthew asked, and he managed to sound as if he was totally on Jose's side.

"The guy was goin' for my little bruvva, and I just lost it, man. My bruvva's only five, you know what I'm sayin?"

Matthew nodded.

"He just threw annuva kid down the stairs, and he was goin' mad, lookin' around to see who next, and he was goin' for Errol, man, so I had to stop him."

"So what will happen to your little brother if you

leave?" Matthew asked.

After about twenty minutes, he convinced Jose that the best thing he could do would be to sit tight, and hope the police caught the other boy. I could feel my eyes stinging, and I tried to dive into my book again to escape. There was a terrible feeling of inevitability about Jose's situation, and I really admired Matthew for trying to alter the course of a life that seemed destined for disaster. The queue moved surprisingly quickly, and by eight fifteen Matthew was finished. He stood up and stretched his arms above his head, and his fingers grazed the damp stains on the curved ceiling of the room.

A train rattled overhead, temporarily rendering us all silent, and then he said, "Gloria, this is Caroline, she's interested in the work of the Law Centre."

"I thought so," said Gloria. She was standing with her back to Matthew, and she looked at me with such a penetrating stare that I physically shivered.

"We're going to get a bite to eat, now that Caroline has observed how we work, and you might be seeing her again," said Matthew, as Gloria filed the papers he had been using, and locked the filing cabinet with an aggressive turn of the key.

"That would be nice," said Gloria, and I wondered why she was saying it when she obviously didn't mean it. She turned to Matthew.

"Shall I leave you to lock up, then, and I'll see you next week. Is there anything I need to pass on to anyone else to handle in the meantime?"

"No. Thanks, Gloria. See you next week, then." He pecked her on the cheek, and she put her hand on his arm. "Be careful, Matthew." After a pause she said, "You don't want to get mugged again, 'specially if you have comp'ny."

"Thanks. Take care. Bye," said Matthew, smiling at her. He grabbed his coat off the rack, and his briefcase from behind the desk.

Gloria went out and waved back through the window as she passed down the street.

"She's like a mother hen," said Matthew as he was pulling down the metal grille and bending down to lock it. His long fingers struggled with the padlock, but it finally clicked into place.

I noticed the hair was thinning slightly on the back of his head, and wondered if he would be bald when he is older.

"She knows there's something going on between us," I said, and I shivered. I had visions of her getting her voodoo dolls out and putting a curse on us. "I sensed that she didn't approve. Maybe she thinks we're mixing work and pleasure."

"She's very protective," said Matthew, dismissively, and he changed the subject, but he was a bit quiet for a while.

We went to the Buzz Bar, because I guessed that in Matt's dire financial straits he wouldn't be likely to go there. The food is great, but not cheap. It's in the crypt of a huge old church in the middle of a major one-way system through Brixton, so you have to cross a busy road to reach it, but it's like an oasis of calm when you get there. We went down the cold stone steps and pushed open the big heavy black wooden door. It really feels like a crypt, with brick pillars and vaulted white plastered ceilings and lots of candles burning in wax-covered brass candlesticks. We were lucky to get a table, just squeezing in between the people having a quick bite before the cinema, and the people who had booked for nine o'clock. Once Matthew started talking about the clients he had just seen, he got completely animated again, and I hoped he didn't notice that I wasn't on top form. I had really bad cramps now, and the tiredness was kicking in. My food arrived and steamed up my glasses, and when I took them off to clean them on my napkin, I knocked over my wineglass. The whole table had to be cleared to mop up the wine, and I looked at it all in a blur, absent-mindedly polishing my glasses until Matthew said, "Caroline, do you think they might be clean, yet?" and laughed. I blushed, and stuck them back on my nose so firmly that they steamed up again, and I stuck my bottom lip out and blew air up to clear them like I used to do when I was a kid. Matthew was laughing properly now, and I couldn't help but join in. What a fiasco! But funnily enough, when he asked me about work and I started telling him about the charity thing, I got a second wind, and when he ordered another bottle of wine, I forgot my intention to get back home before Matt, and realised that it was midnight, and we were on the receiving end of less than subtle hints from the staff that it was time to leave.

Matthew

Jermaine was in again, having survived the magistrates' court unscathed, because two of the witnesses didn't turn up, and one of them admitted that he had had a lot to drink that evening, and couldn't swear that it was Jermaine he had seen. But he was still facing eviction, and he seemed to think that I would come up with some magic solution to his problem. The local councillor still hadn't got back to me, so I didn't have any news for him. I gave him the usual pep talk, which he always takes on the chin, probably because he has a lifetime of practice of listening to parents, teachers, social workers and police officers telling him what to do. Then he went off about his business.

Caroline turned up as I was talking to him, and it was all I could do not to leap across the desk and kiss her. She was wearing glasses, which made her look vulnerable and even younger, and I could tell she felt uncomfortable when she arrived. It's not the most glamorous setting, and the clients can be an intimidating sight, sitting silently waiting for their problems to be solved. I saw her talking to Gloria, and then she had a coffee. I was probably a bit short with some of the clients, I was so eager to get out of there and just to be with Caroline. Gloria must have guessed there was something between us, because she was a bit abrupt with Caroline, and told me to be careful.

I knew. It was the most stupid thing I had ever done, and I kept going back for more, because Caroline was irresistible. I wouldn't put it past Gloria to tell Caroline outright that I was married. She's a Christian, and very uncompromising in her views of the world. I must make sure she and Caroline didn't come across each other again.

I liked Caroline even more when she let down her guard tonight. When she knocked over the wine and blushed, she just looked so beautiful, all pink and bothered, and bordering on tearful. The Law Centre had that effect on me, when I first started working there. Caroline couldn't believe that children like Jose could be living in a home and throwing knives around without someone in authority being there to stop them. The only thing that keeps Jose on the straight and narrow is looking out for his little half-brother. Their mother is schizophrenic, and isn't capable of looking after them, although she is living on the estate nearby with a boyfriend who is father to neither of the boys. Jose and Errol go to visit her after school. The social worker I have talked to thinks this is the only sustainable way of keeping them in contact. Jose has already been cautioned for criminal damage to the boyfriend's car, which he inflicted in revenge after finding his mother bruised from a beating. It can be depressing, but on the good days I feel like I am making a tiny difference, and that is better than nothing. Jose's truancy rate has gone way down since our first chat, when I told him his best chance of escaping this life, and rescuing Errol from it, is to get good school results. At thirteen he's as tough as nails, but he hasn't yet lost all hope, and he's still open to listening. If I could find a way of doing this kind of legal work full time, I would. I'm in that eternal circle of mortgage, nice holidays and imminent school fees that is pretty much inescapable once you have a family. Individual idealism has to make way for family welfare. Liz would have a fit if I even thought about throwing away my City career and money.

I can't believe I was thinking all this, while Caroline was telling me about a charity deal she was working on. Well, I can believe it, because I could see she was excited by it, in a way that I hadn't been excited by my real job for years. Caroline still had the passion that Liz and I seemed to have lost. The head-space for bigger causes has slipped away, as our micro-world of sleepless nights and demanding children has taken us over. When I am with Caroline, I can forget that I must put a new battery in Ben's Buzz Lightyear because he wants to take it to "show and tell" at nursery on Friday and it's no good without a functioning laser. I can forget that I was supposed to buy milk on the way home tonight, and that there is a parents' tour of one of Ben's prospective schools in the morning and I've not told Diana I'll be in late. I can drink lots of wine and pretend that I won't be woken up at six o'clock in the morning. Tomorrow is another day. Tomorrow is another life.

The candlelight was flickering, and Caroline made me laugh. She was really embarassed when she knocked over the wine, and I saw another side to her. A vulnerable, young, less confident side that made me want to hug her and protect her. When I am with Caroline, I can talk about the clients at the Law Centre, and even tell some funny stories about them, without her nagging me to be careful, and not to get too involved. She touched my hand when I reached for my wine, and stroked my fingers as I held the glass. The electric shock was like the one I got when I put my fingers in a socket as a child. It shot all the way up to my neck, and my whole body literally jumped.

"Are you all right?" she asked, taking her hand away, and looking a bit surprised.

"Yes, sorry, I don't know what happened there," I muttered, but I was thinking, "God, I want her." I had to physically grit my teeth to stop myself from standing up and dragging her out of the restaurant – to where, I do not know, but right then it felt like any horizontal surface would do. Crude, animal lust is the only way to describe it. I pushed my chair away from the table, and excused myself. I went to the Gents', locked myself in a cubicle and it took ten deep breaths of air laden with urine and cleaning chemical to bring me back to earth. There is no escaping this kind of lust. I can talk to myself until I am blue in the face, but this is a biological reaction, and I am not in control of it.

"Caroline?" I said when I got back to the table. "Are you doing anything on Saturday morning?"

"Probably having a lie-in," she said. "I haven't got any major plans for the weekend."

"May I join you?" I asked.

She laughed out loud. "That's the best proposition I've ever had."

"Is that a yes?" I asked, desperately hoping that Liz would have the boys for the morning. If she didn't take them out, I would have to think of a very good reason for disappearing.

"No," she said, and she looked down. She was so gorgeous when she blushed.

"Why not? I could be at your place by, say tennish, and we could –"

"I could meet you somewhere for brunch, if you like," she said.

I could hardly say, "No actually, I want to be in bed with you, lying on tangled sweaty sheets, not sitting across yet another white tablecloth, where I can't lay a hand on you." I had a feeling I would get the same reaction as I had before. Gently, gently, I thought to myself. It has been a long time since I have played this game, and I don't want to get it wrong.

We agreed to meet at noon on Saturday, and I had to stop myself from immediately starting to plot how I could contrive it. We spent the rest of the evening talking about work, films, and music. Caroline did most of the chatting. I realised that I haven't been to see a film for about six months, and I couldn't summon the name of one credible band to mention when she talked about a Cold Play gig she had recently gone to at the Brixton Academy. I looked around and realised that we were the only people left in the restaurant, and checked my watch. Twelve thirty-four. I would have to try and get a taxi home. The last train from Victoria goes at 12.38 so I didn't have a chance. Getting a mini-cab in Brixton is not the easiest thing in the world, but the restaurant staff were now almost drumming their fingers on the adjacent tables, so we decided to try our luck on Coldharbour Lane rather than calling a mini-cab company.

Brixton reminds me of Manhattan. It never sleeps. There were at least four cars with vibrating sound systems waiting at the traffic-lights, and I could feel my eardrums resonating. I held her arm as we crossed, because she didn't seem very confident. She laughed it off, saying her glasses made her feel like she was walking around the inside of a goldfish bowl. There was a fight going on outside the cinema, and we skirted around it, just as two bulletproof-jacketed police officers intervened. Sibilant whispers of "Coke, grass, dope," managed to carry above the sounds of shouting, music and police sirens as we made our way down Coldharbour Lane towards the rotating blue light of the mini-cab office. I recognised a couple of my clients loitering outside, but we avoided eye-contact in an unspoken pact. We seemed to jump the queue, and an energetic little Jamaican man came out to escort us to his battered old Ford Granada.

"You lookin' better, sir," he said, as we got into the car, and I was just puzzling about it, when he said, "You go to the pohl-ice, abou' dat muggin' ting?" and I thought he must have seen me outside the Law Centre.

"Yes, I got my wallet back, too," I said, touched that he had asked. He nodded, and caught my eye in the mirror.

"Can we drop the lady off at . . ."

I had turned to Caroline so she could give the address, when the little man said, "Evelyn Gardens, intit?"

She just nodded.

"You goin' on somewhere else, tonight, sir?" he asked me, and I told him. I thought he shrugged, but I was too focused on Caroline to think about it very much. She seemed to have shrunk, and was sitting as far away from me as possible. "Sorry, I don't feel very well," she said, when I tried to move across the seat to get closer to her.

"Oh. Do you think it was the food?" Her starter had prawns in it, but I didn't think food poisoning would set in that quickly.

"No. I'll be fine. I just need to get to bed,' she said shortly, and she shivered when I stroked her leg.

"Do you want me to see you in?" I asked, although I didn't want to lose this cab and have to get another one at that time of night.

"No! Honestly, I'll be grand." She didn't say another word until we pulled up outside her house, and she just got out of the car, saying, "I'll call you tomorrow. Thanks a million for a lovely evening."

I watched as she climbed the steps and put the key in the door.

"She a special lady, intit?" said the driver, as he sucked his lips and did the most expert three-point turn I have ever seen.

"Yes, she certainly is," I said, and sat back on the seat. I dozed off, and he had to wake me up to give him directions as we reached Bromley. The fare was astronomical, and I gave him a three-pound tip. He was probably able to call it a day after that, and go home.

Matt

Zoe seemed to have made friends with Justine, and they

sat together all through the first part of the workshop, laughing and joking, mostly taking the piss out of me. I was taking a bit of a risk. I showed them an Alan Bennett *Talking Heads* video, and then got them to sit in a circle on the floor and did my own East End Cockney monologue, to get them started. I was supposed to be making it up, but I found myself telling them about myself. And about Caroline. Well, about a two-timing girlfriend, actually. I realised what I was doing when Zoe started asking questions like a child who is totally absorbed in a bedtime story.

"And what happened then?" she asked, when I came to a halt, after describing a massive row between the guy and the girl.

"I don't know," I said. "I'll have to tell you next week, I think." I looked around. They were all staring at me, with expressions ranging from disbelief to sympathy. No-one said a word. Even Zoe and Justine had stopped giggling. I stood up and saw my gaunt face reflected in the darkened glass of the window. I pulled the curtains to break the spell and turned around to face them again. "Right, who's next?" I asked briskly, and then wished I had handled it differently. They shuffled around on the carpet, with no-one catching my eye. Who would want to expose themselves like that? It would be worse than an AA meeting.

But Zoe put her hand up, like a child again. "I'll try. Do I have to put on a different voice?"

"No, just do it whatever way you like," I said. "Sometimes a different voice just allows you to say things that you wouldn't normally say."

"There once was a little girl who thought she was really happy. She had a nice Mummy and a Daddy, and loads of friends, and when she got a puppy for her tenth birthday, she thought that all her dreams had come true."

I looked around and everyone was sitting staring at the floor, or the wall, or their fingernails, but there wasn't a sound in the room. Traffic rumbled by outside. Steve's office door slammed, and someone ran upstairs.

"As a special treat, she was allowed to take the puppy to bed with her that night, as long as she promised it would be just for one night. So she took him upstairs and tucked him into his basket by her bedside, and her mummy came to kiss her good night."

I was amazed that these cynical, grubby, hard-nosed teenagers were sitting listening to the childish story.

"In the middle of the night, she woke up. The puppy was awake too, sitting up in his basket, whimpering. She decided to take him downstairs for a wee, so he wouldn't get into trouble for wetting his blanket. Her daddy got cross with her for wetting the bed, and it was the only thing that made her mummy sad. She didn't want anything to spoil the lovely birthday feeling that she had in her tummy, so she sneaked out of bed, and she even remembered to put on her slippers. She picked up the puppy and went to the bathroom first, pushing the door open quietly so she wouldn't wake anybody up. She got a fright when she saw her mummy sitting on the edge of the bath, in the dark. Her head was hanging down and she was crying, and her whole body was shaking. The little girl didn't want to disturb her, so she tiptoed out again, and went back to bed. When she woke up in the morning, she could feel the wetness underneath her, and her nightie was soaked. She leaned out of bed to check on the puppy, and there was a poo and a wet patch on the carpet. Her heart sank. There was no way she could get it all cleared up before they were caught. She froze in the bed, waiting for it. She heard her daddy coming down the hall, and her heart was pounding. Maybe if she stayed in bed he wouldn't notice. She quickly threw her dressing-gown onto the carpet to hide the poo and closed her eyes, pretending to be asleep. 'Please please please, make him go to work and not come in,' she prayed really hard. God wasn't listening. The door opened and he shouted, 'This room stinks! Get out of that bed, you filthy child and get that fucking dog out of my house.' He grabbed the little girl and pulled her out of bed, and his face was all angry and red and he sort of threw her across the room, and picked up the little puppy, who was whimpering, and threw him on top of the little girl's tummy. He ripped the sheets off the bed, and flung them on top of her, so she was in a tent. She held on tight to the puppy, who was really howling now.

She was lucky because her daddy went out then, and she heard him stamping down the stairs and the front door slammed. She waited a minute, and then pulled off the sheets, and they were smelly, but she knew what to do. She took them downstairs, and took off her nightie and put everything in the washing machine, with the dressing-gown and switched it on. She cleaned up the poo and then got dressed and went to find her mummy. It was dark in her mummy's bedroom, and she peeked around the door. Her mummy was in bed, but very quiet. When she got up close, she could see bruises on her mummy's face again. She crept into bed beside her mummy and they had a cuddle, with the puppy wriggling around on top of the duvet, and licking their faces, like little kisses."

Zoe stopped and looked at me.

"And what happened then?" I echoed her question.

"The little girl and her mummy went to live in a special house where daddies weren't allowed in."

"And what happened to the puppy?" asked Justine in a tiny voice.

"The little girl had to give him away. Puppies weren't allowed there. He never even got a name."

What had I done? I shouldn't have opened these doors. I'm just an actor, not a counsellor. This was scary. Zoe leaned against Justine and she hugged her.

I took a deep breath. "Well, that was good work, Zoe. Thanks. You've set a challenge now, for everyone else."

Tommy stood up. "Can I do one?" he asked, and I had a Sidney Poitier moment – I had cracked the toughest kid on the block. I nodded enthusiastically, smiling inanely at him.

"There was a wanker, once, who thought he knew it all, and came nosing into other people's lives, and pissed them off, so they asked him to go away and never come back." Tommy walked slowly to the door, and opened it, standing to one side in a mock butler pose, one arm folded behind his back. He nodded at me and raised an eyebrow. I looked around and the group was silent. Even Zoe wouldn't catch my eye. My chest constricted. I stood up and walked to the door, and my throat was so dry I couldn't even say good-bye. I stumbled out, and the door clicked closed very quietly and firmly behind me.

Caroline

I leaned against the inside of the front door and took a few deep breaths. Matt would be home before me. I hadn't rung him to say I would be late home, and when I looked in my handbag to see if he had called me, I realised I had forgotten to switch my mobile back on when we left the Law Centre. The voicemail icon was flashing, and there were three frantic messages from Matt. He sounded really upset. I actually doubled over and groaned. I went slowly upstairs, and opened the flat door. No lights on. It was very late. Matt would be asleep. I sneaked into the bathroom and got undressed in there. I even brushed my teeth with the ordinary toothbrush so the motor of the electric one wouldn't wake him up. How long had he waited up for me? I felt so bad I nearly wanted him to catch me, and force me to admit what I was doing. Then I'd have to make a decision. I slid into the bed, barely lifting up the duvet. I expected the usual murmur from him, to check that I was all right. There was only silence. A flat duvet. An empty bed. I sat up and switched on the bedside light. The room was empty. Where was Matt? He never stayed out that late. Shit. I went back to the bathroom to get my glasses. I pulled on Matt's dressing-gown and went through to the sitting-room to check the answering machine. There were two messages flashing. I pressed 'play'.

Eight thirty-four. *"Caroline, are you in? Your phone must be out of charge. It's me. Are you in the bath?"* Then a groan, a pause, and a click.

Ten fifty-three. *"Caroline, where are you? Pick it up, it's me."* Another click.

Did his voice sound a bit slurred? I punched out his mobile number with a shaky finger. The stupid electronic woman told me I had dialled incorrectly. I did it again. *"This is Matt, leave me a message. Bye."*

"Matt, darling, it's me. I'm so sorry, are you all right? I'm at home. Ring me when you get this." I flopped down on the sofa. Where could he be? He must have decided to stay over at someone's house, but why hadn't he just said that on the message, so I wouldn't worry about him? I know, it sounds selfish. I had done exactly the same thing to him. I deserved it. After an hour, and a cup of peppermint tea, I was slipping into a doze on the sofa, so I dragged myself to bed. There was nothing I could do until the morning. I pushed away the thought that whether he was lying injured in a hospital bed somewhere, or just sleeping in someone else's bed, daylight wouldn't change the facts. But I might be able to cope with the facts better.

Matt

I stumbled down the steps of the hostel, and I have never ever felt so wretched. I knew I should have told Steve what had happened. I owed it to the kids. You can't just open up wounds like that and then leave them to fester – I had a responsibility to them. But I was completely humiliated. I couldn't admit to Steve that I didn't know what to do next, and I was very close to crying.

I hadn't told Caroline about the workshops because they seemed so trivial compared to the work she does. I wanted to achieve something, to help one of the kids in some tangible way, before telling her, or anyone else, what I was doing. The only preparation I had done was to sit for a couple of hours, scribbling down ideas about what kind of role-plays I would get the kids to do, and skimming through "Icebreakers For Training Events", a little pamphlet from the library with lots of ideas for how to get people in a group to lower the barriers and lose their inhibitions. I thought the whole thing would be easy, and last week's workshop had gone so well, it really did seem easy. My mobile phone rang just as I reached the entrance to the Underground station.

"It's me," I heard when I answered it. Zoe sounded tearful.

"I'm sorry," I said.

"You don't have to be sorry. I told the story. It helped. It really did." I could hear echoes of the brave little girl voice, even on the mobile, with traffic noise in the background.

"Listen, do you want to go for a coffee, and a chat?" I asked, desperate to pick up the pieces. Maybe I could still redeem the situation with Zoe. Tommy would be a more difficult nut to crack. "No, thanks. I'll take a raincheck though," she said, putting on a west-coast American accent, and giggled.

"See you next week, then?" I said. "Same time, same place?" It was my turn to put on a corny accent. I wasn't even sure if I could make myself go back to the hostel next week, but I could still take her for a coffee.

"Sure, see you then."

At least it seemed like she intended to stay at the

hostel in the short term, and there was some comfort in that, as I sat on the tube, not sure where I was going. I really wanted to see Caroline. I didn't care any more about how seriously she would take the workshops. I had to share the whole thing with her. It was too big a thing in my life now, to hide it. I sent her a text message, and when I got off the tube, I rang her twice. Her mobile must have been out of charge. She never switched it off, except for meetings at work. I checked the time. Twenty past eight. Even on a bad day she would be on her way home from work by now. I called the flat. No answer. I couldn't face being on my own right now, so I found myself walking back down the steps and into the Underground, with no particular destination in mind. After Caroline, the only other person I could imagine talking to was my nan. She would have understood. I could have told her everything, and she would put it in perspective for me. I spent a lot of my teenage angst-filled times in her flat, pacing up and down her green and brown leaf-patterned living-room carpet, unloading my troubles on her. She was an East Ender, born and bred in Newham, with a pragmatic view of life, and a very warm heart. Often she didn't say a word, but I always knew she was listening. She would nod sagely, and present me with a can of Coke from the fridge, with a paper straw sticking out as if I was still four years old, or stand up on her tip-toes in her worn-out burgundy slippers and give me a hug. She smelt of old lady, eau de toilette and hairspray, and for a woman of her tiny size, she could give a hug like nobody else.

I found myself on the Jubilee line to Canning Town, drawn to her old haunts. The "integrated transport hub" with underground, train and bus station would have made her laugh, and ask why there wasn't a tram stop as well, just to be sure. "Why would anyone want to come to this godforsaken part of London?" she would ask, conveniently ignoring the City Airport, the towers of Canary Wharf and the evidence everywhere that regeneration and rebuilding will soon make her old stamping grounds unrecognisable. When I was a kid, I didn't see much of Nan, because she and Mum had fallen out for some reason I could never fathom. Only when I became independent, and could get a bus or a tube to visit her, did I see her on a regular basis. She was my escape valve, and my sanity check. The journey to her flat was part of the therapy. I would leave our house in Lavender Crescent, wound up like a spring after the latest tirade from my mother about smoking or a lecture from my father about studying harder. An hour and two buses later I would arrive at Nan's, already starting to unwind. Sitting on her sagging chintzy sofa, listening to her soothing voice, consuming endless quantities of fruitcake and milk had a really calming effect on me. Whatever the crisis, she always seemed to know the answer. What 'A' level subjects should I take? My girlfriend at seventeen thought she was pregnant – what should I do?

Would I get addicted to dope if I had smoked it twice at parties? How could I convince my dad that I wanted to take a gap year before University?

I got on the bus that travels the length of Newham Road, and looked out. Nan would be shocked at the changes. Or maybe she wouldn't. She lived through two wars, and saw London bombed, and the gaps in the skyline filled by the 'sixties concrete tower blocks that are now deemed unsuitable. They are slowly being replaced with yellow London brick apartment blocks and two-up two-down houses, with community health centres, shops and soft-surface playgrounds.

"Can't be bad," she'd say, clicking her false teeth and pouring another cup of tea from her rose-patterned china teapot. "Better for the kids, anyway." She'd delicately remove the tea-strainer from the edge of the cup, one finger crooked. The rituals were as important to her as the actual tea-drinking. She could have been Japanese, except that she wasn't inscrutable enough. You always knew where you stood with Nan. I felt a twist of loneliness. What did I think I was going to find in this bleak part of East London?

It was completely dark, and a light drizzle was falling as I got off the bus outside Nan's local fish and chip shop. It was reassuringly unchanged, and the sharp tang of vinegar mixed with the warm smell of chips in newspaper hit my nostrils as a man came out with a large wrapped packet under his arm. I realised how hungry I was, and stepped into the steamy warmth.

"Hallo, mate!" said the guy behind the counter, and for a second I thought he recognised me. Nan used to send me down to get a "fish supper" on Fridays, and the chippie used to shovel in an extra portion of chips for me. He said that Nan had always had a healthy appetite, and he would wink at me as he shook salt and vinegar over the pile of chips and then, quick as a flash, he would wrap it all up in layers of white paper and newspaper. I asked for cod and chips and realised that he didn't know who I was. He was just being friendly. He used the same tone for the next customer, a wizened little man who looked like he could have been a contemporary of Nan's. I sat perched on the one tall red vinyl-covered stool, and rubbed a clear patch on the steamy window. I watched people scurrying by in the rain, as I ate the fish and chips. Although it had been nearly five years since Nan died, I had a strange feeling of familiarity. I had sat on this same stool many times before. The particular taste and smell of the fish and chips, the squishy feel of the vinyl cushion under my thighs, my feet resting on the chrome crossbar of the stool, the Cockney voices discussing football scores, waiting for the next batch of chips. But most familiar of all was the feeling of confusion and uncertainty that usually led me to Nan. And this time, I wouldn't find her. I scrunched up the paper into a ball, and threw it into the bin. The gesture looked more decisive than I felt. I wandered down the main road, and turned into Nan's street, where most of the windows seemed to be double-glazed now, and there was a general air of modest prosperity. I stood outside the house where Nan had lived for sixty-odd years. During all the time that I visited her, she only occupied the downstairs part. When my mum and her two brothers grew up and left home, and Granda died, she decided she didn't need a whole house, and she used some of Granda's life insurance policy to convert it into two flats. The rental income meant she was never destitute, and in her pragmatic way, she always found "useful" tenants, like nurses, or painters who could look out for her, or "do a bit around the place". The front garden had been paved for car-parking, like many of its neighbours, and boasted a couple of sad terracotta pots sprouting with weeds and what looked like seeded polyanthus plants. Nan's windows were hung with trendy wooden Venetian blinds and her front door had been stripped back to pine, and varnished. I missed her chipped black door with the old-fashioned brass lion's-head knocker. I wanted to see the slightly grey net curtains twitching as she looked out for me coming back with her supper. Suddenly a security light in the porch flashed on, and I felt trapped in the glare. If they looked out, the occupants would think I looked suspicious. But there was no movement inside, and no discreet chinks opened in the blinds. It was worse than I had thought. No spirit of Nan remained hovering over the paved space where she had proudly weeded her flowerbeds until she was too stiff to bend over. No memory of her was imprinted on the outside of the house. She had been concreted up and paved over. I cried. I just let the tears roll down my face, standing still to avoid triggering the spotlight, and looking up at the scudding dark clouds that were whisking the rain away to somewhere else. The orange city glow didn't reach them. They looked ominous as they moved purposefully across the sky. I have never felt as lonely as I was in that moment. It seemed as if I had never grieved for Nan, never let the pain get right inside and really, really hurt. I tried ringing Caroline again, but there was no answer. The thought of summoning the energy required to drag my body all the way back to the flat was daunting.

Ironically, after Nan died, and Dad retired, Mum persuaded him to move from Wandsworth back to East London. I could walk to their house in twenty minutes. I made my first conscious decision of the evening, and turned towards home. Even in the midst of my sadness, I was interested in my mental use of the word "home" to describe where Mum and Dad live, when I have had my own place for several years, and particularly since Caroline moved in, it has felt very homely. My parents were in, as I knew they would be. Their routine had been the same for years, so there was no reason to think it would be different now. Dad was sitting in front of the television with a cup of tea and Mum was ironing, listening to the radio in the kitchen. I took the front-door key out of my pocket, but suddenly it didn't feel right to use it. I rang the doorbell. I could see Mum's silhouette approaching down the hall, blurred by the bubble glass in the door panel. I heard her putting the chain on before opening the door and peering out. "Good heavens," she said, closing it quickly to release the chain, and then opening it wide. "Come in, son. Are you all right?"

I nodded, but she is my mum and she knew better. She rapped on the sitting-room door as she passed, saying, "Dennis, it's our Matthew," and she pulled me towards the kitchen. He came out, carrying his empty mug.

"Hello, Matthew. And to what do we owe the honour?" he said, quite genially for him.

"Nothing, really. I was in the area, and I . . ."

"You sound like one of those travelling salesman!" said Mum, giggling. "Have you got any hoovers to sell us?" She flicked on the kettle. "Are you hungry, love? A sandwich, or just a biscuit?"

"I just had fish and chips, thanks," I said.

"I've got some nice Garibaldis." She bustled around getting the good china plates and cups out of the china cabinet.

"I went to have a look at Nan's old place," I said, sipping my hot tea. Dad was poking around in the aquarium, moving plants, scraping the glass. He wouldn't want to look as if he was only in the room to talk to me. He had other things to do.

"What possessed you to do that, at this hour of the night?" asked Mum.

"I don't know, I just wanted to feel close to her, I suppose," I said, not really sure myself.

"And did you?"

"No, there's nothing of her left there. The house looks completely different."

"I haven't been down that street for years," said Mum, who inherited Nan's practical streak. "No reason to go there, now."

"So, how's work going?" asked Dad, getting straight to the point as only he can.

"Not great, but I have an idea about something that I'm working on," I said, finding myself using the defiant teenage tone that had defined our relationship for too many years.

"What's that, then, love?" Mum plonked down a plate piled high with biscuits, and topped up my barely diminished cup of tea. "Eat up, there's plenty more where that came from."

I can't believe it, but I told them about the workshops. My parents hadn't got the first clue about the Arts. It broke my dad's heart when I decided to study drama. He actually said it was for "poofters". When he finished poking around in the fish tank, he slid onto a chair and poured himself a cup of tea, and listened avidly as I described what I was trying to do with the kids.

Mum made lots of positive and encouraging noises, but it was Dad's silence that led me to continue, and I told them about the disaster of the day.

"Tommy, did you say his name was?" he asked, when I finished talking. I nodded.

"He's the one you want to look out for, not the girl. She'll be fine, by the sound of things."

"I know. He has an aggressive streak. I wouldn't put it past him to throw a punch at me if I try to go back."

"No, that's not what I mean. He's more likely to do himself an injury than someone else." Dad is a man of few words, but they are usually powerful. He has spent all his life managing manual labourers on building-sites, and as they say in East London what he doesn't know about how people tick would fit on the back of a postage stamp. A feeling of dread settled in my stomach.

"Have you got a phone number for the hostel?" Dad asked. "You want to call that Steve and just fill him in." His suggestion brooked no disagreement.

I called from the telephone in the hall, my hands shaking. "Is Steve there?" I asked when the phone was answered.

"No, he's gone out. Police station."

I couldn't identify the voice. "Is there someone else in charge?"

"Me, mate."

Where could I start? "It's just that I have reason to believe that Tommy, one of your –"

"That's why Steve's gone out. Police called about Tommy earlier this evening."

I wanted to throw up. "No!"

"'Fraid so, mate." There was a pause, then he asked, "How did you know him, anyway?"

I could hear in his tone that he realised he shouldn't have divulged anything to a complete stranger. He was trying to find out how much of a problem this might be.

"I do some work at the hostel, with –"

"You're not the *drama* bloke, are you?" The scathing tone and the lengthened syllables said it all.

"Yes, I –"

"Steve's been trying to get hold of you. Bit of trouble after you left."

I actually slid to the floor, my sweatshirt riding up the wall behind me.

"What kind of trouble?"

"He'd probably prefer to discuss it with you himself." Suddenly formal.

"Will he be back tonight?"

"Not sure, mate, depends how long he's tied up with the police, I suppose. Morning would be time enough, prob'ly."

"I'll be over first thing. What time does he get in?"

"About six thirty."

"OK, thanks very much." I hung up, stretching my arm up to replace the handset in the cradle. I sat there for a while with my head in my hands, and my parents, bless them, didn't come out of the kitchen. I forced myself to stand up and go in to the kitchen to tell them the news.

"He might have just got into a fight, or something," said Dad, contradicting completely his previous comment. He handed me a shot of brandy and I gulped it down.

"He used the past tense." I said.

"Form of speech."

"There's no point in worrying until you know all the facts," said Mum, busily folding away her ironing-board and making piles out of the clothes.

"I said I'd go over there first thing."

"The bed in your room has just been aired," said Mum. "I do it every so often. Off you go to bed now, and try to get some sleep. Nothing seems so bad in the morning."

She gave me a peck on the cheek, something she hasn't done since I went to secondary school.

"G'night, son," said Dad morosely. He doesn't do false optimism very well. I inherited my acting ability from Mum.

I didn't sleep much. What could I have done differently? Should I have told Steve straight away about the disastrous end to the workshop? But Zoe had seemed fine, and she was my main concern. After all, she was the one who had bared her soul. Tommy was just being his usual aggressive self when he asked me to leave. I had no reason to think he would do anything. But that was exactly it. I didn't know anything about this stuff, and I was dabbling in areas where I had no business to be. I left the curtains open in the bedroom which was called mine, but where I had only slept twice before. It felt like a guest room, and I felt like a guest. I should be at home with Caroline. That was another thing to worry about. Why wasn't Caroline at home? I keep wondering if she is seeing someone else. Too many late nights working, lately, and too many moments when she seems to be somewhere else when I'm talking to her. In a perverse way, maybe it was good that I hadn't left a message to say where I was. She could stew for a change. I spent the night alternating between guilt and anger about what might have happened to Tommy and anger and guilt about what Caroline might be up to.

Matthew

Liz is sitting on the sofa in the dark when I get in, and I actually yell out loud with fright when she stands up. I had been tiptoeing past the living-room door, and noticed the stereo amplifier light on, so I had gone in to switch it off. Of course I am defensive. If you are already feeling guilty, have had too much red wine, and then you get a fright like that, it is normal to react the way I do.

"What the hell are you doing sitting there in the

dark?" I barely manage to whisper rather than shout again. My heart is pounding.

"Waiting for you."

She sounds tearful, not angry, as I would have expected. Attack is the best form of defence. I decide to hold the moral high ground.

"Why on earth are you sitting up at this time waiting for me?" I ask as if it is perfectly normal for me to come home at this time.

"I got fired today."

"Oh, my God." All the righteous indignation drains away like acid from a pierced battery. I sit down beside her and hug her hard. "Fired?"

"Well, 'made redundant', but it amounts to the same thing," she sobs against my chest. She's so small.

"But why, who's going to do your job?" How could the dynamo of the finance function be made redundant? Liz holds the whole thing together.

"Phil Wilson. They brought him back from the States. He's been hanging around in the wings for a few weeks now. I should have seen it coming."

"But why can't you go back to your old job? The one you did before you stepped up?"

"It's all been re-organised. My old job no longer exists." Her bitterness makes her sound like someone else. Someone hard and cynical.

"When do you finish?"

"Now. I'm on garden leave. I can't believe it. They

treated me like a criminal. I had to clear my office and leave straight away. I couldn't get you on the phone. They let me take the car, just to get my stuff home, but I have to give it back by the end of the week. What will we do without a car?"

We are sitting down now, my arms around her, still in darkness.

"I'm so sorry you couldn't get hold of me." I can't bring myself to make excuses, to tell lies.

"I know you switch your phone off at the Law Centre, but I thought I'd get you at about eight, so I tried loads of times, and then I just gave up. Mum came around to help with bedtime, but I sent her home afterwards. I couldn't cope with her kind of sympathy."

"Yes, I can imagine."

"What are we going to do?" She looks at me and I can see the glint of tears in the reflected light from the hall. I can see that she knows she is losing me, too.

"What do you want to do?" I ask her.

"Try again," she says.

"Yes, we've got to try again."

"I had a call from a headhunter last week, about a big job in Citibank, but I told them I was happy where I was. I could ring them."

"Don't rush into anything," I say. "Garden leave is supposed to mean that you take a rest, isn't it?"

"Yes, but I can't just sit at home, Matt. I would go completely mad."

She hasn't called me Matt for years. Since I became Daddy half the time, and Matthew the other half, usually when I am in trouble for something done or not done around the house.

"The boys would love it if you were around a bit more."

"I know." She blows her nose.

"Even if it ended up just being for the summer, while you're looking for something else."

"Yes, I was thinking that."

"You could pick up with some of the people you met at NCT that you haven't seen since you went back to work."

"Mmm."

"That prospect not filling you with joy?" I ask, trying to be a bit lighthearted.

"Not really. The conversations then were about sore nipples and terry nappies. Now it will probably be the pros and cons of the Montessori method of nursery teaching."

"Let's go to bed. I forgot to tell Diana I would be in late tomorrow, because of the school visit. I'll just call her first thing and take the whole day off tomorrow. We could go for lunch somewhere and talk about things."

"That would be nice," she says, and I stand up and pull her to her feet. We haven't done that for ages either. It used to be a nightly ritual. I follow her upstairs, carrying the milk supplies for the early morning wake-up. We go through the bathroom routine in silence, neither of us wanting to say the words that might shatter the delicate protective shell of illusion we have painted around ourselves.

At the weekend, we play a game at bath-time when the boys climb out of the water, on to our knees, and curl up in a ball. We wrap them in layers of towels so that every inch of them is covered, and they pretend to be baby dinosaurs hatching out of their eggs. They make little squeaking noises, and Liz and I pretend we can't hear anything, until finally they pop out, and we each feign huge surprise that we have just hatched the most handsome baby dinosaur in the world. Their clean smiling faces, framed by otter wet hair, never fail to move me. Their innocence and simple glee seems unbounded. Whatever mischief follows, as they run around refusing to put on their pyjamas, never takes away the warm feeling of having one of them on my lap, damply curled up, wriggling and waiting for the right moment to break out of the egg and surprise me.

When we get into bed, I want to wrap Liz in protective layers, so that she can recover, and emerge restored. I hold her close with my arms crossed around her chest, and she snuggles right up against my stomach. I can feel the vibrations of her sobbing, and hear the catch in her breath as she tries to hide it. I reach up and touch her cheek, and it is warm and wet. I stroke her hair until she mutters, "You know I hate that," trying to soften it with a laugh, and I just say "Sorry".

Sorry for everything. For forgetting what a beautiful woman she is, for forgetting that she is my best friend, the mother of my kids, the touchstone of our family.

CHAPTER 17

Caroline

I managed about two hours of sleep, I think, and at six o'clock I got out of bed and made a pot of coffee and some toast. I tried his mobile again, just so he would know that I was trying, and left another message. *"It's just after six in the morning. Ring me and let me know that you're OK. I love you."*

The phone rang while I was in the shower. I jumped out and ran down the hall, showering the carpet with soapy drips like a manic sheepdog.

"'Hello, ouch!" I said, grabbing the receiver and stubbing my toe on the leg of the sofa at the same time.

"It's me, hi. I'm fine. Sorry I didn't ring last night."

"Hi," I said. My little toe was throbbing and swelling up in front of my eyes as I perched on the arm of the couch and squinted at it.

"Are you OK?" Matt asked.

"Yes, sorry, I just stubbed my toe when I answered the phone. Listen, I was worried about you." I wasn't going to humiliate myself by asking where he slept last night. I looked up at the clock. 6.40.

"I stayed at Mum and Dad's last night."

"Original." For a second I wasn't sure if I'd said it out loud.

"I couldn't get hold of you. I went to see Nan, and then it got late . . ."

"Matt, I'll see you tonight, OK? I was really worried about you. We must talk properly tonight." I heard the voice I used to rehearse into my tape recorder as a teenager, when I was practising how to talk like a lawyer. I hung up.

For an actor, he could have come up with something a little bit more believable than visiting his dead nan and staying at his mum and dad's. The last time he saw them was at Christmas, and only then after I had nagged him for three days. At least I knew he was OK. We could have a proper argument about it all tonight, and hopefully clear the air. I got back into the shower, and stayed under it until all the goose-pimples disappeared, and I was starting to get warm again. I felt strange getting ready for work without Matt around. I missed his laconic summary of the morning news, which I usually get while I'm putting on my make-up in the bedroom. When I finished my cornflakes, I actually went back into the bedroom to kiss him good-bye. The emptiness was bigger than just the empty bed. He would be having a slap-up breakfast at his mum's. She would raid the pantry and use up a week's supply of beans and eggs to make a "bit of a fry-up" to build him up for his day. I'm surprised that he wasn't obese when he was a teenager. His mum's idea of motherhood is to stave off all potential disasters with a stomach full of food.

It was all very well riding my personal wave of righteous indignation, but I wasn't exactly being an angel myself. Maybe there is something fundamentally wrong with our relationship, if we are both going out to look for something else. An adult conversation is what we need. I could cook a nice dinner. We could have a bottle of wine, and sort it all out in a civilised fashion. If it turns out that the time is right for both of us to move on, there is no reason why we can't stay friends, keep in touch . . .

I stopped in the middle of the footpath, the realisation hitting me like a punch in the solar plexus and nearly winding me. I was actually rehearsing my leaving-Matt speech in my head. How did I get here? Was this it? When I walked to the tube station the next day, would I be single? Would I be able to send a text message to Matthew to invite him around for a Saturday morning tangle in the sheets? What a scary but thrilling thought!

I nearly threw up on the pavement. I banished the corn-flakes back to their rightful place on the passage through the underworld, and tinkled the coins in my jacket pocket through my fingers. I kept repeating to myself, "I can do this. I am in control of the situation. I could be single in twelve hours' time, free to do whatever I want." It just needed some words. Words that I would send from my vibrating vocal chords, to float through the air, land on Matt's eardrums, resonate, and come to rest. His brain would translate the vibrations into meaning, and draft the responses. His envoys would reply, traversing the same route through the air, landing, resting. The floating and resonating and resting of those words would tear our little world apart. Matt's flat wouldn't be my home any more. My recorded voice would disappear off the answering machine. My mother would have to put a new entry in her address book, and memorise a new postcode to send the snippets of news from the *Connaught Tribune*. In front of the newspaper stand, I fumbled with the change in my pocket. I was ten pence short. The man didn't even notice how upset I was, and just kept on taking money, handing out newspapers, nodding to the people who said good morning. I stumbled down the steps into the tube station with my head reeling. 7:47. The first time ever I missed my 7:38 deadline. Where had the nine minutes gone? Had I stood on the pavement all that time? Had I walked more slowly than usual? Had I left home later? Was the sitting-room clock running slow? I had to have a paper to read. Like my fellow commuters, I bent down and picked up a copy of Metro from the stack by the ticket machines. For a free newspaper that is supposed to keep Londoners up to date with developments in transport, it has some surprisingly good editorial input.

"Homeless Suicide," read the headline. There was a fuzzy picture of a lanky-looking teenager in a denim jacket, with what looked like a tattoo on the side of his neck.

"Thomas Robert Smith, known as Tommy at the hostel in South East London where he has been staying, was seen loitering on London Bridge for some time. A witness saw him climb onto the wall and jump into the river," the article started. Poor kid. The witness called the police and the ambulance straight away, but they were too late. He couldn't swim. "Rescuers finally found his body just before ten o'clock last night, half a mile downstream, where it had been washed onto one of the river beaches as the tide went out."

How bad must his life have been, to take that step? No friends to confide in, no family to go to, not one single person in the world to give him some hope, and tell him that life could get better? I felt tears pricking the back of my eyes. Then I noticed a quote from the hostel manager, and recognised his name. It was Steve Hartigan.

"Tommy had been in institutional care for most of his

teenage years, following the death of his mother. He was a very disturbed young man. The staff and residents at the hostel are devastated."

I looked up. One more stop to go. I folded the paper and stuck it into my briefcase.

Alison greeted me with a little stack of telephone-message slips. "Matt's called three times already," she said. "Sounded a bit funny, I thought."

"Mmmn," I said. I didn't really want to talk to him while I was at work. I had to rehearse the script a bit more for later.

"Are you two OK?" Alison asked, looking closely at my face.

I had dropped my eyeliner down the back of the radiator in the bedroom and didn't have time to scrabble around looking for it, so my eyes must have looked even more naked and sleep-deprived than they should.

"We're grand, yes, of course," I muttered, and made a quick detour to the coffee machine. The last thing I needed was a professional interrogation by Alison. Without any effort at all, she could extract the most deadly secret from the most secretive person in the world. My mobile vibrated with a message as soon as I switched it on. Matt: *Call me. Need 2 talk.* I managed a single left-handed thumb reply while my coffee spurted into the cup from the machine: *Yes. Home rly 2nite. XX C.*

Then I started replaying the night before. Even with

my glasses on, I know Matthew fancied me. I let him lead me across the road when we went to get a taxi. I've never let anyone do that before. I am the doer, the supporter, the decision-maker. Matt would never lead me across the road. He would think that I'd hate it. He would *know* that I'd hate it. Why did I not mind Matthew doing it? Novelty value? Chivalry? The physical contact? We haven't had much of that. Brief, polite kisses. Fantasy lovemaking, handholding, and Saturday morning foreplay don't count. But soon it won't be fantasy, I thought. I was blushing when I walked past Alison's desk. I sat down in my office, and the images of tall, broad, naked Matthew faded in the face of the piles of paper. I was feeling very virtuous. The thought of illicit sex is really exciting, but I owe more to Matt. I owe him the honest conversation we're going to have tonight, and a clean break so that I can start again. I wonder where I'll end up living? Maybe somewhere nearer to Matthew. It would be a bit easier to see each other after work. I must ask him where the nice areas are down his way, to rent. Maybe six months, just to see how things work out, then who knows . . . He's never mentioned whether he lives in a house or a flat. I presume he owns it, wherever it is. I wonder if he has a garden. That's one thing I miss in Matt's place. A communal garden isn't the same, when you want to sunbathe with the Sunday papers, and potter around in your flip-flops. Alison came in and found me staring into space. She stood there, leaning casually against the door-frame, and not even pretending to do anything else but interrogate me.

"What?" I said, defensively.

"Nothing," she said. "Matt sounded a bit upset earlier on, that's all, so I wondered if he was all right now."

"I haven't spoken to him. I have a lot to do. I'll talk to him tonight. I want to try and get away by six if I can." I shuffled papers around, tapped the space bar on my computer to get my list of e-mails up, and tried to look preoccupied and uninterruptible.

"He sounded really upset," she repeated.

I should have listened to her. She has an instinct about these things. But she didn't know the full story, I told myself. She didn't know that Matt had stayed out all night and not bothered to tell me where he was. And even before all this, he's been gradually changing, getting preoccupied and more distant, and less interested in things.

'What things?' I asked myself.

'Well, in us, in me,' I answered, 'in asking me about work, and seeing friends together, and stuff like that.'

"Do you think he's worried about being out of work?" I asked.

'That's his choice, isn't it?' came the answer. 'He could do loads of different jobs. He just chooses not to. It's really frustrating. We can't plan holidays or anything – one, because we don't have enough money – and two, because he says he has to be available for auditions. When was the last time he had an audition?'

'But have you told him you're getting frustrated with paying all the bills?' I persisted.

'No, because he'd be hurt, and even more frustrated that he can't get work.'

'And you don't want to hurt him?'

"No, of course I don't want to hurt him, I love him!" I said aloud.

"So why are you thinking of leaving him?" asked Alison.

I started. Alison was still there. Looking at me expectantly. So much for internal dialogue.

"What makes you think I'm leaving him?" I asked, failing completely to summon the required sarcasm, incredulity or outrage.

"Classic signs," she said.

"Such as?"

"You obviously didn't sleep a wink last night, and neither did he, by the sound of his voice."

"So?"

"He's called three times this morning, and said he couldn't get you on your mobile. You always have your mobile switched on, so you obviously don't want to talk to him."

"And?"

"You don't want to talk to him because you're planning to dump him tonight, and you don't want to spoil the effect by talking to him now."

Silence from me.

"And you have the newspaper open on the 'flats to let' page. More coffee?" She turned and walked down the corridor. If I didn't really like Alison, I would hate her.

Matt

I got to the hostel and found Steve in his office. He looked awful. His dark skin was dry and dull and seemed stretched across his high cheekbones. His eyes were tired. Even his dreadlocks looked lifeless. He stood up without saying a word and made me an instant coffee from the kettle beside his desk.

"Milk's not here yet, so it's black or black."

"That's fine." I didn't know what to say. I didn't want to hear the words.

"He jumped off London Bridge." Deadpan.

I put my head in my hands, and stared at the broken laminate on the corner of Steve's desk.

"If I'd got hold of you yesterday afternoon I was going to ask 'What the fuck are you playing at?' I won't say it now."

I just nodded, and when I looked up it was the pain in Steve's face that struck me most. "I thought we were getting through to him. Just starting to."

"I thought so too." I said. "I'm sorry I didn't tell you what happened at the workshop. I was embarrassed. Stupid."

"Listen, mate, last night, when they found him, and I had to identify the body, I was really angry. Mostly I was angry with you, because you must have touched a chord in that boy, and I thought you were responsible."

"I feel responsible."

"No, listen, then I thought about it. First, if you had told me about the workshop, I don't know what I would have done differently. Second, Tommy was on a short fuse. It was probably just a matter of time. With some of these kids you can make a difference, and with others, it's all mapped out, and you can't change a damn thing, no matter what you do."

"Sorry."

"The others were asking if you were coming back next week."

"I didn't think they'd want me. Even less so, now . . ."

"They were really annoyed with Tommy for kicking you out, but they were scared of him too, so they didn't say anything. They like the workshops. Don't let them down."

"I'll have to be careful what I do with them. Maybe I'll stick to the safe stuff, and do mock interviews. Steer clear of the more personal things."

"Your call, mate, but they've really latched on to this, and you owe it to them. Too many people in their lives have let them down already."

"Is there going to be a funeral for Tommy?"

"Not sure. We have to try and track down next of kin. Police are coming in at seven to see me."

"How's Zoe handling it?"

"She's OK, considering. She was the last one to see him, before he went off."

"May I talk to her?"

"Of course. Just remember what I said before. You need to draw a line in the sand with these kids. If you cross it, they are the ones who end up getting hurt, when you move on to something else."

I nodded. I had to wait an hour for Zoe to appear downstairs. She came into the TV room, tying her hair into a pony-tail, her bag already over her shoulder. She was pale and her eyes were red-rimmed, but she managed a watery smile.

"Coffee?" I offered.

"Out?"

"Starbucks?"

She smiled properly. We went down the steps together, and turned towards the high street.

"Not much sleep last night?" I asked, not sure how to broach the subject.

"No. You neither, by the look of you," she said, looking sideways at me as we walked along.

"Sorry again about the workshop."

"It wasn't that. Well, maybe partly. Tommy got

reminded about stuff that he didn't want to remember."

"Did he talk to you about it?"

"A bit."

I ordered the coffee and two doughnuts, and we sat on the stools by the window.

"What did he say?"

"His dad knocked his mum about, too."

"Is that why he went into a home?"

"The dad went to prison."

"For abusing the mother?"

"For killing her."

I gulped a mouthful of coffee and scalded my throat and tongue. I couldn't speak.

"He feels . . . he felt guilty that he didn't protect his mum."

"How old was he when it happened?"

"Nine."

"Oh God."

"I know. That's what I said. I was so lucky."

"Lucky?" I said incredulously.

"Well, I've still got a Mum, haven't I? She might leave the scumbag one day, and I could go back. I don't blame her. She doesn't have a lot of choices. She can't work. She's one of those women who has to have a man to look after her. Even if he treats her like shit. Low self-esteem, they call it."

Out of the mouth of babes, I thought. What do you say to that?

333

"We did it in psychology at school."

What was a girl who had studied psychology at 'A' level doing in a hostel for homeless kids? I found myself thinking.

"Do you know where I went last night?" I asked, picking up doughnut crumbs on the end of my index finger.

"No, where?"

"To see my nan."

Her face fell. She nibbled a fingernail, but didn't say anything.

"Do you know what the worst thing about it was?"

"No. Is she a bit senile? Did she not recognise you?" Her anxious face said it all.

I shook my head. "Worse than that. She died a few years ago. I went and stood outside her house, because I wanted to talk to her, and I thought I'd find something of her there. Her front garden was all covered in cement. She would have hated that. She always had flowers in her front garden."

"So did mine."

"But you've still got your grandmother."

"Maybe."

"Would you go to see her if I came with you?" I asked, the idea suddenly striking me.

She looked at me, and I felt like Father Christmas. Her smile is so beautiful. I felt a profound need to stop her being hurt any more.

"When can we go?"

"Tomorrow?" I suggested, aware that I had to talk to Caroline. We had some major sorting out to do, and the sooner the better.

"Today? Have you got anything on today? You could be back by tonight. It's only four hours on the train."

I looked at my watch. Nine o'clock. By the time we got to King's Cross, and got the train, it would be a least ten. There by two, find the granny, back on a train by four or five. I could do it. I would leave a message for Caroline that I would be back late.

"Let's do it!" I said, gulping down the last of the luke-warm coffee. I watched Zoe complete her finger-licking ritual. She looked up at me over the rim of the cup, licking her lips tinged with chocolate powder, and I had two simultaneous thoughts. How could anyone hurt this girl, and how attractive she was – I forced myself to revise that thought to how attractive she will be when she grows up . . .

We walked quickly back to the hostel, and Zoe went upstairs to pack her rucksack. I called in to Steve's office, but the police were in there, so I scribbled a post-it note and stuck it to his office door so he would find it on the way out: *Gone to Newcastle with Zoe. See you next week. Matthew.*

They've never got to calling me Matt, and it seems ridiculous to suggest it now, when I originally introduced myself as Matthew to try and sound more grown-up and credible. I still had something to prove on that front, and maybe my mission to Newcastle would be the beginning of that process. Zoe was waiting at the bottom of the stairs when I came down the corridor, and she grinned at me elfishly.

"Thanks, Matthew," she said.

"You can thank me when we're drinking a cup of tea in your nan's front room after she welcomes you with open arms," I said, grinning. "I checked the train times and if we're quick we can catch one at 10:15 and be in Newcastle by 2:30."

"Wicked."

"Do you still say wicked? I thought that was a bit passé these days."

"No, Grandad, we still say it." She linked arms with me as we strode off to the underground station and the elation I felt was sublime.

Matthew

The phone beeps in my coat pocket while we are having breakfast with the boys. They are surprisingly subdued. Maybe they can sense the mood. Liz looks pale and her eyes are red-rimmed, but she is putting on a brave face. She makes the boys' sandwiches for nursery, and when her friend Alice comes at eight thirty to pick them up, they are scrubbed and ready to go.

She hugs each of them, saying, as she does every morning, "See you later, I love you." Ben says it back now, and sometimes embellishes it with a phrase from his *Nutbrown Hare* book: "I love you all the way to the moon and back."

I check the message while everyone is piling into Alice's car: *Might need to change Sat. Will call u. XXC*

That's a relief. I can't see her any more, but how am I going to tell her? Liz comes back and is surprised that I seem to have turned into a text junkie when I am such a self-professed Luddite about technology.

"I didn't think you could do texting," she says, touching me on the elbow as she goes past me. "Fresh coffee?"

"That would be nice," I mutter, quickly dashing off a reply: *Me 2 c.u. M.* Not bad for a novice. I am particularly proud of the 2. It took me a long time to work out how to do numbers.

"Diana?" Liz asks as I come back into the kitchen.

"No, I must call her now." I get through to her voice-mail and leave a message. There is nothing pressing happening at work. Diana will be delighted at the chance to catch up on her archiving.

"Who, then?"

"What?"

"Who's persuaded you to move into the twenty-first century?"

"Oh, just one of the associates at work, you haven't met her. She's obsessed with texting. Just a quick query."

I am such a lousy liar. Liz knows. I know that she knows. She's wondering if I'm going to do something about it. I am, I tell myself. It's just a matter of when.

We sit and look out at the garden. It looks a bit wild.

"I suppose I could actually do some gardening," she says, with a tiny, brave laugh that echoes slightly in the quiet kitchen.

"We haven't been alone together in this house for almost four years," I say, feeling distinctly strange.

"That's true. Whenever we escape from the children, we escape from the house as well. It's quite nice, really, isn't it?"

We sit in the conservatory, sipping our coffee in a totally companionable silence for about twenty minutes. If thoughts had a soundtrack, the cacophony would be deafening. But the only sound is a scolding blackbird in the garden. The ginger tomcat from next door is on the prowl in the damp undergrowth. It would hate if Liz cut down the jungle camouflage in a sudden gardening frenzy. The bird casualty rate would plummet.

How could I engage in such trivial observations? I berate myself. I have some decisions to make. At this moment in time, even if I wanted to, I couldn't leave Liz and the boys. But I don't want to. The corollary is very clear. I've got to finish with Caroline, before I get myself into deeper water. I haven't actually done anything yet.

I haven't been unfaithful. I can save the situation. It has almost become a mantra: 'I haven't done anything. I haven't been unfaithful.'

"By whose standards?" my conscience yells from the sidelines.

The screeching blackbird is joined by his mate. The cat continues down the path, apparently indifferent to the dive-bombing raids that have started above his head. The noise level outside goes up a notch.

"There's something going on down there." Liz puts her mug on the windowsill and slips on her flip-flops, unlocking the back door. I watch her moving quietly down the path. The cat turns its head once, and looks at her balefully with narrow yellow eyes, then continues on its way. The flapping and squawking increases in intensity. I watch Liz bending down, and cupping her hands. She stands up slowly, and looks around as if she is in a daze, searching for something in the bushes. The birds retreat to the lowest branch of the apple-tree, where they hop up and down agitatedly, directing their vitriole at Liz now that the cat has slunk home through a gap in the fence. She stands there for a minute or two, without looking in my direction. I don't want to add to the birds' distress by joining her. She must have found a fledgling that has fallen from its nest. Eventually, she bends down again, and puts the barely visible brown bundle under the lilac tree. She has tears in her eyes when she comes back.

"Poor little thing. It hasn't even got proper wing feathers, just fluffy little stumps. It hasn't got a chance. I couldn't see a nest anywhere."

"The mum and dad are doing a good job of protecting it," I say, knowing I can't console her.

"The cat will kill it," she says matter of factly, and then in the voice she uses to explain things to Ben, "It's nature's way, I suppose."

"When I was a kid, I found a baby crow in the pile of grass cuttings that masqueraded as a compost heap at the end of the garden," I said.

"What did you do?"

"I tried to teach it to fly. Believe it or not, I sat it on the bristles of a broom, and held the broom as high as I could, and tried to get it to jump off and fly."

"What happened?"

"I called him Chris. The parents were just like those blackbirds. They went crazy, cawing and flying all over the place, and sitting in the pine-trees next door, watching everything. But crows are like pack animals, so there was a whole flock of them, like something out of a horror movie, swooping over the garden, calling to the baby."

"Did it call back?"

"Yes, and he seemed to understand. He had the most piercing ice-blue eyes. I was really struck by them."

"Did it survive?"

"No. My dad and I put him in a box of newspaper in

the shed, and fed him with bread and milk, because he wouldn't eat the worms we brought. But he died after about three days. I tried so many times to help him to fly, but he needed another bird to show him. I felt so futile."

"Did you bury him?"

"Yes, we had a whole funeral ritual, and a procession down the garden, and we buried him under a peony bush, so that when it flowered we would remember him."

"The boys probably won't even see this baby bird," she says sadly. "It won't survive the morning."

We sit there for another few minutes, watching for the return of the cat, but it must have sloped off to do something else. The cat knows as well as we do that the fledgling isn't going anywhere. I've often wondered why my father encouraged me to help the crow, when he must have known how pointless my efforts were. I recently read that you can kill hedgehogs by feeding them bread, because it swells in their stomachs. Maybe it's the same for birds. Did he know that, and choose not to tell me, so that I would feel I was doing all I could? Or even worse, maybe my omnipotent Daddy didn't know everything after all.

"We'd better get going," Liz taps me on the shoulder, and I blink to refocus my eyes. I have been staring at the tiny brown bundle of feathers under the lilac. Even at this distance I think I can see it shivering.

"Do you think we should put it in a nice warm box and try to feed it?" I ask, and she just shakes her head.

The school is quiet, because we have arrived after the children have gone to their classrooms. There are several couples hovering in the lobby outside the headmaster's office, waiting for the tour of the school and the little speech about the values they uphold and their commitment to equal opportunities. We have been to two other schools, and the formula seems to be the same for all of them. There is a school just down the road from us, which seems fine, but there is some kind of peer force that comes into play as your child celebrates their third birthday. It's just like the force that takes you over when you go to National Childbirth Trust antenatal classes, and find yourself with a group of similar people facing an unfamiliar situation. You talk to each other, share theories, listen to other friends' experiences, and lo and behold, find yourself doing what everyone else is doing, despite your deeply held conviction that you are somehow different from them. So now, instead of following the well-trodden path to the "Mamas and Papas" warehouse for three-wheeler pushchairs, we find ourselves on the primary-school trail, without quite knowing why. From the age of nine, I walked to the school around the corner from my house; so did Liz. So did most of our friends. But like all other three-and-a-half-year-old parents, we are intent on the quest for the Holy Grail of the perfect primary school, anywhere within a five-mile radius of our homes.

Suddenly I turn to Liz, who is reading a notice on the

board about an after-school Latin club. "Somehow I don't think that's dancing," she says, grimacing.

"Come on," I say, pulling her arm.

"Where are you going?" she asks, managing to look at her watch as I tug her sleeve.

"We'll be late for our appointment."

I stop and we huddle in a corner of the lobby. "I don't think we should send Ben to a school that's a twenty-minute drive away. Probably forty minutes at school-run time. It's madness, when there's a perfectly good school on our doorstep."

"But that's what I said to you months ago, and you insisted that it was important to find the best," she whispers back fiercely.

"I was wrong," I say, and we look up to see the headmaster and the other couples looking at us expectantly.

"We won't be joining the tour, thank you," I say. "Sorry for any inconvenience caused." I manage to sound like a retail manager apologising for the scaffolding covering the front of the shop. We scurry out into the drizzling rain, and Liz actually smiles at me, and unbelievably, pauses beside a puddle and jumps right into the middle of it. Muddy water splashes up her shins.

"What are you doing?"

"Splashing."

"Why?"

"I've always loved splashing in puddles," she says simply. I suppose even Superwoman must have some way of letting off steam, I think. I'm not tempted to join her, particularly when I see the headmaster escorting the group across the playground to look at the new school gym that cost a million pounds to build.

Caroline

Sitting at my desk, wading through a pile of contract revisions, I knew deep down that no matter how much I fantasised about being single the next day, it wasn't going to be a simple process. Even if I did summon the courage to tell Matt that it was all over, and found somewhere else to live, I would probably be sleeping on Alison's sofa on Saturday morning. Or moving all my stuff into some horrible rented basement flat.

I sent Matthew a quick text but, I couldn't call him with Miss Psychic pricking her ears outside the door. Having waited this long for Matthew, I wasn't going to rush it now. Before I went travelling and met Matt, I had a few short-term boyfriends at home. I remember lots of weekends of hanging around, waiting for them to ring me, or to call for me, or just to let me know if they were going to the pub after the rugby. I figured out fairly quickly that unless I suddenly developed a passion for a totally incomprehensible sport, I probably wouldn't see them before mid-afternoon on Sunday, after the post-match hangover had subsided. Maybe I should take a break, and try being on my own for a while. If Matthew is worth his salt, he'll wait, and if he doesn't want to wait, there are plenty more fish in the sea, as Daddy always used to say whenever I had another heartbreak. I managed to get myself into quite a positive frame of mind before I asked Alison to get me a cab to the meeting in Streatham to finalise the charity deal.

"Done," she said, checking her watch. "It will be here at quarter past."

"Thanks, you're a star," I said. I had just enough time to go to the loo and put on some eyeliner and fresh lipstick. I always keep a spare set of make-up in my drawer, for those emergency situations where you have to look your best. I came back and Alison just lifted her head to say, "It's downstairs."

I know she thinks I'm being horrible to Matt. Maybe she wouldn't let me sleep on her sofa, if I did the dirty on him. The meeting was at one of CityScope's hostels. Only when I told the cab driver the address did I realise it must be the one where that poor kid Tommy stayed. Steve would be devastated. He took his job so seriously, and he really cared about the homeless kids. I was just getting an insight into what it must be like to do a job that makes a real difference to people. I used to think that you had to be a hippy idealistic volunteer type, like I was in Malaysia, or a serious career person, like I'm supposed to be now. Maybe there's something in between.

"Steve, are you all right?" I asked him when he

opened the battered, peeling door of the hostel. He looked terrible.

"Not a good night," he said. "Did you hear the news?"

"Yes, I read it in the paper this morning. It's really sad," I said. I just touched him on the arm, and was fleetingly surprised at the hard muscles under the sleeve. What else should I say or do? He's a client. We don't know each other that well. I never know how to sympathise with people who have had a bereavement. Andy arrived, and the other lawyer turned up in a cab just then so Steve and I didn't get a chance to talk again. The guy getting out of the taxi was a thirty-something guy, wearing a grey turtleneck, Levi jeans and trendy slate-grey Nike trainers. I was a bit taken aback, and it must have shown in my face. You build up a mental picture of someone when you deal with them on the phone and by e-mail. Adrian was a real smoothie, and very bright. After our various conversations on the phone, ranging from his cat's flu to the meaning of life, maybe I should have guessed he would look "unconventional". We legal professionals don't usually engage in anything resembling a meaningful and human conversation while doing business. We stick to the safe legal terminology that obfuscates everything, so that we can argue later about what we really meant. Adrian shook my hand firmly and grinned at me. He was enjoying my surprise. My black pin-striped suit and flat Bally shoes suddenly felt all wrong, even with the chunky silver jewellery from Camden market that is my only rebellion against the corporate uniform. We all squeezed into Steve's office, and after an hour of fairly robust debate, resolved the two outstanding funding issues, which had been deal-breakers for CityScope. The coffee was dreadful. It reminded me of the Law Centre, and I think it might even have been in the same kind of mug. The community sector is fairly incestuous, it seems, even down to the black and yellow freebie mugs. Adrian works for another City law firm, but does pro bono work for a third of his billing time, and he loves it. He told me that his suit was hanging on the back of his office door for a meeting later in the day with a different client, and I felt a bit less stuffy. Despite the generally sombre note cast over things by Tommy's death, I was on a high when we all came out. Adrian leaned across and suggested in a whisper that we sneak around the corner to the local pub for a suitably low-key lunch. We stood outside Steve's office and said our good-byes. My shoe stuck to something on the floor. I found a luminous pink post-it note attached to the bottom of my heel. I unpeeled it and handed it to Steve. He glanced at it.

"Fuck it," he said under his breath, and when we all looked at him, he muttered an apology. "There's nothing worse than well-intentioned do-gooders," he said. "They can really mess things up."

"What is it, mate?" Andy asked, and Steve looked at him.

"I thought that drama guy had got the message, after Tommy. We talked this morning and he said he would just stick to the safe stuff – you know, interview skills, confidence-building exercises."

"So?"

"He's only gone off to Newcastle with Zoe to find her grandmother."

"Oh shit."

"Exactly."

"Is there anything we can do to help?" Adrian asked, sounding as bemused as I was.

"Not unless you can magic yourself up to Newcastle in the next five minutes."

"What's the problem?" I asked.

"We've got this volunteer who does drama workshops with the kids. They've been going quite well, but he's getting too involved. Tommy was at a workshop yesterday, before he . . . "

"Oh," I said.

"And we suspect that Zoe, who is seventeen, has a crush on this guy, and now she's managed to persuade him to take her to Newcastle to find a fictitious grandmother."

Andy interjected. "I thought you gave him the 'line in the sand' lecture?"

"I did. Twice. He's a nice guy, but clueless when it comes to this kind of stuff. These kids have learned to be resourceful, devious and sometimes downright manipulative. He hasn't figured that out yet. Zoe has got him wrapped around her little finger."

"What's the worst-case scenario?" Adrian asked.

"Who knows. I just hope he doesn't do anything stupid."

'Would the hostel be held responsible?' I asked.

"For what?" said Steve. "She's over the age of consent. He's an adult. It's not about where the buck stops, it's about people getting hurt."

I just stood there, wondering what has happened to me, while I've been chasing the golden career dream?

We had a very subdued lunch, Adrian and I, in a grotty pub on the corner of Streatham High Road. I had Shepherd's Pie, with lumpy lukewarm mashed potato on top and stringy mince, cubes of carrot and dark brown gravy underneath. I pushed it around on my plate a lot, and it wasn't just the taste of it that was making my stomach shrink.

"Are you OK?" Adrian asked. He was on his second pint and I was jealous of his ability to drink at lunchtime. I could seriously do with some alcohol, but I would be good for nothing all afternoon. For all his indifference during the process, Baxter was sure to pop in to my office this afternoon to ask how the meeting went. I needed to have my wits about me.

"Not really," I said. "I have some personal stuff going on that isn't very nice. Or won't be nice, put it like that."

"Family, or . . .?"

"Boyfriend. I think I'm going to finish with him tonight." Why was I telling an almost complete stranger something that I wouldn't even admit to Alison this morning?

"Irreconcilable differences?"

"If drifting apart, not really knowing each other any more and fancying someone else fall into that definition, then yes," I said.

"Oh, there's someone else."

"Isn't there always?" I asked. "Isn't someone else the main catalyst, usually? Otherwise, wouldn't we all just settle for the familiar humdrum existence we have with someone who knows what make us tick, whose bad habits we've got used to, whose favourite things are mostly the same as ours?"

"No. I don't think so. Why were you attracted to him in the first place?"

"He's funny, and sincere, and good-looking, and very good in –"

"Well, yes, obviously,' he said, and he actually blushed. Nice to know I'm not the only adult in the world who still does.

"And has any of that changed?"

"He's not so funny any more, because he's a bit stressed about not having any work, so he –"

"What does he do?"

"He's an actor. Well, he trained as an actor. He hasn't

actually, to my knowledge, ever been paid for it."

"Ahh, an artistic, creative, right-brain type of person, to complement your logical, thorough, organised left brain."

"No way, not me," I protested. Is that what he thought of me? Shit, is that what I'm really like?

"Maybe that's only you at work, but that's what I see," he said. "Glass of wine?"

"Oh, go on then. I'll have a small one," I said, just to prove that I could let my right brain have a say at work every so often. While Adrian was standing at the bar, I racked my brain for the other reasons why I wanted to dump Matt. If only he had some work, he probably wouldn't be so moody, and then . . .

"He's not very intellectual, either," I said, when Adrian came back.

"In what sense?"

"We don't ever have deep and meaningful conversations, you know, about stuff that really matters. Maybe he's a bit immature. He's younger than me."

"And you do have these conversations with the 'someone else'?"

I nodded.

"So what's wrong with 'someone else'? Ugly? Married? Too serious?"

"Why do you think there's something wrong with him?" I asked, intrigued, but also irritated that this guy was asking me the kind of questions my best friend should be asking.

"Well, if there wasn't, you wouldn't be so upset about leaving the boyfriend. No doubt you've done it before? Dumped a guy and moved on to pastures new?" Adrian took a gulp of his pint, and pointed at the untouched wine.

"Well, actually, now that you mention it, no, never like this," I said. "Do you think that's part of my problem?" I took a sip.

"It might be. I found the first one difficult too, but it's one of those things you kind of have to experience, at one time or another in your life."

He saw my face change.

"Yes, I am," he said, putting on a campy voice.

Now it was my turn to blush. "Doesn't make any difference," I said, feeling like I had to say something.

"Anyway, back to the main point. What's wrong with number two?"

"Matthew's great. He's good-looking too, but in a scatty kind of way, and I love his hands, and we have great conversations. He can make me laugh, and he makes me think, and –"

"He doesn't do drama workshops, does he?" Adrian nodded back in the direction of the hostel.

I laughed. "No, he's a lawyer too. I met him through work."

"I see." He laughed. "So, what's wrong with him?"

"Nothing, really. I haven't – you know . . . "

"You haven't? And you're thinking of leaving the other guy, what's his name . . .?"

"Matt."

"You're seriously thinking of dumping Matt for someone you haven't . . ."

"You're not suggesting I should?"

"I know, I'm a bit of a tart when it comes to that." He laughed out loud and stood up. "I'm really sorry, but I have to go. Got to put on the threads for the next meeting, and review the papers. Well, it's been a pleasure working with you on this deal, I hope our paths cross again soon." He put out his hand to shake mine. I couldn't believe he was going to leave me in this state.

"Do you want to share a cab?" I suggested desperately.

"Sure, where are you going?"

"Threadneedle Street."

"Close. I'll drop you. Come on, I'm cutting it fine as it is."

I grabbed my briefcase and followed him. Streatham is not exactly humming with black cabs, but one appeared just as we were coming out of the pub.

"Two guys named Matthew, eh?" said Adrian, as I sat beside him and the cab roared off.

"Yes, it's kind of strange," I said, and didn't feel inclined to say anything else. The intimacy had been shattered, and I was already kicking myself for telling him as much as I had.

"They don't know each other, do they?"

"No, that would be a nightmare!"

He laughed. "I managed to have two relationships once, but it all ended in disaster. I dumped one and went rushing around to the other guy's flat, and found him with someone else."

"So you were left stranded?"

"It was all for the best. Both of them were a waste of space. I sometimes think I'm just meant to be on my own."

"I was wondering about that," I said, staring out the window as we were passing the gory pink paint of the Elephant and Castle shopping centre. A 176 bus cut across the lane and the taxi-driver leaned on his horn and swore loudly as only London cabbies can do. We swept around the roundabout, and I was thrown across the seat. I should have learned by now not to cross my legs in the back of a cab. You need two feet on the floor on these occasions.

"Sorry." I pulled myself off Adrian's briefcase.

"Don't worry about it," he said. "'All will be well,' as my dear old mother used to say."

I didn't say anything. Sitting there in the cab, it seemed ridiculous to want to leave Matt just because he was a bit moody, and remote. I should try talking to him to find out what was wrong. We used to have those deep and meaningful conversations when we were travelling. We've just got into a bit of a rut, with me knackered after work, sitting watching telly all evening. I took out my phone.

"Sorry, I just need to send a message," I said.

"Why don't you speak to him?" Adrian was starting to get on my nerves now.

I dialled Matt's number. It rang and rang and clicked into voicemail. I didn't bother to leave a message. Adrian and I stuck to the safe topics of weather, holiday plans and London traffic, which took us nicely to London Bridge. In the spring sunshine, the yellowish stone of Southwark Cathedral glowed. As we were crossing the grey concrete bridge, the hustle and bustle above and the serene passage of the boats on the river below made me wonder why anyone would pick that place to die. We were both quiet. Adrian looked at me. "Sad, isn't it, that he had nothing to live for?"

"It's just so hard to imagine. I saw really poor people in Malaysia and India, with terrible diseases, and disfigurement, and some of them even lost their children, but they had this incredible will to live. They just didn't give in."

"But they have communities, families, and a whole philosophy of life that is completely different," he said.

"You're right. They say that loneliness is the saddest of human conditions. I suppose that poor kid didn't have anybody else to live for."

The cab pulled up outside my office building. "Thanks for the lift," I said, and just before I slammed the door, I added, "and the advice."

"No problem." Adrian nodded. "See you soon."

There was another message from Matt on my desk, to say he would be back late, and I kicked myself. I could hardly blame him for playing games when he must have thought I was doing exactly the same.

Matt

The journey would have been tedious without Zoe's constant chatter. For someone a generation younger than me she has very similar childhood memories of her nan. She sounded like the kind of woman who would take no nonsense, and maybe ultimately could convince Zoe that running away wasn't the answer. Maybe Zoe could stay there for a while, finish school and have some prospect of getting her life back together.

"I can't wait to see Nan," Zoe said. "Have you got any spare money? Could we buy her some Milk Tray? She loves chocolate. My mum used to always bring her a box of Milk Tray when we went to visit."

I rattled the coins in my pocket. "I think we could probably rise to that," I said, mimicking my own mother. We filled in a crossword-puzzle together, and as I sat opposite her, Zoe's intense expression of concentration filled me with a strange emotion I couldn't identify. She looked so vulnerable, with the graze on her temple healing, and her hair tucked behind her ears, her mouth puckered around the top of the pen she was avidly sucking.

"Five down is four letters beginning with f," she said, seemingly expecting me to come up with the answer without the clue.

"Any other letters, yet?" I said absent-mindedly, thinking how much I would miss her if she stayed behind with her nan. I might never see her again.

"No, not yet," she said, looking into my eyes.

She has a maturity well beyond her years, and an intelligence that will get her through, I figure. She's survived so far, without too many disasters.

"There's a great new bridge in Newcastle," I said to her. "I was reading about it in the Sunday papers a couple of weeks ago. It looks very futuristic. It moves to let river traffic through, but instead of opening up like Tower Bridge, it's sort of elliptical, and swings to one side."

"Sounds cool. I like Newcastle. I'll probably stay there," she said matter of factly, and I felt sad again. There really would be no reason for our paths to cross again.

Durham Cathedral loomed darkly on the horizon as we approached the town, or technically a city, I suppose, if it has a cathedral. I knew we only had a short way to go.

"What will you do if your nan isn't there?" I asked.

Dumb question. I'm supposed to be the reassuring adult in this relationship.

"Don't know," she shrugged. "Eat all the chocolates, I suppose," she laughed, and her face lit up, banishing the lines of concentration from her forehead. She is so beautiful. How could her mother let her be hurt?

"Do you want a quick coffee before we get there?" I asked before I thought. I didn't really want to stand up just then.

"No, compared to the nice coffees we've had together, I don't think instant train coffee does it for me, really," she said, looking directly at me again, and I glimpsed the moist tip of her tongue, just grazing her lips.

"OK," I said, gulping. "Let's just finish this, then, shall we?" I pulled the magazine across the grey formica-topped table, and swivelled the crossword to face me.

"It's fate," I said.

And before I filled in the letters, she said, "No, it's not fate, it's destiny."

She put her hand on top of mine.

"That's too many letters." I didn't dare look up. I pressed down on the pen so hard to stop my hand from shaking that I tore the paper.

"*We will shortly be arriving at Newcastle station, where this train terminates. Please ensure that you remove all your personal belongings when you leave the carriage. Thank you for travelling with GNER and we hope to welcome you on board again soon.*"

The metallic voice galvanised me into action. I stood up to get Zoe's bag down from the overhead luggage rack. As I stretched above her, she put her hand on my crotch, and that was the saving of me. It was such a juvenile and obvious gesture that it broke the spell. I decided to ignore it, like a good child psychologist ignoring unacceptable behaviour.

"Come on, girl, we've got a granny to find," I said in my best jolly-adult voice.

She looked crestfallen. Her eyeliner had smudged during the journey and the dark line under her eye made her look younger rather than older. My resolve was strengthened. Steve's words came back to me. I needed to draw a line in the sand. I owed it to her.

When we stepped out of the train onto the platform, I said, "Sit down here, Zoe," pointing to a metallic red bench. She sat and looked up at me expectantly. What was she expecting? A Price Charming kiss? A good telling-off from teacher?

"Listen, Zoe, we're friends, right?"

"Yes, of course," she said. "You're my best friend in the whole world."

"No, I don't think so. I'm a friend who's going to help you to get your life back together, so that you can have somewhere to live, with family, and a chance to meet other people your own age, and make a fresh start."

"You're the only one who understands me." She put her hand on my knee.

I lifted it and gently kissed it and put it back on the bench.

"No, Zoe, it probably feels like that right now, but there are lots of other people who care about you, and your mum is probably frantic by now, wondering if you're all right."

"She hasn't done much to show it," Zoe said sullenly, doing me a favour by looking very much like a thwarted teenager.

"How do you know what she's thinking or doing? She could have the whole Surrey Constabulary out combing the streets for you."

"It hasn't been on the news even once. When other girls go missing, they're on the news for weeks, and their parents do press conferences, and cry on the telly and beg for information. For me, nothing."

"Is that what you want?" I asked, suddenly appalled.

"I'd know that she loved me then. I could go home and tell her everything. But she doesn't care about me. She's probably just glad to get the scumbag to herself and not have to worry about me any more." Tears were streaming down her face now, silently. She didn't even sob. Shit, what was I supposed to do now?

"Let's take it a step at a time. First we'll find your nan. Then we'll see how you feel, and maybe your nan could ring home and tell your mum that you're OK, and take it from there?"

"I haven't got a nan." She said it so quietly I wasn't

sure if I'd heard correctly.

"What?"

"She's dead. Years ago, like yours."

I stood up. "But why are we here then?" I fought the swell of anger that washed over me.

"I wanted to get you to myself for a while. I thought . . ."

"You thought we'd have a shag on the train, did you, and then I'd take you home?"

Her eyes filled with tears. "I thought you liked me."

The smell of the train engines and the nearby bin combined with the churning in my stomach made me want to throw up.

"I do like you, Zoe, as a friend," I said, denying myself as well as her.

"So what are we going to do now?" she asked.

"I don't know what you're doing, but I'm calling Steve to tell him what's happened, and catching the first train back to London." I walked off towards the bank of public phones, because, yet again, my mobile had run out of charge. I refused to look back. I made the call to Steve, but he wasn't in his office. He was probably still tied up with the police investigation. Then I bought a burger and chips, checked the timetable, and crossed to another platform. I had been looking forward to seeing the famous bridge, but there was no point in sightseeing in Newcastle for the sake of it. I should be at home talking to Caroline, not off on some juvenile wild-goose chase. I was still really angry when Zoe sidled up to me.

"Can I come back with you?" she asked in that little-girl voice, and for the first time I wondered how much of the Zoe I thought I knew was just a dramatic persona.

"Whatever," I muttered, knowing that I sounded like a sulky teenager now. "Do you want some chips?" I shoved the bag towards her and she slipped her hand inside and stuffed in a mouthful.

Her mumbled "Sorry" was barely audible through the protruding chips.

"You used to have really good manners," I said, changing to schoolmaster mode.

She giggled. "Must be all the dodgy people I'm hanging around with, having a bad influence on me."

She was irresistible. I laughed too. "You are a nightmare," I said, and she hugged my arm.

"I am sorry, really," she said, and we sat waiting for half an hour, not talking, just watching the other passengers gathering on the platform with various combinations of rucksacks, suitcases and briefcases.

"You going to talk to your girlfriend tonight?" Zoe asked suddenly.

"How did you know that?"

"Well, you've got to sort everything out before next week, so you can tell us the end of the story."

I looked at her. "You really should study psychology, you know. You have a gift for it."

"Yeah, my mum always said I was a little minx. I think

that's what she meant." Zoe grinned. The train pulled in and there was a flurry of activity as everyone tried to line themselves up with the doors so they could nab the unreserved seats.

"We forgot to get you a return ticket," I said, suddenly panicking. We still had fifteen minutes before the train left, but all the seats would be gone.

"I'll run and get one, you find us two seats, and look out the window for me when I come back." I handed over her rucksack, which I had hitched on to my shoulder. She nodded, and climbed through the nearest train door.

"I'll work my way up to the front," she said, turning right into the first carriage. "See you in a minute. Can you get us a Crunchie or something?"

I walked to the ticket office, bought her a single to London, picked up two chocolate bars in the newsagent, and came straight back. No more than five or six minutes had passed. I started at the same carriage door and walked along the platform, looking for Zoe's face at the window. No sign of her. I climbed into the front carriage and walked back down through the train, thinking maybe she could only get a seat on the other side and was afraid to lose it by standing up to get my attention. No sign of her. I continued on down the train to the end, without seeing her. The doors beeped, and shut, while I stood there in a quandary. If Zoe wasn't on the train and I stayed on it, I would be abandoning her.

If she was on the train and I got off, she wouldn't have a ticket. The train started moving off before I could decide what to do. I did a search worthy of an Agatha Christie detective, even waiting outside toilet doors until the occupants emerged, and made my way to the front of the train again. No sign of her. Little minx was too nice a phrase for her, I thought, as I gritted my teeth and sat in a smoking carriage, which was the only place I could find a seat. I stared out the smoke-tinted window, clouding it with my breath, and feeling completely lost.

Matthew

There is a strange sense of optimism about us as we order lunch. "Let's have some wine," says Liz.

I must have looked surprised. "To celebrate new beginnings," she says, and I just nod. We order a bottle of the house red. I almost ask for white. Liz, like me, prefers red, but it is a salutary reminder that I have eaten out with Caroline a lot more often than with Liz lately.

"I'm delighted you didn't want to see that school," she says, glancing at the menu. "The after-school Latin club scared me. We're talking about primary school here, aren't we? What have we got ourselves into? Should we just put Ben's name down for Hartford Road and be done with it?"

"Maybe two, just to be on the safe side," I say, and she

laughs. "I'm supposed to be the risk averse one," she says.

"Not the way you were jumping in that puddle," I say, mock sternly, and she smiles a tight smile. "I am completely devastated about the job, you know. This giddiness is just a defence mechanism. I think I'm in shock."

"I know. Did they talk money yesterday?" I ask, as we fold our menus and sip our wine simultaneously.

"Yes, but it was all a blur. I couldn't take it in, apart from the fact that it's two years' salary and that all my share options will automatically vest. They're going to write to me."

"Two years' salary? As in four hundred grand?" I whisper, looking around furtively.

"Yes. So, as you can see, jumping in puddles was not completely unjustified." Liz lifts her glass and gives me the impish grin that I love. I haven't seen it for ages.

"Wow."

"Yes. So lunch is on me."

"You won't have to look for something straight away, then, will you?" I say.

"No, I was thinking of going on a world cruise for six months."

"By yourself?" I panic.

She looks at me. "No of course not, Matt. It was a joke." Her flat tone acknowledges the reaction of a guilty man. "I think I'll stay at home with the boys for the summer, while I'm looking for a job, and find a new nanny in the autumn. It will be my last chance to spend some time with Ben before he goes to school and starts to grow up on us."

"You've certainly got it all worked out." I mean it as a compliment, but it sounds resentful, and I know it.

"It didn't take much to work it out. I should have seen the signs."

"What signs?" Apart from being late home a couple of times, and those two text messages, there is no evidence of my affair with Caroline.

"Phil Wilson hanging around, and now that I think of it, a couple of meetings happening without me during the last week or so. The usual corporate bullshit."

The waiter arrives with our food, so I don't have to look at her. We seem to be getting double entendre down to a fine art. I am silent, and Liz keeps talking. She has some downloading to do, and sometimes it's best just to listen.

"The thing that really gets me, is the lack of honesty. If they had no intention of appointing me permanently to that board position, why didn't they make it really clear that I was in a custodial role, and tell me the reasons why I'm not ready for the FD job now? I could have taken that. I know I still have some gaps to fill. But I could have done it if they had given me a chance. I know I could."

"I think you could," I say, not having the first clue what a Finance Director would actually do, and whether or not Liz could do it.

"I know it's a publicly-quoted company and they can't afford to take risks, or piss off the shareholders, but. . . " She takes a mouthful of risotto. "This is nice," she says, offering me a forkful. I eat it. I used to hate when she did that. I would get really embarrassed thinking that everyone else was watching. I cut off a piece of my swordfish and put it on her plate.

"Thanks. But Phil Wilson has only a few more years' experience than me, and a lot of it was in the States. Well it's completely different over there. He'll have to forget his US GAAP and start refreshing his memory. We are a UK registered company after all. . ."

"US gap?" I ask, just to show I am listening.

"General accounting principles," she says, gulping her wine. "If I were a different kind of person I could claim sex discrimination," she adds, the alcohol hitting her almost visibly.

"Oh yes?"

"Well, it's obvious, isn't it? The rest of the board is male, even the non-Exec Directors. They probably couldn't handle a woman being up there in the hallowed heights of the ivory tower, challenging their male supremacy." She is really sounding like the idealistic old Liz. "I don't want to fight that battle. I want to just do a really good job and be acknowledged for it. If that means I get a promotion, then great. But I'm not getting on some feminist bandwagon. It's too humiliating." She finally pauses to eat, just as I am about to say her food will get cold.

My appetite is gone, and I push the baby potatoes around on the plate, half-listening to Liz. I couldn't tell you what she is saying. Suddenly she looks at her watch.

"My God, it's two thirty!" She manages to catch a waiter's eye while gulping down the last of her wine. "Alice is bringing the boys back at three. We've got to go." She smiles at the waiter. "Could we have the bill, please?"

I drink my wine and repress the urge to snatch the silver tray with the bill on it. Liz flourishes her credit card and the waiter whisks it off to the till, picking up on Liz's unspoken urgency.

"Thanks," I say. "That was nice."

"If a bit rushed at the end," says Liz, and stands up to go as soon as her card is returned. I follow her out of the restaurant with the sinking feeling that Superwoman is asserting herself again, after a very brief respite.

Matthew

"Daddy, why you home?" Jack asks when the boys come careering into the kitchen, having chased each other down the hall, bouncing off the walls on the way. Why isn't he surprised to see Liz, I wonder, mildly irritated.

"I'm having a day off work today," I say, grabbing him

around the waist and lifting him onto my knee.

"Why?" Ben is absent-mindedly peeling a banana.

"Excuse me, did you ask if you could have that?" Liz asks, hands on hips and her head on one side.

"May I havananaplease," sings Ben, continuing to stuff it into his mouth.

"Yes, since you asked so nicely," says Liz, smiling and tickling his tummy. She fills the kettle and asks the boys what they have been up to at nursery.

"Nuffink," is the predictable response on both fronts, despite the obvious evidence of their rucksacks bulging with works of finger-painting art and salt-dough sculpture.

"I made a boat," says Jack, pulling out a very interesting lollypop-stick construction which immediately falls apart. The glue they use at nursery is probably so politically correct and contaminant free that it hasn't actually got anything resembling the sap from a rubber tree or the gelatin from a horse's hoof anywhere in it, so nothing ever stays stuck for long.

"Never mind," says Liz, consoling him and reconstructing the boat with wood-glue from the kitchen drawer. Jack stops sobbing as soon as she takes over, and watches avidly while she sticks it all back together.

"There," she says. "We'll just put it up here on the windowsill to dry and then you can play with it.'

I have to distract him for a while so we go out to see if the baby bird is still under the lilac tree.

"That's nature's way," says Ben solemnly when we find nothing but three tiny feathers.

"Who told you that?"

"Mummy. She knows a lot of stuff."

"She certainly does." I'm glad that he's too young to hear the ironic tone of my voice.

Jack gets upset all over again, so I give him a hug and we go to look at the seed trays to see if the sunflowers have started germinating. There are some tiny leaves poking out, and I am more delighted than the boys. They'll be impressed only when the sunflowers bloom at a height of six feet, and bend in the wind. The boring weeding, thinning and watering tasks will be left exclusively to me, until the flowers are impressive enough to warrant an argument about whose watering-can is the biggest and therefore the most suitable to use, and whose turn it is to do the honours.

It is nice to potter around with them, pulling up the odd weed, and stopping to listen to the birds, while they slide down the plastic slide, and play hide and seek and generally work off excess boy energy.

Liz is chopping vegetables when we get back inside.

"Shall we all eat together?"

"Fine with me," I say, still full from lunch, but knowing how Liz prizes the "family meals" that are so rare during the week.

"I was thinking," she goes on, as I sip the lukewarm tea she has left on the kitchen table. "Now that I'll be around a lot more, the boys will see more of me during the week, and maybe we could make the Saturday-morning thing your boys together time?"

"That's a good idea," I say, relieved that Caroline has already thwarted the plans for Saturday morning. "I'll take them to Crystal Palace Park to see the dinosaur lake."

"That sounds fine. I've got a hair appointment at ten so you could go out then."

Why does she need to control everything? It really annoys me. If we've agreed in principle that I'm looking after the boys on Saturday morning, why does she have to go into the micro-management of my time?

I stand up. "Just going to catch Diana before she leaves the office, in case anything came up." I go upstairs to get my briefcase out, knowing that if I don't, Diana will tell me something to put in my diary or ask me for a client's phone number and I'll have to sprint upstairs anyway.

There have been no major developments, and our conversation is finished in three minutes flat. I have time to ring Caroline. I use the mobile just in case Liz picks up the extension downstairs.

"Hi, it's me," I say as soon as she answers.

"Hello," she says, sounding cautious.

"Can you talk?"

"Not really. I'm a bit tied up. Later?"

"I'll call you."

"Fine, talk to you later. Bye."

Just hearing her voice has my heart pounding. I have to do the deed quickly while I still have some moral resolve. I should do it face to face. But if I was face to face, I'm not sure if I'd be able to follow through, and tell her we have to finish.

I sit on the bed, and stay there for a while, until Liz calls upstairs, "Matt, are you ready?"

"Coming."

All my limbs feel heavy as I stand up from the edge of the bed. The boys are still full of beans at the table, and it is a challenge to get them to sit still long enough to put any food in their mouths. It doesn't help that Liz and I are picking around the edges of our plates, and not being very good role models. Finally we get Ben to ask for permission to leave the table, which is a slightly moot point by then, because he has managed to slide most of his body off the chair onto the floor, and is trying to tickle Jack's legs under the table, to Jack's extreme consternation. Despite my frustration, I can't help grinning. I look across the table at Liz and she has her hand up to her mouth, desperately trying to hide her laughter. Our eyes connect, dance together for a moment and then I see hers filling with tears. I duck under the table to pull Ben out. I can't bear to look at her sadness. My beautiful Liz. How could I hurt her?

Caroline

I worked until seven. There was no point in leaving the office any earlier, because I would just end up pacing the floor at home until Matt got back. Matthew rang and I pretended to be in a meeting. It was really clear to me now. I had to go one way or the other, and I had to talk to Matt first. Alison left before me.

She made a point of saying, "It's six thirty, Caroline, I'm off now." She's not a clock-watcher. She was reminding me of my promise to leave at six. I looked up at her. "He's going to be late back, so I don't need to rush."

"I know," she said, and the sympathy in her voice made me want to cry. I didn't look up. "See you tomorrow then."

"Yeah," was all that I could manage. I was sitting with my head in my hands, staring at my computer screen and not taking anything in when I heard a noise. Alison quietly put a coffee on the edge of the desk and tiptoed out again. Luckily I heard Baxter coming because he gave his signature cough on the way down the corridor. I sat up and put one hand on the mouse, and sipped my coffee, the picture of concentration and diligence.

"Caroline, how did it go?" he asked, very obviously on his way home, with his briefcase in his hand, and his raincoat over his arm.

"Grand, thanks. We closed the deal today, and

everyone is happy," I said, grinning inanely at him.

"Good work, well done," he said. "We must sit down and review it properly, to ensure that you learn as much as possible from the experience." The phrase sounded familiar. I think it's in the recruitment brochure, under the section, "Professional Development".

"Absolutely," I said.

He left then, and I looked at my watch. It was time to go. I closed down my computer, and had a very strange sense of detachment. When I switched it on again in the morning, something momentous would have happened, and right then I didn't know what. The journey home was the usual sticky smelly experience that would put anyone off working in London. When I got out of the tube station I actually welcomed the heady Brixton smells of ripe market fruit, carbon monoxide and incense.

At home, I had a shower and dug out a pair of lilac linen trousers and a short-sleeved top from the stack of wrinkled summer clothes in the wardrobe. I made a grilled chicken Caesar salad, and looked up a recipe for home-made dressing. Then I found a part-baked baguette in the freezer and stuck it in the oven. There was already a bottle of Chardonnay in the fridge. It had been ages since I made a meal for Matt and me. During the week, he usually cooks, or we have a takeaway, and at the weekends we go out, or survive on snacks. There was something very soothing about pottering around, and when I switched on the radio, it seemed to intrude on the silence so I turned it off again. With Matt always at home, I don't really get time to be on my own in the flat. It has never occurred to me before, but I moved into his place, which was full of his stuff, and even though he made lots of space for me in the wardrobe and on the shelves, my things have always looked like late additions. I have never really, really felt like this flat is my home, instead of just somewhere I live with Matt. At half past eight, I heard the front door closing downstairs, and I had a nervous flutter in my stomach. I had no idea how this conversation was going to go, even with all my planning of a script. I only knew that it had to start with: "Matt, we need to talk." The words were on my lips when the flat door opened, and he walked in. But he wasn't on his own. A skinny blonde teenager followed him into the sitting-room, looking a bit sheepish.

"Matt?" was all that I could summon. He walked across the room and kissed me hard on the mouth, and I was so surprised that I didn't really respond. I just stood there with my arms sticking out like the wooden doll in *Chitty Chitty Bang Bang*.

"Hi, darling," he said, in a strange voice. "This is Zoe. She's homeless, and I've told her she can stay here, *just for one night*." He turned to her as he was saying the last bit, and he sounded like a bossy teacher.

"Hi," she said, with her hair hanging down around her face. She was standing in that gawky way that only teenage girls can do, and I have many a photograph of me doing exactly the same thing.

"Hiya," I said, looking at Matt, completely mystified. "Are you two hungry?"

"Starving!" said the girl. "We only had some chocolate on the train, and Matthew didn't have enough money with him to buy anything else, and he said his credit card wouldn't work, so we haven't eaten since lunch-time."

Matt shrugged, as if the weight and length of the story was too much to bear. He looked exhausted. His face was pale and drawn tight over his cheekbones as if all the moisture had been sucked out of his skin, and he had huge black shadows under his eyes.

"There's plenty for three," I said, pushing Matt gently towards the table. "Sit down, I'll bring it in." I carried the huge bowl of salad and the jug of dressing out to the dinner table, and set an extra place for the girl. I put the bread in a basket, and poured wine into two glasses. I put a glass of water in front of her. My head was racing.

"So you didn't find your grandmother then?" I asked her, as she piled salad and bread on her plate. I know I shouldn't have done it, but I couldn't resist. Matt was astonished. She didn't even look up. "No, I didn't," she said with her mouth full. "Can't I have wine?" She looked at Matt and he shook his head.

"You're too young," he said.

"You've never said that before." She looked at him

sideways with a knowing smile on her lips, and I wanted to smack her.

Matt's eyes opened really wide. I could have sworn his pupils dilated. I have never seen his eyes looking so dark.

"Do you want to sleep on the street tonight?" he asked her, and his voice was so cold I was nearly frightened by it. She shook her head. Her hair was hanging down again so I couldn't see her face.

"Well, stop playing stupid games then. Zoe. I mean it." Matt looked away from her in disgust, and even though he must have been hungry, he pushed his food around with his fork like a picky child.

"Have some bread," I said, and I passed him the basket. He took a piece, and shredded it in his hands. He has never bitten his nails in all the time I have known him, but I could see the raw edges on at least three fingers. His hands were shaking.

I reached out and touched him, and he held my hand, and picked it up and kissed it, his lips lingering, telling me everything he couldn't say out loud. I love him so much, and I wanted to tell him. Why did he have to bring home this silly tart? We needed time together, and she was sitting there, all smug behind her curtain of hair. I had a really strong feeling that she knew exactly what she was doing. It fitted with Steve's description of manipulation and emotional blackmail. I hated her fiercely then, just for that one moment.

"Zoe, why don't you watch TV for a while?" Matt

said. "I'll pull out the sofa-bed for you, and give you the sheets and things, and you can go to bed when you're ready. Caroline and I need to talk." He stood up, cleared away the dishes, and went to the airing cupboard in the hall to get the bedding. He told her where the bathroom was, and to help herself if she wanted anything else to eat.

I rinsed the dishes, and put the rest of the salad in the fridge, covered in clingfilm.

"Night then," I said. I closed the sitting-room door. I couldn't bring myself to talk civilly to her, so it was better to keep quiet. As my mother used to say, 'If you haven't got anything nice to say, then don't say anything at all.'

"Sorry." We said it together. We hugged each other tight and I just wanted to cry. For us, for Matt, even for Zoe.

"Are you all right?" I pulled myself away from him and stroked his cheek.

He just nodded.

"Long story?"

"Let's have a bath." He led me into the bathroom, and turned on the taps. I pulled the blind down and lit three candles along the edge of the bath.

"Don't burn yourself this time," I said, pushing one away from his end of the bath. Last time we did this he burned the underside of his arm when he was reaching for the soap. He still has the scar. It's crescent-shaped, like a children's moon. We got undressed without saying a word, and stepped into the hot water. Matt slid down all the way for a minute, to wet his hair, and when he came up for air, the water dripped down his face, and he flicked it out of his eyes with his fingers.

"That's better," he said.

"Long train journey?"

"How did you know?"

"I was at the hostel today. I heard about Tommy. Are you the Matthew who does drama workshops?"

"Yes." His lip was trembling. I have never seen him like this. Even at his lowest times, he is strong. Matt doesn't cry.

"Why didn't you tell me about it?" I asked.

"I wanted to have some success. I needed to prove to you that I am good."

"I know you're good, Matt. I've always thought you were a great actor. You don't have to prove anything to me." As I said it, I realised what I must have done to him. I hadn't been very supportive. I'd just been judging him because I thought he was too lazy to go out and get other work.

"But being a great actor is no good if I never get any parts. Being great in theory is completely pointless."

"I think the workshops are a really good idea," I said. "It was really unfortunate that Tommy . . . "

"Steve said I wasn't responsible."

"Of course you weren't responsible!" I was shocked

379

that he would even be thinking that. The bathroom door handle rattled.

"Zoe, you'll have to wait," Matt said, using that voice again.

"I've seen you acting about four different roles since you walked in the door this evening," I said, trying to lighten things up a bit.

"This isn't acting, Caroline," he said. "That silly cow has wrapped me around her little finger, and the only reason I let her come home with me was because when I rang Steve he said there was no space at the hostel tonight, and it was too late to find her anywhere else."

"That's what Steve said. That Zoe had you wrapped around her little finger. That she's manipulative and resourceful, and that she had made up a grandmother to lure you to Newcastle."

"He knew?"

"Apparently." It was my turn to submerge myself, and when I came up again Matt was staring into space. "Steve warned me to keep my distance, not to get too involved. And I ignored him. I thought I knew better, and I understood Zoe. I met her on the steps of a tube station, ages ago, and she fascinated me."

"I can see that." I couldn't resist the dig.

"No, Caroline, you don't understand. She wasn't homeless when I met her. She was doing a sociology assignment for her 'A' levels and she was pretending to be homeless to see what the experience was like."

"Wow. And her parents let her do it?" This was getting more complicated by the minute.

"She had to ring her mother every hour to let her know she was all right. It really irritated Zoe because she said she couldn't get into the whole thing properly."

"That's bizarre. So what happened then?"

"Her stepfather raped her. He had been ogling her for months, maybe years, but Zoe didn't tell her mother because she wouldn't hear anything bad said about him."

"Oh my God." The water had suddenly gone cold around me.

"She ran away, and went to the hostel; the one you've been to, because Steve had helped her with her research."

"Does her mother know where she is?"

"No, I've been trying to get her to call home, but Zoe has got it into her head that her mother doesn't love her any more, because she hasn't been on the news, begging for information on Zoe's whereabouts."

"That's pretty melodramatic," I said, my emotions swinging again.

"You can see where she's coming from, can't you?" Matt said. "Other teenage girls disappear from loving families and we don't hear the end of it on the news, for weeks and weeks, until they find a body, or a suspect, or something. We see reconstructions of their last known movements on *Crime Stoppers*, and appeals for information everywhere. Zoe is asking herself why that hasn't happened for her."

"When you think about the number of homeless kids, there must be hundreds going missing like Zoe all the time, without any news coverage at all." It had never occurred to me before.

"She's seventeen, and the way things are going, her life is going to be pretty shit," said Matt. I could see that he was torn, like me, between sympathy and cynicism. He fancied her too, and he was fighting it. All that stern teacher stuff was pretty transparent. You didn't need a degree in psychology to understand that particular dynamic.

"So what are we going to do with her?" I asked. We were in it together now. It was unavoidable. We couldn't sort ourselves out until we got her sorted out.

"I think she needs to get some professional advice. Counselling. She has to face up to what happened, rather than running away from it."

"She has to tell her mother," I said. "The bastard shouldn't get away with it."

"If he did it," Matt said, quietly.

"Do you think she's making it up?" I asked, shocked all over again.

"Well, she did a pretty convincing job of making up her grandmother," he said, and I was starting to see why he was so devastated. It wasn't just Tommy. It wasn't just the fruitless trip to Newcastle. He was questioning the whole thing. Had he fallen for one big made-up story told by an attention-seeking teenager?

"She wouldn't, surely?" I tried to make it a statement, but it came out as a question.

Matt

The bath water was starting to get cold, so we topped it up with the hot tap. When I turned it off, we heard the flat door slamming, and footsteps running downstairs.

"She must have been listening at the door!" Caroline stood up and grabbed a towel.

"Let her go," I said, pulling Caroline's wrist so she sat down again.

"But she has nowhere to go to!"

I looked at Caroline and I just loved her so much. She was desperate for us to talk, and I walked in with Zoe, after a night away with no explanation. Caroline hasn't accused me. She hasn't kicked Zoe out, although she deserved it, with her coquettish little smiles and her calculated comments over dinner. Caroline hasn't even mentioned the obvious. Our relationship is on the brink of disaster. Standing there dripping wet, the only thing she was worried about was Zoe.

"She's survived more than one night on the street before," I said, and Caroline nodded. She lay back and put a flannel on her face. Then she lifted it off to say,

"I'm really sad."

"I know, it's devastating. That's why I wanted to do something, to make a difference . . ."

Caroline interrupted me. "No, I'm sad about Zoe's situation, of course, but I feel really bad that you didn't want to tell me about what you were doing with the workshops. Have I turned into a super-bitch, or what?"

"No, of course not. I just feel like I have a lot to prove. You strolled into that job, and six months later, you got promoted, and you're earning loads of money, and mixing with the brightest and best all day, and then you come home to me . . ." I stopped. I sounded like the disillusioned housewife in a soap opera.

Caroline actually laughed. "You have no idea how pissed off I am about work at the moment. The only thing that has redeemed that job in the last few weeks has been the CityScope deal, where I feel I'm doing something vaguely meaningful."

"Don't you think it's funny that what has preoccupied us both, and what seems to have got between us, is the same thing?" I asked Caroline. She nodded, but the way she gulped her wine to avoid meeting my eye made me wonder if there was more to it for her. "We haven't really talked properly for months," I said.

"Well, lying about the ITV job wasn't a good start," she muttered at me, but her heart wasn't in the accusation.

I thought I'd try an accusation of my own. "Is there

someone else?"

"Matthew," she said, and looked at me. Caroline only uses my full name very occasionally. When she wants me to really listen to her. Or sometimes when we're making love. She caresses me with the extra syllable. I stood up and took her hand, and we dried each other gently in silence. By the time we had patted every inch we were both panting. I unlocked the bathroom door, we ran to the bedroom, and I was fleetingly pleased that Zoe was gone. Afterwards, we lay on top of the duvet, just our little fingers touching. I hadn't felt so close to Caroline for a very long time.

"Are we OK?" I turned my head to ask her, and her eyes were closed. She just smiled with her eyes closed. After twenty minutes of blissful dozing, I shifted my weight gently off the bed so I wouldn't disturb her. I had to see if Zoe had left a note, or anything. I pulled my boxer shorts on and tip-toed into the sitting-room. The sofa-bed was neatly folded, the bedding was untouched in a pile on the armchair. Zoe's rucksack was gone. I had been entertaining a tiny hope that she had just gone out to the corner shop to buy cigarettes, and the doorbell would ring any minute. I sat on the sofa. No note, either. Zoe had really got under my skin, and I was completely unsettled. I decided to ring Steve.

"Hi, Steve, it's Matthew," I said when I recognised his voice. He must work twelve-hour shifts. He practically lives in the place.

"Hi, mate," he said, but from his tone he might as well have said '*what now?*'.

"Sorry to ring so late. I just wanted to let you know that Zoe has disappeared again."

"Listen, Matthew, I am not her keeper. Don't ring me to tell me what she's doing. She is seventeen years old. This is not a children's care facility. It is a hostel. If she comes here, and there's space, she can stay. If not, she can't. I am not responsible for her movements, and neither are you. Let go, for your own sake as well as hers."

The phone clicked off. He must think I am such a tosser. The phone rang again immediately. I grabbed it.

"Matthew?" Only my mum can put that intonation on my name.

"Hi, Mum," I sighed.

"Are you all right, son?" she asked. "Only you didn't let us know what happened at the hostel, and we've been a bit worried about you all day." Had it really only been this morning that I left my old room? It felt like a whole lifetime ago.

"It was as bad as Dad thought," I said.

"The lad? Is he all right?"

"No, Mum, he committed suicide last night."

"Oh. I don't know what to say."

"Neither do I. He was nineteen, Mum." I couldn't hold back the tears. At nineteen, I hated my parents and wished I could move out to get away from them. I took every opportunity to slag them off to my college friends, trying to be cool, and even complained to Nan about how awful they were.

"Don't cry, son, there's nothing you can do for him now." I could barely hear her voice through my sobbing. I had managed to hold it together with Caroline earlier, even though I could feel my voice cracking. But somehow my mum had opened the floodgates. "Do you want to talk to your dad?"

I shook my head, and took a while to remember I had to speak. "No, Mum. Maybe tomorrow?"

"All right, son. Get a good night's sleep. Everything will look better in the morning. Night-night now. Go to bed." She was talking to me like a four-year-old, but I suppose I was behaving like one. I hung up, and I didn't even have the energy to walk to the bedroom. I grabbed the duvet that I had laid out for Zoe and curled up on the sofa.

CHAPTER 18

Caroline

I woke up shivering, lying on top of the duvet cover. The luminous green clock said 3:00. My teeth felt scummy and I was desperate for a wee, so I went to the bathroom. I still felt all tingly. Matt and I haven't made love like that for the longest time. We had slipped into a bit of a 'missionary position on a Saturday night' habit, like some middle-aged couple. That's what working for a living does for you, I thought as I brushed my teeth. You get so stressed out and tired that there isn't time to relax, even when you're at home. What must it be like if you have kids as well? Depressing thought. I went back to the bedroom and only then realised that Matt wasn't in bed. He must have gone to look for Zoe. That little tart was responsible for a lot, and one thing she wasn't going to do was take Matt away from me. I pulled on my dressing-gown and went down the hall to the sitting-room. Surely he wasn't watching telly at three in the morning? There were no lights on, and only the sound of breathing, so I nearly didn't go in. But something made me open the door. There was Matt on the couch, stretched out with just his boxer shorts on, and Zoe curled up against him, supposedly asleep. I took a huge, deep hyperventilating breath, like a reverse sigh. She opened one eye and then the other, and smirked at me. She snuggled up even closer to Matt's body, tucked her hands under her chin and closed her eyes again, with a big theatrical yawn. I wouldn't give her the satisfaction of reacting. I just closed the door really gently, and found myself backing down the hall, with tiny steps. I felt as if I couldn't turn my back on the door. I must have been in shock, I think. I was shivering, and my teeth started chattering. I climbed back into bed with my dressing-gown still on, and lay down, rigid on the pillow. When did she come back? Why was Matt even in there at all? He couldn't have done that to me, surely? Not after, not after . . .

I didn't want to confront Matt with Zoe there. That might just be too humiliating for words. If he was going to dump me for a teenager who was probably half my age, I definitely didn't want him to do it in front of her. Scheming little bitch. The clock said 3:17. Three hours and thirteen minutes later, the radio-alarm clicked on and my eyes hadn't closed once. I threw back the covers and I still didn't know what I was going to do. I had a shower, put on work clothes and make-up, and then I couldn't put it off any longer. My briefcase was in the sitting-room, so I had to go in there. I opened the door quietly. Matt was still snoring. I couldn't see Zoe anywhere. Then I heard the tap in the kitchen running, and the sound of *humming*. I grabbed my briefcase, turned around and left. I banged the front door on the way out, and stomped down the stairs. Then I wished I hadn't. Now she would know that I cared. The newspaper man was surprised when I handed him a fiver. "Sorry, love, can't change that," he said, handing it back. My weekly travel pass had run out, so I stuffed the crumpled fiver into the ticket machine, with the queen's head facing upwards, but the machine just spat it back at me. After queuing for ten minutes at the ticket booth, I finally got going, and looked up at the clock as I went through the barrier: 7:57. The train was much busier than usual so I didn't get a seat. I had my really tight shoes on, and my feet were killing me by the time I eventually got to work.

Alison was at her desk, munching toast.

"Morning," she mumbled in her usual way. She didn't even look curious. Two minutes later, a red mug of coffee appeared on my desk. It had the CityScope logo and a London skyline silhouette printed on it. I looked up.

"It arrived in the post this morning," said Alison, her

mouth thankfully empty. "I thought you'd like to christen it."

"Thanks." I took a sip and burnt my lip.

"It didn't go well then?"

I wanted to cry. She came around the desk to give me a hug, but I pushed her away. "Don't be nice to me, please," I said, and a tear escaped and rolled down my cheek. I brushed it away.

She just patted my hand, and went out to her desk. I wanted to ask her if I could stay at her place for a few days, but I didn't trust myself to talk yet, so I turned on my computer. Everything had turned out so differently to my expectations. Yesterday at five o'clock, Zoe was just some dysfunctional teenager in a hostel and today, she's humming away in my kitchen, making a post-coital bacon sandwich for Matt. Maybe I needed a kick up the arse to make me realise that I loved Matt. Maybe God is telling me to finish with Matt, and this is the sign. Maybe I am meant to be with Matthew after all. How could Matt do that to me? Sleep with me and then with her. If he did.

He did.

She was certainly delighted with herself.

Maybe she was just trying to annoy me.

But what was she doing lying there beside him?

He must have known she was there.

It's possible that he didn't.

Unlikely.

But possible.

"Are you OK?" Alison was in her usual position in the doorway.

"Grand. Thanks."

"You're talking to yourself."

"Am I? Maybe I'm going mad." I felt a hysterical urge to giggle.

Matt

I woke up to the sound of the front door slamming and the smell of frying bacon. I was starving. I was surprised to find myself on the sofa and sat up, scratching my head. Something wasn't quite right. It was definitely Friday, not Saturday. So Caroline should be at work, not cooking breakfast at eight o'clock. Her mobile phone was sitting on the table, being charged. She must be going in to work late. Then I noticed Zoe's rucksack leaning against the armchair.

"She came back, then," I yelled into the kitchen, as I headed down the hall to the bathroom. That was a huge relief. I had a plan. I was going to persuade Zoe to tell her mother everything. I was going to convince her that it was the only way of testing where her mother's loyalties lay. I showered, and luxuriated in the hot water and shower gel. I hadn't slept so well for ages. The sofa was surprisingly comfortable. I wondered when Zoe had come back – hopefully she hadn't woken Caroline up in the middle of the night to answer the door. Caroline hates being woken up. I couldn't believe I had slept through the whole thing. I walked into the kitchen with just a towel wrapped around me. Zoe was looking after the bacon in the pan.

"Hi, Zoe, I'm glad you came back," I said.

"Me too," she smiled at me, and I found myself forgiving her for last night. She's so young, she doesn't know where the boundaries are. She obviously didn't realise she was flirting quite outrageously.

"Where's Caroline?" I asked, wandering out again, drying my hair with another towel.

"Gone," Zoe said, and before I knew it she had come up behind me and pulled the towel from around my waist. "So it's just us," she said, and she reached around and put her hand on my cock.

My brain was shouting "No!" but my body responded predictably.

"Oh my God, it's much bigger than . . ." Zoe said, taking her hand away as if she had been burnt.

"What the hell are you doing, Zoe?" I yelled at her. I turned around and grabbed the towel out of her hand, and wrapped it back around me. I stormed into the bedroom, and yanked open my chest of drawers, pulling out underwear, and putting it on. She followed me.

"Get out of my bedroom!" I shouted.

"But . . ."

"Zoe, get out!"

She backed away, down the hall. When I was fully dressed, I followed her. She was standing in the living-room with the rucksack on her back.

"Don't try the fucking sympathy vote, with me, you little slag!" I said. "Take that rucksack off and sit down."

She sat down, perched on the edge of the sofa with her rucksack still on.

"What the fuck are you playing at?" I was still shouting. I forced myself to lower the volume. "I told you yesterday that I am not interested in you as a girl-friend. I am trying to help you, and all you can do in return is fuck me up. What is your problem?"

She turned on the tears then. She should have gone to RADA. I had never seen a better performance. She didn't say anything for at least five minutes. She just sat there with tears silently streaming down her cheeks. She pulled a tissue out of her sleeve at one point, and blew her nose. I sat there with my arms folded, trying to take deep breaths to suppress the anger, thinking that I must remember to be the adult here, and treat her as a child. In our little game of cat and mouse she was well and truly winning every round. I was still annoyed about the train journey yesterday. When I had completely given up on finding her, and was sitting staring out the window at the miserable sleet washing over Peterborough, she miraculously appeared at my side with a cup of tea and her cheeky grin.

"Give up?" she said, as if we had been playing hide and seek. I wanted to throttle her then, and now found myself wanting to do it again.

"Zoe, I want to ring your mother today and tell her that you are safe, and that you want to meet her somewhere, on neutral territory, to tell her why you ran away from home."

"No, I won't give you the number," she said, sullenly.

"I am not going to accept no for an answer. If you don't give me the number I will call the police and have your mother traced by them. I will not take responsibility for you any longer."

"She knows."

"Knows what?"

"Why I ran away from home."

"She knows you were raped?"

"It wasn't rape."

Why was I surprised? "What are you saying – that you wanted to have sex with your stepfather?"

"I made him up."

"So you weren't raped?"

"No. I slept with my mother's boyfriend. She's much too old for him. At least twice his age. It was disgusting. He promised me that he was going to leave her, and we would run away together, as soon as I was eighteen."

"So what happened?"

"She found us. She kicked me out. Told me never to come back."

"What did he do?"

"He just sat there and let her do it. I couldn't believe it. He made out it was all my fault, that I came on to him, and . . ." The crocodile tears flowed again.

"So you can't go back," I said, deadpan.

"She said she'd kill me if I showed my face."

"Hardly." But I was beginning to believe that in Zoe's life, anything could happen.

"He told me he loved me."

"I bet he did," I said, with my head in my hands. What the hell was I supposed to do now?

Matthew

I left Liz in her T-shirt, trying to lure the boys away from the television long enough to get them dressed, and got into work really early to catch up on e-mails before my day of meetings started. From nine thirty onwards I went from one to the next, and didn't get back to my desk until about five. I was starving – someone had forgotten to order sandwiches for our working lunch and we were so engrossed we just worked through. Diana was packing up. She goes to a yoga class on Friday evenings, and always disappears at exactly five o'clock.

"A young lady called," she said in a faintly disapproving tone. "She declined to leave her name, but her voice sounded somewhat familiar." She passed me a message slip with the time of the call, the "pcb" box ticked, and an emphatic question mark in the space for the caller's name.

"Thank you," I said. I recognised Caroline's mobile number. I had rung it often enough. Diana left, wishing me a pleasant weekend with my *family*. I sat at my desk, wondering if I had the courage to finish it with Caroline tonight, if she was free to meet me. I didn't want to spend the whole weekend being distracted. It really was time to focus on Liz and the boys. I didn't want to leave a message on Caroline's voicemail at work, just in case her secretary checked her messages. I sent a text to her mobile: "Caroline, darling, we really need to talk. See you at the Cabbage and Slipper at seven for a drink?"

Then I called Liz to say I would be late home. She laughed. "It makes a nice change for you to be calling me about being late. I'll have supper ready when you get in. The boys are exhausted so they'll probably be asleep by seven thirty. I'll stick some wine in the fridge. We might be able to stay awake long enough to drink it!"

"Great, see you about nine, then," I said, feeling like the proverbial heel.

Caroline

I locked my office door, put my phone on voicemail and told Alison everything. She didn't know what to say. She really fancies Matt, so of course she was on his side, but I could see the doubt in her face. Maybe he had slept with Zoe. Baxter came past the office twice, and the second time he peered through the blinds. I had the "do not disturb" sign hanging up, and he didn't want to intrude, but I could feel his curiosity emanating through the panel of the door. At one point Alison and I were both crying. What a pair.

Matt

There was a smell of burning from the kitchen so I ran in there to find the grill on fire. By the time I had put it out and opened the window to clear the smoke, Zoe had gone, to my great relief. I checked the hook by the door and she hadn't taken the spare set of keys again, so I didn't have to worry about her mysteriously reappearing a second time. I rang Caroline at the office to see if she wanted her mobile phone. She and Alison were both on voicemail all morning. Maybe there was some kind of team meeting going on. I just left a message. The post arrived, and there was a box of three books from Amazon that I had put on special order weeks ago. I devoured one on group dynamics, and one on practical theatre workshops. I got hungry at about two o'clock and munched a sandwich and some crisps as I read. My notepad was filling up and I was buzzing with ideas. It reminded me of college, when I really got into one of my assignments. The adrenalin rush was great. I tried ringing Caroline again, but Alison answered and told me Caroline was in a meeting. She sounded a bit offhand, I thought, but she was probably busy. I confirmed with Steve that I would be in on Wednesday to run a role-play session. I knew perfectly well that I was keeping myself busy to block out the memory of the morning. My cock had given me away. If Caroline ever found out I would be finished. Her phone rang, but I didn't bother answering it. I checked my watch. If I was quick I could get to her office before she left, and join them all for the Friday-night drink. Her colleagues are not too bad when they're not talking about work, and we could go for something to eat afterwards. To celebrate our fresh start.

Matthew

The evening sunlight was glinting off the river as I walked along the embankment from London Bridge. The pub was very crowded, and people were sitting on the kerbstones and leaning against the river railings, leaving hardly any space to walk past. Seagulls swooped over the water and, although the air was still warm, there was a breeze that ruffled the surface of the river, and emphasised the wash of the passing boats. I was early, so I found a gap in the railings and walked down an old cobbled pier that was sticking out into the river, and must have been built for the river ferrymen when they used to row people across. I sat down on my hunkers, facing the water, not caring that I was creasing my suit trousers. I felt completely alone, even though there must have been over a hundred people just yards behind me. Two children waved from *The Surita*, a tourist boat with open decks and a droning Cockney tour guide, whose voice just reached me across the water. I waved back, and they jumped up and down, waving both arms now. A woman ushered them away from the railings, her maternal body language obvious even from that distance. I hadn't heard back from Caroline yet, but she was probably busy in meetings. I would wait for half an hour, and then go home if she didn't turn up.

Caroline

After my cathartic cry with Alison, I was in back-to-back meetings for the rest of the day. When I came out of the last one at six o'clock there was a message from Adrian suggesting a drink after work. It was a lovely evening, and a glass of cold wine by the river was just what the doctor ordered. I should really have written up my meeting notes straight away, because I would have forgotten all the details by Monday. Even more compellingly, I should go home to Matt, and resolve things once and for all. But I could make it to the pub for half past six, then go home after just one drink to give me Dutch courage. If Zoe was still at the flat with Matt, I didn't think I could be civil to them, anyway. Adrian was the perfect person to ask for advice. He had the gay man's female intuition mixed with male pragmatism. I was digging around in the bottom of my handbag when Alison came in.

"Alison, did I leave my mobile on your desk?" I asked, looking in all my desk drawers, and patting my jacket where it was hanging on the back of my chair.

"Matt rang to say you left it at home and asked if you wanted it."

"Shit." I couldn't remember Adrian's mobile number and of course I hadn't written it down anywhere. I would really have to rush to get to the Cabbage and Slipper for six thirty. "What did you tell Matt?"

"That you'd ring him when you got out of your meeting. Are you going home now?"

"No, I'm going for a drink with Adrian. I can't face talking to Matt yet. I need a drink. Adrian will be on his way already, so I'm just going to run for it." I stuffed everything back into my bag, locked my drawers and dropped the key into the red penholder on my desk.

"What are you going to do?"

"I don't know yet."

"Give Matt a chance," she said.

"A chance to do what?"

"To explain himself."

"I don't think there are many explanations for being asleep on a sofa with a seventeen-year-old who he obviously fancies, and who is drooling all over him. Do you?"

"No, but –"

"Well, then," I said, and I walked past her. "See you Monday. Thanks for listening earlier on."

Matt

I was just leaving when the phone rang. I assumed it was Caroline, so I grabbed it and said, "Hi, darling, I was just leaving to come and meet you."

It was Alison. She sounded embarrassed, but I suppose you would if your boss's boyfriend called you darling.

"Caroline will be at the Cabbage and Slipper," she said. "She's just left."

"Thanks, Alison, I'll meet her there. Have a good weekend."

"See you," she said.

I grabbed Caroline's phone and stuffed it into my jacket pocket. Perhaps if we went for a meal, I could talk to Caroline about my ideas, and see what she thought. I could really make a go of this and take a teaching course in September, so I could work in mainstream education. Then I'd have steady money coming in while I figured out what to do next with my acting career. I didn't want to abandon the dream of being an actor, after holding out this long, but Caroline was right. I couldn't go on as I was. Something had to give, and I didn't want to lose her. I felt hugely optimistic as I waited for the number thirty-five bus. Twenty minutes later the bus still hadn't arrived. I pulled out her phone to tell her I was running late, and I couldn't resist the '*one message received*'.

I pressed the options button and read it.

Matthew

I usually rehearse important speeches. When I proposed to Liz, it took me weeks to finesse exactly what I was going to say. I wanted to have a contingency speech ready in case she refused me. In the end I kept it really simple. "Will you marry me?" has a certain appeal for being unambiguous, short and to the point. There isn't a form of words that's quite so simple to finish a relationship. I could just admit to being married, and having two children. Caroline could be reasonably expected to run a mile, and I wouldn't have to say anything else. But I wanted to tell her why I am attracted to her, how beautiful and clever and stimulating I find her, and how I find myself thinking about her every ten minutes on average, wherever I am and whatever I am doing. But if I start with that bit, I can't then turn around and suddenly finish the relationship, unless I tell her I'm married. Then she won't believe a word of what I've said. She'll think of me as a cheating husband just looking for a bit on the side. I found myself hoping she wouldn't turn up so I could rehearse the speech over the weekend. Then it occurred to me that even if she did turn up we could just have a drink. A drink, not dinner. Liz was at home creating some culinary delight, and anyway, I couldn't keep up the pretence of normality for long with Caroline. Then we could arrange another date, I could decide over the weekend what to say, and do the deed next week instead. The feeling of relief told me I had decided. Postponement was the best option. Now I could enjoy watching the people picking things off the river beach on the opposite bank, and listening to the sounds of the river traffic and the seagulls, while I waited for her to turn up.

Caroline

I nudged my way through the crowd by the door to check inside the pub, even though Adrian was much more likely to be outside. The pub was smoky and very hot. Having battled that far, I thought I might as well buy a round, and then go out and find him. Wielding my Archer's Aqua and a pint of Stella, I managed to elbow my way through to the riverside without spilling anything. I bumped into about five different people from the office, and I was glad I had the drinks in my hand. I just held them up and waved generally in the direction of the river. No-one was expecting me to stop and chat. Adrian's tall, so I would have seen him if he was standing at the railings. There was no sign of him. Then a couple moved away, and walked off hand in hand, leaving a space so that I could see down towards the river. Adrian was sitting on a bollard at the end of a rickety stone pier, talking to a guy whose face I couldn't see. Was it someone from his office, or was he just hitting on that guy? If I wasn't so desperate to speak to him on his own, I would have thought it was funny. They didn't seem to have any drinks down there, but they were chatting away like overgrown schoolboys in their dark suits and city brogues. How I didn't notice straight away when I met him that Adrian was gay, I have no idea, because looking at him now, his body language was so obvious, even from a distance. He was waving his arms around like mad, and throwing his head back when he laughed. I didn't want to be a goose-berry, so I thought I'd wait a minute and see what happened. I could always just say hello, and have a quick drink with the two of them. Deep down I didn't need anyone to tell me what to do. I knew already. I worked my way along the railings to find the gap leading to the pier.

Matt

If Caroline worked in the media, the "darling" in her message wouldn't have bothered me. But she doesn't really mix with the darling set. Who the hell really needed to talk to her? The bus finally turned up and I sat upstairs. The heater was on, blowing diesel fumes and warm air up onto my face. Only last night we made love and she said we were OK. Was she seeing someone else? She'd been working long hours ever since she started in that job, so it could have been going on for a very long time. I wondered how many affairs are discovered through messages on mobile phones.

Caroline was standing at the railings outside the pub when I got there, looking down at the water. As I watched, she picked up a pint that had been standing at her feet, and waved it in the air, as if tempting someone to come closer. I hadn't realised before that you could get down to the riverside at that particular spot.

When I was about ten metres away, a guy in a suit came striding up the pier and said, "Caroline, darling, you made it!" He pecked her on both cheeks. "I couldn't get you on your mobile, so I left a message with Alison."

She smiled at him, and they chinked drinks. They turned towards the river and he seemed to be pointing back towards the pier, telling her something. I should probably have walked away, but I kept going.

"Caroline," I said, and she turned around.

"Matt! What are you doing here?" she asked. She didn't look very pleased to see me. "Your phone." I handed it to her.

The guy was standing there trying to look comical, with his eyebrows lifted and his shoulders hunched. He just looked stupid.

"Hello, I'm Matthew, her boyfriend," I said, holding out my hand. You probably haven't heard about me."

"Hi, I'm Adrian, and I most certainly have," he said, and when he giggled I realised he was gay. That's the other kind of darling not to be afraid of.

I laughed, overwhelmed by relief. Caroline still didn't seem very happy to see me.

"How's Zoe?" Adrian asked me.

"How do you know about Zoe?" I asked.

"I was at the hostel the day she lured you to Newcastle like the proverbial siren luring her victims onto the rocks."

"Very apt description," Caroline said, quite sharply.

"She's gone," I said.

"For how long, though? She was supposedly gone last night too, until I found her cuddled up very cosily on the sofa in the middle of the night." Caroline took a slug of her drink from the bottle and spluttered.

"On the sofa?" I said. "When? And how did she get back in? I didn't even know she was there until I found her burning bacon in the kitchen this morning."

"I'll tell you later," Caroline said to me, looking sideways at Adrian.

"Do tell, now. I can keep a secret," he said. Dressed as he was, his campness seemed bizarre.

"She was curled up on the sofa with Matt when I went to see where he was in the middle of the night." Caroline sounded really surly now. She wasn't even looking at me as she was talking.

"I didn't even know she was back!" I said. At least I was on safe ground there.

"I believe him," said Adrian, rolling his eyes at Caroline.

"So do I." Caroline kissed me on the cheek then, and she was grinning from ear to ear. She looked relieved. Had she been thinking I'd slept with Zoe, or something? "Where's she gone?"

"I don't know. The bacon caught fire, and by the time I'd sorted it out, she had disappeared. I told her I was going to track down her mum through the police. She admitted that she'd been sleeping with her mother's boyfriend, and her mother kicked her out of the house when she found them together. I am so pissed off. I feel like the most gullible idiot."

"Get you a drink?" Adrian asked, as he gulped down

the last of his pint.

"Same as you, thanks, mate," I said. I was gasping for one.

"Caroline, same again?" he nodded at the empty bottle she was tipping up as if she wanted to suck out the last drop. Caroline nodded. We leaned on the railings. There was another guy down on the pier, skimming flat stones on the water. Or trying to. He looked ridiculous, in a pin-striped suit, throwing stones into the water.

"Look at that guy," I said. "He hasn't got a clue. He should be on his commuter train home to Surrey."

Caroline wasn't really looking at him. She squeezed my hand and said, "Sorry for not trusting you."

"She did try it on, Caroline, so your instincts about her were right. But I would never do that to you. Anyway, I was just as bad. I read the message on your phone from Adrian, and I thought you were seeing another guy, so I came here to catch you."

She turned to me. "What?" she said, and I handed her the phone. She looked at the message. "Jesus!" She went red.

"I'm really sorry, Caroline, but who do we know that calls you 'darling'?" I said in my most reasonable tone. She didn't say anything, and just then Adrian came back with the drinks.

"That was quick," Caroline said. She suddenly seemed a bit edgy.

"Hardly anyone at the bar." Adrian sipped his beer, obviously relishing it, and looked down at the river.

"Did you score?" Caroline said, nodding towards the guy throwing stones.

Adrian burst out laughing. "I don't chat up married men!"

"Do you check for a ring, first, then?" I asked him. "What if they're not wearing a ring?"

"I didn't have to in his case. I know him and he's married. He's Matthew Turner, another lawyer who does some work at the Brixton Law Centre. We volunteer on different days so we don't often bump into each other. He's a great guy. I really respect him. He has all the most difficult clients at the centre and he seems to be able to gain their trust, so they listen to him. There are a couple of really tough cases down there, and he's cracked them."

"Why don't you get him to come up and join us?" I said, feeling a bit guilty that I had been ridiculing him. "You're interested in the Law Centre, aren't you, Caroline? You were saying that you might do some volunteering. Well, here are two well-qualified people to tell you what it's like."

Caroline shivered and shook her head. "I'm not really in the mood for talking shop tonight," she said. "Listen, do you mind if we go inside? It's getting a bit breezy now." I touched her arm, and she was covered in goosebumps. "Are you OK?"

"Grand. I'd like to go home after this one, though."

She held up her drink.

"Sure," I said, thinking I might still persuade her to go for a Chinese. We went inside, and Adrian asked me how the workshops were going. I told him I hadn't run any since the day Tommy died.

"You've got to keep going, Matthew. You've had a couple of bad experiences with them, but these kids really are worth helping."

"I know, I have some good ideas. I spent today working up some role plays and characterisation exercises," I said.

"Like what?" he was asking, just as the pin-striped guy walked through the door. He looked familiar, now that I could see his face.

Matthew

I was enjoying the sound of the waves washing against the cobbles when someone tapped me on the shoulder. I looked around. Caroline must have sneaked up behind me.

"Matthew, hi – I thought it was you."

I haven't seen Adrian Woodhouse for about a year. He works at the Law Centre on Tuesday and Thursday evenings, and you couldn't find a more committed guy. He does quite a bit of pro bono work during office hours too.

"Adrian! How are you?" I stood up and shook his hand. "You're looking as impeccable as ever!" I looked him up and down. I was sweating, but I didn't want to take my jacket off. I was wearing one of those stupid pink shirts that Liz persuaded me to buy but I've always hated.

"Well, you know, got to keep the side up," he said, and sat on a bollard beside me. We caught up on a few clients. "Have you got time for a beer?" he asked.

"I'm meeting someone in a few minutes," I said, really wishing now that Caroline wasn't coming and I could just have a beer with Adrian and go home to Liz.

"Me too."

"Male or female?" I asked him as a distraction tactic. I would have to bluff it out if Caroline turned up. Adrian is unashamedly gay, which I really admire for someone in our profession. Gay lawyers usually keep their private lives to themselves, but Adrian has been known to camp it up at conferences or seminars just for the shock value.

"Female, actually." He laughed. "I met her through the pro bono work. She's still young, but she's getting as disillusioned as the rest of us about the meaning of all the corporate bullshit. I think it's just hit her a bit sooner." He looked at his watch. "She's late, so I'll go and scout around in case she's missed me in the crowd. Maybe see you in a few minutes?"

"Sure, yes. Nice to catch up with you. We must have a drink one night when I'm in Brixton." I shook his hand again. Maybe he would get the hint and not come barging in when I was talking to Caroline. I racked my brain for other pubs nearby where I could take her. He walked up the sloping pier, and I turned back to the water. I would wait for another ten minutes. Maybe I should finish with Caroline tonight. Forget rehearsals, just say it as it comes. "Caroline, I'm really sorry to do this to you. It was never my intention to mislead you. I am married, *happily* married, and I think we should finish our relationship before anyone gets hurt."

I started skimming stones, imagining teaching the boys in a few years' time how to do it. I would take them down here, to this very spot. They would love the police launches churning past, and the waste barges with their big blue containers heading for incineration plants further downriver. The greatest number of hops I could manage was three. I used to be much better at skimming, and I was determined to get at least five. I found myself rooting around in the grimy grey sand to find the flattest stones. A whiff of polluted river mud wafted upwards, and I thought I'd better go and wash my hands before meeting Caroline. I scrambled up the pier, not half as agile as Adrian, and headed for the pub. The crowds were starting to clear now, and it was easier to make progress.

Caroline

I couldn't believe it. Matthew was walking in the door of the pub. I was paralysed. I had managed not to react when Adrian told us the man on the pier was Matthew. I had even managed not to burst into tears when I realised that Matthew Turner, my intelligent, funny, slightly scruffy, idealistic and dynamic champion of the underdog Matthew, was married. Mixed in with all that was my huge relief that Matt thought the text message came from Adrian, so I had a chance of getting away with it all. Why didn't I drag Matt home straight away, instead of just coming inside the pub?

Matthew walked towards us, then held up his hands – "Just going to the bathroom," he said, swerving around us and heading for the toilets.

"He looks familiar," said Matt. "Does he work with you?"

"Maybe you've seen him around Brixton?" said Adrian, helpfully. The penny had dropped. I could see it on his face. He was looking at my handsome actor turned drama teacher and my intelligent and compassionate lawyer, both named Matthew.

"You're right," said Matt. "I was in the queue behind him at the police station. Of course, that's it." Adrian excused himself and disappeared into the toilet after Matthew. My knees were weak. I tried to sip my drink, but I couldn't swallow.

"I saw him another time, too. I was with Zoe in a coffee shop on the Strand and he left his wife's birthday present behind so I had to run after him with it."

"With Zoe?"

"Yes, having a coffee."

"His wife?" I managed.

"Yes, he was meeting her."

What was I going to say to him?

'Nice to meet you?' as if we had never met before?

'How's your wife? I'm afraid I've forgotten her name,' as if we had known a little bit about each other in passing?

'Still working hard?' as if we had worked many hours together on lots of deals?

"He's quite a nice guy – do you know him?" asked Matt.

I nodded. "We've done a bit of work together."

"Matthew is his name too, isn't it? I remember now."

"Yes, it's Matthew," she said, sounding a bit strange.

Matthew

The door of the toilet slammed open just as I was washing my hands. It was Adrian.

"Matthew!" he said, standing in front of me and blocking my way.

"Adrian, what's up?" I said, trying to banish the very fleeting thought that he might fancy me, or something.

My mind was already racing. Caroline was out there, and I didn't know what the hell I was going to do.

"Matthew!"

"Yes?"

"Matthew . . ."

"Adrian, will you stop repeating my name. What do you want?"

"I don't know how to tell you this . . ."

"Well, don't then," I said, trying to push past him. This was the last thing I needed. I had to get Caroline somewhere quiet by herself, and I had noticed another chap standing there as well. I was just going to brazen it out, take her by the arm and steer her out of the pub.

"That other man out there. He's Caroline's boyfriend. It's all very awkward. I thought you ought to know." Adrian was looking down at the tiles.

Matt

Pin-striped Matthew had a pink shirt on as well, which is so naff. Where did that pretentious fashion come from? They're really expensive too, the genuine Pinks shirts. His wife probably dressed him. He looks the type. Although to be fair he had been quite pleasant to talk to on the two previous occasions when I met him.

"Caroline," I said, when Adrian followed him into the gents. "Shall we just make our excuses and go, before we get involved in another round of drinks?" At least we wouldn't be leaving Adrian on his own.

She nodded just as they came out of the toilet and walked towards us.

Caroline

Adrian, bless him, did his best to be casual, as if introducing a girl and her two boyfriends was the most everyday social event. "Caroline, this is Matthew. Matthew, Caroline. Matthew, meet Matthew."

We all shook hands. I didn't have to say anything in the end. Matthew held my hand in his beautiful long brown fingers just a second longer than necessary, gently squeezing mine.

"We've actually met before, at the office," he said smoothly.

"And we've bumped into each other a couple of times," Matt smiled at him and shook his hand. While the rest of us were giving the performance of a lifetime, Matt was the only one who wasn't acting. "Nice to have met you both. Caroline and I are just going off for a meal, so we'll leave you to it, if you don't mind."

Adrian interjected, "Matthew, sorry to do this, but could I just have a very quick word about the drama workshops? I've had an idea, and I'd like to run it by you."

Matt looked at me.

"That's fine with me," I said.

"Excuse us, just for a minute." Adrian guided Matt over towards the leaded bay window and they started an animated conversation. I felt like Matthew and I were left occupying a surreal, separate space in the midst of the crowd. I looked up at him.

"Caroline, I've rehearsed this a thousand times in my head . . ."

"I know you're married," I said, trying not to sound accusing. Who was I to judge?

"I wanted to meet you tonight, to talk things over."

"I don't think there's much to talk about, do you?" I said. "Matt and I have been through a bit of a tough patch, and maybe you have too?"

"Yes. Caroline, being with you has been so wonderful. But it has also opened my eyes, and made me realise how precious my family is to me. My whole family. I can't be selfish, and expect to have you too, as much as . . ."

I smiled at him. "You don't have to say any more. I'm really glad we've known each other too, but I think I was looking for something with you that I already have with Matt."

In a quintessential mastery of the English understatement, Matthew said, "Shall we say good-bye then?"

I looked across at Matt, and he was grinning. He came over, and I hooked my hand onto his arm. Adrian waved from the window, and gave me a thumbs-up. I waved back and smiled.

"Good-bye, Matthew," I said, as I was walking out with Matt and we turned towards London Bridge. I could feel tears brimming, but they didn't spill. If they had, they might have been tears of happiness.

THE END

Also published by Poolbeg

Daddy's Girl

SHARON MULROONEY

"You don't want it, do you?"
**"No, of course not, but what are we
going to do?"**

Maria's pregnant but her boyfriend, Joe, is not
ready to be a father. It would tie him down and
what would his mother think?

Maria thought he really loved her but now, it
seems, her only choice is to get rid of their baby.

She can't keep it. Her mother would die of
shame and her father, Sean, would throw her
out of the house.

While Maria heads for London on her own,
an accident leaves Joe's mother in a coma. As
he holds vigil by her bedside he has lots of time
to think about his future.

But in London Maria has made a decision that
will affect everyone she loves . . . **forever!**

ISBN 1-84223-124-3